THE
HALO
EFFECT

Also by M. J. ROSE

Fiction

LIP SERVICE
IN FIDELITY
FLESH TONES
SHEET MUSIC

Nonfiction

HOW TO PUBLISH AND PROMOTE ONLINE
(with Angela Adair-Hoy)
BUZZ YOUR BOOK (with Douglas Clegg)

Watch for the next novel in the Butterfield Institute series

THE DELILAH COMPLEX

Available from MIRA Books in April 2005

M. J. ROSE

THE
HALO
EFFECT

MIRA®

MIRA®

ISBN 0-7783-2080-4

THE HALO EFFECT

www.MIRABooks.com

Printed in U.S.A.

For Mara Nathan

Halo—1: the circle of light with which the head is surrounded in representations of Christ and the saints; a nimbus 2: the ideal glory with which a person or thing is invested when viewed under the influence of feeling or sentiment 3: a more or less circular bright or dark area formed in various photographic processes

Halo Effect—*psychol.,* the favorable bias in interviews, intelligence tests and the like generated by an atmosphere of approbation. A common error in rating intelligence tests is known as the "halo effect." If an individual creates a favorable impression by his excellence in one trait, you are apt to rate him near the top in every trait.

And the day came when the risk to remain tight in the bud was more painful than the risk it took to blossom.
—Anaïs Nin

1

The first thing she saw were the woman's feet, so white they looked like the marble feet on the statue of the Virgin Mary who wears the gold halo and stands in the Catholic church where she attends mass every morning before coming to work at the high-rise hotel on Sixth Avenue. The church where she attended Sunday mass only four hours before. Except these feet oozed black-red blood.

Celia Rodriguez stared, not yet comprehending.

The Virgin's feet do not bleed, though. Christ's feet do. Holes through to the soles, spilling blood.

For the love of God.

No. No love here. Blood. Nighttime pools of congealed blood.

These are still only fragments of thought as her mind raced to keep up with her eyes. She could not make sense of this scene. Not yet.

The mosaic of horror seemed to take forever to fall into place, but in reality, from the time the maid walked into the room to the time she finally opened her mouth to attempt—and fail—at a scream, only one minute passed.

Holy Mother of God.

In random order Celia Rodriguez registered that there were fifty-dollar bills, no longer green but soaked dark brown, dozens of them, surrounding the woman's head. Like a halo. And what she had first thought was a blanket was a voluminous black dress pushed up to show shapely naked legs. No, revealing more. Pushed up farther to reveal a chestnut patch of hair between the legs. Too bare. More naked than naked.

The fifty-year-old housekeeper and mother of three stared, sure that what she saw was a vision of some kind.

The woman's pubis had been shaved in a particular shape. She knew this shape. But before she could focus on that, she saw that there was blood oozing from there, too. Celia's eyes shifted from right to left, taking in that the woman's hands were outstretched in a T position and lying in yet more viscous blood.

Celia could not believe what she saw. None of it. Especially not the shape the hair had been shaved into. She knew this shape. It was engraved on her own heart. It hung around her own neck in gold.

It was a cross.

With that, everything finally slipped into place: the plentiful and flowing dress was a nun's habit.

The Spanish woman who opened the door only seconds before fell to her knees and touched the corner of the robe. Her hand came away, stained with bright crimson. She was mesmerized by this horror that made her think of a shrine in the back of her church. Our Lady of Sorrows.

Her eyes returned to the shape carved out of the wiry hair. Why did she have to keep looking there? At that cross. At that blasphemy.

And then she saw more. There was more?

Dripping from the woman's nether mouth was not just blood, but something that was alive, moving, almost crawling. No, it was a rosary that was dripping blood, drop by drop from bead to bead. The blood had washed over the oval medal of the Virgin and had painted the Christ figure. What had flowed off of him had soaked into the carpet. And still it came. And still it came. Christ's blood. This poor woman's blood.

The housekeeper opened her mouth and tried to scream but no sound came. She called for her God, and even if he heard her, no one else did.

It would be nearly half an hour before she could make any noise. Then hotel security came, followed ten minutes later by three uniformed policemen. But it would take an hour for Detective Noah Jordain of the Special Victims Unit to get the phone call while he was sitting in a steamy and crowded restaurant in Chinatown, finishing up a spicy bowl of hot and sour soup and about to start in on a platter of crabs in black bean sauce.

Twenty-four hours later, Jordain learned that the woman who had been brutally murdered was not a woman of God at all, not married to Jesus Christ or pledged to charity or good works, but rather a call girl who had one prior and had just finished up her last stint in prison four months before.

"At least she had a head start at getting into heaven in that outfit," Jordain said after leaving the autopsy room, while he and his partner, Mark Perez, examined the nun's habit the woman was wearing.

"Noah, if you say prayers, you'd better start praying," Perez suggested.

"To help her get in?"

"No, that this isn't the beginning of something."

Jordain nodded. He'd already been there, thought that. A murder like this, ritualistic and designed, was not just an act of passion. It was, in all likelihood, the calling card of a sociopath on a mission.

Statistically, things would get far worse before they got any better.

2

"Good girls don't kiss and tell." She stroked the cushion she had put in her lap and the movement of her fingers was mesmerizing.

"Does that mean you're not a good girl? Or that you aren't going to tell your story?" I asked.

Cleo Thane laughed. A child's laugh that was all delight with only an innocent hint of sensuality. "I'm good, but not a good girl."

To look at her shining blond hair, the flawless skin, the light makeup that highlighted rather than hid, to take in the classic diamond stud earrings and the watch—subtle platinum, not gold—the designer blazer and slacks, the chic shoes and the status bag, you might guess she was an executive at a cosmetic company or the president of an agency or an art gallery.

But the night before this lovely woman had been whispering lies into the ear of a television newscaster whose name you would recognize, while she brought him to a violent orgasm in the back of a stretch limousine, with only a thin layer of glass separating them and their hot breaths from the driver. And before she met him,

she'd charged his credit card two thousand dollars for the privilege of spending three hours with her.

The contrast of who she was and how she presented herself was
just one of the many things I was intrigued by.

"Dr. Snow, no matter what kind of gentle words I wrap it up
in…I sell sex. That's what I do for a living. How could I be a good
girl?" She kicked off one of her very high-heeled shoes and noticed my glance. Even though I'd looked at her shoes before, she'd
never paid attention until today. I made a mental note of that.

"In my line of work, you always wear stilettos."

"Because they are so sexy?"

"Because they are weapons."

That was the last thing I had expected her to say. I certainly
knew how dangerous prostitution was for street hookers, but the
way Cleo had described her extremely exclusive business, the
need for weapons hadn't occurred to me. I covered my surprise.
"Other than your shoes, you make a real effort to look like a good
girl, don't you?"

"It's how I look. Why is that so hard to reconcile? I look like
this. And I sell sex. And since I do, I can't possibly be a good girl,
now can I?" By repeating the question, she made it impossible for
me to ignore it or how important an issue it was to her. We'd
talked about this before in the last six months, but there was obviously something about it that we still hadn't uncovered.

"Well, we aren't necessarily what we do, are we?" I asked, then
leaned back in my chair, crossing my ankles, noticing my own mod-
estly heeled pumps. Classic and not inexpensive, but not sexy like
Cleo's shoes.

She cocked her head and thought about my question. Not
everyone did that. Some patients just blurted out whatever
came into their minds. But because we'd been meeting for a
long time, I already knew Cleo was more calculated with her
words, sometimes saying what she wanted me to hear instead
of what she really thought. That was what we'd spent most of
her sessions talking about: not that she was a prostitute, or her
conflicts with her lifestyle, but her inclination to please people

too much—both sexually and in other ways. And not just her clients. That would have been natural. But the other people in her life.

With her forefinger she drew circles on the pillow. Her eyelashes were long and dusted her skin, and for the first time since she had been coming to see me, twice a week, at 10:00 a.m. each Monday and Wednesday, a single tear escaped from her eye and rolled down her cheek.

She kept her head bowed.

I waited.

Still, Cleo didn't move. I took the opportunity to tuck my hair behind my ears. Straight, dark hair—almost black—that hung down to the top of my shoulders. Cut to curve and frame my face. My twelve-year-old daughter liked to experiment with it: setting it, braiding it, putting it up with clips. She also liked to do my makeup. Other kids dress up in their mother's clothes; Dulcie preferred to dress me up and prepare me for the makeshift stage that doubled as the far side of our living room. And then, once I was in costume, she'd make me act out plays with her.

"Morgan Snow appearing as the lead in—" she'd say, and fill in the part I was playing at her direction. She'd act opposite me. Happier with this game than any other.

My daughter wanted to be an actress. Which wasn't surprising since her father was a film director, and I, being an overindulgent mother despite my better instincts, accommodated her. I didn't mind that it was her hobby and her ambition, but she wanted to try to act professionally while she was still in grade school, and I didn't want her to.

Acting is a tough business and I wanted my daughter's life to be filled with acceptance and success—not rejection and frustration.

Cleo finally looked up. Her gray eyes were soft and wet.

"What is it?" I asked.

"I am really confused. I wish I'd found you sooner. I wish I had known you a year ago. Two years ago. I needed someone like you who I could trust not to judge me, but who would push me to judge myself."

"That is not what I want to do. This isn't about judgment at all."

"Is it about redemption?"

"Do you need to be redeemed? Do you think of yourself as a sinner?"

More laughter. Even though Cleo, at twenty-eight, was only seven years younger than me, she reminded me of my daughter. For all that she had seen and done in her life, she remained untouched in some fundamental way.

"Not necessarily a sinner. No. But I'm not a good girl, either."

"You say it as if you are proud of it. What would be so bad about being a good girl?"

She grinned at my unintentional word play. "There are some very good things that I do. If I talk about them it will sound like propaganda from some dogmatic pamphlet."

"Let me worry about that. I think you are much harder on yourself than you need to be. And we need to talk about that. It plays in to you doing too much for other people. You deserve to feel good even if you don't want to be good."

She reached out and touched my hand, to thank me. Her skin, even on her fingertips, was like finely spun satin. It was unusual for my patients to touch me, but I didn't pull back, didn't flinch or show any reaction. Touch is telling. Lack of touch is even more telling. There is nothing as sacred as one person reaching out to another with their body to offer connection, and I would never treat such a thing lightly. There was nothing sexual about the way she put her fingers on the back of my hand and exerted a small but real pressure, but it woke me up in a momentarily sexual way. It made me think about sex, not with her, not with a man, but just inside of myself. Two fingers on my skin and she made me crave something I couldn't quite name.

"I don't meet many people willing to forgo making judgments about me," she said.

The current of connection between us was strong. It was not

something I ignored with my patients. I intrinsically understood some better than others.

"What do you think would make you feel good?"

"Having my book published."

Cleo had just finished writing a memoir, a tell-all about what she had learned about men and sex, based on the clients she had worked with over the last five years. She'd submitted an outline and the first five chapters to a publisher and just two weeks ago had received a substantial six-figure deal.

Now she was dealing with the reality of what she had signed on to do. Reveal secrets, albeit anonymously, about men, albeit disguised and not named, who had paid her and trusted her to never do exactly what she was doing.

My phone rang and Cleo glanced at it with a slight frown, but not nearly with the consternation that some patients do. I don't usually answer the telephone during sessions, but I do look at the caller ID in case it is Dulcie, or her school.

It was neither, so I let the machine pick up, apologizing to Cleo.

"That's all right. But you asked me another question and I never answered it. What was it? I don't like unanswered questions."

Her voice was soft with a faint hint of a Southern accent. Too soft to be talking about such hard facts and harsh realities.

She sighed and crossed her legs at her ankles. It was a dainty movement. A woman sitting on a veranda sipping iced tea and wearing a soft summer dress would cross her ankles like that.

"A patient after my own heart. I asked you what was wrong with being a good girl."

"Can you think of anything that would be more boring?"

"Can you?" I asked.

"Okay. You don't answer questions, I do. I forgot. So, no, I can't think of anything that would be more boring than being a good girl. They have no power, no clout. They are so easy to dismiss. Wives. Girlfriends. Sweethearts." She grimaced. "I know their husbands. I look into their lovers' eyes." She shook her head and her golden hair swung around like a sheath of silk. "You know, everyone talks about men having all the power, but it's easy to take it away. Especially if you have the one thing that they want so badly."

"What is the difference between you and those women? What do you know that they don't?" I wanted to hear her answer as much to learn about her as to understand more about the men she serviced.

"I know what they want and my entire energy is focused on giving it to them. And to make sure they don't have any reason to fear me. I'm not about approval or disapproval. Men are scared, Dr. Snow. Some worse than others. Some men, who have trouble getting an erection, or who have trouble with premature ejaculation, are just scared of what is between a woman's legs. Did you know that? Of course you do. You know even more than I do about all this. One man told me that he imagined it as a big gaping hole with rows of tiny sharp teeth inside and he was worried that if he stayed inside of me for too long, I'd bite him off. Have you ever heard that from a patient?"

Not for the first time, I was reminded of how much Cleo and I actually had in common. In figuring out what her clients wanted, in satisfying them, she had to listen to their fears and phobias, which was exactly what I did with patients.

I leaned forward just a little, to make the connection between us stronger. "Did it bother you when that man told you that?"

"Bother me? No, but it made me sad. And it made it much easier to do what I could for him. I never took him inside of me. But I saw him for months. Talking, soft touching, listening to him. I'd go to his hotel room every time he came to the city on business. He'd order whatever I wanted from room service and then we'd get into bed with the food. He liked me to feed him. And then he liked to feed me. And he liked me to massage him. Just lightly, you know, with oil. He was strong, worked out a lot, and I liked looking at him. All stretched out on the bed. He never closed his eyes, though. And we never shut off the light. I'd use the oil to loosen him up, and then I'd..."

She cut herself off and looked over at me.

"I guess there's no reason for me to go into all that?"

"If you want to tell me about it, I want to hear about it," I offered.

She'd pulled me in and lulled me with the cadences and nuances of her speech. If Cleo Thane wanted to become a sex therapist, she'd be very good at it. The only problem was as much as I earned—$225 an hour—she made more than three times that.

"It hurts. This confusion. These conflicts..." Her lips trembled for a minute; she looked away.

"What scares you the most? What is the most confusing?"

"I'm not sure. Maybe it's the book...." She hesitated. And then in a quieter voice said, "No. Not exactly the book. But it's related to the book. It's really the man I'm seeing."

"Seeing? As in seeing a client?" I was surprised. In all the time she had been in therapy with me she had never mentioned that she was seriously dating anyone, and I'd been waiting for a revelation like this.

Six months may sound like a long time for a patient to hold back important aspects of their personal life, but opening up was not always a simple act. Cleo had been obfuscating since she started with me. It was my job to be patient and do the best I could and trust that she would tell me her secrets when she was ready.

She shook her head. "No. He's not a client. He's my fiancé. A lawyer. At a very prestigious white-glove law firm. I hired him a year ago to help me set up an off-shore account for my company." She let out a delightful peal of laughter. "How ironic is that? I hired him. After a while he asked me out. This love shit is worse than the guy who pulled the knife on me in bed when I first got into the business. Him I knew what to do with, I just reached out and grabbed him by the balls. I squeezed so hard, his little baby fingers opened and the knife just dropped out. But this love stuff? I don't know where to grab."

When you are a therapist, you often become preoccupied with a patient's body language and voice. Obsessed with those things, in fact. From an inappropriate smile you understand a conflict, from crossed arms you pick up on an unwillingness to open up, from closed eyes you detect a reluctance to face the truth. In listening to a client, you learn the subtleties of inflections, pauses and rhythms because a voice is telling. Not just the words said, but also the beginnings of words that almost come out but are aborted, the sighs, the hints of tears. For me, voices are a rich source of information, especially when a patient is lying down on the couch and I can't see his or her face.

But Cleo was sitting up and facing me. She had been clear from the first: she didn't want to lie down on my couch. That, she said, would make her feel too much like she was back at work.

"What is so confusing about the love stuff, as you call it?" I asked.

"I never believed in romantic love. I once read that it's something that was invented in the twelfth century. And up till now every experience I've had was just more proof. This has never happened to me before. And I'm not sure I'm cut out for it." A faraway look in her eyes suggested she was trying very hard to deny the very opposite feeling.

Doctors were not supposed to admit this, but we like some patients more than others. And I liked Cleo. She was refreshing and honest. She was authentic. And that went far with me. But mostly it was because I—Morgan Snow, not the doctor part but the woman part—identified with her, mostly because of the similarities in our professions. But also because I had to work hard at not trying to please the people in my own life too much.

Identification with a patient is a healthy, normal part of therapy. In fact it helps us to get deeper insight into the men and women whom we are helping. But it is important to be aware of identifying with someone we are treating so that we don't lose our objectivity.

"Why don't you think you can be in love, Cleo?"

"That's not what I said."

"Isn't it?"

"You are too clever." She gave me a smile along with the compliment.

This woman was seductive in the most delightful way. Her charm was like a song that made you happy, and just for a little while, while you were listening, it enabled you to stop worrying about everything else that was going on.

And if I reacted to her that way—me, her therapist—then I could just imagine how the men she met reacted.

"You do ask good questions," she said, trying to get me off the track.

I nodded. Waited. Knew she had more to say.

"The man I am in love with thinks I might be in danger." A slight frown creased her forehead.

This was not what I had expected. "Why?"

Outside a cloud passed in front of the sun and the office was cast into shadow. Just for one second. But in that second, Cleo looked frightened. And even younger. And vulnerable.

How could this woman, who ran a successful twenty-first-century brothel, who teased and tortured and pleasured men to the tune of two thousand dollars a session, look so innocent and vulnerable?

"Cleo?"

"Yes?" She had been so deep in thought she couldn't remember what I had asked her.

"You said that this man thinks that you might be in danger. Have you been threatened?"

"No. Nothing has happened, not yet. But he's afraid of what will happen when word gets out about the book."

"Has the deal been announced?"

She shook her head but didn't say anything. The clock on my desk ticked, making a slight but distinct sound as each second passed. We were running out of time, but I didn't want her to leave before she answered me.

"I really am in love," she said.

"You say that as if you have to convince me of your feelings."

"Maybe…maybe I have to convince myself."

"Why?"

"Because how can I love someone but not be able to make love to him?"

"And you can't?" This was an important revelation, and I watched her carefully as she composed herself and then answered.

First she shook her head no. Once. Twice. And then for a third time. Finally she began to speak. "No. No matter how hard I try.

I can't do the simplest things with him. How can I feel the way I do about him and not be able to go down on him without gagging? He puts one hand on my breast and I freeze. He kisses me and I get sick to my stomach. You know, even though I'm getting paid to do it, I still like sex. Always have. It's what I do. How can I not be able to do it with the one guy who really matters to me?"

Her tears caught in the reflection of the sun in her eyes. Cleo even cried in a lovely way: her eyes didn't get red; she didn't scrunch up her face. Her lips quivered and a small sob escaped from her lips. "I'm really confused."

She had just told me more about herself in the last fifteen minutes than she had in all the days and weeks that she had been coming to see me. I nodded. "I know."

"Do you think this is what I'm really here to talk to you about? Not how I want to please people. Not the book, but what is wrong between this man and me." She shook her head vehemently. "Is that what happens in therapy? People come to you for one thing and find out something completely different is bothering them?"

"It might look like that, but everything is connected in some way. However, figuring that out isn't your job right now. You should just feel free to tell me what's on your mind. Whether it seems connected or not."

She didn't say anything.

"What are you thinking?" I asked.

"How he'd feel if he knew that I had just told you all that. He's sort of private."

"Cleo, is there a reason you won't use his name?"

"Occupational hazard. I never use men's real names. To protect their privacy. I just give everyone nicknames."

"But you said he's not a client."

"No. No, he's not."

"If you were to give him a nickname, what would it be?"

She laughed. "I've given him a few nicknames."

"Okay. What one comes to mind first?"

"Caesar."

I must have arched my eyebrows, because she laughed. "Do you think it's silly?"

"No, but I'm curious. Why Caesar?"

"The real Caesar was so commanding and powerful. Did you see the movie? His passion for Cleopatra was so all-encompassing. It just reminds me of how he is."

"Is he understanding about your sexual conflicts with him?"

She nodded. "No. Yes. Well, intellectually yes. He understands that I am having some sort of resistance to doing what he wants me to do to him—what I want to do to him—and confusing it with what I do with my clients...." She broke off, close to breaking down again.

I've been a therapist for ten years, a sex therapist at the Butterfield Institute for five of them, and have had more than fifty long-term patients. One thing I've learned is that, if we are sensitive to our patients, if we listen to what they say as well as to what they don't say, they reveal all the clues we are going to need in order to help them in the first five to eight weeks of therapy. It can take an infinite amount of time to move the pieces around until they lock into place and present us with a whole picture, but we get the clues early on. I was getting them now.

Cleo's head was bowed. Her eyes lowered. Her body remained quite still. I didn't know if she was crying again or not, but clearly she was distressed. I looked away for just a second, toward the windows and the balcony outside my office—the narrow terrace that is just wide enough for me to stand on and sip a cup of coffee as I watch the pedestrians and traffic on the street below. Beyond that are two lovely magnolia and dogwood trees that filter the strong summer light as it spills into my office, sending shadows of dancing leaves on the wall and across the Chinese art deco rug.

Cleo started speaking while my head was turned.

"Caesar seems more worried about the book than about our sex life. He doesn't understand why my sense of accomplishment at having written the book isn't enough. He thinks I should burn it now that I've gotten it 'out of my system'— as he says. He is afraid that one of the men I am writing about might try to get back at me. Oh, it's just so ridiculous." Her eyes filled up again. "I'm afraid he is going to give me an ultimatum over this. Over a book!"

The minute hand on the small silver clock on the table by my chair swooshed forward. It was ten-forty-five. The session was technically over. But I didn't mind giving her a few more minutes.

She was twisting the emerald ring on her ring finger, twirling it around so that every few seconds the stone caught the light, sending reflections on the wall, then disappearing just as quickly.

"Has he read the book?" I asked her.

"No. No one has. Not yet."

"Because there's something in it that you don't want Caesar to know about?" I guessed.

She nodded. "I haven't lied to him about what I do. I just haven't gone into the kind of detail the book does. Caesar thinks that for the last couple of years I have been behind a desk sending out the girls. And I have been doing that. But I've also been doing some calls."

"You told him you stopped?"

"He thinks I stopped about a year ago. I didn't. I still have a half-dozen regular clients who I've been taking care of for a long time. I know these guys. We have...hell...we have a relationship."

"Cleo, I'm not sure that I understand. Does Caesar know that you are still going to bed with other men?"

"Well, see that's the thing. Technically I'm not. I don't have what you'd call regular sex with most of them."

"Regular sex?" I laughed. "I don't make judgments, but there is no such thing as regular or irregular sex, as far as I'm concerned."

"See, that's why I like you. We're on the same side of all this. The logical side. The side that doesn't make sex into some religious experience that saves souls or plummets you into hell."

The clock chimed and the bell-like sound drew her attention. "I guess my time is up?"

I nodded.

"Just one more sec?"

I nodded again

She reached down and pulled out the Tiffany shopping bag she had brought with her. I'd noticed it when she walked in but hadn't though much about it.

From inside, she extracted a bulky manila envelope, which she held in her hand for a few seconds and caressed as if it was a velvet pillow, or a man's thigh.

"I printed this out for you. Like I said, no one has seen the whole thing yet or even knows I finished it. It's my first draft. I still have a lot of work to do. Not to mention disguising the guys I write about much better..." She smiled. "But I really want you to read it."

"Does Caesar know you're giving it to me?"

"No." She stood up.

Even though she was getting ready to go, I didn't want her to miss what I thought might be a moment of insight for her.

"Does keeping that from him make you feel good or bad?"

Her head tilted to the side and a half smile played on her lips. "Good. And. Bad." She sighed. "But here's the thing. If we are going to talk about whether or not I can really go through with publishing this book, you have to read it. I mean, if I do this, I need to be able to give Caesar a really good reason why. I want to publish my book, but I don't want to lose him in the process. So..."

She took the last step to the leather chair where I sat.

Holding out my hands I took the package from her.

It wasn't light and somehow that surprised me. Everything about Cleo Thane was. From the lilting voice to the blond hair to the pastel-colored clothes she favored—so different from the almost all black uniform most of us New Yorkers wore—to her pale gray eyes and barely pink lips. Even her perfume, which reminded me of spring and had a base note of lilacs, was light.

There was nothing heavy or dark or ominous about the woman who handed me her confession.

Nothing except for what was actually in that envelope: all the secrets she hadn't yet told me, or anyone else, but that would, in the end, be like the pins collectors used in the process of "pinning" a butterfly's body to a board after they have captured and killed them.

3

After Cleo left my office I pushed the play button on my answering machine, and while the morning's messages repeated, I walked to the window, opened the door to the balcony, stepped out and looked down.

The first message was from my divorce lawyer, telling me that the papers had been signed by the judge and my divorce was final. We'd expected it to happen that day, but there was always a chance that the paperwork would be delayed.

I rubbed my fingers against the gritty stone surface of the balustrade. I was conflicted about having ended my marriage. Yes, it was the right thing to do, and I would have championed this divorce if it were for any one of my patients. But, despite our problems, I had liked the calm of my life with Mitch. That we had wound up at a place where there was a lack of passion hadn't been a surprise to me. Many marriages wind up lusterless. But it depressed my husband and he couldn't live with it. Ex-husband, I reminded myself.

The next message, from an insurance company, droned on

while the sun disappeared behind a cloud and peeked back out. It was early June, and the scent of the climbing rose bush that winded through the railing and up the side of the brownstone perfumed the air. I leaned over, looked down.

Below me, on the street, Cleo emerged, stood in front of the building and lit a cigarette, her gold lighter flashing in the sun.

Cleo worried me.

No one who did what she did for a living, who had been with so many men, who had made money having sex with lonely or worse—with disturbed or sexually addicted men—could remain as untouched and blasé as she appeared.

Despite how long it had taken for us to get to the heart of her problems, I didn't feel manipulated. I didn't see any deception. I didn't feel—in that intuitive way that a therapist sometimes does—that she had been holding back. She just needed more time to open up. So then, what didn't I trust?

My own preconceived notions of what someone who did what she did for a living must feel?

I had other patients who were prostitutes. None, however, who had their own businesses, or who got paid what Cleo did.

One day a week I did my duty and visited women behind bars to counsel them so that when they were released they would stay off the street. And pigs can fly and there is a Santa Claus. But occasionally we did help. And for that one patient a year who didn't go back to where she just was, I could give up fifty-two days.

Cleo had never even been near a prison. And to look at her, you would believe that. With her lustrous hair, refined clothes and shining eyes, she presented a very pretty picture. I knew better than to assign personality traits based on appearances. But there was a real guilelessness about her. Were her defence mechanisms so strong that she just did not allow the reality of her life to bruise her?

Or was she disturbed in a deeper way? How buried were the fissures and flaws? How long would it take us, working together, pulling and pushing, to find them? Was she just an excellent actress playing one role with her clients, another with me? I didn't think so, and I knew a little about actresses. My mother had been one. Not a very famous one, though. She never became a bright star, except for a short time, in one little girl's eyes.

My machine beeped and another message started.

"Dr. Stone, this is Officer Tom Dignazio from the Twenty-fourth Precinct," the somber voice said. I stiffened. This was the last message, the one I had ignored while Cleo had been in my office.

"Someone who we believe was a patient of yours has been found. A young girl you were seeing earlier this year when she was in prison. I'm afraid she's been murdered. And we need you to identify the body."

He rattled off his phone number and requested I call him as soon as possible.

The body?

Which one of those girls whom I'd been seeing was now just *the body?* I knew I would call him back, but not yet. Not that fast. I was too stunned.

Below me, Cleo was still standing on the stoop smoking her cigarette. Two men, walking east from Madison Avenue, slowed just a little as they approached, watching her standing there in the street having her cigarette. She must have smiled at them—her back was to me—because one of the guys' faces lit up as if he'd been anointed. The other just stared. It would have been rude if his expression hadn't been filled with admiration. They passed her. Then one turned back for a last look.

Cleo took one more puff and threw the cigarette down on the sidewalk, stamping it out with that high-heeled shoe that showed just enough toe cleavage, then she started to walk west, away from me. Just as I was about to turn back to my office, I noticed a third man in the shadows of the building across the street, a bulky briefcase by his foot. He gripped an umbrella with a shining silver handle despite the sunny day.

Clearly, he was watching Cleo.

He stood, unmoving, just staring until she was almost to the corner, and then he began walking in her direction. He moved as if mesmerized, as if pulled forward because of her.

I crossed my arms, shivering despite the warm air. I was suddenly scared for Cleo.

She didn't sway her hips. There was nothing lascivious about the way she held her shoulders or head. What signal did she telegraph, what was it that men instinctively knew just from looking at her?

I wanted to follow her, to protect her and to watch her interact. It was one thing to hear her talk about seducing men, but I wanted to see her do it, to note the steps of the process, to study the interaction.

If I was totally truthful with myself, the reason I was so curious about this client of mine was because I wanted to learn from Cleo Thane.

I had been studying human sexual response and counseling patients with sexual problems for years. But living with the same man for almost fifteen years, I had forgotten so much about how to deal with men. Now that I was once again single, I felt naive.

Physician heal thyself.

If I could have followed her around for the rest of the day, I would have. Even into the darkened rooms where her clients waited for her, desperate to have her work her magic on them.

We want what we don't have. We take what we have for granted. I was curious about what it would be like to be hungry for someone again. I had not tasted a man's skin or licked a man's lips for too long. What would it be like? How easy or how difficult would it be to find that part of myself again?

My husband and I had separated two years before. And for a few years before that we had not been very physical with each other. Early on in our relationship we'd fallen into being friends and parents first, and lovers last and infrequently.

That's what I mean. You want what you know you cannot have. Cleo didn't want what I wanted. She had men's desire. She wanted what I'd had—unconditional love that didn't depend on sex. That was what my marriage with Mitch had become. What I really still had with him, despite our divorce. We couldn't generate any heat anymore, but we cared about each other. That was what made our breaking apart so bittersweet.

To be a therapist, you have to go into therapy yourself. I'd started that part of the process when I was a teenager, and over the years I had gone back several times. I knew that I had some issues with control, with wanting to please the people I cared about—sometimes too much. And I knew I'd lost the connection to my own sexual energy. Only in the last few months, once I knew my divorce was imminent, had I started to think about it again: about seduction, passion. About the hot rush of pleasure that I hadn't felt in a while.

Cleo talked about standing in front of a man and watching his face grow slack with need. Seeing his eyes half close and have him fight his urgency. Listening to him beg her to take him in her mouth or let him slip inside of her so that he could, for just a little while, swirl off into that soundless, sightless place where everything falls into waves of blues, greens, reds, yellows, and bursts into feelings. Explosions of sensation. No words.

I wanted to see what she saw.

The man in the street was still twenty or thirty paces behind Cleo, his footsteps not intruding on her shadow. Was he being cautious not to go faster? Was he measuring his steps? Was this someone who just happened to be walking in the same direction she was going? Or was he following her?

I knew about trailing someone, even though it had been more than twenty years since I had done it. I'd followed my mother, sneaked out of the apartment after her, waited on the street corner to see which direction she took and then crept forward, staying in the background. Not to spy on her, but to make sure that she was, indeed, going where she had told me. To make sure she was not going to get more pills or alcohol. Or to meet another man whose name I would never hear.

If you don't want to be seen, you are careful. The way the man in the street below was being careful.

Cleo had reached the corner, still unaware of him. Men's glances couldn't be important to Cleo anymore. When someone was willing to give you thousands of dollars to look at you, and touch you, and have you touch them, when you were desired that way, a mere look must have been meaningless. There were other things that might have caught her attention, but a man's attraction?

This guy was good at what he was doing. To anyone else on the street who had not watched this aerial ballet of suspense that I had, there would be nothing suspicious to see.

But I believed she *was* being followed. And I didn't know what to do with the information. Call her on her cell phone? Warn her?

Except what if I was wrong?

She turned the corner. And ten seconds later he turned, too.

And then they were both gone.

Maybe, it didn't mean anything.

A woman walked west on Sixty-fifth Street at 11:00 a.m. on a Wednesday morning, and a man, who happened to be going in the same direction, noticed her. He hesitated when he saw her, not to hide in the shadows, not to make sure that he wasn't seen, but to enjoy the lithe body as it walked by. To smile at the shining hair. He was just appreciating her. And the fact that he went in the same direction? Well, everyone on the street has to go either east or west, north or south. It was a meaningless encounter.

It was not the first time my overactive imagine was trying to turn an innocent moment on a lovely spring day into a portent of imminent danger.

Where are you going? When are you coming back? I would ask my mother, and she would smile and run her fingers through my hair and promise that she'd be back soon, leaving me, again, to wonder if this time my mother was telling the truth or a lie.

Until she went away for good.

4

The officer who was supposed to meet me at the morgue wasn't there yet, so I sat in the anteroom, trying not to smell the antiseptic harbinger of death and mystery that hung in the air.

Before that spring, my patients didn't die.

While I deal with the heart, the head and the sex organs, I don't wield a scalpel or saw. I have never sliced through the top layer of skin, through fat and muscle, to discover the growth that does not belong, find the tear to sew up, or cosmetically alter an appearance. I have never immersed my hands in a human cavity to move aside a pulsing organ or feel the heat of blood spurting out of a wound.

Instead I probe with words for the secrets we learn to keep from others—and even more critical—the secrets we keep from ourselves, buried just as deeply as a bullet lodged in bone.

I have never signed a death certificate or had to walk out into a waiting room to find the expectant, anxious faces of a family

member clinging past logic to the hope that I could save their ail-
ing loved one.

My office is not in a cubicle in a hospital and does not smell of
disinfectants. Rather I work in a turn-of-the-century building on
the Upper East Side in New York City. Nothing about the building's elegant facade or classic lines suggests that past the Ionic col-
umns and through the wrought-iron door is the most progressive
sex clinic in the country.

There is a small brass plaque on the outside of the building,
identifying it but giving little else away: *The Butterfield Institute.*

The black cursive letters are etched deeply into the metal plate.
Run your fingers over them and you feel the edges pushing into
your flesh. Could you cut your skin on those edges and draw
blood? Probably not, but even if you did, none of us inside could
offer more than a Band-Aid.

There are only those three words on the bronze rectangle. We
do not advertise. Not because we are ashamed of what we do—
each of us could work twice as many hours and still not see all the
patients who are waiting for an appointment—but because we respect our patients' privacy: their secrets are ours.

Inside the marble-floored foyer a glittering chandelier casts a
sparkling light on the reception area. A young woman sits behind
the ornate desk, complete with gilded lion's-claw feet. Behind her
you can glimpse the marble fireplace, thick molding around the
perimeter of the ceiling and another chandelier. One flight up the
stairs are our offices.

That spring there were trees in bloom on the street outside my
window, and I had seen them go from tight-pinked buds to lush,
provocative blossoms to brown-edged and withering petals. It had
been a glorious, slow seduction, but the trees had come into leaf
and the show was over. And I was waiting at the morgue.

"What about Sheba Larcher's parole officer?" I asked Officer
Dignazio as he escorted me into the cold tiled room. "Why didn't
you call her?"

"Her parole officer is out of town. We wouldn't have asked you if we had any other choice, Dr. Snow."

A lab assistant in green scrubs pulled the metal drawer out. The mound under the pale blue sheet looked so small, more child-size than adult.

And then the M.E. lifted a corner and pulled it down.

I didn't look. Not at first. I had to force my head to turn, propel my feet forward, look down.

Sheba was only twenty. Only eight years older than my own daughter, but aged in ways I prayed my daughter would never be. This girl had still been beautiful, despite the hard edge. Hope could still leap into her eyes when we'd talked about how she was going to leave New York and find another way to make money.

I turned away. Not able to look at her anymore.

"Yes, that's her," I said to the M.E.

And then for just a second, under the antiseptic scent, I smelled something else. Not flowery like a woman's perfume, but heavy and almost a little sweet. And then the sharper astringent odor took over again.

I had seen her last in February. In prison. Four days before she was to be released. She had told me her mother had wired her the money to come home to a small town in West Virginia. That she was all right with giving up the dreams that had brought her to New York. But just in case, I gave her both my phone number and my address. An invitation to use either if she felt the need.

But she hadn't made contact. And obviously she had not made it home. The next contact I had had with her came from a police officer who called, asking me to come down and identify her body.

Every day for the last five years I had gone to my pale yellow office five days a week, sat in my comfortable chair flanked on my right by an end table on which rested an agate ashtray and an innocuous clock and looked across the room at this patient or that one. I'd elicited secrets and listened as hard as I could to revelations so that I would be able to help heal or restore their sexual wounds and integrate that one aspect of their personality back into the whole, to align love and lust, to balance who they were with who they wished they could be, to bring the passion back after grief or loss or pregnancy or divorce or a loss of self-esteem, to work with the fetish as well as the fantasy.

And no one who had ever come to me for help had died because of my advice.

Until that spring.

Until that spring I had never seen any of my patients laid out on a hospital gurney. Not breathing. I took one last look at the waxen face of the woman I had worked with——all the vitality and expression that had illuminated her, gone.

Butterfly collectors trap living creatures and suffocate them. Then carefully, and with precision and a certain obsessive passion, pin these glorious creatures down and lay them out so that in death they can be admired. Even if they cannot flutter or fly, their colors shimmer and shine inside their glass tombs forever. In death, these creatures retain some of their glory.

Not her.

She did not shine anymore. Her hair was limp, her skin was dull, her cheeks bloodless.

She would never shimmer again.

I had started working with prostitutes in prison while I was getting my Ph.D. I was not so naive to think that I could do enough for all of them. Most of them would go back to their pimps, or their e-mail accounts, or worse, the streets. Yet, I kept at it. Hoping that some of them might get away.

Some of them.

She had asked for help and I had gone to see her. She had welcomed me for what was ahead of her. Had wanted to change the direction her life had been taking, to have me light a fire to help her melt the past. None of this would happen. Not ever. She was lost now. To everyone who had known her. To her potential. To her promise.

She was one of *the lost girls.*
Not the first one I had tried to save.
Not the last one I would fail.

5

I was back in my office twenty minutes later, sitting at my desk thinking about the still, pallid body when Nina stuck her head in.

"Morgan?"

I turned, startled out of the moment.

Dr. Nina Butterfield, the owner of the institute, my mentor, my godmother and my friend, stood in the doorway to my office.

"You okay?" she asked.

I nodded.

"You look like you saw a ghost."

I saw ghosts all the time and she knew that. No answer was needed. And she knew that, too. She spoke to fill in the silence, so that we could move past it.

As if I would ever be able to move past it.

"Did the paperwork come through?" she asked, referring, I knew, to the divorce.

I nodded.

"Well, weren't we going to have lunch?" She was watching me carefully, as she always did. "You were hoping I'd forget. That doesn't surprise me. You don't want to talk about the divorce and you know I'm going to force you to."

We both laughed at that.

When Nina laughed she looked much younger than her sixty-two years. She had shoulder-length copper-colored hair, warm caramel-colored skin and bright amber eyes that bored into you and dared you to look away. She had sculpted features that would seem masculine in a less sensual woman. Dressed in a honey suede jacket, black slacks and a rust silk shirt, she looked professional, but easy-going. And she was. The most fluid woman I'd ever met. With the biggest heart and the smartest head. She had swooped down and picked me up, opened her wings and sheltered me under them when I was too little to know how scared I was or how much I needed her.

Now that I knew, I was grateful every day that she was in my life. She'd given me support and helped me find my way. And for her, I was as close to a daughter as she'd ever have. For someone so maternal, so caring, Nina had never had children. And because of me, and my daughter, she said she never regretted it. We were her family, she said.

"Get your bag, we have a reservation," she said.

"A reservation?"

Usually we walked during lunch. The point of going out together wasn't necessarily to eat as much as it was for us to leave the institute. To spend time together. We walked Manhattan in every direction, often without any destination in mind: two pilgrims, not searching for a shrine, but for the hour with each other. I'd grown up taking walks with Nina. She'd been my mother's best friend—they'd met when they were both students at NYU and lived next door to each other in their Greenwich Village dorm.

After my mother died, when I was eight, Nina had stepped in, not trying to replace my mother, because she knew no one could do that, but to at least be there for me, to offer a hand, a hug and a heart. Even after my father remarried, Nina remained the most important woman in my life.

Grabbing my bag, I followed Nina into the hall. She stopped at the head of the staircase, put her arm around me and gave me a companionable hug. Her spicy, Oriental scent was familiar and, instead of smelling sexy, was reassuring in its constancy. Especially that day, I liked knowing that some things remained the same.

"It's actually easier than I thought it would be," I said as we separated from the hug.

"I'm glad." Her voice told me she didn't believe a word of what I was saying, but she was going to allow me the charade for at least a while.   •

Nina knew far better than I did what going through a divorce was like. She'd had three.

"Well, you don't look like you've been weeping copiously in your office."

"I haven't had time." And then I told her about my trip to identify Sheba Larcher's body.

At the restaurant, Nina ordered us both glasses of champagne and I didn't bother to protest. She always drank it, and after what I'd seen in the last hour, coming right on the heels of the call from my lawyer, I welcomed the aperitif.

She raised her glass. "I know you are still conflicted over the divorce, but I'm proud of how you handled it."

Yes, the divorce could have dragged on a lot longer, it could have turned ugly and have hurt my daughter even more than it already had, but Mitch and I had worked hard so that hadn't happened.

"There isn't much I can do about what Dulcie is facing or how hard it has been on her already. The least I could do was not make it any worse," I said.

"You have done everything you could. You have a strong little girl and an ex-husband who is a good friend. Nothing is going to get worse anymore, it's going to start to get better now."

I nodded.

"The joint custody will work. It's been working since the separation. Dulcie needs to be with both of you. I've seen her, Morgan. I know she's going to be fine. Every kid struggles with something. This will be what she struggles with. But the way you and Mitch have worked it out, she'll have less strife over it than many kids do."

Custody had been the one issue that I wanted to fight. During the separation, Dulcie spent two weekends and one entire week each month with Mitch at his apartment across town from ours. She'd handled it well and Mitch wanted it to continue. I didn't. I wanted to grab my daughter and keep her with me every day and every night. Not keep her from him, but keep her with me because when he picked her up and took her with him, away from me, something in me wrenched. I could barely breathe for the first few minutes she was gone. The separation from her was the most painful emotion I'd experienced as an adult. If you can love someone too much, I loved Dulcie too much.

And yet, I knew, when I was logical instead of emotional, that Mitch was entitled to his time with our daughter. It was my problem that I couldn't bear to have her out of my sight.

"He is a good father," I said to Nina, and sipped at the tulip-shaped flute.

"He is a great father," she corrected.

"He *is* a great father."

"There wasn't anything else you could do. This was not your failure. Not anyone's failure," Nina offered.

I nodded.

"No one tried harder than you did. But it just didn't make sense to keep it going."

"It did to me. I was perfectly content with our life. He's my friend. We had Dulcie. It was enough." I was going over the same ground, but Nina didn't remind me of that or sigh with impatience or boredom.

"I know, sweetie." She paused, drank from her glass, and then went on. "For some people it works. For others it doesn't."

"I have had more than my share of clients who were in marriages where the people drifted apart. Where the husband felt the wife was too connected to her work. Where the sex got boring. And I've helped those couples to stay in those relationships or leave them, but I just never thought… I guess it's just that I feel like such a failure, Nina."

"You aren't. The two of you didn't bring out the best in each other—except where Dulcie is concerned."

"He says that when he is with me, all he can feel is the dark side of me, the side that is connected to my patients' problems, that I treat him too much like a patient with a problem to solve." I had repeated this, thought about it, obsessed over it, and discussed it with Nina before. And yet I still needed to say it again. "But I'm not dark all the time. I'm not, am I?"

She shook her head. "That Mitch connects to that one part of you is as much his issue as it is yours. Another man whose psychology is different from his would identify with all the other parts of you. You know that. You just have to give someone else a chance to show you that."

I picked up the menu. I was sick of talking about it. I'd tried to solve it alone in therapy, and then in marriage counseling with Mitch. I hadn't been able to. We hadn't been able to. That was that.

Following my lead, Nina picked up her menu, too, and together we read through the two pages of offerings.

"I'll have the niçoise salad," she said when the waiter appeared.

"The warm goat cheese salad for me."

The waiter left.

"You have that look in your eyes, Morgan."

"What look?"

"The *I-should-have-done-better* look."

"No, I have the *so-this-is-how-your-life-turns-out* look."

We smiled ruefully at each other.

"For two women who spend their working lives helping people with their sexual problems, we can be pretty pathetic."

We both laughed.

"Better luck next time," she offered.

We clinked glasses. She drank from hers, but I just held mine.

"Do you want a next time?" I asked.

"Sometimes I do. Other times…I'm not sure." She shook her head.

"I know."

"But we will."

"Do we have to? Life is really much easier to deal with if you cut romantic relationships out of the equation."

She burst into laughter.

Our salads arrived and we dove into the beds of lettuce, attacking the leaves with a voracity that was almost predatory.

"*Freedom* is just another word for being alone," she said.

"But being alone means not having to make allowances for anyone else's screw-ups."

"And not having to deal with anyone else's screw-ups means never having to clean up after them."

Nina knew a lot about that.

"Sex and love and marriage and attraction and fantasy, and flirting and seduction, are all other people's problems—at least for today." I speared another lettuce leaf with the tongs of my fork.

Nina put her lips around an olive and scraped off the meat with her teeth. "Passion is passé," she said. Then, daintily, with her manicured nails, she put the pit on the side of her plate and just as delicately did not mention that tears were streaming down my cheeks.

6

It was the end of the day for most people, but not for Detective Noah Jordain and his partner, Mark Perez. Tana Butler, the thirtysomething officer who was a whiz at noticing things that other people overlooked, had just arrived with her report, and the three of them had work to do. The evening was just beginning.

A fresh pot of coffee perked on a battered table in the corner and Jordain stood above it, waiting impatiently to pour himself a cup.

"The problem with a hotel room—" Tana was saying when Jordain interrupted.

"Don't even bother telling us. You've got too much contamination to know what has to do with our perp and a hundred perfectly acceptable guests," he said in the slow New Orleans way he had of speaking.

Tana Butler nodded.

"Is there anything you can isolate? Under her fingernails? Toenails? In her mouth, for Christ's sake?" Perez asked, almost shouting.

Anyone who worked with Jordain and Perez found out quickly that, while they were completely efficient, they were extremes. Perez had a quick temper and wanted data even before the evidence was collected. Jordain was thorough. Overly analytical. Almost to a fault. Almost to the point of taking too much time.

The two of them—one laid-back, the other in-your-face—balanced each other out.

Tana flipped through her file. "No, Mark. Sorry. Of course, there are fibers under her nails—from the rug, from the nun's habit, other detritus from the room. Nothing that helps. Soap residue. Matched the soap the hotel puts out. She took a shower or a bath in the room. Either before he got there or while he was there."

Jordain paced. "So we know either she liked to be clean or he wanted her to be clean."

"That's a hell of a lot to learn. Boy, are we the lucky bastards or what?"

As he did when his partner's sarcasm went too far, Jordain gave Perez a sidelong glance. Perez saw it, got up, grabbed a can of Diet Coke and popped the tab. He took a slug.

He was addicted to the beverage but Jordain matched him can for cup of the chicory-laced coffee that he drank all day long.

"The rosary? The nun's habit?" Jordain asked.

"We are working on it."

"Not good enough, Tana," Perez said. "You know that we need a lead while this is fresh. The first forty-eight hours…"

"What about the hotel tape?" Jordain interrupted his partner on purpose. Tana was a professional. She didn't deserve a lecture just because they hadn't turned up anything yet.

Perez took another sip of his soda.

"How are we doing on the hotel tapes?" Jordain asked.

Tana looked down at the report on the table. "It's the same story. A crowded lobby of a midtown hotel. Hundreds of people coming and going. She checked in at five-thirty. Died at two in the morning. He could have come up to the room anytime before, say, midnight." She shook her head. "Along with about a hundred other people. We've got tons of head shots—mostly from the back."

"Why do these idiots put the cameras in such ridiculous places?" Perez asked.

"It's worse than that, Detective. Like almost every other hotel, the system is ancient. The quality of the pictures is horrible."

Jordain sighed and pushed his coffee mug away from him, then pulled it closer and took a long sip.

"Let's not walk away from the tapes. I want blowups of every man who went up and down every one of those elevators. It might not help us now, but if this guy is a repeater, I want to be ready."

"There is one thing," Tana said.

Both men turned to face her. "It's not much. It looks like the girl was given last rites."

"Details?" Jordain asked. It was his most-oft-repeated phrase. Some younger cops, who didn't know him well enough yet to respect him as much as most people did, called him Detective Details behind his back. Jordain knew about it. And it didn't bother him in the least.

God, his father had taught him, is in the details. That's where you solved a case.

"She had a smear of olive oil on her forehead and that's—"

"We're both good Catholic boys," Perez said. "We know priests use olive oil. Blessed olive oil."

Tana didn't react to his sarcasm as she continued with her notes. "And she'd recently consumed a small amount of red wine."

Jordain was up, pouring himself more coffee. "The sacraments? The archdiocese is not going to be happy about this. But we are going to have to call them."

"It's a priest? A priest did this to her?" Perez asked, mostly muttering it to himself. "When I was a kid, there were no church scandals. The sacred was never mixed with the profane. Or if it was, it was so well hidden that no one ever found out. Now there are priests in the news all the time." He walked to the window. "Do you think it's a priest doing this shit?"

"I don't know. It could be. But it could also be someone who was a priest," Jordain said. "Or someone who wants us to think he is a priest," he added.

"Okay, let's get on it," Perez said. "We are looking for a male. Religious affiliation. N.Y. metro area. Usually they don't stray too far from home."

7

Because it was raining when I left the office, I hailed a taxi and popped a peppermint mint in my mouth before I opened the door. I have a very sensitive sense of smell, and taxis often harbored too many stale scents. But with the candy in my mouth, most of them could be diffused.

I gave the driver the address of my apartment on the corner of Madison Avenue and Eightieth Street, and then opened my briefcase and pulled out the package Cleo had given me.

Inside the manila envelope was a manuscript printed out on three-hole paper with shiny brass brads holding the heavy load together.

The paper smelled clean and inky, a pristine copy. It must have been printed within the last twenty-four hours, because usually the smell of ink didn't last any longer. There was another scent on the paper, too. But I wasn't sure what it was. I shut my eyes and breathed it in. Menthol. Faint, but persistent.

For Love or Money
by Cleo Thane
Chapter One

The room is in a five-star hotel. It could be any one of the luxury hotel rooms in any one of a dozen cities in the United States that have such hotels. At least four hundred dollars a night. Sometimes five hundred. Often six hundred. And so the rug is thick and the linens on the bed are from France or Italy and have thread counts as high as the cost of the room.

It is nighttime. The only light in the room comes from the lamp on the desk. The drawn curtains hang, heavy and rich, and pool on the floor.

The wallpaper is pale blue with a slight diamond pattern. The furnishings are ornate and gilded. The man is about forty-two years old. He has dark hair, slicked back, and a slightly receding hairline. He is in decent shape. You can tell because he is practically naked. His arms are muscled—he probably plays tennis every weekend and goes to the gym at least twice a week. And with his arms pulled above his head, the muscles are bulging against the awkward position. His chest is broad. Good skin. A slight tan. You are surprised that he is good-looking, aren't you? She isn't. She wets her lips, not to be purposely provocative but because she needs them to be wet, and then she leans down and puts her face very close to his, so close that if he reached up he could kiss her. But they are not playing at romance. This is seduction. And there is a difference.

"Wet enough?" she asks him.

He shakes his head no.

She lubricates her lips more.

"Now?"

He nods.

"Don't move."

"I won't."

"No, you won't. If you do, you know I'll stop."

He nods again. But he does move, he stretches out his legs just a little against the constraints that keep his ankles tied together.

The man who is tied up is waiting for her to put her lips on his nipples and suckle him. First he feels the tips of her hair tickle the smooth skin of his chest. He wants to arch up, to get her mouth on him sooner, but he knows that if he does she will stop. And he doesn't want that.

The sound of her wet lips on his skin is the melody he is paying her to play. It fills his ears. He shuts his eyes. Her tongue swirls on his skin, her teeth pull at him, taking small nibbles. The muscles in his back are pulled tight and he can feel the heat moving from his fingers, toward his elbows, toward his chest and traveling down, meeting the heat that is traveling up his legs. Everything converges dead center in his body at his erection.

Her hair is fanning his chest now. She raises her face to him and shows him how she is licking her lips once more and then she bows down again before him to take his other nipple in her mouth.

She sucks on it as if she is a baby and starving and he does not even realize, so focused is he on her sucking, that milk of another kind does flow from him, spurting out, arcing over his body, wetting his chest, and her arm and the back of her neck.

She feels it and lessens her hold on his nipple. Slowly she straightens up, still smiling. There is an art to disengagement. She does not just stand up the minute the man has ejaculated and say, "Well, that's done now, so I'll be taking off."

She finesses the rest of the encounter without breaking the fictive dream. She is a poet, and even if she is writing disturbing poetry full of putrefied images that make some people want to vomit, she has to finish the poem. She has to complete the last stanza.

After all, this man has paid for this evening in this chic hotel. And he has been paying for evenings like this for the last two years. He is the son of a man who owns a very large media empire. He is the second in command there, appearing on the cover of the annual report next to his dad.

She knows this because as a bonus last year he gave her stock in this company, and two months ago the report arrived in the mail. Despite a fluctuating market, the stock has performed.

The least she can do is to stay awhile and have something to eat or drink and show her real appreciation. Because this man likes to show off and brag a little. He likes to tell her about what the company is doing so she will be impressed. So she asks as she works the knot, "How is business?"

"We are starting a new magazine," Clark Kent says as she unties his left hand. This is not his real name, but this is what she has named him. After Superman, after the mild-mannered reporter who is other than he seems.

"It is aimed at women who aren't going to stop working no matter how many kids they have."

She unties his right ankle.

"The demographics show that this is the largest part of the work force."

The knot on his left ankle is harder to untangle.

"We were thinking of putting—" he names a celebrity she has seen often on television "—on the cover. But instead I had an idea that the cover should be made of Mylar so that the woman who picks up the magazine sees herself."

He is free now and he sits up and reaches for the clean white terry-cloth robe that the hotel provides guests. It is pristine.

"Would you like a drink?" she asks. He nods. She makes him a dry martini the way she knows he likes it from the tray room service has provided, and then she settles down to talk business with him, helping him to forget that she knows things about his personal business that he does not want her to know.

This is how she earned her living last night.

8

I closed the manuscript. Felt the goose bumps on my arms. I had been so deep into what I was reading that for a second I was disoriented. Cleo had transported me to the hotel room. My lips had been on her client's nipples. I was feeling his muscles stretch. And I was uncomfortable.

Looking out the window, I saw that we were already at Seventy-eighth Street. The rain had stopped, leaving the sidewalks glistening and giving the air a loamy scent.

I usually used the time it took to get home to morph from a therapist into Dulcie's mother. I always came down more slowly than I'd like from my professional role to settle into mother mode. Perhaps because I'd had to learn mothering secondhand.

Some women became the mother their mother was. I did not have that luxury. Even before mine died, she was not the kind of parent that I wanted to be. There was no road map; I did this one blind. Too many mornings I woke up thinking, I'll get it right today. I'd been doing it for so long, I should have been comfortable with it by now. It will all flow naturally today, I'd tell myself. But it didn't always.

Why did you have to go so soon? I wasn't ready. I wasn't old enough. Why couldn't you have stayed with me until...until when? There never was a good time to become motherless.

Part of me was always watching, from the wings, looking at the woman who I was, interacting with her daughter, judging, questioning, comparing this mother to another who was not as steady on her feet and a daughter who had grown up too fast.

The cab pulled up to the curb.

I thrust the manuscript back in its envelope, shoved it under my arm and reached into the side pocket of my bag to get my wallet.

Fifteen minutes later I was sitting in the kitchen drinking a glass of iced tea when I heard the front door open. I saw the flash of blue jeans and white shirt as Dulcie walked by the kitchen on her way to her room.

"Hon? I'm in here?"

She doubled back, came in and dropped her bag on the floor. My eyes flew to the stark white bandage on her arm.

"What's wrong?"

"Nothing major. I burned my arm."

I got up and went to her. "How?"

"Stupid hot soup at lunch. Gretchen tripped, her soup, tomato soup, went flying. My arm was in the way."

"Let me see."

As she lifted her arm to me I saw splotches of blood on her white shirt.

She saw my eyes widen. "Mom?"

"Is this blood?"

"Soup. I told you. Gretchen's tomato soup. Don't spiral over this, okay?" I ignored her exasperated tone.

My daughter was at the age where no matter how controlled my concern was, it was still overbearing.

I bent to inspect the bandage. "Does it hurt?"

"Nope."

"No?"

"A little when it happened. But not enough that I cried or anything. It's just a burn."

"Okay." I reached out and hugged her, carefully avoiding her arm. She let me hold her and then pulled back. I brushed her bangs off her face and let my fingers linger on her skin just for a moment longer than I needed to.

She went to the refrigerator.

At twelve, Dulcie's chest was still flat and her hips were still narrow, but there was a grown-up look in her eyes that hadn't been there six months before and an impatience with me that went with it. I wasn't sure if it was just her age or a reaction to her father and me separating, or both.

"Maybe we should go see Dr. Kulick and have him look at your arm."

"It's not a big deal. I am really fine." She opened the top of a container of blueberry yogurt. She let the fridge door slam and grabbed a spoon from the utensil drawer. "The nurse gave me a note to give to you," she said between mouthfuls.

She fished in her backpack and pulled out a crumpled sheet of paper with a prescription stapled to it.

I read it quickly once, and then read it again more slowly. The drama school where Dulcie was spending the summer had a doctor on call. He'd come over and inspected Dulcie's burn, said that it wasn't serious, but had prescribed an antibiotic cream and some painkillers if Dulcie needed them.

My daughter looked at me with her huge eyes—the same cornflower-blue of my mother's eyes—and touched my hand as if she felt just the littlest bit sorry for me.

"Don't worry about me," she said, and tossed her head. Her hair, the same black color as mine, was long and straight and gleamed in the overhead light.

I watched her eat the rest of her snack, searching for clues as to how she really felt, but she didn't seem to be in pain or crisis. Her eyes weren't swollen, there were no tearstains on her cheeks. I took her emotional temperature whenever I came into her presence, checking my daughter for signs of distress or sadness. And I was always mildly shocked that she rarely showed any. Despite everything I must have done wrong, my daughter was a secure and mostly happy teen. Smart, charismatic and more than pretty enough, she had a large extended family and friends circling around her, ensuring she was traveling through childhood with relative calm.

Dulcie plopped down beside me. "Is Gretchen a klutz or what?" She picked up Cleo's book.

"Don't," I said, taking the manuscript from her.

"Why?"

"It's not mine. It belongs to a patient."

Dulcie nodded. One thing she understood was the sacrosanct relationship between a doctor and patient. She needed to trust something about me. Know, at least, that her mother never broke that commandment between her patients and herself. Maybe if she knew this, she would believe other things that I would not be so good at showing her.

"Oooh. A patient," Dulcie said sarcastically. "One of Dr. Sin's sinners." And then she laughed. I joined in. Even if I wanted to be angry, I couldn't. I understood her too well. I appreciated her too much.

My daughter was not unhappy with what I did for a living, she just wished it was more noble. "She's a doctor," I'd hear Dulcie tell her friends, not admitting what kind of doctor I was and what kind of help I offered my patients.

I looked from the white bandage on my daughter's arm to the white first page of the book. For all the pieces of information I had added to my already-crowded brain that day, the last two were twisting up like some double helix. Interwoven with my fear of what had happened to Dulcie was my fear for Cleo, and I flashed on the image of the tall man following her down the street.

Dulcie got up and fussed with the CD player and put on something that she liked and that I could tolerate. She was sensitive that way, and it made me smile. I noticed the bandage again and thought it looked too large on her slim arm.

Suddenly a name popped into my head. Barry Johnson. He had to be the man lying on the bed in the hotel room who had paid Cleo two thousand dollars to tease him to orgasm. It shouldn't have been that easy for me to figure out who he was, but I had. A media mogul who was in business with his father. In his forties.

"Besides the arm, how else was your day?" It was our routine. To go over the day. Usually we did it at dinner, but I was doing it now. The rule was we had to state one good thing for every bad thing. As many bad things as you wanted. But always a balance.

"Besides the arm...well, we had auditions for *Our Town*." Her eyes grew wider. She'd been looking forward to these twelve weeks at the American Academy of Dramatic Art's summer program since she'd been accepted back in February. It didn't even matter to her that she hadn't had much of a break between one school ending and the next one starting.

"I love this play, Mom."

I smiled at her, picked up the manuscript and put the stack of papers in my briefcase.

"It's a wonderful play, isn't it. What part are you trying out for?"

"The main character. I didn't think I should, but Mrs. Harte said she thought I was ready for it."

I leaned over and kissed her. "I'm proud of you."

My daughter preened. And then she picked up the thread of the game.

"And you, Dr. Sin? How was your day?"

The divorce papers dissolving your father's and my marriage came today. You hurt your arm. You called me Dr. Sin, twice. I had to go to the morgue to see one of my ex-patients, a girl not even ten years older than you, laid out and cut open. And I figured out who one of my patients' clients was and not because Cleo had told me herself, but because her description of him had been too clear.

But I couldn't tell Dulcie any of those things. Not just because she was not old enough to hear them, but because I couldn't think of anything at all that was good to counter them with. And the rules were the rules. You could only tell the bad if you found some good.

Later we took a walk together to the drugstore to get the anti-biotic cream at the pharmacy. I didn't fill the other prescription for painkillers. My daughter had my high tolerance for pain. And short of being masochistic, I encouraged it. Prescription painkillers were a godsend, but they were also a far more dangerous drug than I wanted to expose her to if I didn't have to. Some people have a physical propensity toward addictions. There was no reason to test my daughter's ability with a codeine derivative when she wasn't even in enough pain to take an extra-strength ibuprofen.

Afterward we stopped at her favorite place for dinner—the overpriced food shop and restaurant, E.A.T. at Eighty-first and Madison. She chose the same comfort food that her father would have picked: macaroni and cheese and a Coke.

I had my second salad of the day, hating every piece of verdant green. Dulcie was chattering about the classes she was signed up for at drama school when my cell phone rang.

"Hello?"

"Hi." It was my now ex-husband. "I just got your message. How is she?"

"Fine." I looked over at her and mouthed—*It's your father*—and her face brightened. "It really is just a simple burn. We're having dinner. She's talking about drama school, nothing's changed." I smiled at Dulcie, who was listening intently to my conversation. She reached out her hand. I saw the bandage and winced. "Do you want to talk to her?" I asked him.

"First tell me if you are okay. I know how you panic about her."

The problem with still being friends with the man I used to be married to was that he wanted to know how I was, too.

"Like I said, it's really only a minor burn. Here's Dulcie."

I handed my daughter the phone, and while she told her father the whole story, from the moment of impact with the soup, I tried to figure out why Cleo's book was as much on my mind as anything else. A distraction? Something to dwell on other than the randomness of fate and the horror that I had to go on sending my daughter off to school every day not knowing when something else would happen to her?

"And then the doctor came and he looked at it," Dulcie was saying, still only halfway through the story. She was making it dramatic, stringing it out and turning it into performance art for one half of her best audience.

I was surprised that Cleo's book had affected me as much as it had. I listened to people talking about sex all day, about their issues with their bodies and brains, and how they functioned or didn't function. What was different about this woman and what she was saying?

As I watched my daughter, I realized my own arm throbbed. Ever since my child had been a baby I'd experienced the same pain she did. I knew that it was psychosomatic and that if I worked on it I most probably could stop it from happening. But I didn't mind. She was my girl. I would have preferred to take all of her pain than to stop feeling it.

I motioned to Dulcie to wrap it up.

9

Saturday night Detective Noah Jordain had played piano till almost 12:00 a.m. in the same restaurant in Greenwich Village he had first found when he moved to New York City nine years before.

He'd been homesick for New Orleans that night. And that led to him thinking about his father: a good cop whose name had been sullied and then had died before he could clear it. Whoever had set up Andre Jordain, a thirty-year veteran of the New Orleans Police Department, might have thought he had gotten away with it, but Noah was still working on the case.

Andre and his partner, Pat Nagley, had busted a cocaine ring. It was cut-and-dried. Or so everyone thought. Until the defense attorney got the evidence thrown out of court by proving that Andre and Pat had been on the take, accepting payoffs from the dealer for five years until finally turning on the dealer when he refused to increase the payoffs.

There was a string of evidence presented that, on the surface, damned the two New Orleans detectives. But Noah knew, just as his mother and his brothers and sisters knew, it had all been fabricated. His father had upheld the law every day of his life. He'd been a devout Catholic and faithful husband. Yes, he drank too much sometimes, he could let his temper get the better of him, and he was a big flirt. But a bad cop? No way. The documents and evidence had to have been manufactured after the fact.

There was no question of collusion, and there was some connection between the drug dealer and someone higher up with more power than Andre Jordain. One day Noah would find out who'd been involved and clear his father's name. He owed him that.

A year after the indictment, his father had died. A few months after that Noah had broken up with his live-in girlfriend. His mother had three other sons and two daughters and six grandchildren around her. That left him free.

Noah had come to New York to get away from a police department that was as corrupt as often as it upheld the law and so that he might see things more clearly from a distance. No, that was bullshit. At least he could be honest with himself. He had come to Manhattan to work the case from the New York angle, since there was evidence that the drug ring was tied to someone in the NYPD. And he'd also left home because he hated walking down the streets and smelling the river and doing all the things that made him remember.

The restaurant that had become his regular haunt was two blocks away from Noah's apartment. Caroline's had a long mahogany bar, a fireplace in the dining area and a beat-up old upright Steinway in the front that no one had touched since the previous owner had died twenty years before. After a few months of getting to know the current owner, having drinks or dinner there at least three times a week, occasionally bringing a date—never the same woman twice—Noah asked if he could play.

His slow, soulful jazz was like New York. Moody and energetic, dark then bright. He played like they played in the twenties and it fit the restaurant. Caroline's had had a musical history; it had been a popular jazz club and speakeasy during prohibition, catering to a crowd that sat and sipped their illegal gin, listening to music just as sorrowful as Noah's.

Now he had a regular gig. Friday and Saturday nights. On Sundays he slept off the homesickness and the nightmares that followed the purging music. Usually he slept late. Till at least noon. His one sin of the week. Well, maybe not his one sin, but the one he felt the guiltiest about because he'd been brought up to be in church on Sunday mornings. Not in bed.

It had been four years since he'd walked into any house of God. The day of his father's funeral. It wasn't a loss of faith so much as a break of faith. A jagged cut that bled and bled and wouldn't heal, and until it did, he'd rather sleep.

But that Sunday morning the phone call had woken him up at 9:00 a.m. It was the second Sunday in a row that he'd been woken this way.

"Were you sleeping?" Mark Perez asked.

"Umm."

"Having a nightmare?"

"No."

"Wrong answer," his partner said.

"Oh, no," Jordain said, anticipating the next sentence.

"Looks like we might have a serial killer, after all. You were right."

"Damn, this is one time I wish to God I'd been wrong."

"You have no idea." Perez then gave Jordain the address of the hotel where the woman's body had been found fifteen minutes before.

10

As he walked through the bedroom of the hotel suite, Noah took it all in: the unmade bed, sheets pulled back, pillows indented. Nothing violent. Nothing alarming about the scene. The rest of the room was relatively undisturbed. A bottle of mineral water was next to the bed. A glass was partially filled with clear liquid.

The television was set to an all-day news station, and a familiar reporter was talking about a suicide bomber in Israel who had blown himself up along with seventeen people in a supermarket. It happened so often, Noah realized, that you became so inured to it you could walk by the TV and not stop to listen.

Not right, Noah thought, and for a few seconds, he did stop and said a silent prayer for the people who had died suddenly at the hands of an overzealous lunatic.

And then he walked on, toward the world of another madman, the sound of the newscaster fading into the background.

Her back was to the bathroom door, and she was on her knees in front of a makeshift shrine. A plastic Jesus on a cross nestled in the niche of the soap dish. It was a crappy plastic religious artifact. Not like the heavy and sacred gold cross in the cathedral at home that the priest touched with reverence and that gleamed in the soft lights of the church.

This one glared.

Like the woman who had preceded her, she was wearing a nun's habit. That much was obvious, even though they were pulled up and exposed her bare ass as she prayed at the tub, her head bowed.

Noah didn't rush. She was past saving.

The perfect pale skin of her back was streaked with murky marks; the dark red color of dried blood. They were not arbitrary smears but crosses. Finger-painted crosses all over her back, her backside, the backs of her thighs and the soles of her poor feet.

Of all the horrors, it was the sight of her feet that made Noah sad. The wrinkled soles were small. There was something so fucking innocent about the woman's feet. He wished he could wet a towel and wash them off, clean them of the offending finger-painting of a devil.

Something was moving between her legs.

No. That wasn't possible. He focused. Even before he consciously figured it out, memory informed him of what it was going to be. He should have been prepared because it had been there at the first bloodbath.

Like a reptile, like a living thing, the rosary dangled between her legs, half stuffed into her vaginal cavity, half exposed, and dripping with the poor whore's blood.

It was the constant trickle that caused the holy prayer beads to sway to some rhythm that Noah did not recognize from anything he had ever played.

No one would have listened.

Down each bead of the rosary, down over the medallion of the Virgin Mary, down over the Christ figure on the cross, drops of blood fell to the floor where they pooled on the white tiles.

Like Mrs. Rodriguez, the maid in the hotel on Fifty-sixth Street, Noah subconsciously intoned a prayer: *Our Father, who art in Heaven, hallowed be Thy name.*

Taking a few steps forward, he stood as close to the dead woman's body as he could without contaminating the crime scene and looked down into the oversize bathtub. Its gleaming silver heads reflected her face, with her closed eyes, back at him.

On the bottom of the tub were ten fifty-dollar bills, soaked in blood, laid out in the shape of the cross.

The photographer had arrived and Noah stepped out of the bathroom to give him room to do his job. He and his partner talked to the uniformed cop who had arrived first on the scene, asking him questions and listening to his detailed answers.

"She checked in last night at 10:00 p.m."

"Not dressed like a nun, I'm guessing," said Noah.

"The desk clerk who was on duty isn't here. But I've got his name and phone number at home. Do you want it?"

"We're done," the photographer said, coming out of the bathroom. "She's all yours."

Tibor Mercer, the M.E., took over then, making a preliminary examination before moving the woman. He was a middle-aged, overweight man who had curly red hair and had been with the department for his entire career. After being an expert witness in an important televised trial, he had become one of the most trusted M.E.s in the country, appearing on crime shows and being quoted in newspapers. But even with all his experience, he had never become hardened to his job, which earned him the respect of many of the people who worked with him. Including Noah Jordain.

Finally Mercer pulled her away from her porcelain prie-dieu.

"How long do you think she's been dead?" Noah asked.

"Probably died shortly after midnight."

Noah watched the man do his job. A few minutes passed.

"Look at this."

Noah knew Mercer well enough to not like the sound of his voice. "What?"

"See for yourself."

The M.E. held the prostitute's mouth open with his plastic-sheathed fingers. Noah peered in and saw a communion wafer.

No. That's not what it was, damn it.

On the corpse's tongue, the same shape as a wafer blessed by a priest, was a perfect, carefully placed, pristine and unused condom, still coiled and flat: a circle of pale translucent latex.

As if in the hour of her death, she was taking communion.

After all, it was Sunday morning.

11

After I dropped Dulcie at drama school on Monday, I started to walk uptown to my office. On the corner was a trio of kiosks holding the morning papers. While I waited for the light to change, I scanned the headlines on the *New York Times,* but it was the three words on the front page of the *New York Post* that screamed out at me.

Second Holy Horror.

And then in smaller letters: Magdalene Murderer Strikes Again. Hooker Slain in Nuns' Habit.

I put two quarters in the slot, pulled the handle, and the smell of the ink wafted up from inside the metal cage.

I read the article, missing the first green light, and the next. According to the reporter, the murder was almost identical to the first crime, which had occurred a week before.

This woman had also been found in a midtown hotel frequented by business people and tourists. Rooms went for two hundred dollars. She, too, had paid for the room with cash. No one had seen who she was with. There were no discarded clothes found in the room, and the desk clerk claimed that he had most certainly not seen a woman in a nun's habit signing in.

Her name was Cara De Beer. Twenty-two. From Austin, Texas. Had been working in New York since she'd left high school at seventeen. She had two priors.

In as lurid language as the reporter could use, he described the nun's habit, the pools of blood left on the bathroom floor—because he had gotten to the room after the body had been taken away—and he quoted one of the cops as saying that "a rosary had been inserted into one of her body cavities."

But the police wouldn't elaborate. Just as they had not said any more about the first woman who had been found the week before. The rosary might have been in the hooker's mouth, her ear or any other opening.

I reread the woman's name and her stats. I didn't know this one. She wasn't one of the women I'd ever treated in prison. Moving on to the next paragraph: "Someone is obviously targeting prostitutes," said Detective Noah Jordain of the Special Victims Unit. "And we urge every sex worker to be careful. If anyone has any information, please come forward. We need to catch this man."

I shut the paper but held on to it.

I wasn't smelling the newsprint anymore. The scent of thick blood was in my head. We have all smelled it. A bad cut, a birth, our baby's bloody nose and our periods. Not the violent bloodletting described in the paper. But that didn't matter. The odor of blood does not change depending on why it flows. I watched people passing by, but they didn't distract me from the imagery of the girl's death. We have all seen so much violence on television and in the movies that it has become too easy to picture a body on the floor, the pools of blood, the lifeless face.

I wanted more coffee. No, needed more coffee. And stopped at the first Starbucks I passed and ordered a double espresso.

For the past few nights I hadn't slept well. Not since Dulcie had burned her arm. Not since the divorce had gone through. Even though my daughter hadn't had any pain, I had kept waking to check on her. My own arm had throbbed worse in sympathy than the actual injury, and the phantom ache had kept me awake. And when I couldn't fall back asleep, I'd been reading Cleo's book, but was still a hundred pages shy of finishing.

As she had warned me, Cleo hadn't done a very good job at disguising the men. While she had given them all nicknames, like Midas or King Henry or Valentino, she had written so much about the businesses they ran or their occupations that I was engaged in playing a guessing game.

No wonder Caesar was nervous about her publishing this book. Once the men she'd written about discovered their private lives were going to appear in ink, there would be a lot of anger and fear among them.

Her exposé was not like one of those bestselling suspense novels by Dan Brown, Doug Clegg or Stan Pottinger that kept me turning pages. Instead, Cleo's insights into the men who came to see her and her "troupe," as she called the prostitutes who worked for her, were too rich and complicated to read quickly. If she wanted to become a therapist, or a sociologist, or write more books on the same subject, she would have no trouble. Her writing style was simple but clear and her passion for and knowledge of the subject matter came through. Her empathy for the other women who worked in the industry was sincere, and she understood them and explained their lives in a refreshingly unmelodramatic yet dramatic way.

But it was the empathy she had for the men who came to see her that made me stop and reread what she had written.

Cleo seemed to have shut down the part of herself that made judgments. No matter what a man asked for, she understood that his need came from a wellspring that was vital and strong and could not be simply dammed up. Her ability to grasp the reasons for the humiliations that titillated one man as opposed to the physical prowess another needed to believe he possessed impressed me. But her own distance from what she had done disturbed me.

And I was hoping I could get her to talk about that when she arrived for her 10:00 a.m. appointment that morning.

* * *

But for the first time, Cleo was late, and when she arrived at ten-fifteen she apologized for the delay but didn't give me a reason. Sometimes, with patients, I pursued tardiness if I felt there were unconscious reasons for it, but Cleo was so anxious to be in therapy, I didn't think this was the case.

As soon as she sat down, she hauled out a large bottle of water and took a long gulp. And then a longer breath. In previous sessions she had eased into talking about what was on her mind, but that morning she didn't waste any time.

"Those murders. Did you read about them?"

I nodded, but I did not tell her that the first victim had been one of my ex-patients. All of that was privileged information, details that the police had not yet revealed to the press. None of the specific ways the woman's body had been defiled had made it into the news. The police were obviously trying to keep it quiet to prevent copycats and to make sure that if they got any leads they were legit. Only the broad strokes of the killing had been reported.

"That shouldn't happen. It wouldn't happen if prostitution was legal."

"Did you know the woman who was killed?" I asked Cleo.

She shook her head. "No." She shook her head again, and for the first time I noticed a tiny pink-diamond cross that she was wearing on a fragile chain around her neck as it caught the light and gleamed. It looked lovely and expensive.

"The news has made things worse. Caesar is preoccupied with the story. Worried about me. And the last thing he needs is more reason to worry about me. So we had a fight. A bad fight."

"Tell me about it."

"It started with the news, then segued into the book again. But it's really all about me and sex, isn't it?" She stopped and drank her water as if she had not had anything to drink for days. "He's confused. And he's impatient. And I just feel all this pressure to get better faster."

"Does he know you are seeing me?"

"Yes."

"Does he think it's a good idea?"

"Yes, but he also has his own idea of how to cure me."

"Cure you? His word or yours?"

"His."

I nodded. "Go on."

"He thinks we should act out a scenario where he is one of my clients. He wants to pay me to have sex with him and play out his fantasy. That maybe this is a way to break down my resistance. To just see him like any other client. Is this making any sense?"

"Does it make sense to you?"

She shrugged. "Not really. But I think I am willing to try it."

"What is the fantasy?"

Cleo leaned back against the couch as if she was pushing herself away from me. As if she could disappear into the furniture and avoid the revelation. For the first time I saw a look in her eyes that reminded me of women who are missing from themselves. The lost women. Lost to drugs or alcohol or fear or abuse.

I waited.

She shook it off. "It's the Caesar and Cleopatra thing." Now the look on her face was one of embarrassment, but she continued. After reading so much of her book and knowing how little inhibition she had with her clients, her shyness in describing this fantasy that she and her lover had talked about was almost charming. It was also a signal I needed to pay extra attention, too.

"He wants me to be Cleopatra, brought to him in a carpet, unrolled at his feet. The queen coming to the conqueror. He wants me to play-act at being this potentate willing to give herself up to the Roman. He thinks that if I can get into that role, that I will feel real things for him. Sort of what happens to actors in a play. How they fall in love with one another and feel things within the personalities they inhabit."

"And how do you feel about it?"

"I wanted to ask you that. How should I feel?"

"There are no shoulds."

She got up and walked over to the window. While I certainly didn't mind that she needed to move, so few patients do it. There are reasons that a patient should remain seated and focused for the whole session, but they, by no means, should feel as if they are strapped down to the couch.

Cleo roamed. Like a dancer she covered the length of the room in long strides and her eyes took in everything. She glanced at the knickknacks on my desk, looked out one window, then the next. She walked past my bookshelves and ran a finger over the smooth stone marble egg that rested on my mantelpiece.

I had carved that egg, and as her forefinger ran down its surface I felt as if she was touching my arm. The physical sensation surprised me. And I knew I'd need to tell Nina about it the next time I saw her.

Sculpture had once been my passion. Now it was only a hobby. My preoccupation with carving started when my father remarried. I was fourteen and Krista, the woman he married, was a sculptor. She wasn't maternal, and I never looked to her to fulfill that role—Nina had been offering me motherly sustenance since I was eight.

But Krista did bring her art into my life. When she moved into our apartment the cool stone pieces that she strategically placed around the apartment attracted me.

And still, today, on vacations, or sometimes late at night when I can't sleep, I'll pull out my tools and work on a reluctant stone.

Cleo sat back down again. "I don't know if I should act out his fantasy."

"Why?"

"Does it make sense? Do you think his idea will work? If I do with him what I do with clients, will that make this problem any better? I don't know if I want to turn into an actress and play a role with him. He thinks that will help me jump the divide, that once I am in character and start to make love with him, I'll just segue into being myself and enjoy it."

"And what do you think?"

She shook her head. "I have no idea. All I know is that I feel pretty desperate. The irony of me having a sexual problem with the one man I actually want to sleep with is not lost on me, Dr.

Snow. I'm upset. But he's even more upset. He's already taking it personally. He thinks he's not sexy enough. That he can't turn me on."

"Do you think it would help if you brought him with you, here?"

She shrugged.

"Why don't you suggest it?"

"I did. He saw someone once. Not too long ago. He said it was a waste of time." She shrugged and her eyes filled with tears she didn't make any effort to wipe away.

Crying made her look younger and more vulnerable. Neither of us said anything. She wept and I watched.

It is a very special privilege to be privy to these moments in people's lives, when their defenses drop and the essence of who they are and what they feel is unmasked. Like watching a butterfly break free from its cocoon. When someone goes into any kind of therapy, if the process works, for a time they are as delicate as that butterfly. You must not reach out and touch their wings, or you will destroy the pattern and the iridescence—the illumination— will come off on your fingers. You can only sit back and wait and hope that you are a good-enough guide to do justice to the gift.

"What are you feeling?" I asked her, speaking softly.

"I wish it could be different." The pain in her voice was so raw I felt it. The way I felt my daughter's pain. The same empathetic connection had developed between Cleo and I. And why shouldn't it have? That is the art of therapy, Nina Butterfield had taught me.

For a time, you as the therapist also have to become vulnerable so that you can connect in such a way as to build trust and understand things that often have no obvious logic but can be sacred to your patient.

Our forty-five minutes were over and Cleo noticed it before I did.

"I have to leave on time. I have an appointment downtown," she said with a sorry shake of her head that made me think she was off to see a client.

"I'll see you Wednesday," she added.

I nodded. "Cleo, maybe you shouldn't make up your mind about whether or not to do what Caesar is asking until then. Would that be okay with you?"

She didn't say anything as she gathered her leather bag and straightened her skirt.

"Yes. You're probably right."

But she had a look in her eye that reiterated that she was feeling desperate and that she was running out of time.

I wished later that I had taken the look more seriously. I wished I had called out to her and told her to be careful. Be extremely careful. But she had convinced me, by the way she tossed her hair, looking me in the eye with her cool gray eyes, that she knew how to take care of herself.

Eyes had lied to me before.

12

After Dulcie and I had dinner, we watched *My Fair Lady* on television. Then my daughter went to her room to study the part she'd won in *Our Town* while I stayed in the living room and picked up Cleo's book.

I read it that night and another hundred pages the next night, and with every page became more and more aware of why she was worried about what would happen to her if she did, indeed, go ahead and publish this book.

I was anxious to see her on Wednesday morning, but for the second time in a row, Cleo was late for her appointment.

During the first fifteen minutes, I assumed she was still on her way. But by ten-thirty, I realized she wasn't coming.

Had we delved too far in the last session? Had she run scared? I hadn't expected she would react this way to opening up.

Maybe she just woke up with a sore throat and meant to call but fell back asleep, I reasoned. Or maybe she got an early-morning call from a client that she couldn't ignore.

I did some paperwork and made some calls and gave up waiting.

* * *

When a patient misses a session without calling, they get charged the full price of the appointment. I don't call to find out where someone is. At the start of the next session, I ask him or her to explain what happened.

And so I put Cleo out of my mind and left my office at twelve-fifteen. My next appointment wasn't until two o'clock, and I needed to walk.

It was a lovely June afternoon and I headed into Central Park, crossing by the Bethesda Fountain and going west. I passed nannies with children holding on to toys, their faces smeared with food; dog walkers trotting along at a fast clip, each with a pack of ten or thirteen dogs; and young couples full of the romance of spring, holding hands and walking lazily in the sunshine.

I looked at them and thought of my daughter, thankful that she was two or three years away from her first pass at love. And I hoped it might not happen even that soon. And then, without consciously being aware of it, I was thinking about Cleo again and her confusion now that she was feeling the stirrings of a powerful emotion she wasn't that familiar with.

Love isn't a germ or a virus. We can't put it under a microscope to examine it. Nor is sexual attraction or desire or lack of desire. Or any of the fetishes and anxieties that haunt us. But I try, along with everyone else at the institute and therapists all over the world, to treat people who succumb to love or passion or lust or any variation of those and who get sick with them.

The wind picked up and debris scattered. My eye caught the headline on the sheet of newsprint that had snagged on the bottom of the stone water fountain.

No Headway in Hooker Killings.

And then the wind blew the paper away.

I went over the stats I'd read earlier in the paper, thinking that at least all the girls I worked with in prison were safe. Safer behind bars than they would be on the street.

And Cleo was safe. She was too savvy to get messed up with anyone she didn't know. I knew enough about how she worked and how careful she was about screening clients. She would never go to a hotel with a complete stranger. Would never allow herself to be put in a position where she wasn't protected.

And yet, and yet, what if some man was smarter than her? What if this psychopath was clever enough to—

I sat down under the wisteria arbor on the West Side and pulled out my cell phone. I dialed my office number, listened to it ring and then punched in the code to play back my messages.

I wasn't usually this nervous about a patient. But the news preyed on me. And Cleo mattered to me.

I had three messages.

The first was from a client requesting a second appointment that week.

The next was from another therapist at the institute requesting a consult later in the week.

I waited for the third message, desperately wanting it to be Cleo, worried that it wouldn't be, concerned that if it wasn't, my imagination would take off like the newspaper had.

The third message was from my ex-husband to say hello and talk about the rest of Dulcie's summer schedule with him.

There was no word from Cleo.

13

On the other side of the world from my office at the Butterfield Institute lay the women's state penitentiary in upstate New York. Almost three hours from the city, the redbrick building sat at the bottom of a hill on a lonely stretch of road near a state park. Every Thursday morning Simon Weiss, a fellow therapist at the institute, and I drove there. Between us we met with anywhere from two to six patients, prostitutes who had either requested to see a therapist or who were required to see one.

This gig started as part of my graduate school work, but I kept doing it, because I was still innocent enough, or dumb enough, to think that I might actually make a difference. And Simon, who was one of my closest friends, in addition to being an associate, had been doing it with me for the last year.

Since the first prostitute's killing, the women were more angry and sad than usual. Worried about their friends on the outside, and about themselves when they would be released.

As Simon navigated the city traffic we talked about office gossip and then fell into a companionable silence. I was looking out the window, but I could see him in my peripheral vision.

Between the curly dirty-blond hair, dimples and lively blue eyes, and a mind that leapt ahead when other people were still trying to figure out what direction to take, he was impressive. But it was more than that. He had that rare male attribute: he loved women. He loved to talk to us, spend time with us, listen to us and bond with us. Sometimes, when we were out having a drink along with a heart-to-heart, he joked that he was a chick with a dick.

"You know, you are really quiet," he said.

"How does that make you feel?"

He laughed. It was our joke, the jargon we used on each other. We made each other laugh by dipping into patient-doctor talk. One day we'd have to dig deep and find what we were covering up with all the teasing. But I was hoping it wouldn't be for a while.

"Seriously," he said, "what's going on?"

"I have a patient who missed an appointment yesterday and didn't call. I hate to admit it, but I have a feeling that something might be wrong."

"Did you call her?"

"I tried to. Late yesterday afternoon. I wasn't sure I should."

"Why?"

"I don't usually."

"But she's special?"

I nodded.

Simon smiled. Every once in a while, a patient got to me the way Cleo had. But it had been a long time.

"She didn't call back?"

"No."

"Who is it? Cleo Thane?"

I nodded.

During weekly meetings, all ten therapists at the institute discussed our patients so they all knew about Cleo.

"When is she scheduled to come in next?"

"Monday. I'm assuming she got a job that took her out of town."

"Is that all that's bothering you?"

Simon had been a friend for a long time. "My divorce came through last week."

"And you waited a whole week to tell me."

For a moment I was embarrassed.

"Morgan?"

"Hmm?"

"Do you want to talk about it?"

"Not yet. I just want to be in denial that anything in my life has to change any more than it already has."

"Change is not always bad."

"I know that professionally. But on a personal level, let's just say I am not yet convinced."

We were out of Manhattan and on the highway heading toward the George Washington Bridge. In the sunlight the metal girders and trusses gleamed and the Hudson River glinted.

"It looks like a postcard, doesn't it? All that blue sky and green trees and that gigantic bridge," he said.

"From a distance it's easy to see things in symmetry."

He reached out and took my hand and held it in the seat between us. I relied upon all of my training and insight and intuition to figure out if this touch was the same as the million touches he had given me over the past five years. He was a physical person, and hugs and brotherly kisses and things like holding my hand to make me feel as if we were connected were just how we were.

But now I was divorced. And he was a flirt. And what would have been innocent before could be interpreted differently now. His skin was warm and his fingers were long and strong. What would happen if I moved my fingers against his? If, instead of letting my hand lie limp in his, I pressed my fingertips into his? What would it feel like to channel energy into the touch? To use the proximity of our hands to give him a message? To say to him with my flesh that I wanted more?

I would ruin a wonderful friendship. Of that I had no doubt. If I was going to experiment with a side of myself that had been dormant for too long, it was not going to be with someone I sat across a conference room table with several times a week.

The sun was coming through the window and making me warm. I shifted in my seat and extracted my hand.

As if nothing had happened, because it hadn't, Simon put his hand back on the wheel. We drove another few minutes before he asked me something I was surprised we'd never covered in all our hundreds of hours of conversation.

"Why do you do this prison work?"

"Because of 'grace.'"

He knew my shorthand for "There but for the grace of God go I."

There were too many things I'd seen that made me stop, catch my breath and be grateful that I was not there and that was not my life. Dulcie had picked up on it and sometimes came home from school with a "grace" story.

"That is a wonderfully Morgan thing to say." Simon smiled.

In my lap, I put my right hand over my left and let my fingers play with one another.

But you can't make a connection with your own skin.

14

The walk from the parking lot to the prison itself was bizarrely lovely. It was about a quarter of a mile down a path that bordered on a state park with trees spilling into the grounds of the institution. Towering old oaks, maples, cedars and pine trees bathe the path in shade, and you could easily forget where you were. Until you reached the summit and saw the guardhouse, the barbed-wire fence, the huge spotlights and a fleet of police, prison and state cars in the smaller parking area flanking the building.

The prison sat on the estate of a wealthy industrialist whose three-year-old son was brutally murdered in the house while everyone slept. The murderer was his mother: a woman who had been troubled and in and out of doctors' offices and hospitals for years.

Regardless of her mental history, she was sentenced to life in prison and hung herself the first week she was there. The noose was made of her bedsheet, ripped with her teeth.

Her husband, Al Serwin, moved away, leaving the property, the house and an endowment to the state with the express desire that it be turned into a women's prison. But a special house of incarceration, one where the most hopeful cases would go, with a generous fund to ensure that every prisoner got psychiatric help. The best, brought in and paid in full. Not the sad social workers who took whatever work they could get and sat through appointments being only slightly more capable than the people they were counseling.

It was warmer than I'd anticipated and I took off my jacket as we approached the doors. Just as well, as I had to be patted down and all my pockets emptied before I could go in.

Once inside we were greeted by Mary Kathryn Evans, the guard whom we had seen every Thursday for the last few years.

"We had a little scene here last night," she told us with a rueful smile. She was heavyset and always chewed cinnamon-flavored gum.

Her hands were on my hips.

"What happened?"

"One of the ladies had a visitor. Turns out he was the ex of another one of our ladies."

Her hand moved down my legs, pat, pat, pat, feeling for something that wasn't there.

"There was quite a fight. Scratching, biting. Turned into a party."

"Anyone hurt?"

Her hands were on my arms now.

"Stitches, concussions. Some of the bites broke skin—and, you know, with AIDS, that can be serious business."

Mary Kathryn was finished and moved on to Simon. "I don't know where Joe is. You want to wait? Or do you mind if I do this today?"

"I'd rather if you did it, darling," he joked.

She started her hands down his hips and I watched the way her fingers so impersonally felt for the nonexistent contraband.

"One of your patients was involved," she said to me as her hands moved around Simon's ankles.

Now she had my full attention.

"Who?"

"Coffey Gerard."

I was hoping she wasn't going to say her name. "Did she get attacked or was she the instigator?"

"She's the one who got attacked. Caty Laine attacked her."

Coffey was a gorgeous African-American prostitute whom many of the other girls were jealous of.

"But I can see her?"

"Guess so—you are on the sheet with her at eleven." Mary Kathryn nodded to a printed sheet of doctor appointments for the day. And with that she buzzed Simon and me through.

We walked down the hallway to the waiting room reserved for doctors and therapists and correctional officials. We usually didn't have to wait long.

The smell wasn't too bad in that room, other than the use of too much disinfectant. But I knew that once the next guard came to escort me to the room where I conducted my sessions, the stench would be overwhelming.

The prison was crowded, even though this was one of the better places to be holed up. But there were no good prisons. There were no easy ways to do time.

"Dr. Snow?" A male guard stood at the door. I didn't recognize him. Standing, I turned back to Simon and said goodbye.

"See you later, alligator," he said.

I smiled and followed the guard out.

As soon as I left that room and started down the hallway, I bit into the mint I'd put in my mouth so that the peppermint would overwhelm every other odor. If I focused on breathing through my mouth it was always better. But the stale body odor, the whiff of urine, the cigarette smoke and the cheap perfumes and shampoos that some of the women used to try to pretty up themselves were still stifling. It was like inhaling desperation.

Dante wrote about the three circles of hell: every Thursday I walked through purgatory.

I took a seat in the windowless room. There was a couch and a chair next to a desk. An approximation of a therapist's office. At least it was not filthy. The women here had to do cleanup, and they worked harder in some rooms than others. The therapy office was one of the rooms that they took pride in keeping pristine. Many of them wanted to come to therapy. They said they felt better after it. We treated our patients the same way here we treated the patients we saw in our own offices, and that dignity was precious to them.

While I waited for Coffey, whose real name was Sarah, I popped another strong peppermint into my mouth and breathed in, placing the pack on the table, knowing that I wouldn't leave with them. At some point when my head was turned, Coffey would carefully roll them off the tabletop and secret them in her pocket.

Eventually we'd get to her petty thievery. But in the meantime we had bigger issues to deal with.

"Morning, Doc," she said after the guard had opened the door and let her in.

I tried not to look surprised. One of her eyes was swollen shut, and if her nose hadn't been broken, it had been badly beaten. A long scratch, crusted with dried blood, ran the length of her neck.

"You should see what I did to her," Coffey said, bragging a little.

"Yeah?"

She smiled. "It was self-defense, but not the guards or nobody knows that."

"How come?"

"Just because I am mad at Billy I was not going to rat on Caty. She had a nail file. Shit. Who knows how she got it. But she had it and she was heading for my eye with it."

"Because?"

"I had a visitor yesterday."

"Who?"

"Tyson." She gave me the self-satisfied smile of a woman who knows that she has a man so hot for her that he will come all the way out to a prison and look at her through a wire-and-glass partition.

"So he's back?"

Coffey nodded. We'd had a few conversations about her pimp,

and she knew that if she wanted to get out of prison and stay off the streets she was going to have to break off with him.

"He is going to try to get me an interview with someone really big when I get out. He thinks I can do more. He thinks I have something extra. He is worried about me. This guy who is killing girls, and dressing us up like nuns? He's got everyone freaked. And Tyson cares about me too much to let me back on the street. So he's gonna get me an interview."

"An interview?"

She leaned forward like she had a secret.

"Did you ever hear of a woman named Cleo Thane?"

I was not an actress. That was what my mother had done with her life. So it was an effort to keep my face expressionless.

"Who is she?"

"Only the most successful bitch in the business. A pretty-as-a-picture princess who you'd guess lived in one of them fancy-dancy high-rises on Fifth Avenue and did nothing but shop and work out all day."

"She is a prostitute?"

"She is a prostitute?" Coffey mimicked me and laughed. "Yes. She's the Patron Saint of Sluts."

I laughed along with her, but something inside of me contracted and the skin on the back of my neck prickled.

"Funny moniker. How did she get it?"

"Yeah, well. You gotta understand how this bitch treats her girls. She gives them health insurance. Starts those retirement accounts for them. It matters to her that we get taken care of, do you know what I mean?"

It's not often that you got to talk about your patient with someone else. You were generally forced to accept the version that the patient wanted you to have.

"And how does Tyson come into this?"

"He says he knows someone who knows her and that when I get out he will set up a go-see. She runs her place more like a modeling agency than a whorehouse. You gotta be able to speak and think and have insight to work for Cleo. But Tyson says I've got all that. And he says her girls are safe. The safest in the business. That the Saint just takes care of things right."

Coffey was a twenty-four-year-old prostitute who had stabbed one of her clients in self-defense when he pulled a knife on her and demanded that she make him come, blaming his own impotence on her failure. It was only then, with his knife at her throat, that he was able to finally ejaculate, and while he disappeared into a few pathetic moments of ecstasy she pulled the knife out of his hand.

In the fight that ensued she cut him and he started to bleed. She had no way of knowing she had sliced through his carotid artery.

He died at her feet. His pants down around his ankles, his sperm drying on his stomach. And now she was serving a sentence of six to thirteen years, hoping to get out in three.

"So you have a hero," I said.

Coffey shot me a dirty look. "What the hell is wrong with me looking up to someone? Having a role model? Huh?"

"It's not going to get you off the streets if you pick a prostitute to emulate."

I said it without any inflection, but inside I felt as if Coffey had pierced me a little. Cleo was my client. I didn't want to start thinking about her in any kind of demeaning way. That wasn't my job.

Not back in Manhattan, it wasn't.

But it was here.

Coffey was biting her thumbnail and looking up at me from under her eyes. Despite her battered face, you could see the strong bone structure and how good her skin was. Her hair was still thick and lustrous. But she hadn't been in prison that long. She hadn't hit bottom yet. This was her first fight, but there would be more. And there might be worse.

"Coffey, let's talk about this. Isn't there anyone else you can think of who you look up to?"

"You have a problem with me thinking the Saint is special?"

"Can you think of any reason I would?"

"Don't you ever answer a question with an answer?"

"Fair enough. I think that there are other women who might be more positive role models for you. I want to help you realize that there are other jobs you can do besides being a prostitute."

Coffey cackled. She'd gone from winsome, sad prisoner to witch with one sound.

"You do not get it, sister. You have got to meet her. You have got to listen to her talk about what we all do for a living and why we deserve something other than undercover cops on our tails all the fucking time. You keep talking about her like she is some low-down, dirty whore. She's not. This woman is shining. She stands up against anyone who gets in her way. She wears Jimmy Choo shoes and fucking designer clothes. You should see her. There is not a hair out of place, not a crease in her jacket that doesn't belong there. She is beautiful."

And then Coffey gave me one more big, openmouthed laugh that revealed the silver cavities in her back teeth.

"You remind me of her, Doc Snow. In fact, if you had blond hair like her, the two of you could be fucking sisters, you really could."

15

I was quiet as Simon drove away from the prison and headed the car toward the city.

The sky ahead of us was gray, streaked with clouds. The closer we got to the city, the darker the sky became, and as we crossed the George Washington Bridge, it started to rain.

Traffic was backed up. The rain turned to a downpour. The cars came to a standstill and humidity fogged the windows in Simon's car.

Up ahead was the coffee shop we usually stopped at on our way back to New York. Simon parked and we ran from the car into the restaurant, only getting a little wet.

He ordered a Coke and a grilled cheese sandwich. I was used to him eating what I called "kid" food whenever he wanted. And envious. I ordered a salad and an iced coffee, and when the drink came I used artificial sweetener. Even though I tried to walk and go to the gym a few times a week, I always needed to lose ten pounds.

Finally he moved the conversation away from the light banter we'd been enjoying in the car. "What's wrong, Morgan?"

"I know depression is anger turned inward, but I can't seem to use that information to help myself as much as my patients."

"You get angry for your patients all the time. It's your Achilles' heel. You feel for them. You want to solve their problems for them. You want to save them. And you know it's not good for you."

"There isn't enough love in the world. Or enough compassion. Or even enough pity. There certainly is not enough time to give to all the people who deserve it."

"You just have to remember that you deserve some of it, too."

"I have a supervisor, thank you very much, Dr. Weiss."

He smiled. "There's more. Spill."

"Cleo Thane. These girls look up to her."

He nodded and watched the waitress set down our food. "I know. Is that why she's getting under your skin?"

I ate a forkful of my salad and then answered, "I don't know."

"First thought."

"She's seems so tough. Except it's all an act. She is the best actress in the world and no one will ever know it except for a few dozen men."

"Hmm. And who else could that be a description of?"

I nodded. It was too easy. When you are good friends with a therapist who really knows you, you speak in shortcuts. Between Simon Weiss and Nina Butterfield, I never got to stay confused for too long.

"You see your mother in her, don't you?" he asked gently.

"I see something of my mother in her."

It was raining that day, too. We were living in that hellhole on the Lower East Side and the water was seeping in the windows through the space where the frame was pulled away from the glass. My mother was lying on the couch, her silk shirt wrinkled, her jeans loose on her lean frame. Her lovely black hair framed her pale face. My mother's electric-blue eyes were half-shut, and her trained voice was slurred with the effects of the painkillers she popped like sweet candy and the liquor she used to wash them down.

She had a friend there when I got home from school that day. Jim, she called him, and she held his hand.

When he pulled it away, she tucked something into her pocket.

Tell me a story, Morgan, she whispered after he had gone while she lay there on the couch.

And I, too young at eight to understand, thought that my talking to her would bring her back from almost dead and make her whole again.

"Once upon a time there were two lost girls...."

The rain stopped as quickly as it started, and the sun was coming out as we turned onto Sixty-fifth Street and pulled into the parking garage down the block from the institute. It was five o'clock. We had an hour and a half till our Thursday-night group therapy sessions started.

Simon and I walked through the wrought-iron-and-glass doors and each said hello to Belinda, the receptionist. And then we parted, he to his office, and I to mine. In the time remaining before the session started I wanted to call Dulcie, who spent Thursday nights with her paternal grandmother and grandfather.

I opened the door to my office and stopped on the threshold, sensing something was wrong even before I consciously saw it.

A window must have been left open and the wind must have blown in. No...not just a wind.

Only gale-force gusts could have made this mess.

The cobalt-and-emerald carpet was hidden under a thick layer of papers, like litter in the street after a parade. I didn't even know I had that much paper in my office. The top of my desk was clear and the file cabinets were all open, the drawers pulled out, empty and gaping like hungry mouths.

Scattered among the papers were my books.

My bookshelves had been dumped onto the floor along with everything else. Dozens of books lay open, their backs broken and their spines split. The late-afternoon sunshine coming through the windows and illuminating the melee was obscene.

No window had been left open. And there was no wind that could have caused this amount of destruction.

"Belinda?" I yelled. I knew I might be disturbing someone in session but I couldn't seem to stop myself from bellowing out her name.

Footsteps came quickly; she had heard the urgency in my voice.
"Dr. Snow? Are you all right?"

She was at the threshold of the door to my office.

"Oh, my God," she whispered.

"Did you see anyone come in here this afternoon? Did you let
anyone in? Was my door shut all afternoon?" I knew this was hope-
less questioning. She sat partway down the hall with her back to
my office door. But maybe she had walked by. Maybe she had
turned around.

"Open or shut?" I asked.

"It had to be shut. I would have noticed if it had been open. I
walked by here at least four times since lunch. What do you
think—"

"You'd better call Nina."

Nina and I stood in the middle of the room assessing the mess.
There was nothing of monetary value in the office except for the
computer—which was still sitting in the middle of the desk—and
the carpet. But we were both worried about the patient files.
What if someone had taken any of those? Each file had private and
sensitive information in it. While no one even blinked anymore
when you said you were going to a therapist, when you said—if
you even said it aloud—that you were seeing a *sex* therapist, people inched closer. They wanted to know, even if they didn't dare
ask, what was the problem. Impotency? Frigidity? Lack of desire,
too much desire? Worse? Some deviant fetish?

We are still such a puritan society.

"Let's try to make some sense of this mess and see if anything
is missing. Do you have a group?" Nina asked.

I nodded.

"Well, let's hurry, then. We have an hour. Forget the books, let's
work with the papers and see what's what. This could be a disaster."

As we shuffled through the papers and I saw the names of past
and present clients on my notes, I grew more and more concerned.

"Most of these notes are fairly cryptic, but if someone
wanted to blackmail a husband or a wife—or if someone is in

the midst of a child custody case—there is stuff here that they could use." My voice was rising toward a hysterical pitch. "There's no way for me to know what is missing. *Anything* could be missing. Someone could have taken just one piece of paper that could upset a—"

Nina came over to me and put her hands on my shoulders. We were the same height and she looked right into my eyes. I remembered when I had been a lost little girl and she had been a grownup. She'd ignored my smelly clothes and matted hair, ignored my mother lying on the bed beside me, half out of her mind on painkillers, and she had just lassoed me with her amber eyes and held me in a kind embrace.

"You didn't do anything wrong, Morgan." Thirty years later she was still the only one who could tell me that and make me believe it.

I took a breath. The way she had taught me. Square breathing. It calmed you right down. Inhale, one, two, three, four, hold it, one, two, three, four. Exhale, one, two, three, four, hold it, one, two, three, four. And again.

"Should we call the police?" I asked.

Nina shook her head. I knew she wouldn't want to do that. While I had worked with the police a few times over the years as an expert witness and had a good working relationship with the D.A.'s office, Nina didn't.

In 1996, her husband of only two years and founder of this institute, Sam Butterfield, had been arrested and charged with running an illegal prostitution ring. He was a brilliant, aging hippie who had a child-of-the-sixties hatred of the police. As a radical revolutionary who believed America was backward and puritanical when it came to sexual attitudes, mores and rules, he broke laws and made up new ones without fear.

The police used a writer named Julia Sterling in a sting operation to infiltrate the institute. Six months later, Sam was convicted. He died of a heart attack the second week he was in prison.

Nina, who had always had a healthy skepticism balanced with

respect for law enforcement, had become embittered. She completely blamed the police and the slick and effective sting operation they had put in place for Sam's death.

All they had to do, she'd said more than once, was come out and tell Sam what they'd wanted from him. Investigate him out in the open. But instead they had gone undercover. Played lip service to the idea of justice. And the shock of that, Nina said, was what did him in. And now she mistrusted the police as much as her husband ever had.

"What I want to know is how the hell did anyone get in here? Was your door locked?" she asked.

I shook my head. "I never lock my door."

"When was the last time you were in here?"

"Yesterday, around five."

"There were half a dozen groups here last night. That's more than fifty people between 6:00 p.m. and 9:00 p.m. Someone could have slipped in without the receptionist noticing."

"Belinda would have noticed," I said.

"She wasn't here last night. We had a temp on the front desk. Serena something. I don't remember her last name."

Nina walked over to the windows and tried first the one on the left and then the right. Only one of them was locked. My office was on the second floor. At night, in the dark, during the few hours when New York City's residential neighborhoods really do go to sleep, it might have been possible for someone to climb up the stone wall and steal into the building.

"Do you lock the windows and the balcony door at night?"

I was searching, sifting through the papers, but I wasn't focused. Was this the act of an angry ex-patient? Had someone broken into my office looking for valuable information that would allow them to destroy one of my patients?

"Yes, of course," I said. But had I forgotten to?

"Do you have any idea about which of your patients might be at risk for blackmail?" Nina asked.

"Which one? It's more like which *ones.* I have one patient who has finally decided to ask her husband for a separation. He's been sexually abusing her and has even been here with her several times. I guess he might be angry enough to do something like this. He'd know the layout of the office. And he might have gotten in. Anyone might have gotten in with a temp at the front desk."

"Who else?"

"There are dozens. I don't even know where to start." I felt overwhelmed by the melee and confusion everywhere I looked.

"I'm going to talk to the temp and look through the appointment books. There has to be a way to make sense of this."

A half hour later, she was back in my office.

"Have you noticed anything missing?" she asked as she began picking up the books off the floor and putting them back on my shelves.

"No. But who knows. It could be one single sheet of paper with my notes on it. Did you find out anything?" I asked.

She shook her head. "No. Too many options. We had sixty-five people in here last night between single appointments and groups. Five first-timers. We also had someone from the phone company working here. And about five messengers delivered packages. Any one of them could have stayed behind in a bathroom. We're going to have to keep track of all the new patients who came in yesterday but don't come back."

"That will only work if the person used his or her own name. If not, we might never be able to figure out who it was. Or what they wanted." I smoothed the endpapers of a book on Freud's whore-madonna complex before I returned it to the shelf.

16

The stone spires of St. Patrick's Cathedral only reached up 330 feet, but despite being dwarfed by boxes of glass and steel, it exuded an importance those taller buildings didn't have. From the minute its doors opened in the morning to when they shut each night, more than seven thousand people walked up the steps and through the doors to behold this magnificent Gothic house of worship. And no day was more crowded than a Saturday in the summer when people were visiting the city from all over the world.

That was why he had chosen that morning at 11:00 a.m.

It simply was the safest place for him to hide in all of New York. He could spend as long as he needed in the sanctuary, thinking out what he needed to do next without anyone paying attention to him. He never sat in the same pew two visits in a row. Never visited the same shrine more than once a month.

People who prayed sat under a shroud of invisibility. There was still the sense that it was wrong to stare at someone with their head bowed, eyes closed. And so that was the pose he struck when he needed to escape from the streets outside and the people who knew him and expected things of him.

This was his refuge. And today it was also his shopping mall. The tableau he'd constructed required simple black rosaries. And there was no safer place to buy them than in the gift shop of this holy edifice.

Commercialism had taken over the church with the same voracity as it had taken over the art world. For all the people who stood rapt in front of a van Gogh, there were two dozen who bought the coasters for sale in the museum's store. For all the people who came to this grand cathedral to reach out to their Lord, hundreds more worshiped in the small shop buying medals, prayer cards, bottles of holy water and any one of the dozens of rosaries offered for sale.

No one would remember the man who purchased the black rosary. No one would think it odd that he had been there once a week for the last few weeks, each time buying the exact same prayer beads. And no one noticed that he managed not to touch the beads with his fingertips but only held on to the tag when he handed it over to the saleswoman.

He chose black again. Because they were simple. Because he liked how they looked against ivory-colored skin. He chose the medium-size beads, with the silver roundels and Virgin medal and crucifix. The gold was ostentatious.

The act of handing over the money and taking the bag holding the rosaries was an act of faith in itself. He was doing God's work. He was bringing another woman into the fold. He was introducing Jesus to another lost soul. And if they did not appreciate him for it, if they did not understand what was happening in the moment, he was sure that their souls did.

The woman smiled at him as she gave him change. He smiled back. Easily. Without fear. Knowing that she would never remember just another man. He left the gift shop and walked into the apse of the church. He would go to the confessional and ask the priest behind the mesh window to bless these beads. Dozens of people made this request every day. Tourists in the house of the

Lord who had no respect. Who took pictures. Who bought souvenirs. If he could push them all out, he would. If he could make the cathedral pure again he would.

But then he would no longer be invisible. And until his job was done, until he'd completed his task, being seen, being recognized was not anything he could risk.

"Father, it has been one week since my last confession. I have taken the Lord God's name in vain and coveted my neighbor's wife. And I would like you to bless my rosary. Would you do that?"

"Yes, my son."

17

The following Monday morning at eight-fifteen, Dulcie and I were in a taxi, heading downtown to her drama school.

"I wish I could go to this school all year long," she said longingly.

As the cab worked its way through the traffic, she kept up a steady stream of chatter about how she liked the academy so much more than regular school and how her new friend, Gretchen, and she thought that the earlier you got started with your career, the better chance you had of making it as an actress.

I had not minded that Dulcie was going to spend the summer at the academy instead of going to a sleep-away camp, although I would have preferred she spend the summer months outdoors, swimming and playing softball and tennis. Of all the things for her to be fascinated by, the theater was the last one I would have chosen for her. And not just because I'd seen what my mother's early success as an actress, and then later failure, had done to her. How it had destroyed her. I just wanted Dulcie to enjoy her childhood and not face the pressure and rejections of an acting career before she had the coping mechanisms of an adult. It could be a cruel business no matter how old you were—but she was only twelve.

Except acting was in my daughter's blood.

The cab pulled up to the school on Madison and Thirty-ninth Street and Dulcie jumped out while I paid the fare. We stood outside the school and she kissed me goodbye, her high-voltage blue eyes beaming.

"Have a wonderful day," I said to her.

"Oh, I will," she said, and ran into the building. Her happiness was contagious and I found myself smiling.

But my smile didn't last long.

I got to the office in time for my nine o'clock patient, who left at nine-forty-five, which gave me a fifteen-minute break until Cleo was supposed to show up.

Ten o'clock came and went without her appearing. I waited at my desk until ten-fifteen and then went outside onto my balcony. Ostensibly I was watering the many plants that lived out there, but I was really watching the street.

For the second time in five days, Cleo Thane had not shown up for her appointment. And she hadn't called to cancel. Maybe I was overacting, but I was worried.

The sun was shining and a warm breeze was blowing. The geraniums in the terra-cotta pots in front of the institute were in full bloom and the white and pink blossoms bent in the wind. From above, they looked as if they were praying.

I scanned the street, watching and waiting to see Cleo turn the corner and walk down the block.

At ten-thirty-five I went back into my office, called her and got her answering machine. I left a brief message, then sat at my desk wondering what else I could do. How worried should I be?

I opened her folder and found the form she'd been required to fill out when she first came to see me. I scanned past her insurance-company data, home address, phone number and place of work. In the space where we required the patient to list his or her next of kin and contact information in case of emergencies she had written the name Gil Howard. And then a New York city phone number.

I assumed this was the man she referred to as Caesar, but calling him raised an ethical dilemma.

Cleo had told me that he was aware that she was in therapy, but that still didn't give me the right to contact him if, by doing so, I wound up giving him information about her that she didn't want him to know.

What if, for instance, she had taken an out-of-town job and not told him? If I called and said she'd missed appointments, I might be giving him knowledge she didn't want him to have.

And what if she'd just walked away from therapy and decided not to come back? Patients occasionally did that. A therapist could dig too deep and get too far too fast and a patient could bolt. And what if she hadn't told him that she'd quit?

I put off making the call.

My 11:00 a.m. patient was on time.

As soon as she left, I picked up the phone and called Cleo's number once more. When the machine answered, I hung up. I'd already left two messages—one last Wednesday, one earlier today.

A jagged bolt of fear rippled through my stomach. Until then, that particular feeling had been reserved for Dulcie and, when I was young, for my mother.

The sixth sense that mothers and daughters have—or that at least I had had with my mother and my daughter—was kicking in for the first time with a client.

At noon I left my office. A walk in the park would help me clear my head and allow me to figure out why I was reacting so powerfully to Cleo's disappearance.

With every step I took under the thick canopy of leaves, I became more and more certain that Cleo was in trouble. If she simply had gone away or taken a job she would have let me know. And if she had forgotten, I'd left messages. She would have picked them up. She was a successful businesswoman; no matter where she was, she would monitor her calls. She took in more than two million dollars a year. She was involved with dozens of important, wealthy and well-placed men. This was not a teenager acting out and running away from home. Cleo was a responsible woman.

Something was wrong.

On the way back to the office, I stopped to get a double espresso at the café but didn't bother with any food. Now that I had decided what to do, I was in a hurry to get upstairs.

Opening her file, I found Gil Howard's number and dialed.

"Diablo Cigar Bar," said a sweet-sounding woman.

"Gil Howard, please."

"Who can I say is calling?"

I didn't know what to say. Give my name or not?

"This is Morgan Snow."

The man who came on the line had a New York accent and sounded concerned. "Hello?"

"I'm calling from the doctor's office. Cleo Thane had an appointment with me earlier today but she didn't keep it. Since she gave me your number as next of kin, I just wanted to find out if she was ill?"

"No… I…" He clearly didn't know what to say.

"Do you have a number I could reach her at?"

"No."

I had no idea who he was, but still I could tell the man I was talking to was distraught.

"Are you all right?" It slipped out. A professional knee-jerk reaction. A person's voice goes into a certain cadence and rhythm of distress and I ask if they are all right.

"Cleo's not here."

It wasn't an answer to my question. "Can I leave my number? If you hear from her, will you let her know she missed her appointment?"

"When was it?" he asked.

"This morning at 10:00 a.m."

There was a long silence. Then he said, "Right. That's right. I know that. She told me. Mondays and Wednesdays at ten. Was she there last Wednesday at ten?"

But he sounded as if he already knew the answer to his own question.

"No."

"You are her therapist, aren't you?"

"Yes. This is Dr. Snow. I'm sorry to be cryptic, but I had to be careful—"

He cut me off. "I'm going crazy here and I'm worried as hell. No one has heard from her since last Tuesday night. That is six days. Six fucking days. Cleo has never done anything like this. And I am scared out of my mind. I'm still making phone calls. Looking for her. Can I call you back later? Will you be there?"

"Yes, I have patients all afternoon. The best time to call is ten minutes before the hour."

"Yeah, yeah, I know. Been there, done that. That's the other phone. I'll talk to you later."

And without waiting for me to answer, he hung up. The sudden dead quiet was immediate and alarming.

But there wasn't time to think about the call because my two o'clock patient had arrived.

18

My last patient left at three-forty-five. On any other day, I would have gone home early, but I was hoping Gil Howard would call. I did some paperwork for a while and tried to ignore the headache that lay right behind my eyes.

When the phone rang at four-thirty, I picked up the receiver quickly.

"Dr Snow?" This man didn't sound like Gil, even though I'd only spoken to him once.

"Yes."

"I... I..." He hesitated.

"Can I help you? Who is this?"

"I'm sorry. My name is Elias Beecher." He paused.

I didn't recognize the name any more than the voice. "Can I help you?"

"I don't know..." He paused once more.

I was used to people hesitating when they first called. Making the decision to see a therapist can be a difficult one. As much as someone might know that he or she wants help, actually asking for it is something else.

"Can I help you?" I asked again.

"I'm not sure. This is awkward. Especially over the phone."

He had a cultured voice, deep and resonant. A handsome voice. And at the same time, vulnerable. I liked him right off. Even his hesitancy. Most people I knew hid behind too many words, spoke too quickly.

"Well, we don't need to talk about anything over the phone. We can make an appointment. We can talk when you come in."

With the phone wedged between my ear and shoulder, I walked over to the bookshelves, and poured myself a glass of water from the silver carafe. It was cold, and before I took a sip I held it up to my forehead. The headache I'd had for the last hour was getting worse, and I hoped the cool glass would offer some relief. I should just give in and take two aspirin. But even though the pills were benign, I had a difficult time taking them.

All these years later and I still would rather suffer pain than succumb to taking pills.

"You don't know who I am, do you?" Elias Beecher asked.

"No. Should I?"

"No, I guess not. I'm sorry. It was rude of me to assume that you would." His consideration surprised me, reminded me of someone, but I couldn't think of whom. "For some reason I thought you'd know my name," he said, but still didn't explain.

I took the bottle of Bufferin out of my top desk drawer and put it down in front of the phone. The white bottle. The blue label. It was harmless. It would make my head ache less. Yet, still I hesitated.

"I'm sorry, should I?" I asked.

"Yes. Well, she told me that she had come to you for help. And that you were helping. And I was so grateful. I should say that first. How very grateful I was that you were going to help her and that she was feeling that she might get her—our problems resolved. God, I love her. And that's all I want."

Was this the husband or the father of one of my patients? There was so much sadness in his voice. Nothing pulled at me like someone's melancholy. I wanted to help him. Now. As soon as possible. And I was impressed that he was willing—and able—to talk openly to me even though we'd never met. It reinforced the vulnerability I'd heard in his voice. There are so many people closed off to their own emotions, but someone like Elias Beecher was a therapist's dream. It is much easier to help someone when they weren't fighting you. When they wanted to let you in.

"Mr. Beecher. I know that you are very upset. But I can't even begin to figure out if I can help you or not unless I understand who and what you are talking about. Do you think you could start at the beginning? Who was talking to me? And why was she talking to me about you?"

He took a deep breath. "Dr. Snow, the woman I am engaged to is one of your patients. And she has been missing for almost a week. I've gone to the police. I'm a lawyer, I know how it works. She's a missing person until she shows up dead and only then will she be a priority. There were no threats on her life, no sign of foul play, no break-in at her apartment. If she was kidnapped, no one has made any contact with me for ransom. I just don't have anything to give the police to entice them to take this more seriously. And to complicate it further, I know they think I might be responsible for her disappearance. The boyfriend or husband is always a suspect, isn't he?"

Elias Beecher had been talking so quickly and with such urgency I hadn't had a chance to interrupt, but he'd finally stopped long enough to take a breath.

My hands were as cold as the water in my glass, and I clasped them together in my lap.

"Who is your fiancée, Mr. Beecher?" I had to hear him say it.

"Cleo Thane."

19

I reached out to my desk and put my hand around the plastic bottle of aspirin. Wasn't Gil Howard Cleo's boyfriend?

"Dr. Snow?"

"Yes. I'm sorry. And, yes, she did mention you but not by name. As far as you can tell, how long has she been missing, Mr. Beecher?"

"Six days. That's what I told the police. They said they couldn't do anything. Yet. I filed a missing-person report. But from the way they treated me, from the questions they asked me, I think all I accomplished was making myself a suspect."

I popped the top of the bottle, but I didn't shake any of the pills out, I didn't want to distract him with the sound, I didn't want to change the tenor of this conversation. I needed to listen hard and glean everything I could from what he said.

"A suspect? In her disappearance?" I asked. I knew they would. First and before anyone else, the police would look at those who were closest to her. But I wanted to hear how he responded to my questions. His reactions were critical in helping me understand whether or not he, indeed, was a suspect.

He laughed. And like his voice, the sound was intimate and resonant. "I've been in love twice in my life," he said. "The first time when I was in college. She left me for the one man I could never compete with. And now with Cleo. And this time she made me feel that no man could compete with me. The others are just clients."

"Did the police ask you about Cleo's business?"

"Yes. But I didn't exactly tell them. What would I have said when they asked me how I felt about it? How would I explain it so they would understand that, yes, I minded what she does...of course, I wouldn't be human if I didn't. But not enough to put her in harm's way. Cleo is young. She's lovely. And she's magical— the way she's untouched by it all somehow."

I was nodding. I had felt this myself, I knew what he meant. But I didn't say anything. I didn't want to interrupt him.

"I don't know how else to explain it," he continued. "Cleo is only acting with those men. She becomes someone else. With me, she has this light...this delight...in things. A perspective. I'm rambling. I'm sorry. None of this is pertinent. I should know better than to go on like this. The point is that she is missing and has been for six days and I have to find her and I want to know if you can help me."

"I've been worried about her, too. I've been hoping she'd gone on a vacation or a business trip and just forgotten to let me know."

He laughed. A different laugh. This one was...what? Harsher? More ironic. I was listening to him with an intensity that made my head pound even harder.

Who was he? What kind of man? Was he involved in Cleo's disappearance?

It wasn't unheard of for the guilty party to be the one who went to the police. It was in the news every day. A wife is missing. The husband reports it. Six weeks later, he's arrested for her murder.

But nothing Cleo had said about Caesar—or Elias, now that I knew his real name—had suggested that he had been at a breaking point with her.

"Can I see you?" he asked. "Will you talk to me? Will you help me? Between the two of us, maybe we can figure out what happened."

"I can try. I'm not sure how much I can tell you. Everything that Cleo talked to me about is confidential. But certainly, I'll do what I can."

"I know you will. From everything Cleo told me about you, I'm sure that you can help me. You are very important to her. She really respects you."

I thanked him, feeling even worse than I had before I'd picked up the phone. We made an appointment for the next day, and as soon as I hung up, I grabbed hold of the bottle of aspirin again and held it as if the medicine inside would seep into my bloodstream through the plastic.

But it wouldn't. In order to get any relief from the pain I was going to have to shake out two pills, put them in my mouth and swallow them.

And once I did, I could try to figure out the new piece of the puzzle. Who was the man I'd called earlier that afternoon? The one I'd assumed was Cleo's lover? Who was Gil Howard?

20

Five minutes later I was still sitting at my desk, staring at the bottle of pills, feeling the pain throb behind my eyes, knowing it was not going to go away by itself, when there was a knock on my door.

"Come in."

It was Belinda, and behind her was a tall man whose face was in shadow.

"Dr. Snow, there is someone here to see you." Her voice was tight.

"I don't have any sessions scheduled and I was just getting ready to leave. Is someone giving you a hard time?"

In the background I heard a male voice. "I don't have an appointment, but I'd appreciate you just giving me a few minutes." He had an accent that I couldn't place, except that I knew it was Southern. Then he stepped into the doorway. He was tall and lanky, wearing blue jeans, a white shirt and a dark jacket.

"I'm sorry to barge in, Dr. Snow." He stepped over the threshold. "I'm Detective Noah Jordain. And yes, this is official business."

"Is my daughter all right?" My heart jolted and started pounding, adrenaline releasing in a nanosecond. The pain in my head stabbed me between the eyes.

He was fast. He knew. "This isn't about your family. I'm here to see you in your professional capacity."

I'll see you as soon I recover from this fucking heart attack you just gave me, I wanted to say, but I didn't. Instead my response was polite and professional. "Come in."

I wanted to put my head down on my desk and close my eyes. Instead I did one quick round of square breathing. Shit. Why was my panic always so close to the surface? It was as if I was always waiting for the phone call, the knock on the door, the explosion. Expecting it. Anticipating the awful call that something was wrong, that Dulcie was in danger. In my head her safety was at risk every minute of every day. I fought it and blocked it and I lived with it, but sometimes it morphed into the fear I'd had about my mother's safety when I was a child. She hadn't been safe and I hadn't been able to save her.

I was no wimpette. I was no victim. Yet I suffered anxiety along with most of the rest of the world. To cope I'd learned exercises, did visualizations. Had worked on my issues in therapy. And most of the time I mastered my weakness. But if it caught me off guard the way it just had when this detective walked into my office and introduced himself, I lost the ability to control my feelings.

I gulped the air.

It didn't matter that this man whom I'd never met before was standing there watching me trying to come up from under. He just waited and smiled at me with eyes that were surprisingly kind, and then walked across the floor toward my desk.

"Can I sit?" he asked, with his hand on the back of the chair facing me.

And as I nodded, I realized why he was here. Of course. It had been the leitmotiv of my whole day. This detective was here about Cleo. Something *had* happened to her. They'd found her.

The words were already forming in the back of my throat... Has something happen to Cleo Thane? Is it connected to the other prostitutes who were killed? Was she the last victim of the Magdalene Murderer? Is that why she missed her appointments and hadn't been in touch?

After my call with Gil Howard and Elias Beecher's plea, I was primed to hear the solution to the mystery. And who else would have it than a detective? This detective.

He was watching me, and I wondered how much of what I was thinking he could glean from the expression on my face.

All I wanted to do was find out if Cleo was all right, but I couldn't just come out and ask when I didn't know for sure that she was the reason he was here. Besides, even if she was why he was here, I couldn't reveal that Cleo had been coming to see me.

Not until I knew she was dead. If she was alive there was nothing I could say. I would have to wait to hear what he wanted before I could ask about a patient who had come to symbolize a tight ball of anxiety that I could not dissolve.

"I should let you catch your breath. Do you want me to get you some water?" He looked around and spotted the ubiquitous water carafe. I shook my head no and picked up the glass already on my desk.

"I do apologize, Doctor. I hate that about what I do…show up unannounced and have people look at me like I am the grim reaper. Just once, I want to introduce myself to someone and have them throw their arms around me and hug me tight and say, Oh, I am so damn happy you are here."

I smiled.

How easily he'd brought me around. Expertly, I'd have to say. The man had to have some psychological training.

"I'm Detective Noah Jordain."

"Hello. I'm Morgan Snow."

In the last few years, I'd been asked to work on several cases with the NYPD. I'd appeared in court to give testimony dozens of times. I had met dozens of policemen and detectives, some of whom fit the stereotypes of what a law enforcement officer was and others who eschewed the role and just cared about doing their jobs the best they could.

Noah Jordain, on first impression, was one of the latter.

Some people inhabit their skin with comfort, others are never at ease. He was. His clothes—a blazer, jeans, a white shirt and tie—fit him. Elbows, knees, stomach that didn't push at the seams, creases were where they should be. Even from a distance, I was sure he smelled clean. Like lemons, I guessed.

But when he leaned in to shake my hand I was surprised to find it was rosemary and mint. Not as expected. Just as sharp and invigorating. He looked as if he was in his late thirties—early forties at the most—but there was something aged and ragged in his voice. You could hear all that he had seen behind his words. And you could see all that he had heard in his eyes. Sorry blue eyes that analyzed as they searched. And they always searched.

He squinted, stared, roamed, looked from me to the windows, behind me, to the right, to the left, back to me, to my face, then my hands, then he looked right into my eyes. Dared me to look away. A police trick—did he even know he was doing it? I dared him to look away first. A therapist's trick. We were evenly matched. Involuntarily I smiled just a little at the thought. He held out his hand and I shook it, aware of it being large, pleasantly dry, but not too rough. I could tell he had enormous strength in his fingers but that he was aware of it and was being careful.

"*Dr.* Snow, right?"

I nodded. "Do you want to sit down or are you going to stand over me and talk down to me?"

"Whoa. I know I upset and scared you. But that much sarcasm? I don't talk down to women. Especially pretty ones who have more degrees than I do."

With a smile, he sat opposite me at the desk, leaned back and gave me some more time. He was so completely at ease, and so few people were in my office that it was a pleasure to watch him.

How someone acted when they first met you and then came into your space told you something about them. Especially this space. Some people needed to give themselves time, were nervous, or intimidated; others had too much bravado, needed to own the area even though it wasn't theirs. He didn't do any of those things. His actions were not informed by any neurosis. At least not yet.

I offered him coffee and he accepted.

I was glad for a few minutes of busy work to observe him and get a beat on him.

My curiosity was like the pain in my head, insistent and determined. And as much as I wanted to just ask him to tell me why he was here and find out what was going on, I would be better served this way. Knowledge, even subtle knowledge and intuitive information, was a weapon. And since I was sure he had his gun in a holster under his arm or strapped around his ankle, it seemed only fair for me to have some ammunition of my own.

"Milk? Sugar?" I asked as I poured the still-steaming Italian roast from the thermos into one of the four mugs that Dulcie had made for me in school. The one I picked for him read: *Was Freud Wearing a Slip?*

I turned for his answer.

"Light and sweet."

I knew he hadn't meant there to be anything even slightly lascivious about his answer. I knew he was being straightforward— I could see it in his face. And I almost laughed at the way his eyes widened slightly when he realized his words had sounded suggestive.

And then, the tall, strong detective blushed. And something kicked awake in me. But it wasn't anything I could even think about. Not there and not then.

I was used to being only one kind of person in this room—a doctor listening to my patients through a filter of learning, weighing every word uttered. I had never been a woman sitting in that office, and I couldn't remember ever hearing a line that I responded to. Of course over the years, a few of my male patients and even one or two of my female patients had been flirtatious with me, but my reaction had always been clinical.

This was different.

And it was stupid, I thought as I stirred the cream-colored

brew and handed it to him, careful not to touch his hand by accident. This was ridiculous.

He was inspecting the mug.

"Cute."

"My daughter's handiwork."

"Clever kid."

"Much too clever."

"How old is she?"

"Twelve. Going on four sometimes. Twenty other times."

"You're lucky."

I smiled. "I know." I looked down at my own mug. It read: *Jungry? Or Thirsty?* I showed it to him and he laughed deeply.

"So. How can I help you, Detective?"

Now I was afraid I was blushing. Everything sounded like a ridiculous line. Why? What was going on? This was serious. An NYPD detective was sitting in my office on official business and I kept hearing innuendos.

In the middle of this awful day, a day I'd spent worried about Cleo, a day punctuated by talking to two men who were both disconsolate over her disappearance, I suddenly realized that probably for the first time in a few years, I'd met a man whom I was actually attracted to. He wasn't a friend like Simon, whom I was trying the thought out on. This was a man I'd never met before and I was curious about him.

There was nothing special about him. Well, he had nice hair. Salt-and-pepper, which fell in soft waves across his broad forehead and down his neck. But his eyes were sort of small. And his nose might be a little bit too big. Except all put together, he was striking. Handsome, even. And he had great hands.

Shit. What was I doing noticing the man's hands?

He saw that I was staring at his hands and his eyes sort of crinkled and his lips spread into a grin, and I felt his whole stupid smile in the pit of my stomach and my head pounded more.

I picked up the bottle of pills and finally, after hours of suffering with the damn headache, shook two out. But still I didn't take them. Holding them in the palm of my hand, I looked down at them. Two tiny pills that scared me and reassured me at the same time.

He just watched. Took it all in. Sipped his coffee, then said, "You might as well take them. I'm afraid this is going to be a complicated conversation."

I nodded, surprised that he had almost read my mind. "You already know that?"

Now he nodded. "We have reason to believe that one of your patients is missing. And I'm hoping you might be able to help us figure out why." He was watching me the way I watched my patients, and I wasn't sure if I liked it.

"What patient?" I knew, but I wasn't going to let on that I did.

"Cleo Thane."

I could not allow any reaction. Not yet. I had to protect her until I found out that I no longer could. "Detective, you know there is nothing I can tell you about any of my patients. I can't even confirm or deny that someone is seeing me."

"She is. Her fiancé already confirmed it. He's the one who reported her missing. There's not much we can do about a missing person other than put out a report and wait. Unless it's a child. Or there has been a threat. Or there is proof it was a kidnapping. Or there's something to suggest foul play. We went to her apartment, but there is no sign of any foul play. Nothing to suggest that anything has happened to her. One of her suitcases is gone, according to her boyfriend. And some of her clothes. On the surface there is nothing even slightly suspect about that.

"But with what has been going on with the Magdalene murders, I don't want to assume anything. We know who your client is and what she does for a living, and since there is some maniac out there who's brutally—"

"If there is nothing suspect about her apartment, why do you think there is a connection?" Could he hear the panic in my voice?

"How 'bout we trade. An answer for an answer."

I nodded. "But you first. Do you think this is connected? Do you think she is still alive?"

"That's two questions, but I'll answer them. We don't know

anything about her disappearance at this point. For all we know she went away for reasons of her own and just didn't tell anyone what they were. And, yes, we think she's alive. Again, we have no reason or information to think otherwise.

"Now, my turn," he said. "Have you heard from Ms. Thane?"

"No."

"Is she a patient?"

"Yes. She is a patient."

"When was the last time you saw her?"

"Last Wednesday."

"How many appointments has she missed?"

"Two."

"Had she ever missed appointments before?"

"No."

"And she didn't call you to cancel?"

"No."

"Is that unusual?" he asked.

I nodded.

He took a long drink of his coffee. Down the hall a door opened and shut, and I was aware of the sound and then the ensuing silence. Even after he put down his mug, he didn't speak right away. As if he was figuring out what to say or how to say it.

"I need you to help me," he said.

It was such a personal plea that it took me by surprise. The official tone was gone and there was a real pain in his voice. How could he do his job and still have room to connect with that much feeling? I knew what he faced, and I couldn't have done it.

"I'm not sure that I can help."

"You can. It's more a question of if you will."

"There isn't anything I can tell you. Everything Cleo told me is confidential. Privileged and private information."

"Dr. Snow—"

"Morgan, please."

"Morgan, you have a terrific reputation. You've got fans in the department. My forensic psychiatrist says you are one of the best in your field." He took a breath and then blew the air out of his mouth. "Will you help us?"

"As long as she is alive there isn't anything I can—"

He held up his hand. His fingers really were impossibly long, and graceful. I imagined them holding a gun. It was an incongruous image.

"Here's where we are. We don't know where Cleo Thane is. We don't know if she's in trouble or not. But we have a man out there who has brutally murdered and defiled two prostitutes, and we don't want Cleo Thane to be the third. Right now, I'd just be happy to find out where she is so I can rule her out. We've been to her apartment with her fiancé and it doesn't look like anything is missing. But we don't have her appointment book or her Palm-Pilot or her beeper or whatever it is she uses. We don't have her cell phone. We only know that she hasn't used it in the last six days."

"But what can I do?"

"You can tell us what you know about her. Was anyone bothering her? Was she planning on leaving the city? Was she dissatisfied with her business? Did she have any clients who—from what she told you—might be psychotic? And what about the boyfriend? Was she really happy with him? Did they have problems? Does he have any issues we should know about?" I could tell from the way he was leaning forward, from the way he had placed his hands on my desk, how badly he wanted the answers.

I shrugged. "I can't tell you any of those things. I am sorry. I really am. But Cleo is my patient and everything that she has told me has been told to me in complete confidence. As long as she might be alive, I have to protect that confidence."

"Even if it means putting her in jeopardy?"

I opened my hands, fingers splayed, as if I was holding the answers and had let them all slip out. But all that dropped to the floor were two round white painkillers.

21

The next day was bright and sunny and hot, and Nina and I took a walk into Central Park at lunchtime. We entered through the zoo entrance and as soon as we left the traffic and the exhaust of Fifth Avenue, I took a deep breath, inhaling the fresher air. If you live in the suburbs you don't understand how important a park becomes to city dwellers. Especially in the summer. Most of us knew every inch of it, the way you know your own backyard.

"What's wrong?" Nina asked.

"Am I that transparent?"

She shook her head. "No."

"You are just that good, right?" We both laughed. It was an old joke. She could see through me just as she had been able to see through my mother, no matter how dense the thicket of lies.

"Dulcie okay?" she asked.

"She's at drama school. I've never seen her happier. She hasn't argued with me about anything for days."

"Okay, so it's not Dulcie. Are you going to tell me or are you going to make me pull it out of you?"

"It's a patient."

She raised her eyebrows. "So someone's gotten to you?"

I laughed sarcastically.

Since graduate school I'd endured the joke that my last name should have been Ice, not Snow. Of all the traps in being a shrink, I rarely, if ever, got too close to my patients. I hardly ever stepped over the boundaries. Almost never had countertransference issues, even though they were common with therapists and were, in fact, often a good way to stay in touch with your patients as long as you were aware of what was happening.

We'd reached the dead center of the park, where a huge abandoned amphitheater stood like a comforting parenthesis mark.

The ear, I had called this structure as a child.

I'd learned to ride my bike and use my roller skates on the esplanade just beyond this spot. And I brought my boyfriends here when I was in high school to make out in the shadows of the shell.

I filled Nina in on my concern over Cleo's disappearance and my phone calls with Gil Howard and Elias Beecher. I explained who they both were, having more information now after talking to Gil a second time that morning.

"Elias is Cleo's boyfriend. A white-glove lawyer. I've talked to him once. Not sure yet what I think of him. I've talked to Gil twice. He's her business partner. They've been working together for five years. And I think they've also been lovers. He implied they still are lovers. In any case, he doesn't know about Elias."

"Do you think either of them have anything to do with her disappearance?"

"Gut reaction is no. They are both distraught. Going on instinct, their fears and distress appear heartfelt. But we both know that if either of them is a psychopath, they'd be able to fool me. The business partner could be upset about the book, knowing that if she does publish it, clients could very well stop coming to the club. It would be a terrible scandal."

"And the boyfriend?"

"The police think he's a suspect. Just because he is her boyfriend. And he knows that. He told me that right off the bat. But I don't think he's involved."

"Why?"

I went into detail about Cleo's sexual dysfunction. "She told me he's been patient with her. Willing to work with her."

"Or that's how she wants to see it. You don't really know. He could be insanely jealous of the other men she's been with. How does he feel about the book?"

"I don't know if he's read it. She just finished the first draft. But she told me he was worried about the idea of it."

"He could have gotten his hands on it and flipped out when he actually read about what she's done with these men. It's one thing knowing it in the abstract but another having read the details."

We walked through the empty space, sending the assembled pigeons flying.

"There's a third scenario," I said. "Last night the detective who has been working on the Magdalene murders came to see me."

I watched Nina's face harden into an angry mask. Before she had a chance to say anything, I spoke. "This has nothing to do with what had happened with Sam. This is about a beautiful young woman."

Nina was shaking her head. "You think that's what's bothering me? C'mon Morgan. You know why I'm upset. This is about ethics. I understand how worried you are about your patient. But there is a clear line here, and you know you can't cross it." She squinted. But the sun wasn't in her eyes. She was looking at me hard. "You aren't considering talking to the police about your patient, are you?"

"Of course not. I'd never do that unless I knew she was in danger and I had information that could save her." My voice was tight.

"Do you have any information?"

There was a sudden fluttering of wings as a flock of pigeons settled on the stage of the amphitheater and began hunting for crumbs of food.

I explained that Cleo had given me a copy of the book and that I'd been reading it. "No. I don't have any real information. Only that her boyfriend was right to be worried about her publishing it. Her clients are powerful and wealthy men who've trusted her with their peccadilloes. Not one of them is going to be happy about this memoir. Even if she does disguise them."

A group of kids Dulcie's age came roaring down the aisle on bikes, hollering and listening to their voices echo off the bandshell.

"Does she name the men in the book?"

"No. Well, not quite. She goes into enough detail about several of the men whom she sees on a regular basis for me to guess who they are. But she doesn't name them."

"Is it incendiary?"

"If you knew who they were, for sure it would be. She talks about what they want from her...some of it's sad, some dark. All of it is potentially explosive. The question I keep asking myself is what if one of these men whom she's written about knows that she is about to reveal his secrets? He'd worry she would leave in just enough detail so that someone close to this guy might recognize him. That could make someone desperate. And if that's true, if I keep Cleo's book and don't turn it in, I could be preventing the police from finding her."

"Not so fast. You don't even know she's in danger. And you don't know that any of her clients knew about the book."

"Right. But I can't just sit on the book and not do anything, either."

"You have to. You understand that, don't you, Morgan?"

I nodded.

We started walking back, taking a different route that led us past the Bethesda Fountain. A film crew was shooting and there were large trucks obstructing the view of the bronze statue.

"Nina, what if I'm the only—"

"You can't solve everything, Morgan. You have to stop trying."

I kicked at a fallen branch in my way. Took a step. Kicked it another few feet. "What if I tried to meet the men in the book and—"

"How would you figure out who they are?"

"Gil Howard, that's Cleo's partner and the guy who owns the Club, might be willing to help me. There are a lot of men in the book who have a lot to lose."

Nina stopped, not saying anything right away. It was almost as if she was waiting for everything to line up in some order in her mind. "What would meeting them do? How would that help you figure out what happened to her? *If* anything has happened to her."

We started up a small incline, past a playground on one side and a meadow on the others.

"I could assess them."

Nina was shaking her head now. "No."

"I have to do something."

"Morgan, what if she just went away to get some space from her boyfriend? Or to get plastic surgery? Or she had some kind of psychotic break? What if you met the men, suspected one and then were to tell the police enough about him for them to figure out who he was, and what if the police exposed him and then it turned out your client wasn't in any danger at all?" She shook her head again. "Not only would you have jeopardized Cleo's business, and her clients' privacy, but you could also lead to her getting arrested. After all, prostitution is illegal. I know we aren't supposed to make judgments and I'm not making one now, but you are dealing with someone who is breaking the law every single day. And if you give the police any information, you are giving them a key to arresting her."

"Arresting her? But she might be in danger."

A sly smile crossed Nina's lips. "You sure? You really sure? I'm not. Do you remember what they did to Sam? They acted as if they were investigating some poor girl who was in trouble, but they weren't. They were laying a trap for Sam. What if they are laying a trap again? The police know about Cleo and her business. They have been watching her and waiting for just one slipup. And now they have a very convenient situation to play with. The boyfriend has told them she's missing. Since when does the NYPD do anything about missing people? Thousands go missing in this city every single week. Without any sign that she was kidnapped or taken against her will, believe me, they do not investigate a case like this. What if they are using the serial murder to fool you into helping them nail Cleo? It could be just another sting."

The kids, having made one huge circle, were back again and shouting too loud for us to talk over them.

"That's impossible," I finally said. "You are mixing up your past with this present. That's not what this is about. Not this detective."

"You don't think the police can be that duplicitous? You think that some detective you have never met before would hesitate to use you? Give me one shred of one reason that a woman like Cleo would allow herself to get taken in by a serial killer who meets with hookers in midpriced hotels? From everything you said, her clientele is about a hundred steps up the social ladder from that."

Nina was right about that. I couldn't see Cleo making that kind of mistake. Especially since she had been forewarned. But what if the man committing this crime was someone she already knew? What if he had relationships with several different kinds of prostitutes in the city?

"I understand what you are afraid of, but Nina, Detective Jordain isn't lying to me."

"I know that for some reason you want to believe that, but you can't be sure."

"But I am."

"Just because you have that damn Geiger counter in your head that can measure bullshit doesn't mean you can't ever be wrong. People act all the time. And some of them are very good at it. Why can't the detective just be an excellent actor?"

I didn't have an answer.

But I knew he wasn't.

22

When I got back to the office, there was a message from Elias Beecher, and we made plans to meet at the end of the day for coffee in the bar of the Mark Hotel a few blocks from my office. When I arrived, he was waiting for me in the reception area.

He was midheight, extremely thin, with high cheekbones, a sharp jawline and haunted dark brown eyes. Even though I'd never met him before, he looked tired. So tired, he might be ill.

"Mr. Beecher." I held out my hand.

His was strong, so strong I felt my fingers pinch.

He motioned to the maître d', who led us to a corner table.

"Thank you for meeting me here," Elias said as soon as we were seated.

"No problem."

"My client is staying here and I have back-to-back meetings in just a little while, but I wanted to see you before—" he started to explain.

"It's okay," I assured him.

"I need you to help me."

"I will. I'll do everything I can."

"I'm going crazy. No one will listen to me."

"I'll listen to you."

He played with the small china vase of flowers in the middle of the table. "I'm going crazy and I just don't know who else to speak to."

His pain and distress were palpable.

The waiter arrived and hovered.

"I'll just have coffee," Elias said. "Espresso." Then he looked at me. "I'm sorry, that was rude. I'm just not thinking. What would you like?"

"I'll just have an iced tea," I said to the waiter, who gave a slight nod and walked away. He was barely out of earshot when Elias started talking again.

"None of this makes any sense. It's a nightmare that just keeps growing." He was playing with the vase again. "And the police won't do anything. In good faith, I went to them and asked for help. Begged them to start looking for Cleo. I even took them to her apartment. I told them everything I knew, and what did they do? They turned around and questioned me. Treated me as if I'm the lead suspect even before they know if there has been a crime. They need to concentrate on Cleo. Not on me. They need to start looking for her. What good can I do them?"

"And you don't think they will look for her?"

"I don't know. I don't have much confidence in the NYPD. But more important, I can't wait for them. I have to do something now."

"That is completely understandable."

"So help me."

"How?"

"Talk to me about Cleo. Tell me what you know about her and the men who were her clients. Of course she never told me that much about them. I didn't want to know. I'm sure you can understand that. But maybe one of the men she worked with had it in for her. Because of the book. You know about the book? Right?"

"I do."

"Have you read it?"

"Even if I had, I couldn't tell you that."

He shook his head, violently. "You don't understand, Cleo told me everything. We are in love. She trusts me. I know she gave you a copy. I am just asking you if you read it."

Was he telling me the truth? Or was he fishing? There was no way for me to know. I was going to have to gamble on him. But I wasn't ready to do that yet.

But how or when would I be, and by then would it be too late?

The waiter was back with our orders and neither of us said anything until he had put the drinks down.

"I have a copy of the book," he said.

How did he get a copy? I wondered. Had Cleo given it to him after she gave one to me? I was fairly certain she had told me that I was the only person whom she wanted to read it at this stage. But Elias had keys to her apartment—he must—he said he'd taken the police there. Maybe he found her copy and took it.

"You have a copy?" I asked, as innocuously as I could, hoping he'd elaborate.

"I brought some of it with me. The pages that have to do with her clients. Read about them from a psychiatrist's point of view. And you tell me if you think I'm right—that one of these men might have a reason to harm Cleo. The point is, almost all of them might wish she was dead if they know about the book. But that doesn't mean shit. Wishing and having the ability to act are other sides of the moon. I know a lot of people who think things but can't carry them out. It's action that makes heroes. Or villains. You understand that, don't you? It's doing something that matters. It's too easy to sit it out and let someone else worry about it. I'm not like that, you're not."

He looked at me, straight into my eyes. His were bloodshot. And sad. Only Cleo, who'd known him before, knew how his eyes looked when they weren't so damn sad.

"You're not too scared to help, are you?" he repeated. "I know. I can tell. You will. We're in this together. We're both worried about her. We were both her caretakers. We have to save her. You'll help me save her, won't you? That's what you were doing before someone took her away. Saving her. And she was so grateful to you for that."

23

That night after Dulcie went to bed, I went into the kitchen. If I was going to help Elias figure out who might have had a reason to hurt Cleo, I was going to have to really study Cleo's book, and to do that I was going to need help staying up. The strongest stimulant I'd indulge in was coffee. While I waited for the water in the kettle to boil, I measured out six tablespoons of espresso and poured them into the French press.

My kitchen was testament to my fantasy of being one of those women who could do it all. It looked like something you'd see in an issue of *Martha Stewart Living*. Stainless-steel stove with six burners, plus a double oven, a state-of-the-art refrigerator and dishwasher, also fronted in the same brushed silver. The countertops were black granite. The cabinets were glass and showed off two different sets of dishes and glasses—everyday thick white stoneware and an indulgent set of Limoges. Underneath the counters were more cabinets, but these were painted a glossy black to match the black-and-white-tiled floor. You would think I knew how to cook. You would think I baked pies and knew how to ice a cake and squeeze butter-cream rosettes out of a pastry bag. You might imagine huge turkeys, golden-brown and still tender, coming out of those ovens and being carved with one of the German knives from the butcher block sitting on the countertop. And the stuffing would be oyster-and-chestnut and the gravy would be homemade.

But I was only a dreamer in my own apartment. I wanted to bake and sew and cover walls with photographs hanging from grosgrain ribbons. I yearned to set the table with hand-painted napkins and create centerpieces inspired by Japanese simplicity. But I was a fraud.

The water boiled and I poured it over the ground beans that I did not grind at home but bought at Starbucks. Fitting the filter into the glass beaker, I sat down at the marble-topped table on one of the French bistro chairs and waited for the muddy mess to brew.

My apartment was indicative of what happens when you grow up with a mother who feeds you TV dinners or canned soup and steals you away in the middle of the night and takes you on a road trip to hell and then dies before she ever makes it back home.

When I was eight, my father came and rescued me from the two-room walk-up on Avenue A, bringing me home to his luxurious apartment on East End Avenue in Manhattan. I'd only been a few miles away, but he hadn't known it. He blamed himself for not finding me sooner. For not keeping me safer. But it wasn't his fault. My mother took me when he wasn't watching. She didn't register me for school for that year we were gone. She didn't ever venture uptown.

The only person we saw from our old life was Nina. My mother cleaned up when her friend came over and tried to act as if our new life was working out. Nina knew better, but she never knew how bad it was. No matter how far my mother fell, she was still a good actress.

That last day, when I found my mother, I called my father on the phone. And he called Nina to find out our address. I didn't know it. They both arrived within fifteen minutes of each other.

After she died, my father took me back to the place I'd grown up. My old housekeeper, Mary, was still there. I begged her that year to let me watch her cook. To stay in the kitchen. I suppose I yearned for something that I could only get from watching butter melt in a pan or smelling chicken fry or licking the bowl of brownie batter. But Mary was elderly and ornery and she cooked while I was at school and didn't want me in her kitchen.

Eventually my father remarried, but Krista was not much better in the kitchen than my mother had been.

Longing to be the kind of mother I had not had, I invested in every gadget I read about in the pages of lifestyle magazines and looked at them lovingly. But when it came time to use these clever apparatuses, I was inept.

At twelve, Dulcie was a better cook than I would ever be. She loved to impress me with her skill, and have me taste and "ooh and aah." She even tried to teach me.

My miniature little woman, who already could cook certain things without recipes, tried to show me the ropes that her grandmother, Mitch's mother, had taught her. Sarah had handed down the time-honored traditions of women in the kitchen to her granddaughter. But it was something the two of them shared without me.

I still attempted adventures in this kitchen that, if they did not lead to delicious dinners, at least led to laughing fits. We never went hungry, but that was only because we both learned to suffer through my pathetic attempts to be creative or else my daughter took over.

The rest of the apartment was indicative of the same homebody yearnings. I had projects started but never finished in every room. Attempts at needlepoint, quilting, knitting, the materials to make my own frames, to stencil my own walls, to hook my own rugs.

What was it about homemaking that kept calling me back and enticing me? This time, I would think, I will be able to get the hang of it. So I couldn't knit, I will be able to learn to arrange my own flowers. If I can't baste a turkey, I will be good at staining a wall.

But I wasn't. Nothing ever turned out the way it did in the glossy pages of the magazines I pored over late at night while I watched the Food Channel and sipped burned hot chocolate made from the finest Valrhona the way the diva on the TV said Angelina's in Paris had been making it since the nineteenth century.

But after I filled a mug with steaming coffee, it wasn't a magazine I opened. I had work to do. I pulled out Cleo's manuscript. This was one thing I had started I would finish. Someone's life might depend on it.

24

He is not who you think he is. You imagine a bald, overweight man who smokes cigarettes and is lonely and pathetic in some way that allows you to put him outside your world. People I know, men I love, do not go to prostitutes.

You have to close your eyes and picture this man, you need to understand that human need is not disgusting. You have to wipe the stereotype away. You have to, if you want to see something more about men than you already know, understand that he is a catch. He wears three-thousand dollar suits and has his shirts made. His salary is in the stratosphere.

And he is with me tonight instead of you because he can be. Peter Pan is married. To a lovely woman whose pictures you have seen in the style pages and society pages of *Town & Country* magazine. He is a real estate mogul. Only forty-

seven. Already one of the most successful builders in New
York City.

He is sitting in a darkened theater. He has rented this private screening room from a film company. It has cost him
eight thousand dollars for the night.

On the screen is the film *The Graduate*. The soundtrack is
turned down lower than normal so that only bits and pieces
of the dialogue are distinguishable, but you can hear the
music. Especially because Peter Pan sings most of the Simon
and Garfunkel songs along with the soundtrack. We have a
bottle of Cristal champagne in a silver bucket and are sipping the pale gold wine out of fine crystal glasses that were
waiting for us in a box from Fifth Avenue's Tiffany & Co.

I arranged for the champagne and the glasses and the pound
of Sevruga caviar that sits in a glass caviar dish on the table.

Peter Pan is wearing jeans. And a white shirt. And a tie. A
tie from the prep school he went to. On his feet are loafers
and crew socks. And a blazer lies on the empty seat next to
him.

I am wearing a navy-blue pleated skirt, a powder-blue
button-down shirt. Knee socks and almost identical loafers.
My hair is loose. Underneath the skirt I am wearing a pair
of white cotton underpants.

We are back in tenth grade. We are sixteen. The age Peter Pan was when *The Graduate* was released.

I will not ask the scion of real estate why we are dressed
like this or why we are watching this movie. Just like I did
not ask him last week and will not ask him next week to explain the scenario he requests that I enact for him. He has
provided me with the money to make this dream come true.
And that is all I do. I pander to my clients' dreams. Some are
darker, but many are surprisingly simple. Rarely do I have
to turn clients away or say no.

And tonight I will not only do as Peter Pan wants, but I will enjoy all of it. Will I feel what you feel when you look into the eyes of a man who you love? Who makes your heart beat faster and makes you wet between your legs? Is this coming together something I long for the way you do when you lie in bed and imagine your lover kissing your lips and stroking you gently?

No. This is how I make my living. But I do enjoy my job. Especially when I have clients like Peter Pan.

The play is about to begin. Shh. Sit back. Let go of your preconceived notions. Watch the action. And don't judge. Just watch.

We have not touched. At all. We are both properly dressed. The movie has been playing for fifteen minutes.

Now Peter Pan puts his arm around the back of my chair. He leaves it there for a minute. Just resting it on the edge of the movie seat. I am aware of his arm being there. I wait.

The scene on the screen shifts. Benjamin is going to meet Mrs. Robinson for the first time in the hotel. We watch the film. We laugh. My laugh is more authentic than Peter Pan's. He is really more interested in making his next move than watching the movie. And as soon as the music comes up again, I feel his fingers on my shoulder. I shut my eyes.

I am sixteen. I am sitting in a movie theater with my boyfriend. He has just touched me. It is helpful for me to be in character. The better I can be at my role, the more authentic it will seem to Peter Pan and pleasing my client is my only true role.

Ah. You see. You get the first glimpse. You don't like where I am going, do you? Of course not. This is not about equality. This is not about a relationship of two people building a life together. Yes, there is sex in that equation. But sex of a different nature. In a relationship you both have needs, you must each bend, give, take, learn and understand. That is right. It has its place. But it has its restrictions, too. It has its problems. It makes for issues. It is constricting, limiting.

I, on the other hand, want nothing from Peter Pan. I am an actress in his play. The money has already changed hands. He is the director.

Too pretty? Too easy? Am I sugarcoating? Oh, sugar, I wish I was. I wish I could tell you how ugly and deranged what I do is. But the truth is, it just isn't. Men are not all monsters. Most of them just want to believe for a little while that they really are the center of the universe and that the power they yearn for is really the power that they wield. They want their fantasies to come true. And they are used to buying what they want and making it happen.

There are other women who will tell you different stories. Maybe there are more of them than there are of hookers like me. But listen, there are wives and girlfriends who will tell you other stories, too. There are women who wear diamonds on their fingers the size of olives in a martini, and they get treated worse than I do and perform far more demeaning tasks in bed. Whore, mother, wife, mistress, lover, girlfriend. We are all giving up something to get something. I just chose to get my alimony payments or divorce settlements without having to go through the emotional turmoil of love and marriage.

Peter Pan's hand plays with my hair. And it feels good. He has a light touch. He leans over now, closer to me. And I pull away just a little. This is my role. I'm supposed to be shy. I have never been to bed with a boy. I'm sixteen. I am in love with him.

And to tell you the truth, it is not hard at all to imagine this.

Peter Pan smells of a cologne called Fahrenheit. And beneath that scent he is clean. He is trim. His nails are mani-

cured. He has thick black hair. Yes, his hairline is slightly receding. He has dark green eyes and an engaging smile. A
small scar on his chin makes me curious. I don't ask, though.
Not now. His eyebrows are expressive. His mouth isn't. His
secrets are words. You can tell this, too, the better you get
at this. Everyone has secrets that they hide. Peter Pan's secrets are words he has spoken. His mouth is pressed tight.
Another man's secrets are actions he has taken; he will keep
his hands pressed tightly in his lap.

There is no more time to think about this. My sixteen-
year-old boyfriend leans forward and then turns in his seat
so that he can kiss me. It is tentative at first and I pull back.
Stare at him with a mixture of surprise and confusion. He
whispers, please, just let me kiss you. Once more.

I do not say no.

He presses his lips against mine with more certainty this
time. And more pressure. It is a sweet-smelling kiss and I
taste champagne. The kiss moves in me the way the bubbles
in the wine did a few minutes ago.

If I were to break role now I would tell you that I am not
feeling this the way you would if this were a man you were
having a relationship with. But the man you are in a relationship with will not tell you that in his fantasies he is always
sixteen, always just falling in love with his first girlfriend, always hot and horny and needing to make out in every dark
corner he can find. He will not tell you because you are his
wife or his girlfriend now, and what would you say? Go to
a therapist. Stop fantasizing about someone who dumped
you. Don't you love me?

I don't say any of those things. I act the part. I make the
money. I pay the bills.

I kiss him back. His mouth opens just a little. I open mine.

Sixteen. Summertime. The movie is *The Graduate*. The

music is Simon and Garfunkel. The theater is dark. His hand is moist but not unpleasant as it works its way from around my back to my shirt buttons.

I pull back.

I'm not sure you should—

Shhh. He kisses me quiet.

He knows how to kiss. And what he has forgotten by being married to the same woman for the last eighteen years, I am making him remember.

The problem is, the woman he's married to has his balls in a vise. She is a good, hardworking woman who is obsessed with her image and her notoriety and her power. She came to it later in life and she adores it. As well she should. She is brilliant and she has worked like a slave for her success. But sexually, she's not interested. She provides but isn't passionate. She loves him but isn't "in" love with him.

You know about this. Either you are in a relationship like this or you know someone who is. The marriage is fine. The couple are friends. But the fire's gone out a long time ago.

Peter Pan's wife isn't his fantasy. Hell, she isn't even his lover anymore. And he worries, more than he should, that if she finds out what he's doing with me she'll leave him. And if she does that, he's afraid of what else she will do. Because the trouble is her father's inheritance started his business. So in effect she owns his business. Or at least half of it. And that is half more than he ever wants to give up.

I tease him with my tongue and he teases me back. I have to go slow, play my part and not be too eager. His hand is inside my shirt now, his fingers moving over the fabric that keeps him from making the contact he wants so very badly to make.

I don't help. I let him fumble with the cotton bra. I actually have forgotten what this was like. And for a while, I, too, slip back and I am sixteen again. Going out with one of the handsome guys. In a movie theater making out.

He unclasps my bra and has access. As he cups my breast he sighs. A long, slow, deep, sweet sigh. His first goal. He touches my nipple as if he has just discovered that such a thing exists and I harden under his touch. He kisses me now with more ardor and some urgency. On the screen, a new song starts. "Feeling Groovy."

He is. I am, too. I like this role. Being Peter Pan's girlfriend feels groovy, and as long as I concentrate on that, I can make him happy.

Each kiss is longer now.

The space between them is shorter. He pulls away to look at me. His face is flushed, his lips are wet and the Technicolor movie images are reflected in his eyes. Wide boy eyes. This is real. He is as lost in his dream as he can be. And now, watching me, holding my eyes with his, he moves his hand to my thigh and under my skirt and up the rest of my leg. He moves the elastic of my underpants with his fingers and feels around. Seeking heat, seeking warmth, he finds the space he has been heading for all along and his fingers slip into the wetness. He smiles. A satisfied smile. He loves the wetness. This is his proof. This is his hope. It is not an aborted attempt but an equal want.

He moves in for another kiss while he continues to stoke me. He knows how to do this. I benefit from what women before have demanded of him. A forty-seven-year-old man cannot be a groping sixteen-year-old boy no matter how much that is all he wants to be. He knows how to move his fingers in slow circles. He cannot unlearn this just to have his fantasy, and so I benefit.

I do not come often with my clients. It is my job to have

sex. Not my desire. Just like an actress does not fall in love with every leading man she plays opposite.

But sometimes she does. And tonight in the theater, this fantasy is too sweet. And Peter Pan's fingers are too expert.

He strokes harder, then softer; he kisses me in rhythm to the tension he is building. I almost forget. But I can't. This is not my game.

I reach out. Oh, so slowly, scared, unknowing. I touch his knee, I hear him sigh. Encouragement. His fingers stop moving. Desperately I want to get them moving again. But this isn't my game. I move my fingers up his thigh and find the bulge in his pants.

Still sixteen, I stop, react, then try again. My fingertips run up and down the length of his erection. Testing it. Learning it.

"Is this what you want?" I whisper.

"More, Jenny, more." He is using her name; he has paid for the right to do that. I don't mind. I am enjoying being Jenny, who is the teenager he was in love with thirty-one years before.

I get braver and unzip his fly and fumble in his pants to release him. I stroke him with my hand and he moves in his seat, thrusting out. And rather than this be the end, his fingers begin to circulate deep within me again. He mimics my movements so we are doing the same thing to each other now. My hand slides down and up, his fingers probe. We are in tandem.

Faster. He pushes forward. So do I. Faster yet. He pushes his lips at me, presses hard, I can feel his teeth and his fingers in me and my fingers on him and the sounds of a guitar in the background and the feel of mohair velvet on the back of my thighs and my breasts loose under my shirt.

The first wave hits me with a shock. It is very rare that this happens. But I don't fight it. I give him the benefit of the feeling, I let him hear the pleasure, and it is what he needs to take him over the edge. The forty-seven-year-old man, who has never quite stopped wanting Jenny, whoever she was, throws his head back and lets me milk him to orgasm.

Not bad for a three-thousand-dollar-night's work.

I'm sorry.

I know you don't want to believe it. I know it hurts. You want to be his Jenny. You are his wife and his friend and the mother of his children. But you just can't be her. At least not in real life. That's for the movies and the make-believe. And that is what I'm in the biz of doing. Making make-believe real—for a few hours, at least.

25

Later, looking back on it with a level head, it would be hard to explain my decision. But at the time, it seemed inevitable.

Mitch came to pick up Dulcie that Saturday so she could, as per our custody agreement, spend the next ten days with him. The fact that Dulcie was out of the house and safely ensconced with her father left me untethered. As used to her being at Mitch's as I was, I still didn't sleep well when my daughter was gone. I lived in a doorman-guarded building, but still, I worried. Not that my twelve-year-old daughter kept me safe, but I felt secure when I knew where she was and could be certain she was fine.

So it was with this uneasy edge that I spent the weekend obsessing about a man who had so far killed two prostitutes and the fact that one of my patients, who was also a prostitute, was missing.

I rationalized my decision because there obviously was a chance that Cleo was missing because of that same man. Or that one of the men whom she had written about in the book had her.

Either way, chances were she was in danger.

And there weren't many people who could help her.

* * *

I spent most of Saturday in a pair of old jeans and a T-shirt sitting in my living room with my copy of Cleo's manuscript, the pages Elias had given me of the same manuscript with his notes in the margins, and a pad of yellow paper, making my own lists and notes.

From early in the morning to late that night, while the sun traveled in its westward arc, I pored over her pages, no longer reading for the overall meaning. I was mining the book. I made detailed lists of each man she referred to, and underneath the name that she had given him I wrote any and all identifying information. The type of job he held, where he lived, who he had introduced her to, what other clients he had brought into the fold, the kind of tips he gave, if any, and, of course, what his sexual proclivity was.

In all, she mentioned more than twenty men. Fifteen in detail. And in enough detail in every case but one for me to figure out, along with the help of the Internet and a few dozen phone calls to friends who knew people who knew people, who they probably were in real life and what their actual names were.

Cleo had a method to her rechristening of these men: they were either named for what they liked or for what they did. For instance, Lindbergh was a politician who was also an amateur pilot; Lord Byron was a bestselling author; the Marquis was an actor who had played the role of the Marquis de Sade in an Academy Award-winning film; Perry Mason was a public defender who had won a well-televised case and had gone on to become a TV commentator; Superman was a high-ranking and very charismatic ex-D.A. who was an NYC politician; and on and on. Each page of the manuscript would be cause for a lawsuit unless she did a much better job of disguising the men.

Surprising perhaps to someone who did not study human sexuality for a living, it would seem that most of what these men wanted was tame. Boring, even. It was the newness, the lack of commitment, the nonrelationship, nonresponsibility of the act, the desire for someone young and beautiful, the need for someone discreet who could be trusted, the lack of interest in the woman herself, the ego and the narcissistic needs of these men that sent them to Cleo or her girls time after time.

These were not the men who went with the street whores I worked with in prison. So, maybe, there *was* no connection between the Magdalene murders and Cleo. Maybe she had just taken herself out of circulation for some other reason and just hadn't even wanted to tell the two men she was closest to. Her business partner and her lover.

But I didn't think so.

I worked on the lists and reread sections of the book for the whole day. Then I checked my list against Elias's. We had both identified the same four men as those with the most to lose. But I had put a fifth man on my list that he hadn't. I went on to make another list of second choices.

By the time I stopped to make dinner, my instincts were telling me that one of the men in this book, knowing that she had made a deal with a publisher, had taken matters into his own hands.

In the bowl, the tuna fish looked pathetic. I hadn't remembered to dice the celery small enough and I used too much mayo and then too much pepper. I was embarrassed. The simplest meal. The most meager dinner. And I screwed it up.

I dumped the mess on some rye bread I had found in the refrigerator, added pickle slices and brought the sandwich over to the table. I nibbled on it and sipped a glass of cold white wine and read my notes over again.

So many men had motives that it became less and less likely that there was any connection with the serial killer. It had to be one of these wealthy men who couldn't stand the thought that his carefully constructed lie was going to be revealed.

The bread got soggy way too fast. What had I done wrong? Damn. It was the water. I'd forgotten to drain the water.

I threw it out. Opened a second can. Drained the water. Then grabbed the bread. But all that was left in the plastic bag was the heel. Great. Out of bread. There was, however, a bag of prewashed lettuce. So I put that in a clean bowl, added the tuna and tossed it up with my fork.

It was dry. I found some dressing in the fridge, shook it and driz-zled that on the salad. Better but by no means good.

I had another salad in my mind. One I had seen in *Gourmet* mag-azine, a niçoise salad served poolside at a five-star hotel in the south of France. With tiny black olives glistening in the sun, and ele-gant string beans layered with anchovy fillets on top of the mé-lange of different types of lettuce.

My best intentions were never realized. I could never translate the artful into the actual. Not as a cook, a decorator, a craftsperson or a sculptor. I had worked at stone and wood for years, in art school and after, to chip away and find the object I could see so clearly in my mind. But my fingers could never bring the vision forth.

There was one thing I was good at. Listening. Listening very hard to words and nuances and pauses and silence, and understand-ing and taking what I'd understood and helping someone to un-derstand it for themselves.

When the phone rang at eight, I jumped. The whole day had been so quiet. I picked it up, hoping it was Dulcie. When she was at Mitch's I tried not to call her more than once every day. It was hard but I usually held out, knowing that she was safe and sound with her father.

"Hello?"

"Dr. Snow?" A man's voice.

A little breeze of disappointment that it wasn't Dulcie blew over me.

"Yes?"

"It's Noah Jordain. I am sorry to bother you at home."

"So then why *are* you bothering me at home?" It came out harsher than I meant, but it was how I felt.

"We have another murder on our hands. A third woman."

"Oh. No. That's awf— Do you know who she is?" *Is it Cleo?* was what I'd wanted to ask but I was still under my own self-imposed gag rule.

"She's not your patient if that is what you want to know."

"Thank you for telling me."

"I think we should talk, though."

"Now?"

"I'm not asking you to come down to the station house. I can come to you."

I ran my fingers through my hair. I hadn't even taken a shower that morning. "It's Sunday night. Can't it wait till tomorrow?"

He didn't seem to care at all that I was both annoyed and indignant. "The thing is I don't want to wait until tomorrow. I'm up against time. This one came faster than the last. I'm afraid we may soon have another one. I know that you assisted our department before, and my partner says your insight into profiling sexual deviants was stellar."

"But you have your own forensic psychologist, Detective."

"This girl was twenty years old, Dr. Snow. Her scalp was shaved like a nun's. She was wearing a hair shirt. Do you know what that is? An instrument of torture that religious zealots used to martyr themselves. But she didn't want to be a martyr. That was the role our perp assigned to her. He tortured her." He paused. "In more ways than one. And most of it we think while she was still alive. Her back was flayed open. Slivers of skin hung like ribbons."

He had obviously paused for effect. And it had worked. Shivers pinpricked my skin, up and down my legs and arms. I shut my eyes against the vision, but of course that didn't make it go away.

26

It was going to take the detective twenty minutes to get to my apartment, he said, and I spent one-third of that time figuring out where to hide Cleo's manuscript pages. It was unlikely that he was bringing a court order to search my house for the book. It was unlikely he even knew that the manuscript existed. But now that I had read it all and studied it so carefully, I knew how explosive it was.

I wanted it put away.

Safe. I wanted it hidden.

The pages had taken on an unearthly glow. They hummed. They emitted an odor. A dog trained in searching for explosives would run right toward them.

There was a doll's cradle on the floor of a storage closet. An old toy of Dulcie's that she hadn't looked at in years and wouldn't ever look at again. It was made of rough-hewn wood, about two feet long, standing about eighteen inches high, filled with a doll resting on a mattress made of flannel. I lifted the doll and the mattress and placed the manuscript on the bottom wooden panel, then put the two-inch-thick bedding back in place.

In the remaining time I exchanged my T-shirt for a fresh one, brushed my hair, washed my face and then put on some lipstick, mascara and blush. I looked at myself in the mirror. The makeup had helped, but I couldn't erase the worry from my eyes or the fear from my expression. My nerves were showing. I added some concealer under my eyes to try to hide the circles. I wasn't primping for him; I'd do this even if one of Dulcie's friends came over. Just to be presentable. Just to be cleaned up.

And then I waited. Getting more and more nervous as each second passed. I went into the living room to make sure I'd put everything away and stopped to look at the photograph of my mother on the étagère. It was a shot of her with me, when I was just two years old. My head against her shoulder, her fingers playing with my hair.

She was still so lovely in that photo. Before the pills and the booze started to wreck her looks. It didn't really surprise me that I was thinking of her again. Most of the time she was a distant memory that blew across me once or twice a month. But since Cleo had gone missing, since Dulcie had been accepted into drama school, my mother was more on my mind.

She is lying on the couch, and I am trying to pull her back from the limbo of the pills' effects. Nothing else has worked, and so I decide to act out a story for her. One of the many extended stories I will make up about The Lost Girls.

The Lost Girls was a television show about two orphaned teenagers who were taken in by a married couple—both professors—at an Ivy League school in Boston.

The girls always got into terrible trouble, and then one of them—either my mother or her co-star, Debi Carey—would solve the insurmountable problem and save the day. Meanwhile the charming but clueless elderly couple never guessed how close the girls had come to danger and sometimes death.

The Lost Girls ran from the time my mother was sixteen to nineteen, thirty episodes in all. And then it had been dropped. My mother did a few movies after that but was never the success she'd been on TV.

The year I was six, the series was in reruns. And night after night at 7:00 p.m., I sat rapt in front of the TV, not moving, entranced as I watched my very own mother be someone I did not know.

Every Thursday night, for one hour, I watched a kind of magic I could not understand. For years I have been searching for copies of those shows. But the company who owned them has been sold and sold again, and I haven't been able to track down anyone who knows about them. But I remember them.

And after my mother left my father and took me with her, we went to live in a tiny, messy apartment in a tenement building on Manhattan's Lower East Side.

Some nights, when my mother lay on the couch in her self-induced haze—which at eight I did not understand—I retold her the story of each episode. And when I ran out of real ones, I made them up.

Trying so hard to engage her, entertain her, make her sit up and get excited about something. Trying so hard just get her to talk to me.

After I acted out the stories, I always ended the way the shows did with me playing the part of my mother's sidekick and delivering the next-to-last sign-off line.

"And what happened next?" I'd say to the pale, beautiful woman lying on the lumpy couch.

"They all lived happily never after," she'd say.

Half drugged, half asleep, sick with her addiction, it didn't matter: she always knew her last line. The line her character had ended every episode with.

Just once I had wanted my mother to tell *me* a story. For her to be the mommy and me the little girl, with me under the covers and her sitting up.

And in my imagination, when she would ask me what happened at the end, I would say something very different: I would smile and say, "They all lived happily *ever* after."

Because that, of course, was my dream.

The doorbell rang.

As I walked from the kitchen into the living room, I wondered how it was going to end for Cleo. If there was any chance she would live happily ever after. Or if she would even live.

27

We sat in the kitchen while I made coffee. The detective was dressed more informally than he had been when he came to my office. Instead of the white cotton shirt and blazer with his jeans, he was wearing a blue chambray shirt and a windbreaker. Same loafers, same sunglasses stuck into the top button of his shirt, hanging precariously, as if he might need them at any second.

Instead of being nervous, once he was there, I felt calmer. I don't like admitting that part of it was simply that he was a big man and he was in my apartment and he certainly was armed. Feeling unsafe wasn't something I thought about. Until I felt safe. And then I became aware that I often felt frightened. I operated from a constant stance of being just slightly afraid.

Knowing too much about how the brain works, about the fragility of sanity, about the very thin line that separates the functional human being from the madman, made me wary of people. Even people whom I should have been able to trust.

I put the coffeepot, mugs, sugar and milk on the table.

"Spoon?" he asked.

It took a minute for it to compute. I picked up a spoon and handed it to him. Long fingers reached out. I looked away and my eyes settled on his face. A flash of his serene blue eyes. And then I looked away from his eyes, too.

I don't know where he looked. Turning my back on him I rummaged in the cabinets for something else to put out and found a package of Dulcie's favorite Pepperidge Farm Milano cookies. So I got a plate and spent a few minutes laying them out. My Martha Stewart consciousness causing me to try to lay them out in some kind of pattern.

When I put them down on the table, I didn't look back at him, but poured myself a cup of coffee and then used his spoon to stir in a teaspoon of sugar.

"We have had our profiler on this since the first woman was found."

I nodded, waiting.

"And what we have put together is fine as far as it goes. But we are up against it on this one and time isn't on our side anymore." He shook his head. "Not that it ever was, but it's worse now. He's speeding up and we haven't caught a break. No one remembers seeing him. We don't have a clue what he looks like. He picks the busiest hotels that have hundreds of guests. And there are so many fingerprints, fibers and hair samples, it's like looking for the proverbial needle in the haystack.

"Our teams are working on it. We have some leads with the religious supply houses. But even there I'm not holding out much hope. It's not like he's bought any one item to the exclusion of others. We've got it all. Nuns' habits, communion wafers, what we think is holy water, and anointing oil. Basically, we are as on top of all the physical aspects of this case as we can be, but we're just not moving as fast as I'd like."

He reached out, took one of the cookies and ate half of it before continuing. "I can't sit around and wait, I have to get ahead of him. But to do that I need to get into the mind of this man."

"And your forensic psychiatrist can't do that because...?"

"He is trying to do that. But I want to involve you. Perez says you are the best person he has ever met at getting into the mind of someone with a sexual problem. He and Hobart—that's our guy—you remember him?"

I nodded. He was good, Jordain was right. But he wasn't always creative enough when it came to the more bizarre sex crimes.

"Well, Hobart agreed with Perez. I was surprised. It takes a healthy ego to agree to consult with someone from the outside." He stopped, waiting, looking at me, and expecting me to comment. I didn't. But I did note that Jordain was talking shrink talk.

He sipped his coffee. When I didn't say anything, he continued.

"Let me lay it all out for you. Show you the pictures. Go over the details of the cases. The ones that the reporters don't have. All I'm asking are two things of you.

"One is that you let me tell you what we know. Get any insight you might have. The other is, I know that you are worried about Cleo Thane's disappearance and you are going to, in your own way, try to find her. No, don't argue with me. Just listen. I know you will. Even if you don't know it yet. Because you can hardly even sit still when I talk about her. And what I want is an open communication with you in case you come across a connection. You won't recognize it unless you know what page I'm on. Are you game?"

"No. The last thing I am is game." I shook my head. "The one time I agreed to consult with you guys, Hobart second-guessed everything I said and didn't follow up. And I had nailed the guy's psychosis. I don't play well with teams."

"I did my homework. Perez told me all about what happened last time. And about Sam Butterfield."

I didn't even acknowledge that but asked, "So why do you think I'd change my mind?"

"Because you care about Cleo. Besides, I'm not asking you to work with us. I'm just asking you to help me. And keep your eyes open. Take my cell phone number and call me whenever you want and let me know what you are doing and thinking, and if there is anything—anything at all—that strikes you as a possible connection."

He had been looking at me the whole time he was talking, but his gaze was becoming more intense. As if he was trying to see inside of me. To find someone there.

I knew the problem. I am so damn good at putting up a wall. At separating the patient from the shrink. And the shrink from the patient. At closing down emotionally so that I could just absorb and compute the information, the other person's emotion and his or her dilemma. I made myself disappear. It made me a good therapist.

I was doing it with Jordain, and he had not only noticed, he was fighting me for entry. Two points for the detective. Most people don't. I don't want my patients to, and don't expected it of them. They are caught up in their own dramas—and the very point of the therapy is for them to connect to their own selves, their secrets, their souls. Not mine.

But my problem was, since Mitch and I had separated, I'd gotten into the habit of closing myself off and staying in my comfort zone with everyone, not just my patients. Cut off and removed— that's what I called it. No one could get to me when I was there. It was not only easy to venture forth without connecting, it was painless. And lately I had been afraid of pain.

"Dr. Snow, I will not take advantage of you."

I wanted to smile. His voice was just a shade too intimate, and it made totally acceptable comments strike me as absurdly flirtatious, even though there was nothing at all flirtatious in his demeanor or attitude.

In fact he was dead serious.

"You know you have to help me," he said, making it sound personal. As if this was not about the police, or the women at risk, but just about him.

"Why?"

"Because Cleo Thane is still missing and you can't tell me anything about her, and the only way you can involve the police is if you consult with me. That way you could really be helping her. All without you compromising your ethics. Can you take a chance that you don't need me with you on this?"

"Clever. The one thing—the only thing—that would influence me and you got it."

He smiled, that same smile I'd seen in my office. His eyes squinted and the laugh lines around them deepened and his mouth went up at the corners. It was an off-center smile that was almost a smirk. It wasn't arrogance, exactly, or self-assuredness that showed in that smile, but there was an audacity that I responded to.

And there were other things I responded to. The way his fingers picked up his cup with a grace that a cop didn't usually have. The way he looked at things as if he was seeing past them. Even me. I couldn't help it. His intensity was interesting. Atypical. And the analyst in me was intrigued by his contradictions.

"If I decided to do this I would have some rules."

"Yes, ma'am," he joked.

"No questions about Cleo Thane. Not one. Not one single question."

He nodded and a lock of his thick hair fell into his eyes. He brushed it away and looked right into my eyes. "No questions. I promise."

I didn't know if I was right to, or if I'd regret it later, or if I was making a mistake, but I believed him.

28

She was scared by the darkness. By the idea that she might not be alive this time tomorrow. She was frightened because she had no idea what was expected of her or when she would escape from the nightmare she was shackled to.

But nothing terrorized her more than the silence. For hours at a time there was simply no noise, no sound. Nothing but her own heartbeat.

She had never been anywhere in her life that was this silent. Had never known how important noise was until she had been deprived of it for days.

How many?

How many days had she been here? Again she tried to figure it out. But when she thought back, she couldn't count. There were not enough markers to tell her what time it was. She could not even tell sometimes if it was night or morning.

It was always dark in the cell. Even when he came to see her, he often kept it dark. But when she was alone, as she was now, the blackness was dense and thick. As if it had dimension. As if it had weight. The weight of time passing without her knowing it.

In the darkness, Cleo could never see more than the ghostly glow of her bound hands and feet. They were so pale and thin she didn't recognize them. She had always been thin, but now she was thinner. He did not give her much food. Sustenance. But that was all.

Other than craving sound, Cleo wanted to be able to use her hands. She wanted this desperately. She couldn't touch her face or her hair. These are things you take for granted, she thought. Brushing a lock of hair off your cheek, rubbing your eye, resting your chin on your hand. Scratching an itch. And her arms and legs and her torso and breasts and back and neck itched. Everywhere the robe touched, her skin prickled. Her robe was abrasive against her skin. Where had it come from? This was not her clothing. She never would have bought anything so coarse. Or so heavy. Or so somber.

No client had ever asked her to wear a uniform like this.

Until now.

And until now, she had never minded doing what the men she'd been with asked of her.

But this had not been asked of her. This had been forced on her. He had stripped off her own clothes—the gray skirt and white silk blouse, the pale pink silk-and-lace bra and thong—and he had bathed her and then dressed her in this outfit.

When the blackness had first enveloped her head, when she felt the heaviness of the robe, in that one claustrophobic moment she had acknowledged what she had been afraid to accept until then. This was not a game. There was not going to be an easy end to this endless night.

She was not with a man who craved a simple sexual release or comfort or kindness.

If only she could hear a car horn. A bird chirping. A child calling out. If only there was some music playing nearby, wafting in through an open window. If only there was a dog barking. Or a leaf falling. Or the sound of a kettle boiling.

If only she could whisper her own name out loud and hear her own voice. If only she could touch her own face with her fingertips. If only she could lick her own lips.

Instead she felt the pull of the tape across her mouth and the taste of it—a fresh strip put on her twice a day—chemical and metallic.

She waited.

She waited longer.

She heard nothing.

She wanted to hear anything.

Anything except the one thing that was inevitable: the tapping of his shoes on the floor, coming toward her. The tread of the madman who wanted something from her that was not hers to give. That one sound was the only thing worse than this silence because it meant that she would have to endure his bizarre requests and pleas for an hour. Or sometimes two or three hours. But he had just left. She had time before he returned. But how much time?

If only she could hear a radio. Or the chiming of a clock. Or the ticking of a wristwatch. Any sound. To distract her from the confines of her dark prison where she sat and waited for the man who prayed at her feet for a deliverance she didn't think would ever be hers to give.

29

My last appointment on Monday before lunch was with Gil Howard, Cleo's business partner and the man she had put down on her chart as next of kin.

"Do you mind?" he asked, holding up his pack of cigarettes.

I did but he was so distressed, I told him it was all right. As he lit the extra-long, slim brown cigarette with a silver-and-lacquer lighter, his hand shook and the sun bounced off the glass of his paper-thin Piaget watch.

Gil was older than I'd guessed he would be from his voice on the phone. About sixty, but rugged and in shape. He was wearing an exquisitely tailored suit, but with a white shirt open at the neck. It was a mix of the relaxed and the elegant usually reserved for those who are used to wealth. But I knew from Cleo's book that he had only come into money in his late forties as a day trader on Wall Street. He had cashed out early, retired, gotten bored and then started the Diablo. He and Cleo had met, she'd written in her book, when he'd hired her for the night.

"I am at a total loss," he said, tapping the nonexistent ash off the just-lit cigarette into the ashtray I'd put on the table in front of him. "She didn't say she was leaving town."

"Has she ever done anything like this before?"

"No. Occasionally one of her regular clients has asked her to go away with him. And usually, if the location is enticing enough, she'll go. The money is usually too good to turn down. But we've known each other for years, and she's never just disappeared before."

He tapped the ash again. This time a quarter inch fell.

"You can imagine how upset I am. I even thought about going to the police, for Christ's sake." He laughed, and for a second I glimpsed the man he must be when he wasn't stressed out and worried, friendly and easygoing.

"She likes you. A lot," he said.

"I like her, too."

"She told me you donate your time to the girls in prison. She does things like that. There is no one like her."

I nodded. I still wasn't sure why Gil Howard had wanted to come see me, but I was glad he had. He'd saved me a trip.

"So, I know you were talking to her. But I don't know how much she was telling you about what was going on with her. And I'm not asking." Another drag of the cigarette, another tap on the ashtray. "But she was different the last few months. And I'm wondering if that has something to do with her being missing."

"Is that what you would have told the police if you had gone to them?"

"This is all sort of tricky, you know? Our business is run legitimately. We pay taxes. And people know who Cleo is. Or at least they think they do. But she has never publicly acknowledged what she does, and she's never been arrested or caught in any kind of compromising situation."

I nodded.

"So I'm in an awkward spot. I can't compromise our clients. And I don't want to get Cleo in trouble if she's just—" He didn't finish the sentence. "But the truth is, I don't think she's just taken off or is on some sudden vacation. I'm worried."

"So how do you think I can help you? I'm in pretty much the same situation you are. I can't talk to anyone about what Cleo and I discussed. It's all privileged information."

"But if you thought she was in danger, if you thought you had some information about where she was, would you be able to help her?"

"What are you asking—if I'd risk her privacy to save her life?" He nodded.

"Only if I was sure that was what I was doing. Her privacy mattered to her. So much. What do you think she'd want?"

"She's not embarrassed by what she does. Just cautious. But I don't know." He looked down at the cigarette. Then shook his head, and, with an angry motion, ground it out in the ashtray. A thin plume of smoke rose into the air and dissipated somewhere above his head. He expelled his breath and ran a hand through his hair.

"Anyway, I never had to make the decision about going to the police. They came to me and—big surprise—I think I'm on their list of possible suspects. That's fine. The boyfriend is always a suspect."

"How long have you been together?" I tried not to act surprised by his admission that they were not only partners but lovers.

"For a while." He was remembering. I could see it in the way his eyes glazed over and he looked out into the middle distance of the room as if he could see something there. "I never thought, when I first met her, that I'd wind up with her. Never thought I could love someone, really love someone who does what she does. Do you think that is strange?"

"I don't deal with words like *strange*. I don't believe in making judgments."

"It's more than the sex. Except it's hard to separate the sex from the rest. With Cleo almost everything is tinged with sex. Just the way she leans forward to listen to you talk, or the way she puts a hand on your arm when she is about to say something. It's not like other women, who are just who they are all the time, and then in bed they get a little sexy. Or a lot sexy. And it's not like Cleo is some sex symbol. Not like some show-off with implants and a Brazilian bikini wax. Cleo is just a completely sensual creature. That's what makes it so easy for her to take a man to bed."

He stopped to light another cigarette. I didn't say anything. Not wanting to interrupt him and break his mood. No matter who he was to her, this man was in love with my patient, and he deserved to be able to talk about what he was feeling. And I wanted him to. Suddenly there was a motive for Cleo's disappearance. Two different men thought that she was in love with them. Had she run away from both of them? Had one of them been so jealous of the other that he'd done something about it?

If, for instance, Gil *had* been her lover and now she had a new lover, then there was every possibility that he could have struck her in a rage.

"I never thought I'd be able to forget about the other men she was with for work when we were in bed. But she made me. It wasn't just what she did for me, but what she let me do to her. She was shy. Can you believe that? She was actually shy with me. But I relaxed her. I was good for her. She told me that she could separate it all——that what went on at work was work, but what we were like was different."

What was he saying? She was able to separate from what she did at work with Gil? This didn't sound anything like the relationship that Cleo had described to me. She had told me that she had serious problems making the leap from work to love and was uncomfortable in bed with Caesar. Was "shy" to Gil "uncomfortable" to Cleo? Or was she fine with Gil, because she wasn't in love with him? Was that problem reserved for Elias Beecher?

"Of course I can believe that she was shy with you. And you were happy with that?"

"Yes. And happy because she was letting me see another side of her. And most of all because I was able to make her happy."

"Was? You are saying it all in the past tense." I couldn't imagine I'd caught him on anything this obvious, but I had to ask.

"A few months ago, something started to change. She pulled back. Not sexually. The sex stayed fine. She still needed the sex.

Or wanted it. Whatever. But emotionally she wasn't...I don't know...present. We stopped spending as much time together. Then it got worse. In the last eight weeks I hardly ever saw her except at work. She blamed it on the book. But why would the book have made her so—" he groped for a word "—distant?

"What is it, Dr. Snow?"

"How else did her distance manifest itself?"

"Mostly she wanted more time alone. You know, since she's been missing, I've tried to reconstruct the last two months. Hell, I can't even remember the last time we were together. It wasn't abrupt. And I've busy, too, with the club. Opening another branch in Las Vegas. I wasn't around. I was jet-lagged. I was haggling with architects and interior designers. But now, looking back at it, she seemed relieved I was preoccupied."

"Any other changes?"

"Yes, she started spending more money on herself. She has never been frugal, but she'd never bought herself the kinds of things she started buying. An Hermès bag. A Cartier watch. A diamond thing around her neck. That's not hundreds of dollars... that's tens of thousands. I asked her if it was a client buying the stuff for her. But she said it wasn't. So I figured she was just treating herself. And I figured she deserved it. But how dumb am I? What if it *was* someone else? Maybe there was a client who was more involved with her than I knew. Maybe he has something to do with her being gone." His voice had become more and more rushed as he talked about the possibility of another man.

And maybe he did know there was another man and couldn't handle it? What better way to put off suspicion than asking for help?

While I waited for Gil to keep talking, I realized that I had seen those things—the bag, the watch, the diamond thing, as Gil called it, around her neck. She had told me that Caesar had bought the necklace for her. So if that was the truth—and there was no reason I could think of for Cleo to lie to me about who was buying her gifts—then there was another man. Gil wasn't Caesar, but Elias Beecher was.

But why hadn't she told Gil she was seeing someone else?

Why hadn't she ended things with him? Maybe she was hedging her bets, afraid to end something with a man she was sure of while the new relationship she had begun was still so fraught with problems. Or maybe she knew Gil was so jealous he wouldn't be able to handle it. Was that it?

"She told you all about the book, right? She gave you a copy of it?" he asked.

I couldn't tell him. The book might be yet another motive.

As Nina and I had discussed, what if Gil was afraid that if the book was published, the men whom Cleo wrote about would stay away from the club? And what if other men, afraid that their privacy would be compromised in the future, stayed away also?

My skin goose bumped. Was that it? But if it was true, why was Gil here? To find out how much I knew? To set up some kind of psychological defense?

"Mr. Howard, I can't talk to you about what Cleo and I discussed or if I have or have not seen a book."

"But she might be in danger."

"I know that. But that doesn't change anything about my responsibility to my patient."

"But what if she is in danger? And what if one of her clients is responsible?"

"I'm terribly worried about that. But I still don't understand how I can help you."

"If I could read the book, then I might be able to figure it out. If I could read what those different men asked of her, what kinds of tricks they wanted, what they were into, then maybe I could figure out which one of them was crazy enough to do something to her."

"I can't help you with that."

The conversation was making me afraid. Not for myself, but for Cleo. As worried as I had been, there was something much more frightening now that this man was sitting in front of me, chain-smoking, nervously tapping his cigarettes against my ashtray. Dropping dead ash into the bowl.

"But you have the information," he insisted. "I know you do. I know she gave you the book. And I think you are the only one who has a copy. I went to her apartment. I have the keys. I always have had the keys. And her laptop is gone. All her notes for the book were in there. There were no paper copies of the book. She worked on her pristine white laptop late at night while I lay beside her, the glow of the monitor shining on her face. She told me she was going to let me read it when it was done. She was proud of it in a way that she wasn't proud of anything else she had ever done. It was going to set her free, she said."

I nodded. There was nothing I could say to him. But he had more to say to me. And I was not at all prepared for it.

"You know you are very beautiful."

I heard his words on more than one level. I was a therapist, listening to a distraught man, I was a psychologist helping the police, and I was a woman who could not really remember the last time anyone had told her that.

I knew I was attractive enough. You don't grow up in the last few decades of the twentieth century and not know what you look like. You judge yourself against every other woman you meet. Confronted with a culture that puts more value on the right features arranged correctly on your face than the quality of your thoughts or your accomplishments, you are aware of how you measure up. But I had been married to the same man for more than fourteen years. A man who was my closest friend and who was the father of my daughter. But not someone who looked at me the way a stranger does.

Under Gil's scrutiny, I felt my cheeks grow warm, and rather than try to understand that, I focused instead on the psychology of this man, who was worried about the woman he loved, telling me that I was beautiful.

"You could help Cleo."

The segue was nonsensical.

"I have already told you, Mr. Howard, that I'm not at liberty to talk to you or anyone else about anything Cleo and I talked about. Not as long as there is a possibility that she is alive."

This last part made him cringe. And unleashed something desperate in him. He sat forward, his arms on his legs, leaning toward me, pleading.

"You can meet her clients. I can introduce you to them. You can pretend to be someone whom she's asked to fill in for her while she is gone."

He'd come up with the same idea I had. I didn't say anything but I nodded. Gil continued.

"I know you have a copy of the book. Knowing Cleo, she had to give you a copy. You've read it. You can meet those men and you can test them. You can look at them and listen to them and judge them and try to figure out if any one of them could have been the one who has taken her away. Just the way you are doing with me."

This last comment startled me.

"I'm a therapist, not a mind reader," I said, surprising myself that I hadn't just said no. Even though I'd brought up the possibility of doing just this, when I'd talked to Nina, it had only been an idea. Gil was making it all too possible.

"I'm not asking you to be a mind reader. Dr. Snow, Cleo told me that you knew things about her that she didn't even know she knew about herself. She said that you knew more about human nature and human sexuality than anyone she had ever met. And Cleo knew people. She was damn good at knowing what men wanted. At knowing how to touch them, even the ones like me who were made of ice before they met her. It was this way she had of making you feel like your happiness mattered to her. As if she got transfusions of happiness from doing these things. It wasn't just the sex, it was the way she could listen. And it's the same way you listen. As if all that matters is that I am here and I have something to say."

Even though I knew that Gil was a suspect himself, his words were reaching me.

"I couldn't do that."

"You mean you won't."

"I mean that there is no way I could pretend to be—" I didn't even know what to call it. I could no longer call Cleo a prostitute, or a call girl. Or a sex worker. All those words came with attitudes and judgments attached. She was a woman who had feelings and thoughts and loved, even if she also played games acting out scenarios that brought pleasure to the men she worked with, who paid her too much money for what she did because it was not anything they could get anywhere else.

"You don't have to pretend to be anything. Just meet them. Let them interview you. You interview them. Cleo always set up free first dates between the girls and the prospective clients. She didn't want any man to pay two thousand for an evening with a woman who wasn't what he wanted. All the guys know about the first-date policy. Of course, with the out-of-towners, or the gift girls whom clients hired for their friends or associates, that wasn't how it worked. But Cleo didn't see those guys. Her clients, her regulars, the ones she saw herself, have been calling. They want to see someone else while she's away—because that's what I told them—that she was away. Her guys expect to have a date before they commit. They are the heavy hitters. The ones who come in regularly. The ones who count on her. And the ones who have something to lose if they are exposed. One of these men might be the one who has her."

"You have to go back to the police, Gil. You have to give them these men's names." But even as I said it I knew how impossible that would be for him to do. For the exact reason I couldn't think of doing it. What if Cleo was really away on a trip? What if she wasn't in danger?

If we gave out information that was not ours to give we could destroy her.

"You know I can't do that," Gil said. "I've tried to figure out another way to do this. To set up Cleo's clients with one of the other girls and try to get the information that way. But they aren't smart enough. Or intuitive enough. They're college girls. Out-of-work actresses. None on them have any psychological training. None of them could find out anything."

I shook my head. Even though I'd told Nina I wanted to do this,

confronted with the reality of it, I knew I could never go through
with it.

"I know it sounds crazy. But I promise, you don't have to have
sex with any of them. Just meet them. Just take their psychological pulse."

I stood up. "Mr. Howard, I'm sorry, but there are ethical con-
siderations here, and what you are suggesting breaks about every
one of them I can think of."

He stood up, too. And we faced each other. Extending his hand,
he held out a white card. I took it. It was his business card, with
the name and address of the Diablo Cigar Bar embossed in blood-
red letters.

"That is my private number. Just think about it, please."

He paused as if he wasn't sure that he should say anything else.
I tried to read his face. But whether it was grief, worry or guilt, I
couldn't tell.

"She told me when she met you that she felt as if she had been
lost and had finally found the person who was going to help her
find herself. She came off as so assured and strong. But she wasn't.
She was vulnerable. Just another woman who didn't even understand her own worth."

He left me standing there in the middle of my own office.

The sun was out and the room was flooded with the morning
light, but it seemed like the dead of winter to me.

Wrapping my arms around myself, I tried to stop shivering, but
all I could think of were those damn words he had used. As if they
were some kind of code.

But he couldn't have known. Not about *The Lost Girls.* There
was no way that Gil Howard knew how important saving those
girls was. Even though the one who mattered most was long gone.

30

I called Gil the next day and told him I was willing to proceed with his plan and that there were five men who, based on Cleo's descriptions, I wanted to meet. Then I gave him their nicknames and some information I'd gleaned from the manuscript. It was too easy. He knew all but one from the nicknames alone—clearly she'd referred to them that way with him. The fifth, he said, he wasn't sure about and would need to think about it. It might be someone she hadn't seen in a long time and he'd forgotten who it was. We got off the phone after planning that I'd go to the Diablo the next evening at around seven-thirty for my first meeting.

I spent the rest of that day and most of the next trying not to think about that night. And when my last client left, I shut the door and changed my clothes.

Gil had explained that the entrance to the Diablo Cigar Bar on East Fifty-fifth Street was through an unmarked door in the lobby of a small and exclusive hotel called the Bristol-Trent.

There were other private clubs hidden behind unmarked doors in Manhattan—Raffles in the Sherry-Netherland Hotel, for instance—so the location in itself wasn't that unusual. An exclusive club tucked away inside another establishment protected a patron's privacy. But certainly not all private clubs offered the same extras as the Diablo.

Cleo's book had described the way Diablo worked in detail. Membership was a onetime fifty-thousand-dollar bond. Nonrefundable. There were yearly dues in the amount of twenty-five-thousand dollars, which was applied to drinks, cigars and light meals. Through the club's concierge, men could book a room at the Bristol-Trent Hotel. And for an additional fee they could book an assignation through Cleo.

It was as safe and private as possible.

I stood across the street for more than ten minutes, staring at the hotel's facade, trying to get up the nerve to finally cross the street. I was worried I didn't know how to be the kind of woman that I was expected to be. Acting out a charade wasn't my trade.

Cleo Thane's voice wasn't the one I heard while I stood there. It wasn't Gil's voice or the voice of the detective who had asked for my help.

It was my daughter's.

"But why aren't you a real doctor?" she had asked me a year before.

"I am a real doctor, Dulcie."

"No. You just talk to people about sex." She made a face. "You don't heal them."

"I make them feel better. Doesn't that count? I help them to make their lives better."

She had shrugged. "I guess. But I wish you were the kind of real doctor who saved people."

I crossed the street, feeling wobbly and ridiculous in my get-up.

My black skirt was shorter than the length I usually wore, my legs were encased in expensive hose, my heels were the highest and pointiest I could find. Remembering Cleo's Jimmy Choo pumps, I'd run out at lunch and bought a pair of the ridiculously expensive stilettos, horrified at the price tag and wondering how I was ever going to walk in them.

I'd spent more time and money than I'd planned on the shoes, but after making that purchase, I stopped off at Victoria's Secret and purchased lace underwear. Light green satin. If I was going to play the part, I wanted to feel the part; I remembered that from my mother. It might be easier to fake it if I was at least in character.

Except I felt like I was wearing a costume.

I smoothed my skirt down and noticed my hands. Damn. I hadn't done a good job of preparing at all. My fingernails were unpolished. And of everything, that unsettled me.

How many other mistakes was I making? How silly was this whole charade?

I'd never pull this off. And besides, what did I hope to accomplish? Did I really think I'd be able to psyche out these men well enough to figure out if one of them had done Cleo harm?

The doorman opened the front door for me and I stepped over the threshold. Inside the mirrored lobby, just as Gil had described, was a door to the right, almost behind the concierge's desk. Anyone could open it, but only the men who had enough money and cleared Cleo and Gil's rigorous credit check and police-record check were allowed in.

Once through the door, I walked across a lovely Persian carpet trying not to trip. Overhead a crystal chandelier cast glints of soft light on the paintings of devils hanging on the walls.

"Can I help you?" the maître d' asked.

"I'm here to see Gil Howard."

"May I have your name, please?"

"Morgan White."

Gil had suggested and I'd agreed to use another last name. Morgan Snow. White. Seven dwarfs. Exactly how many suspects I had. It had been easy to come up with the pseudonym.

"He should be right inside. Do you need me to point him out to you?"

"No, thank you. I can find him."

The large room was smoky and smelled of cigars and whiskey.

It was such a male scent that it caught me by surprise. I'd never been in a place that was so exclusively devoted to and created for men. And rather than find it off-putting, I was attracted to it. The walls here were wood-paneled. The club chairs had obviously been chosen for their comfort. The bar on the left wall was long and gleaming. Behind it was a delightful mural of nymphs romping in an enchanted forest, being chased by very cheery-looking devils with extremely long and pointed tails.

The devil motif was on the ashtrays and etched more subtly onto the heavy crystal glasses that I saw a waiter carrying.

Ella Fitzgerald was belting out a song on the stereo.

There was nothing about the scene before me that was any different than what you would find at any restaurant in New York. Walk into the bar at the Mark Hotel, or the St. Regis, and you'd find the same men, sipping the same Scotch or martinis.

But while there are always some beautiful women in restaurants in New York, here there were nothing but beautiful women, and all of them were under forty. Many of them under thirty.

And none of the couples at any of the tables look tired or bored or were arguing.

I found Gil in the corner at a table with two other men. He rose and welcomed me with a grateful and relieved hug.

"This is Morgan," he said as he introduced me to Ted and Bernard. Like most of the club members, these two would have looked at home at any boardroom meeting. Polished, buffed and slightly tanned, Ted was in his early forties. Bernard was a bit younger, wearing a European-cut sport coat and a crisp white shirt, opened at the top. Both of them shook my hand.

And then I realized something: the men were openly staring at me.

I wasn't used to it. In fact, I couldn't ever remember being looked at that way except by Gil the day before in my office. People glanced at you all the time. They assessed you and judged you and made rash decisions based on those first impressions when eyes swiftly swept over you. But this was not subtle. These men looked at me shamelessly and I felt naked.

There was something so frank about these appraisals that, while they made me uncomfortable, I also appreciated the lack of pretense about them. They were just men, staring at a woman. Intellectually, I may have had issues with mating dances, but sociologically I understood them. Men are hardwired to find women alluring by looks alone. And not just one woman at a time, but many women. And for good reason.

It is all about survival of the fittest. The men who were the most prolific at producing progeny were the ones whose genetic imprint was passed on. Just as the women who got pregnant often, and nursed and nurtured their babies best, were the ones whom we descend from.

Men thrusted. Women held. Of course in some cases it was reversed. Of course women could do what men could do. Intellectually we were, if not identical, then certainly equal.

But our most basic hormonal sexual selves were not always similar. Men were more excited about a woman they had never tasted or touched before than one they already knew intimately. A stranger whose pheromones a man had not yet become immune to, was more desirable than a trusted lover.

But all this scientific jargon, this polite way to try to make the best of something that irks, pains and annoys women, didn't make it any easier to do the dance.

Some enlightened men did more than pay lip service to the idea of change, could outsmart their instincts, but they were not at the Diablo Cigar Bar. Here, protected by a steel door with a fine wood veneer, and armed guards who sat almost invisibly by the front of the room, there was no pretense. No wives or girlfriends allowed. This was a men's club and every woman present was for sale.

And so, even though in any other circumstance I would have turned away from the stares, I could not do that here. Not even allow myself the indignant narrowing of my eyes. I could not shoot back a comment that would put the guys in their place. This *was* their place. I was either the interloper or the entertainment. And I had two seconds to make up my mind what it was to be.

If I chose one way, I would have to leave and be no closer to helping Cleo—if, indeed, she was in trouble, if, indeed, it was not already too late. The other way, I could stay and take my chances, betting on my ability to find something out.

And if I didn't, there was no one else who could.

Gil excused us and took me off to the bar.

"What would you like to drink?" he asked.

"I'll just have a sparkling water."

"No. A drink. You look like a deer caught in the headlights. You need something. What will it be?"

"A vodka martini, then."

"A Diablo martini, then."

When the bartender put it down I took a sip.

"What is it?"

"Do you like it?"

I nodded, though I couldn't quite figure out what made it taste just a little hotter and saltier than I was used to.

"A few red peppercorns dropped in for color, a splash of the brine from the olives."

I took another sip.

"A dirty martini," I said. And then smiled. "Appropriate."

He gave me what was an attempt at a smile, but it slipped at the end and wound up marking his face like a wound.

"I appreciate your doing this," he said.

"Don't thank me yet. I have no idea if I can pull it off. And even if I do, there's no guarantee we are going to find out anything."

"No, but it's better than sitting and waiting. The police haven't done a thing. It's been over a week."

"They don't have any evidence that Cleo is—"

He interrupted me. "We shouldn't talk about this. Not here. Not now." He looked around. Besides his fear of us being over-heard, I knew it wasn't smart for me to be having this conversa-tion. I was slipping back into being Cleo's therapist, and I had to get out of that frame of mind if I was going to be meeting her clients and pretending to be a possible assignation.

"He just walked in," Gil said as he got up to greet his client.

Cleo's name for the first man I was going to meet was Judas. According to her book, he was fifty years old, married, with two grown children. His wife was a judge who heard children's rights cases.

A client for more than two years, Judas had seemed like the best place for me to start because he had a lot to lose if Cleo's book was published, and because, sexually, he was one of her least-demanding clients.

I'd only had a few sips of my drink when Gil returned to the bar with a man who looked familiar. Of course. I knew who he was from photos that had been in the newspapers and magazines over the years. Judas wasn't only married to a high-powered woman, he was one of the leading fund-raisers for the Democratic party in New York and was often seen at gala events and balls for the state senators, the governor and the administration.

"Morgan, this is Nelson."

Unlike the two men I'd met minutes ago, Nelson—or Judas, as I thought of him—didn't give me an immediate once-over. He was too practiced and political for that. I was still a stranger to him, and he was too used to meeting people to let go of the routine of shaking hands, focusing on your eyes and offering back a sincere look of comradeship for the introduction to have any sexual over-tones. He could have been meeting me at a fund-raiser instead of in a men's club where high-class prostitutes discreetly took men to a room in the adjoining hotel and engaged in the ancient art of the courtesan.

"So let's sit you two down so you can get to know each other a little bit," Gil said as he led us over to a table against the wall, exchanged a little more small talk and then left us.

Almost immediately a waiter appeared with a beer in a frosted glass for Judas and what was still my mostly full martini.

For fifteen minutes we talked about politics. Judas made no pretense about what he did for a living. That was part of their attraction to being with one of Cleo's girls. The men knew they could be themselves, however and whatever that meant, and trusted that not a word would ever get out. They paid for that privacy.

Which was why Cleo's deciding to write a book, no matter how well she would ultimately disguise the men, would be such a total betrayal.

Which was why she had been so very careful about who she had told.

Was it even possible she would have confided in one of her clients? There might not be a single man among her regulars who knew that she had a brand-new laptop and had been typing out a tell-all tale of the sexual innocence and depravity of some of the richest men in New York, L.A. and the world. And if that was the case, this whole charade might be a waste of my time. But I had nothing more to lose than a few evenings. Dulcie was at her father's for the week. I certainly wasn't dating anyone. Working on Cleo's disappearance this way was better than sitting at home alone, brooding on it and feeling helpless.

"Well, at least I know you are a Democrat. That's one hurdle we've jumped," Judas said after I'd admitted to my political party affiliation.

"Is that part of your criteria?" I tried to tease with my voice. But I hadn't flirted in a long time. And it was awkward for me to ask questions and lace them with attitude. As a therapist I did the exact opposite. I cleaned my questions up, erased the emotional tones and tried not to give away how I was feeling.

He smiled. I felt relieved. My question had been all right. Under the table I felt my legs shaking. This was never going to work if I was this nervous. But I had nothing to draw upon from my own life to help me with this. I had foolishly assumed that, because I wanted to figure out this mystery, I would be able to. What made me think I could just walk in here wearing a low-cut silk blouse, a skirt that was four inches shorter than I normally wore, and shoes that were like nothing else I'd ever owned, and just pretend to be someone I wasn't?

"I could never have any kind of meaningful arrangement with a woman who votes for an ass."

Laughter, from both of us.

* * *

Dulcie had been telling me about her acting classes over the phone that afternoon. She'd had an assignment to be a liquid. Any liquid she chose. And act the essence of it. She'd chosen honey. She'd told me that she'd thought about how slowly it spilled and how she'd walked across the stage making each step take forever and all the while just thinking over and over that she was honey. How, after the first step, just lifting her foot had been such an effort that she hadn't been sure she was ever going to get to the other side of the room. Finally she'd just slid to the floor. She couldn't walk. Then she inched her way across, moving her arms, then her torso, then her legs, all separately. And when she reached the other side and the teacher told her how good a job she'd done, Dulcie had said that it had taken her a minute to remember she wasn't honey and just get up normally.

If my daughter could do that, then how hard could this be for me?

I imagined Cleo. Her mouth in a tortured O, her eyes wide with some kind of terror. I didn't know where she was or what was happening to her, but I could conjecture. I knew the kinds of sadistic things a man could do to a woman if he wanted to.

I tried to hear her, talking to me, telling me how to act this part. What would she say? What kind of advice would she offer? She'd tell me to take my time. To be the honey that Dulcie had been. That her clients would like honey: heavy, sweet, golden, viscous liquid.

I reached out and touched the hairs on the back of Judas's hand. Lightly. The way Cleo might. Not the way I ever could.

"I'm sorry if I'm not who you expected," I said softly. "But I hope you aren't too disappointed. I know you were expecting Cleo."

"Well, I am certainly surprised." But had he seemed surprised when he met me? I didn't think so. Perhaps he meant when Gil had first told him, before he'd brought him over to see me. But even if Gil had just told him, only a few moments had passed.

On the other hand, if he was involved in Cleo's disappearance, he wouldn't be surprised.

"I've been seeing Cleo for two years. I didn't know she was taking a vacation. Last time she did that she told me in advance. Why wouldn't she have told me this time?"

I gave a shrug. "I don't know."

I try to teach my patients the power of not always answering a question. There is no rule of the universe that you must respond to what people ask. You have every right to hold your thoughts inside and not reveal them. In a time when revelation was fodder for the constant news and talk-show-type entertainment, questions were usually answered. But in real life you didn't have to do that. And I didn't. And Judas, as I had hoped he would, just kept talking.

"But I can't stay mad at her for too long."

"Have you ever been mad at her?" I put my hand on his.

To anyone watching, it would look like my fingers were courting his hand, but I had the pad of my forefinger on his pulse and I was feeling the steady flow of his blood through his veins. My own, not very accurate lie detector test. It would never, like its more scientific sibling, be admissible in a court of law, but I knew that it was a good way to judge. When people are telling the truth their heart rate tends to stay consistent, but when they lie, especially about something that might be making them nervous, the rate can speed up.

"I don't know if it's fair to talk about her," he said.

His pulse seemed slightly faster.

"I don't mind talking about Cleo," I told him. "She's very special. I don't expect to take her place. Just fill in a little while she's gone if that's what you'd like."

"Fill in." He gave me a wicked grin. And then it disappeared. "It's not just what we do together that matters to me. It's that she doesn't judge me."

His pulse was definitely more rapid now.

"There isn't anything to judge. What makes us happy, what gives us pleasure, isn't about other people's opinions. It's not up for debate. We're really fragile inside our skin, and the reasons that some things excite us and others don't is a very mysterious science."

He was nodding, but I was horrified. I had just slipped back into jargon. Luckily, he not only didn't seem to mind, but he actually became more attentive. But I had to be careful. I knew Cleo was smart and knew that her clients would expect someone who was equally intelligent. But I also knew there was a difference between pleasing someone and pandering to their desires, and being their therapist.

"You know, this is ridiculous, but I actually missed her last week. And it surprised me."

I nodded.

"Do you think that it's strange? That I could get attached to someone I see once a week?"

I almost laughed and I might have if my heart wasn't pounding in my chest, because he had just reached out across the table and pushed my blouse off my shoulder.

"No. I think you must be a very sensitive man. Of course Cleo can mean something to you."

I had no idea what to do. Gil had said that these meetings were "dates" in order to give both the client and Cleo's girls the opportunity to see if they wanted to do business together. All the girls had twenty-four-hour veto power. Cleo relied on them to follow their instincts about the men they met. She didn't want anyone to go with a man she didn't feel comfortable with. Certain girls didn't mind going with strangers, but they were the ones who usually did the "outside" dates and trips.

I wouldn't have to go to a room with any of these men; just meet them and get a sense of who they were and see if I could pick up on anything untoward or hint that they were capable of harming Cleo. Then Gil would take it from there and go to the police with one name.

If, indeed, she was even missing. If she had not just decided to run away from her life and not tell anyone. The idea kept repeating like the chorus of a song I couldn't get out of my head.

Cleo was a very confused young woman in love with a man who had issues with her profession, whom she couldn't make love to, and at the same time she was writing a book that she knew was going to create havoc and possibly cause a lot of pain. She was also a woman with two boyfriends, neither of whom, it seemed, knew anything about the other.

Judas trailed his fingers across the inside of my wrist and up my arm. It was an unfamiliar sensation. I wasn't used to the feeling of having a man touch me like this.

For the last few years of my marriage to Mitch and all the nights we held each other, there had been love and there had been comfort, but there had not been much more. And now a total stranger was making me feel something that I hadn't remembered forgetting.

Skin is alive. It breathes. It is made up of nerve endings. It sensates. His fingers were doing something to me that had nothing to do with us knowing each other or liking each other or even caring if we ever found out anything more about each other. My skin didn't care that this was obscene, that I was playing a very dangerous game. My skin was enraptured by the ever-so-slight pressure of a man's fingertips sailing across its expanse. I shut my eyes, not pretending, not being coy, but rather finding myself in this unusual place, sitting across the table from a successful and nice-looking middle-aged man who liked to touch women's skin and knew how to do it with exactly the right pressure.

The rest of my body was jealous of that thin line of skin. It hadn't been touched, either. It hadn't touched. There was a war going on between my mind/body and sensation/intellect.

I moved away. "Not yet," I said as coyly as I could but not really sure what coy sounded like.

"I know I'm being bad. But your skin is so luscious."

"Should I know anything about you being bad? Is that something you do? You need to tell me. I have to make sure that I can be who you want."

There were things I knew from the book that had made me nervous about Judas. He was conflicted. He cared about his wife and their children and his life. His professional stature was immensely important to him. But he was sexually impotent unless he felt that he was doing something wrong. It was the thrill of danger and deceit that turned him on. Not only was it something he didn't know how to explain to his wife, the judge, but out of every possible scenario of what could turn him on, the need to be bad—to do illegal things—this was the worst.

"I like to be afraid."

"Of what?" I whispered.

"Of being found out."

I nodded. "What else?"

"To know I am doing something that could blow the whole fucking lid off my life," he said.

I wanted to ask him why. To get him to talk about that. I wanted to help him. But I was the honey, I wasn't Dr. Morgan Snow. I didn't have those two letters before my name in here. I didn't even have a last name. I was just Morgan. Someone whose job was to figure out how to give pleasure.

This was far more confusing than I had imagined. But I couldn't stop. I needed to understand what kind of danger he meant. How far that danger would go. Would it translate into taking a woman and hiding her away somewhere, or to hurting her, or to making her tell him if she really was writing a book and if he was in it?

It was strange to know things about Judas that he didn't know I knew. To have read about him and studied his psychology as Cleo had laid it out.

"If it would be okay with you, can you tell me what you'd want me to do? So I can figure out if I'm right for you? If I'm not I can find someone who would be."

He leaned forward. Even closer. "I'd like to tell you. But first you have to take this." He pulled out a wad of cash from his pocket and peeled off five one hundred dollar bills.

The soft light from the small lamp on the table shone on his money clip, which was in the shape of a snake, curling around itself. The sinuous creature had a small tongue—black enamel—and two tiny ruby eyes. It was unusual, yes, and worth looking at on its own, but what stopped me was that I had read a description of this money clip in Cleo's book.

But not in the part about Judas.

In Cleo's book, the money clip belonged to a man she called the Healer—that fifth man whom Gil hadn't recognized—and she had described seeing it every time he took it out of his pocket. That fifth man had handed her bills exactly the way Judas had just handed me bills, putting the money in my palm, then closing my fingers around it.

There wasn't supposed to be a charge for this evening. Gil had explained that. "What is this?" I asked Judas.

"If I am going to give you my secrets, I need to make sure you have an incentive for keeping them."

If only I could have told him how safe his secrets would be with me. But the question that was on my mind was, did he trust Cleo with them or was he worried that she was going to tell on him?

I shook my head. "You don't have to." I handed the money back to him.

"I want to. Please." He pushed it back at me.

I didn't want to make a fuss over the money and disrupt any confidence he was about to share, so I took the bills and put them in my bag. I would figure out what to do with them later.

"You were going to tell me what you liked," I reminded him with what I hoped was an inviting smile. But what the hell was an inviting smile? How was I ever going to get through meeting four of these men? Or five if Gil ever figured out who the Healer was.

Judas smiled. "What I like to do is go places. In public. Places where other people are."

I nodded.

Cleo had listed a few of the places that he had taken her. Into his wife's chambers once at night. Into the dressing room of a men's department store in New York. Into an empty room off the stage at the opera the night of a huge fund-raiser while his wife was sitting in their season box. He had gotten Cleo a ticket and a date and had arranged to meet her there.

But I wanted to hear him tell me about it. See if, since Cleo had written about him, he had changed any, if he now needed to push his fantasy, to go further to the edge of his boundaries.

"Where was the last place you took Cleo?"

The smile on his face wasn't what I expected. It wasn't suffused with pleasure the way it had been a minute ago when he was giving me money. What was I seeing? Was this a deeper darkness of someone who didn't have any boundaries?

"I took her to the bank. To the vault. I gave her money. It gave me pleasure. I miss her." His voice was suddenly thick. He lowered his eyes.

"We all miss her," I said.

We did. And we were all worried about her. Very worried.

31

At six-thirty the night maid opened the door to room 1543 in the Pallard Hotel, and within twenty minutes Noah Jordain and his partner were speeding out of Manhattan to the large hotel in nearby Newark, New Jersey, both of them hoping that what they were about to find in that room was not another notch in the belt of the man whom they now referred to as the Magdalene Murderer.

For Jordain, this series of crimes was worse than most, if in fact there could be such degrees of horror when you dealt with the depths of depravity. Not only were they more personally disturbing, but he'd never had such a cold case before. So far forensics hadn't turned up any serious leads.

The M.E. said the murderer hit the women over the head with a blunt object, which was slightly convex. After he knocked them out, he strangled them with latex-sheathed hands. They were the kind of gloves you could buy in any drugstore.

Conjecturing, the M.E. also said he didn't think the women regained consciousness after they'd been knocked out.

At least there was that—they never knew what happened. So

they never knew that once they were dead, the man defiled their bodies, dressed them as nuns and posed them in blasphemous tableaux.

Dozens of people had probably seen the murderer passing through the hotel on his way to his assignations. But to them, he was just one more man in the lobby, in the elevator, in the hall.

"We need to get someone to compare the surveillance tapes from all the different hotels and see if by chance the same face shows up more than once," Jordain said to his partner as he drove across town.

"Oh, great," was Perez's sarcastic response.

It was not going to be easy. All they could do was assume the perp was dressed as a businessman so that he blended in and probably carried a small suitcase that held the nun's clothes and accessories he needed.

"I know." Jordain nodded. "It's not much, but he's not making any mistakes, and so far the hotel rooms are just too damn full of crap. If he'd only picked more expensive hotels with better surveillance, or if some desk clerk had paid more attention to whom had checked in. Or if someone had had a bedspread washed in the last month...." Jordain let the sentence trail off in frustration. There was no point in going over all the scenarios that could make their job easier. So far, the three crime scenes had offered up such a mess of hair, fiber and prints, that the lab had not isolated anything meaningful. Inevitably, the same scenario would be repeated at this newest location.

"He has to make a mistake sooner or later," was the best Perez could offer.

"I want it sooner, damn it."

"It sure doesn't help that he's killing women that no one is watching out for."

The light changed. Jordain nodded and pressed down on the accelerator.

It was a warm night. Breezy, full moon, not much traffic, the lights of the city sparkling as if it were a magical place full of hope instead of the terrors that Jordain knew were there. For every light there was a darkness. For every window that blazed there was a man or woman who was capable of slipping from grace into garbage.

The church, his church, the same church that ordained men to spread God's word and women to do God's work, said that children were born innocent. But as good a Catholic as Jordain was, he no longer believed that. He had seen too much carnage. And he knew he was about to see more.

32

She was young.

Younger than any of the others. Not a line on her face. Not a shadow of age. Not a shadow of life, either.

"Eighteen?" Jordain asked the M.E.

"Maybe."

They were all jaded, but Jordain still wanted to get down on his knees and cross himself and pray that in her hour of need an angel had come down and eased this woman's way and she had not known what the monster had done to her.

All she had expected was to have to get naked and give the john a blow job or to spread her legs and pretend to enjoy it.

But this? No, she had not counted on this.

The young woman was lying on the bed. The first one they had found on a bed. And somehow that, too, made it worse. For the comfort the bed pretended to offer. For the pain that she had to have felt there.

Like the victims before her, she had been dressed in a nun's habit pushed up to reveal the devil's handiwork, which in this case included wrapping her naked body in barbed wire. One length of it encircled each leg. Another few yards girdled her torso and spiraled upward around her breasts. And the smallest piece was wrapped around her head. A crown of thorns.

She had been turned into a human pincushion. Everywhere the wire touched her skin, the sharp metal barb had pierced her skin and she had bled.

The room smelled of the sickly sweet liquid that still oozed out of the hundreds of punctures and dripped down in rivulets, making rivers and streams of blood. It had flowed from her and saturated the white sheets beneath her. Jordain imagined the stain went deeper, past the sheets to the mattress. Did it go deeper still? From the mattress had her blood dripped on the floor and into the carpet and into the wood and then into the ceiling of the room below?

"We might have something here," Perez said.

Jordain looked away from the rosary that hung from between the woman's legs, his perp's very distinguished signature.

"What is it?" Jordain asked when he saw Perez lean over and bag something that had been on the floor. "Is it something we can use? Did he slip up?"

"Hardware-store sticker. Must have come off the wire."

"Maybe he didn't notice it."

"Maybe it got stuck to his shoe."

"True Value." Jordain moaned. "There must be what? Two thousand of those stores?"

It wasn't his style to be negative. To let the frustration come to the surface. But this case was torture. Maybe Morgan Snow would turn up something. Maybe her ability to twist along into the tunnels of someone's mind would illuminate just one thing that had eluded the rest of them.

He'd call her when they were done. Maybe she would have something to tell him.

"No, you're right. It is something. It's a big something. It's got to be in the area. New York, New Jersey, Connecticut. There can't be more than a few dozen stores."

Jordain turned back and looked at the poor girl on the bed, because no matter how hard he tried to make her into a tough street hooker who should have known better, he couldn't.

She was a kid. Someone's daughter. Someone else's sister.

He sighed and leaned up against a wall and waited while the photographers finished up.

"You know what is going to happen?" Jordain was only forty years old, but he knew he sounded like someone who had already lived a whole lifetime. It was in every weary syllable and the lethargic cadence of his words.

Perez shrugged.

"We'll find all the stores that carry this wire. We might even narrow it down to a few stores that have sold this exact length in one purchase. We might even be lucky enough to find the clerk who sold it. But when we look there will be no credit card to check. You know it will be a cash purchase and, of course, the purchaser's face won't be memorable. Who would remember a man who had bought a few yards of barbed wire along with a few other things that he'd thrown in there to make certain he was a forgettable customer?"

"Maybe he slipped up with that." Perez didn't even wait for Jordain to respond. "I know. Don't even tell me how unlikely that is. We are dealing with someone who is as smart as we are. If not smarter. At least so far."

Jordain looked back at the young girl. Just stared at her for a few seconds. "We could still catch a break on where the nuns' habits come from."

"How the fuck does a man buy nuns' habits and not be noticed? Even if he was a priest, he would be remembered."

"Hobart doesn't think he is a priest, neither does Morgan. Although she thinks he might have once been a priest."

"You know, I don't hold out any hope for what the shrinks think. Mostly they guess. And it's only after we find the perp that suddenly they claim they always said he was a whatever all along. How often does any of their bullshit make a difference? When was the last time we caught anyone from a profile?"

Jordain shrugged. "It's a moot point. We don't know anything. We don't have anything."

"We are gonna crack this on the habits," Perez insisted.

"From your mouth…"

Perez gave him a half smile. The detective was used to Jordain's appropriating his expressions by now. But it still made him grin to hear the Southern detective with the New Orleans patois use his grandmother's favorite saying.

While the M.E. and his team worked the scene, the detectives filled out their reports. Then Perez's cell phone rang.

"Anything?" Jordain asked when the call was over.

His partner shook his head. "Yes, no. They've worked their way through another half-dozen religious supply stores and no luck with the habits yet."

"But they've had that first outfit for two weeks. How long can it take to figure out where the thing was bought?"

"Because he cut the fucking labels out of the habits. And this particular model is the most basic and popular one made. You do not want to know what our guys now know about nuns' clothes."

"Well, they better find out a little bit more. The commissioner is getting anxious," Jordain said. But the truth was he was the one getting more and more anxious, and his partner knew it.

"It would have been easier a few years ago to track down those costumes. But now that you can buy anything on the Internet…"

Jordain looked away as one member of the M.E. team extracted the bloody rosary out of the girl's vaginal cavity with a pair of tweezers.

"Hey, Perez. You just said something. Costumes. Has it occurred to anyone that these are not real habits at all but costumes? Has anyone—"

But he didn't have to finish. Perez was already on the phone calling in the suggestion.

Jordain's eyes returned to the cop who was holding out a new evidence bag for the M.E. tech. The rosary was still hanging in the air. One drop of blood, dark red like a precious stone, hung on the end of the cross, glinting in the light, shining. It held for a few seconds, then dripped off and fell onto the cop's shoe.

Only Jordain had seen the spill. And it made him nauseous. Just then his cell phone rang, and he answered it with a sharp "Jordain." It was one word he pronounced with the full, slow drawl of his hometown. Playing the word for all its music. He'd heard his dad do it for years, and he was barely aware he was doing it himself.

"Hey, boss, I wanted you to know. She's leaving the club."

"Alone?"

"Yup. Want me to follow her home?"

"No. Just follow her until you are sure no one else is."

33

I didn't feel dirty. I didn't need a bath when I got home. But I did want a drink and was opening a bottle of wine when the phone rang. After checking the caller ID first, I answered it.

"Hello, Detective." I checked my watch as I talked to him. It was earlier than I'd thought. Only nine.

"I'm in the neighborhood."

"Again? What excuse do you have this time?"

"No excuse. You are too smart. You'd see right through me. But I could wait till tomorrow, if this is too inconvenient. I will call you at your office. Ask you if I can come up. You'll remind me that Dr. Buttercup doesn't want me there. Then I'll ask you if you can come over to the station house. And we'll spend ten minutes trying to find a gap in your schedule—"

"How far away are you?"

"About fifteen minutes," he said.

"Okay," I said, and heard him hang up.

* * *

In the bathroom, looking at myself in the mirror as I washed my face and then reapplied just a little lipstick, I wondered why he thought it would be okay to call me at night. Or how he managed to phone just minutes after I got in.

I checked my answering machine on the off chance that he had been calling for a few hours and finally found me home. But no one had called. Then I checked my caller ID to see if anyone had called but hung up without leaving a message. Nothing there, either.

So how did he know I'd just gotten home?

Maybe I was being too suspicious.

I brushed my hair, shut the light off without checking my reflection again and went into the kitchen to open a bottle of wine. The day had been long and the night had been longer. And now it would be longer still.

Pouring the wine, I took a sip and tasted, focusing on the sensations: the cold liquid, and the slightly sour and fruity scent, the way it felt filling my mouth, sliding down my throat and leaving me ready for the next sip.

When Detective Jordain rang the bell, I offered him some but he shook his head.

"You are still on duty? It's almost ten."

"I might have to go back to the station after we finish up."

He looked exhausted, not from lack of sleep, but the way people look after they have been through a trauma or shock.

As he followed me inside, I sensed that he was walking more slowly than usual. And then found myself astonished that I would have noticed something that obscure about him—the speed of his gait. But he was tall, so much taller than me, and his legs were so long, that the last time we had walked across my living room floor he had overtaken me.

Not tonight.

He sat down on the couch.

"Do you want some coffee? Something to eat?"

"You know, I haven't eaten anything all day. I didn't even realize that till right now. Yes. Anything. Anything easy."

"Come with me into the kitchen, then. I'll see what I have but I'm warning you, the best I can offer is probably a can of soup, a frozen vegetarian entrée or maybe you'll be really lucky and I'll have an English muffin and some peanut butter."

In the kitchen he leaned against the counter and looked at me with a kind of sardonic sadness. "Soup, frozen stuff? Did *you* eat tonight?"

I shook my head.

"Are you hungry?"

"Now that you mention it, I am. Ravenous."

"But you really don't cook?"

I shook my head again.

"Sit down."

There was something so matter-of-fact about the way he said it, so easy, that I obeyed. And felt a little jolt of pleasure. I couldn't remember when anyone had taken over before. Ever? Surely. My father used to. Nina Butterfield did. But my ex didn't.

"So, let's see what we have," he said as he opened the cabinets and foraged around, searching for ingredients.

"You have everything," he said after a moment. "This is one of the best-stocked larders I've ever seen."

"That doesn't mean I can cook it up for you. I'm a Martha Stewart wanna-be in the kitchen, as my daughter says. But I'm all wishful thinking. I have no food skills."

"Well, then, you just sit down, have some more wine and I'll see what I can do with all this exotica."

Everything about him was easy. The expansive way he smiled and the slow way he spoke. So much slower than any easterner. And compared to New Yorkese it sounded almost excessively languid.

From my overstocked but underused supplies he pulled out cans and boxes, smiling, reading some of the contents aloud, and then putting most of them back.

What he finally assembled on the countertop included a frozen bag of precooked shrimp, a French baguette, a jar of tomato sauce, olive oil and bottles of dried spices, including red chili flakes, cayenne pepper, white pepper and salt.

In the vegetable drawer he found a slightly dried-up garlic clove, an equally sad-looking red onion and a shallot. From the middle shelf he took out a carton of eggs that I hoped were not past their expiration date and a tub of butter that I was afraid might be empty.

First he heated the oven. Then he boiled some water and defrosted the shrimp by dumping them in for just a few minutes. Next he put a frying pan on the stovetop, dropped in a knob of butter and a pour of olive oil.

"Olive oil *and* butter?" I asked.

He gave me a look. It made me start. Not because he was looking at me, but because of how it reminded me of how the men looked at me in Diablo's. I had forgotten about them and the night and what had gone on. Suddenly, I felt odd sitting there in my own kitchen being one person, while I had been someone so very different only an hour before when a stranger had given me five hundred dollars just to keep some secrets.

Noah threw the onion into the sizzling fat, gave it a few quick stirs and then added the garlic. While he stirred that some more he said, "You can handle one tablespoon of butter. What the hell is it with you women up east? In New Orleans a woman would never get that hysterical about a little bit of butter."

But he didn't say it like that—the words were half sung, in his New Orleans drawl that had a sound all of its own.

While Noah continued with the prep work, I set the table, glancing over at him every once in a while, astounded that such good smells were coming out of my kitchen.

I'm just hungry, I thought to myself.

Leaning against the kitchen sink, I watched him move: stirring one pot, working on the batter for whatever was coming next and getting the French bread into the oven.

Only minutes later, he had dished up the food and set the plates on the table. The first bite was peppery and smooth and made me want another right away. "Does this have a name?" I asked.

"Sort of. It's a frittata. That's the egg part—"

"I know what a frittata is. I mean the whole dish."

He shook his head while he took another bite.

"I don't use recipes or sheet music if I can help it."

"You're a musician, too?"

"Piano. Jazz. I like to cook the same way I play. Loose. Whatever strikes my fancy."

We ate without much more conversation for a few minutes.

"Well, that was delicious. Thank you," I said when we both were done. "Do you want some coffee?"

I watched him rip off a hunk of bread and wipe up the sauce from his plate.

"I don't suppose you have any chicory?" he asked.

"No. Just Starbucks."

"Okay. As strong as you can make it."

He was delaying whatever he had come here to tell me. He'd been in my house for an hour and hadn't said a word about his case or asked me one question about Cleo. That was when I got nervous. What if he was here to tell me bad news? Awful news. About Cleo. What if... Just ask, I said to myself.

With my back to him I filled the French press with ground beans. "So do you have any news?" I asked.

"It can wait for the coffee."

"But I don't know if I can." My heart started to speed up.

"There was another Magdalene murder tonight."

The steel coffee scoop I was using fell out of my hand and onto the tile floor. The grounds scattered. It looked as if there were ants—hundreds of dead ants—on the white squares. I moved to wipe them up just as Noah came over to help. As I bent down, he did, too, our heads close together. We both looked up at the same time.

I could see into his eyes, which were a blue so light, they almost didn't look real. I could feel his breath on my face.

For a minute I got confused. Started to sway. Felt as if I was reaching forward, as if I might actually be moving closer to him, as if he was inching toward me. And then I lost my balance just enough for him to notice, and he reached out to steady me with his hand.

My skin reacted. For the second time in one night, a man's fingers were on me. It stopped everything. I couldn't move. It was different from Judas. It was, in its own way, much more frightening.

But how could that be? How could this safe police detective, with his trusty weapon strapped under his arm, frighten me more than a total stranger who liked to pay women to fuck him in very public places where he might get caught?

"I'll make the coffee," he said. "You sit down. Let me tell you what happened. You just listen. Then you can tell me what you think. We know what we have on our hands now. There's no question about that. But we still don't know enough to outthink him." Noah's back was to me as he cleaned out the French press.

It was a wide back with a lot weighing on the shoulders. And I wanted to help him. Not only, I knew, because of Cleo. But for his sake too.

Because when I'd looked into his eyes, I'd seen more than a startling color of blue. I'd seen pain.

34

The following night, I met the second man, who, from Cleo's description, was suspect. Exposure for him would mean excommunication from his life's work, a job that had made him a hero. Cleo had called him Midas, but when he put out his aged hand, Gil introduced him as Keifer. He smelled of cigars and had deep wrinkles around his eyes and his mouth.

At sixty-eight he was the head of the largest Christian charity in the United States. Independently wealthy, he had devoted his life to amassing even more wealth and giving as much of it away as he could. And while I knew this from Cleo's book, sitting down with him over drinks that night, I pretended I had no idea.

"I haven't been doing this for very long," I offered. It had occurred to me that I could use my nervousness to my advantage. Put the men at ease by having them think I was uncomfortable, and perhaps they would be less self-conscious with me.

"Well, that's even better, isn't it? Is it your first time?" he asked.

"It would be, yes. If we both decide that this will be pleasurable."

"Giving is what gives me pleasure." He smiled at me.

Despite his age, he had a full head of white hair, with no sign of a receding hairline. Tall, with square shoulders and a long face, he leaned back in his chair at the club and watched me answer. It was not yet any easier to be looked at in that unapologetic way, but I steeled myself against his gaze and played along with his banter.

He was the kind of man you would notice in a crowd because of his presence. I've had patients who were like this, so secure in their persona, so successful and so wealthy that they radiate an aura of success. And I've had female patients who were receptive to men like this and their attention.

"The thing about me, Morgan, is that I don't demand much but for you to enjoy what you are doing."

I arched my eyebrows.

"I'll confess why if you'd like to hear."

It was an effort to stay still, to not say anything, to not rush him. All the patience I usually had was gone.

"Yes?" I said.

"I like giving out money. It's what I do every day. I enjoy making it, but I love giving it away. In fact, that's really all I like to do. I'm an easy date."

"You have me totally confounded." I laughed.

"I can tell. You should see your face. Lovely, but definitely confounded. It's very simple."

He reached into his jacket and brought out a two-inch-thick pile of bills. The flickering lights were bright enough to see that they were hundred dollar bills, and there must have been at least fifty of them in the pile.

"Your eyes just got a little bigger."

"I don't think I've ever seen that much cash."

"But you are worth this much cash."

"I am?"

He was looking at me again, up and down, appraising me. And that was when I started to slip into the role I'd assigned myself.

It didn't matter that I was in a place I didn't belong, pretending to be someone I wasn't. It was still my face, and my eyes and my mouth and hands and breasts and it was still my voice and mannerisms. He was looking at me, and on his face was a look that told me he wanted me.

My breath caught in my throat. His blatant hunger was affecting me. It was a physical thing, like a wind that blew over me. Like a warm rain that dropped and ran down my cheeks.

"Feel this," he said, and took my right hand, putting it gently on the pile of bills. The paper was smooth under my fingertips and involuntarily I ran my thumb over the edge, fanning them out, feeling their thickness.

"Can we go to a room now?" he asked.

"No. But you can tell me about what would happen if we did take a room. Tell me what you'd expect. We can start there, can't we?"

He nodded but not happily.

"What would we do in the room?"

"I would lay down these bills on the bed. Ten rows of bills across and ten rows of bills down. A five-thousand-dollar bedspread."

My face must have showed my surprise. Cleo had never indicated in the book how much money Midas gave her.

"I like what I do," he said in response to my expression.

"Giving money away?"

"Can you imagine anything better?"

I shook my head.

He called the waiter over. "Would you like some wine, a drink?" he asked me.

"Whatever you are having." I wanted to connect to him and this was a simple way.

"Champagne, please. Cristal," he said to the waiter. And then to me, "I don't drink anything but champagne. And only Cristal."

There was something familiar about this, but in the moment I couldn't focus on it.

"If we were up in the room, I'd baptize you with it."

"How?" I tried to keep my voice even, but I was afraid it was quaking. The religious overtones of his comments were hard to ignore.

"I'd put the glass up to your lips and feed it to you."

His sensuality was overwhelming. His voice, low and deep, brought me in toward him. Was there a connection between the prostitutes who had been so brutally killed and Cleo being missing? Was this man part of that connection?

Unlikely.

I knew the odds. More than two hundred people were reported missing every day in Manhattan.

Midas stopped talking as the waiter appeared. He uncorked the champagne and carefully poured out two glasses.

"Here, let me show you," Midas said as soon as the waiter was gone. He picked up my glass, and without taking his eyes off me, as if he were, indeed, offering some kind of blessing, he poured just one mouthful of the dry wine into my mouth.

"Tell me how delicious that is," he said.

I swallowed. "It is." It was.

"Let me give you some more." He held the glass up to my lips again and I sipped.

"What else would happen up in the room?" I asked.

"I'd feed you goodies. Caviar. Chocolate. Strawberries washed in cream. Whatever you liked."

"Chocolate," I said, remembering this part from the book. Cleo always chose chocolate.

He smiled.

I was two people at that table. One playing at being seductive with an older man who seemed to care about nothing but giving women pleasure, and the other, a psychiatrist making every effort to pay attention to the man's every nuance.

"And then?" I asked.

"I would ask you to open your shirt for me."

Cleo had written that this was all he wanted. For her to open her blouse so he could look at her lingerie. She said she never minded that. The lights in the room were low. She didn't even have to get naked.

"And then I'd ask you to lie down on the bed. On the money."

I flashed on the description that Noah had given me of the bills positioned at the crime scenes. Fifties always soaked in blood. I shivered.

What if everyone was wrong and Cleo's disappearance and the murdered prostitutes were connected? Could this well-known and charitable man be the one to commit such deranged acts?

I couldn't imagine it.

But was he capable of doing something to Cleo to stop her from publishing a book that would expose a secret that he was trying so hard to hide that he overpaid her?

Maybe.

Secrets don't come cheap.

And keeping them is often worth killing for.

"You would have to close your eyes then."

"I don't know if I could do that."

"You would have to. Close your eyes and tell me how much you like the money. Tell me what you are going to do with it. How much pleasure it's going to give you. I need to know that I can give you pleasure." He was slipping into his fantasy. Even though we were just sitting in the bar, he was starting to imagine that we were actually in the room.

"If I gave you all that money, what would you do with it?" He was whispering, his voice was low and urgent. He sounded almost desperate.

"I don't know..." I hesitated, not knowing what to say. And then I thought I should do what I had done before. Stay with the truth. He would think it was a lie, anyway. All that mattered was to keep him satiated until he was lulled even deeper into his pornographic dream, when his guard was down, and I could look right into his face, right into his eyes and ask him the question I had come here to ask and watch his reaction.

"It's not what I am going to do with it. It's that you think I am worth this much that makes me so happy. It's the fact that you giving me money is making you excited. The idea of that is amazing to me. That I could be attractive enough, desirable enough, that you would want to give me all this."

I hesitated long enough to listen to his breathing, which was now slightly belabored.

"I have never been wanted five thousand dollars' worth," I continued. "And it makes me really appreciate you. It gives me pleasure."

"Will you touch yourself? Just there on your neck?" He pointed to a spot under my chin. It seemed an innocent-enough place, and tentatively I put my fingers up high on my neck. I knew the scenario, all he wanted was the tease. And I could oblige him if it helped me figure him out.

Running my hand up and down my neck, my fingers drifted on my skin, not going anywhere near my breasts. The idea that someone was getting pleasure out of watching me, that I was arousing a man with just this little bit of foreplay, that I was almost starting to enjoy my amateur performance was the last thing I had expected. A small "Oh" escaped hoarsely from his throat.

"What else would you give me besides the money?" I asked, using his distracted state to set my trap. "Would you give me pain in addition to all that money if it gave me pleasure?" I asked. "Would you hurt me?"

He looked startled.

"Hurt you?"

"Yes. Don't you also like to inflict pain with that pleasure?"

He shook his head. "No. Not me. I've never done that." He looked horrified at the thought. Was he bluffing or was he serious? His eyes did not flicker. The pulse point in his neck did not jump and throb. I only had a small window of time left. "Where is Cleo? Tell me," I said.

"Cleo? I have no idea. Why are you asking *me* that?"

I could see it in his eyes. He was confused and he was telling the truth. And I felt a little bit sorry for him, sorry that I had lulled him into this erotic state only to shock him out of it with my questions.

"All I want is to give pleasure...." It was almost a cry.

35

I met Elias Beecher the next afternoon at a Japanese restaurant near my office. When I arrived, he was sipping a sake and looked even more exhausted than he had the last time we'd met.

The dining room was quiet and the table he'd chosen in the corner created even more of an illusion of privacy.

"I feel guilty even trying to eat," he said after the waitress took our order.

"I know, but it won't do Cleo any good if you get sick. Have you slept at all?"

"I fall asleep okay. Sleep for about two hours and then I'm wide awake. Lying there, imagining... Oh, I can't even tell you the things I start to imagine. There are so many disgusting people out there, capable of doing such violent, disturbed things I—"

The haunted look in his eyes, the pallor of his skin, the way he spoke just one level above a whisper, all pulled at me, and I put my hand out to cover his and then left it there.

He looked down at my hand on top of his as if it were a foreign object that he had never seen before. This touch was strange for me, too. Elias was halfway between a patient and a partner.

"We're all alone in this. It's just you and me looking for her," he said.

"Gil is looking for her, too."

His eyebrows arched and the soft look in his eyes hardened for a second. "Gil?" This he said with a derisive twist to his words that I hadn't heard from him before. "I don't trust him, Morgan. He is as much a suspect as anyone else. That book could destroy his business overnight."

"I know," I said, and then told him about our conversation.

"And you don't really believe he didn't know about Cleo and me?" he asked when I was done.

"He didn't seem to."

"But if she told him, if she finally told him, then he might have gone crazy. Did you see that movie...with Richard Gere and Diane Ladd, *Unfaithful?* When this mild, warm man finally is confronted with his wife's betrayal he becomes capable of murder." Elias was playing with his chopsticks, rubbing the tips against each other as if he could light a fire with the thin wooden utensils. "And the other movie like that was..."

He was starting to fragment and disappear into a list of films and books that would illustrate his point. I had to stop him.

"Elias?"

He looked at me, still lost for a moment and then reconnecting.

"I need you to help me. We need to find out more about all these men."

"You're meeting them, right?"

"Yes, I've met two, and so far I don't think either of them were capable of doing anything to Cleo."

"Then you have to move on to the next two. And then the next two."

"I only identified four who had serious motives—" I hesitated. I was avoiding mentioning the fifth man.

"But there's something else. What is it?"

It wasn't the first time he'd been in tune with what I was thinking.

"Cleo was so specific in her descriptions. So many things are accurate. But there is one specific thing about each of the men that I've met that she didn't use to describe them. She used those things to describe a fifth man. It's like he's a composition of all of them."

"But that shouldn't matter, should it? You still know there are four men who have motives. Who would absolutely be ruined one way or the other if that book were published?"

The waitress came with lacquered plates of glistening sushi and sashimi, and while she placed them before us and poured puddles of soy sauce into porcelain dishes, we were quiet.

Elias returned to rubbing the chopsticks together and the noise was like fingers on a blackboard, setting my teeth on edge.

When she left, I broke my own chopsticks apart, lifted up a piece of tuna, dipped it in the soy sauce and put it in my mouth. There was enough wasabi to inflame my taste buds and make my eyes tear, but it was a good kind of burn.

Elias was dipping a piece of cucumber roll in his dish of soy over and over, and while I watched, it fell apart, the grains of rice no longer sticky.

"This isn't going fast enough," he said. "I know you are doing the best you can. But it's still taking too long. Why won't the police do something? Why won't they help?"

I shook my head. "There's no evidence for them to get involved yet."

"Do you realize how ineffectual they are? How screwed up that is? I went to them and begged them to help and they turned around, treated me like a suspect, and they still aren't doing anything to find her. This is why I became a corporate lawyer. Dealing with law enforcement on the police level is far too frustrating."

He picked up another piece of sushi, went to dip it in the soy sauce, noticed that the round dish was full of rice and put the piece back on his plate.

"Haven't you found out anything you can take to them to

get them to stop putting all their effort on me and instead onto whoever really has taken her? Why would I take her, anyway? We were together. She is in love with me. Why haven't they connected her disappearance with those Magdalene murders? Every time I ask, the detective acts as if I am just trying to throw him off track. 'We need something to go on, Mr. Beecher, just one lead and we'll jump on it. But in the meantime there is no connection.'" He was mimicking Detective Jordain's New Orleans accent. I was about to ask him not to but why did I care if Elias made fun of Noah's way of speaking?

"If I thought it would get them moving in the right direction, I'd tell him that I did it," Elias continued, his eyes taking on a desperate intensity. "That I killed those three women. I'd tell them that I am responsible for all of those women being murdered and that Cleo is absolutely part of the plan. Maybe that would get them off their asses and onto the case. They'd have to find her. And then they would give her back to me and you would finish helping her and she'd get better. She'd be fine then. Whole. Finally, holy."

He pushed away the soy sauce dish filled with the uneaten sushi. He had not touched a single bite of his food.

I noticed that he'd used the word *holy* instead of *whole*. An obvious mistake because he was talking about the Magdalene murders. He was still talking, almost ranting now, the words tumbling out faster and faster and running together in pools of ideas.

"If you'd had more time with her, if you'd had another two or three weeks, what would you have done to help her? What would you have said to her? Could you have fixed this problem she was having? Could you have made her better? How would you have done it? What would you have done?"

"I don't fix problems."

"Yes, you do. That is why she went to you," he argued.

"I help people to work things out."

"Well, what would you have said to her to help her work things out?"

"I can't talk about that with you," I said as gently as I could.

"You can. I love her. You know how I love her. You can talk to me easier than you can talk to anyone else. Do you think you really could help her? Really?"

I nodded.

"How?"

"Just by getting her to talk about what had happened to her—" I stopped. He had almost lulled me into talking about my patient, and that was something I could not do. Would not do. Even with him.

36

Going to the police station where Noah Jordain worked wasn't how I wanted to spend the rest of my afternoon, but I'd made a commitment to meet him and look over what he and his team had collected.

I found Detective Jordain in a big room that had a large cork wall covered with a collage of photographs of the victims and evidence. The table that dominated the center of the room held piles of papers, videotape cassettes and more photographs.

Noah was standing, rifling through a stack of computer printouts when I got there. Hearing my footsteps, he turned to see who had come in and then made no effort to hide his smile.

"Well, it's certainly nicer to see you than another detective with more bad news."

"I could have bad news."

"It wouldn't be as bad coming from you." He pulled out two chairs. "Sit down. Do you want some coffee? It's fresh. Made it myself. Have to. Boy, do most cops make bad coffee."

"Sure, I'd love some."

He poured me a cup. I asked him about his investigation, and as I listened to him describe the small progress they'd made, I sipped the strong, bitter but surprisingly delicious coffee.

He was wearing a blue-and-black-striped shirt that made his blue eyes even more prominent. But there were deeper shadows under them than there had been on Sunday night.

None of us were sleeping well anymore. Not Gil, not Noah, not me.

That was something to remember. The man who was involved in these crimes would probably not be sleeping well anymore, either. He would be on a high from his rampage. Peaceful rest would probably be eluding him. I told him that and he made a note of it.

"But I don't think that he's getting a thrill from the murders," I said. "These are not glory killings. If they were, he'd be doing more to alert the press. He'd be playing some games, making sure the bodies were discovered sooner. He'd want to get the attention from the crimes if that was the case. That's not what is going on here. He's got some real need to kill these women."

"Can you elaborate on that? What kind of things would he need from them?"

"He's taking prostitutes and dressing them as nuns. Killing women and turning them into saintly figures. There has to be some personal scenario he is acting out."

"You still don't think he is a priest?"

"No. But I think he is religious."

"We agree there," Noah said. "He has all the right accoutrements and accessories. The communion wafers, the unguents, the wine. He not only knows about the sacraments, he knows how to deliver them and he knows where to get them. One thing that has checked out is that everything he uses is authentic."

"You mean he's not using Necco wafers?"

Noah shook his head and got up to get more coffee. "You want more?"

"No, I'm fine."

He sat down and jostled a pile of papers, looking for something. A photograph slipped out. A morgue shot of a woman—a hundred tiny pinpricks all over her body. I was sorry that I'd seen it. I knew it would haunt me.

"Do you think the women are being offered up as sacrifices?" he asked, seeing me looking, staring, at the picture.

"Do you mean is he killing the women as some kind of offering to God?"

He nodded.

"No. I don't think so. Do you?"

"Well, there is nothing in the Catholic doctrine that would fit that."

"What he's doing is more transformative. It's as if he's trying to turn them into holy women."

"Some misguided effort to save them?" Noah asked.

I shrugged. "That almost sounds right. Have you found any evidence that he has had sex with them?"

"No. Not before he's killed them or after."

I nodded. "The case is getting to you, isn't it?"

"They all do. But this one is one of the worst."

"You'd have to be made of steel for it not to."

"I thought I was. I thought I could handle it."

I leaned closer. He looked up. Away from the photographs. For a second neither of us said anything. His eyes were on me and I held them. In the middle of the sad, sick pictures and proof of a man gone wild was this other man who was sane and caring.

"You're a good man," I said softly.

"Is that going to help me here?"

It was another one of those ambiguous comments. I couldn't be sure whether he was referring to the case or to the attraction that seemed to be growing between us. But until I was sure he was feeling it, too, I wouldn't acknowledge it. Not because I didn't want to, but because I didn't know how to. What would I say? Making the first move was my style professionally, but not when it came to a man. It had been more than fourteen years since I'd had any dating experience. It wasn't even that I was out of practice; I was unknowing.

I broke the gaze, picked up my coffee and drank. "You know

you shouldn't drink too much of this. It's very strong. No wonder you are not sleeping."

"How do you know I'm not sleeping? Is that part of your psychiatric ability? What did I say that gave me away?"

"Nothing. And no, it's not my ability, either. It's the circles under your eyes."

"I lie down but I'm bombarded with all the unanswered questions."

"I've had patients that keep me up at night, too. You just keep running the facts and the suppositions and the ideas over and over in your mind, hoping that if you just keep examining them you'll see the pattern. And that's all you need. The beginning of one solid idea of how it all comes together."

"Morgan, what is going to get this lunatic to stop?"

"Either he is going to find the magic that he is looking for—which is unlikely—or you are going to have to stop him."

From the expression of Noah's face, it looked as if he thought the magic was a more likely scenario.

"I have to ask you something," he said.

I nodded.

"It's about the Diablo Cigar Bar—"

"I am not going to talk about Cleo," I interrupted.

"I am not going to ask you to. I want to know about you. I want to know why you are going there. What are you doing, Morgan?"

How did he know? It only took me a second to realize. It was how he'd known exactly when I'd arrived home the other night. "Are you having me followed?"

"For your own protection."

"This consultation is over, Detective." I stood up, and without saying another word, walked toward the door.

"Don't. Don't misinterpret it. I am worried about you. You could be in the middle of something much more dangerous than you know if these two cases are connected. I just have someone making sure you are okay, that's all."

I turned and looked back at him. "No, it's not all. You are smarter than that. You think there *is* a connection, don't you? But you're not telling me about it. You're treating me like a novice who needs special handling."

"I am treating you like someone who might potentially be in danger. I don't want anything to happen to you. How could I live with that on top of everything else that is going on?"

"Cleo is my patient. This all matters more to me than it does to anyone in the fucking NYPD. She isn't just a statistic, not just another missing person. This is a woman I sat across a room from for hours and hours and listened while she talked—opened up to me—about her secrets and her dreams and her problems. I watched her cry, Noah. Saw her wring her hands. What I do about trying to help her boyfriend find her is not something I need to be lectured about."

"I'm sorry."

I didn't say anything. The last thing I had expected from him was such a sincere apology. Hell, I hadn't expected any apology at all. But as unexpected as it was, something about it didn't surprise me all that much.

"Will you sit down, please?" he asked.

"Will you call off your watchdogs?"

"No. I'm protecting you, Morgan. Not spying on you."

"Then don't ask me about why I've gone to the club."

"I won't ask you. But you know you should tell me. I'm no shrink but I have eyes, too. And you look as tired as I do. And just as worried. And you even look a little guilty. But we'll put that aside for now, okay?"

I nodded, not wanting to think too much about what he'd just said, neither the insight it exhibited, nor the way his concern made me feel. No, now was not a good time to think about any of those things.

"One thing you can do for me," I said.

"Okay."

"Cleo wore a tiny diamond cross on her neck. Normally it wouldn't be the kind of thing that would be easy to track down. Except it was made of pink diamonds, which are extremely expensive. I'm not sure...maybe it's a long shot...but it's a cross,

Noah. Maybe you can find out what stores sell pink-diamond crosses. Maybe you can find out who bought one. Maybe there is a connection."

It seemed, at least for the moment, that I'd succeeded in taking his mind off me. And mine off him.

37

"You understand that this is a sin?" he asked the young woman whose brown eyes followed his every move, never looking away for a second.

"You understand that I am washing you of your sins?"

He did not need her answer. He knew. He could feel the silt and filth washing off her. "Can you feel your sins sloughing off like dead cells?"

Of course she was frightened, but once she got beyond her fear, he knew she would be grateful for his attention and ministrations. Once she was new again. "You don't need to be afraid. I am not doing this to hurt you." But despite his words, the expression in his eyes did not soften.

He leaned back, away from the tub, looking at her naked body sitting in the shallow pool of water. There was sweat on his upper lip and at his hairline. Under his arms. The backs of his knees. He was naked, too. To keep his suit from getting wet and wrinkled.

The hot, hot water had turned the marble bathroom into a steam room, but he did not temper the water coming from the tap. It had to be this hot. If there was any way to use boiling wa-ter he would have. He needed it to destroy the bacteria. To kill the living filth.

The duct tape on her mouth pulled her skin into an unnatural grimace. He hated this need to silence her, but he knew better than to trust her. Her simple mind could not rise to meet his. No mat-ter how carefully he might explain it, she would never be able to comprehend that this was for her own good.

For her own good.

For her own goodness.

Her skin was bright red now, and there was sweat all over her face. Tiny droplets of water that looked like translucent pearls. She deserved to look beautiful. She was giving herself to a great cause. Her sacrifice would help other women. He whispered this to her, but it did not becalm her.

Enough of trying to make her understand and appreciate what he was doing. The time was coming for the next step. Just a few more minutes of the ritual bath: the christening that was cleansing her and then he would be ready. The adrenaline surged through him. He knew it would work this time. He'd never gotten this far before.

The water smelled of the expensive liquid soap the hotel of-fered to all guests. He inhaled its sweetness as he rubbed the wash-cloth down her neck. Down her back. Around her shoulders, under her breasts.

"We're almost done," he said. "You should be clean now."

But was she? How could he really know? It wasn't surface dirt on her skin he was after. It was deep underneath. The filth had been in her. And he was sure he had sensed it, smelled it: she had been stinking of the dirt deposited on her, inserted in her by the men she had been with.

Yes, she needed this. This cleansing. She would thank him.

If only he knew how clean was clean enough.

After he'd been at it for another ten minutes, he pulled her out of the tub and lay her down on the bathroom floor and stared at her naked body. At the long neck and full breasts and nipples the color of faded roses.

She was so beautiful, she had been given so much and yet she had abused and defiled her body. She had taken this body that God had given her and she had given it away and ruined herself.

He began to shave her. Carefully. He didn't mind blood. But blood in the right way at the right time.

And that time hadn't come yet.

Her frightened eyes went to the erection between his legs.

"It's only a temporary aberration," his whispered in a reassuring tone. "I won't abuse you. My job is not to violate you further but to restrain myself and do my job."

That was his sacrifice to make. Just as she would make hers.

He blew on her pubis, and the short curly hair flew away, leaving the three-dimensional tattoo. It was the best one yet. A perfect cross. Jesus died for our sins. But he left behind so many sinners.

So far he hadn't accomplished his goal. He hadn't found the formula. But he was not searching for some mythological alchemy. He was certain this transformation was possible. He knew what had gone wrong. Until tonight he had not cleansed the women properly.

He had forgotten how Jesus had washed the feet of the sinners. How could he have forgotten that? It was the most basic of Catholic rituals. The first one. Spilling the water on the baby and anointing its forehead: the baptism.

With an innocent baby all that was needed was a slim trickle of water. But with a woman who had laid open her legs for hundreds of men, who had taken them in her mouth, her hands, her vagina, he had to clean her very well, indeed.

That was what he had missed. The one step he should have remembered. The one part of all this that he had forgotten. He lost his erection thinking of his failure. How many nights had he wasted? How much money had he lost? All because he'd forgotten this one step.

No. He would not berate himself. Not now. Not when he was so close.

The steam in the bathroom was dissipating and condensation

was dripping down the mirror and onto the tiles. The lights were still slightly diffused. This was like a heaven on earth.

Yes. He would do it tonight. Learn the lessons. Know the secret. And then put it to use on the one who deserved it the most.

Now that she is clean, you can prepare her for the rest.

In his mind, he was not hearing his own voice talking him through the steps. It was a holy voice, deep, professorial. The voice of the Holy Father. He could close his eyes and see his savior, halo around his head, hands outstretched.

If she is cleaned, if you have rid her of the stain on her soul, then she will not die, she will be saved.

He knew that this one would be the first of them to survive the trauma. Her salvation would lead to the salvation of others. He was sure of it. And it excited him.

He saw himself in the mirror. A naked man, dripping with sweat, his hair curled from the heat, his arms held high, a bright and shining gold object high about his head. It gleamed like the sun on a perfect day. He lowered the chalice. Precisely, carefully. But quickly with all his strength.

Her eyes went even wider. And in them he saw himself and the golden chalice reflected back. Shining. He was shining in her eyes. He was going to save her.

38

I didn't really have enough of the right kind of clothes for all the evenings I had to spend at the Diablo Cigar Bar. For my third excursion into the dark and smoky lounge, I scrounged through my closet before I went to work and tried to put together an outfit.

I could repeat the short black skirt and the Jimmy Choo pumps that showed more toe cleavage than any other shoes I had ever owned. But I'd already worn the off-the-shoulder Donna Karan black top twice. The fact that this was the best I could do would have been funny if it weren't such a sad statement about how little sexy dressing up I did.

I pushed all the hangers to the right, the way you do when you go to a department store and see a rack of sale clothes, not wanting to miss anything. Taking inventory at the same time, I went through a dozen white, light blue, bone and black tailored silk shirts—the staples that I wore almost every day with gabardine, linen or wool slacks in black, gray or khaki. No emerald shantung bustiers, no cobalt-blue dresses with plunging necklines. No golden silk blouses that were almost see-through.

No symbolic clothes of seduction were hanging in my closet.

Every day for the last thirteen years I'd faced women who were unhappy and frustrated by not measuring up. I had seen what the pressures of being attractive, of being sexy, had done.

There was no way we could compete with what we saw every time we opened a magazine, turned on a television or watched a movie. The media instructed us—albeit subliminally—that other people were better-looking, more successful, having more sex, better sex, were happier about their sexual selves and had figured it all out.

We were inadequate no matter how much we accomplished or how happy we might be with ourselves or our mates. In the world of more and more, it was all too common to feel less than enough.

And now, I had to dress the part of a woman who bought into those superficial values.

Disgusted, I looked through the rest of my clothes finally finding an Armani jacket that I'd once gotten on sale that was short and only offered two buttons. With one of my safe shirts it was not a daring piece of clothing. But when I put it on over the black lace bra that I'd bought at the lingerie store, it was perfect. The odd combination of classic design that seemed to say one thing, juxtaposed with too much skin would work.

I undressed, packed up my costume, got dressed again in my typical work clothes, grabbed my briefcase and left for the office.

As I walked downtown, I thought about the Healer, the one man I had described to Gil whom he hadn't been able to identify. The man who Cleo said had a fixation on saving women and who had treated her so differently than all the others. And I thought about the odd coincidence that two of the most telling things about him were shared by Midas and Judas.

The Healer had a money clip that I had seen Judas pull out of his wallet.

And like Midas, the Healer only drank champagne. And only Cristal.

What did that mean? That the Healer wasn't real? Or that Cleo was so concerned about anyone recognizing him, she had completely disguised him by giving him other people's attributes and accoutrements.

At noon Nina stopped by my office. "You up for a walk?" she asked.

It seemed as if it had been weeks since we'd taken a walk at lunch. The argument we'd had over Cleo and me helping the police was still hanging between us. I hated the coolness.

Having her angry with me was very difficult to tolerate. I'd worked on this in therapy, but it was still an issue. Without a mother for so long, and so needy for maternal attention, I had never rebelled as a teenager, instead always trying to be a good girl, at least in Nina's eyes. Considering who she was, that had nothing to do with sex, drugs or rock and roll, and everything to do with facing adversity head-on, being honest about my emotions and trying to come clean when she asked a question, no matter how tough it was.

I nodded.

"Good. I need to stretch my legs and we need to catch up."

A month ago I would have welcomed the company. Now the last thing I wanted was to have her ask me anything. Anything at all. I was breaking about a hundred rules. Doing things that were just on the line where ethics were concerned.

But wasn't I doing them so that I would not cross that other line? The most important one? The patient-doctor privilege. That was what was sacred. That was what had to be protected.

It was a lovely June day. Seventy degrees with a slight breeze lightly scented with the curious NewYork City smell of car fumes, expensive perfume wafting off of the coiffed and well-dressed women out on their way to lunch, and the flowers blooming in hanging baskets, window boxes and planted in the sidewalk gardens up and down the street

"Madison Avenue, Fifth, or the park?Your pleasure," Nina said.

"The park."

"You always choose the park. I didn't need to ask, did I?"

"No. But you always do ask."

"Why do you think?" she asked.

"Occupational hazard? You get so used to working with patients, taking nothing for granted, knowing if you don't ask you might miss finding out the one fact or the one feeling that could change the whole picture and offer up the missing piece."

We crossed the street and entered Central Park through the zoo. Everywhere were children and mothers. Many of the little ones holding blue, red or yellow balloons that bobbed in the sky, swaying in the breeze. Other kids had messy faces from hot dogs smeared with mustard, or chocolate mustaches from ice-cream cones. I could feel the sticky fingers as I remembered when Dulcie was this age.

"No-o-o-o," a child wailed in agony. He was standing rigidly, staring up at the sky, pointing with one small finger. Tears streamed down his face. "No-o-o-o-o."

A bright blue balloon sailed upward, its white string trailing behind as it ascended past the tree line and then higher and higher toward the clouds.

How many balloons floated up from this part of the park every day?

"Kelsey, don't cry, we can get another balloon. Come on. Let's go. A red one. Would you like a red one this time?" asked the exasperated mother.

"No-o-o-o-o."

The smell of the zoo, animal and raw, was all around us, assaulting us. Nina's nose twitched and she frowned, but I liked it and breathed in deeply.

Leaving the zoo, we walked deeper into the park, engulfed by the trees that were thick and heavy with leaves. Up ahead a bed of delphiniums swayed in the breeze.

"You used to love balloons. But only green ones. You were so stubborn. Never blue, never red. If they didn't have green, you wouldn't take a balloon."

I laughed.

She continued to reminisce. "You were so stubborn about everything. When your father and I came to get you, you were sitting on the edge of your mother's bed, holding her hand and telling her a story. She was deep into her drugged sleep, but you were still trying to reach her. And when we tried to take you away from her, you didn't cry, or scream, or argue. You simply refused to move. You just held on to her hand and kept talking to her. Trying to save her with your story."

I felt an old surge of loss come up and overtake me, the same way that a sudden spray of perfume could overwhelm your senses. And for an instant I could still smell my mother's perfume— roses and lemon and lavender—a scent memory. The only real memories I had of my mother. I knew her face from photographs, and there were fragments of images and words, but they were never whole. A smile, her blue eyes glassy and unfocused. The mess of the apartment on Avenue A. The kitchen sink that always had dirty dishes piled in it. Her lovely hand with long fingernails painted pink, trembling as she reached for the amber pill bottle. The feeling of her thin arms around my back. The whisper of her voice, *My little lost girl.*

I remembered the crystal bottle of perfume that sat on her dresser, still half-full, and the way she so carefully tipped it over every morning and wet her fingers with just enough to dab behind her earlobes and mine. It was her last vanity. No matter how broke we were, or how pathetic the meals she managed to make for us were, the one thing that she never gave up was her French perfume.

The only thing I wanted to talk about less than what I was doing to help find Cleo was the year I was eight when everything changed and I lost my bearings.

"Morgan, do you know why finding Cleo matters so much to you?"

"Because she is my patient. Because I was helping her. But I didn't help her enough. Because I failed. Because I can't fail."

"Haven't you ever failed with another patient?" Nina's voice was a curious cross between doctor and mother. Probing but warm. Inquisitive but caring.

"You know that I have."

"So why this one? Why are you going up against what you know is ethically questionable?"

"Because if I don't, no one else will."

"But you are becoming obsessed with this."

"Listen. There is a woman who confided in me. Only in me. And so I am the only one who has what might be the clues to her disappearance. How on earth am I supposed to turn my back on her?"

"You need to be needed too much, Morgan."

I stopped. She took two more steps until she realized that I wasn't still by her side, and then she stopped, too, and turned around, smiling.

"You once did that to me, at Rockefeller Center when we went to see the lighting of the Christmas tree. You were what, thirteen? We got separated. Do you remember?"

"You do that, you know, play unfair. Play mother one minute, supervisor the next, family member, colleague, confidante. I'm not the only one who breaks the rules."

"I just use all the tools at hand. And they still aren't getting me anywhere, are they? You are still a stubborn rod of steel that I cannot bend."

"Oh, I bend. Just not over everything."

"Morgan, what are you doing?"

"Why do you think I am doing anything?"

"I know you. Whatever it is, I want you to stop."

"I can't, Nina. If I do that, if I give up, then..."

A trio of ten- or eleven-year-old girls ran by, screaming out to one another, laughing and shouting. The noise was too loud to talk over, but as soon as they had passed, Nina interrupted what I had been saying.

"Just stop. Get out of whatever you are in the middle of and let the police do their own job of trying to find her."

Smiling, I took her arm. "Yeah. Walk away from a patient. You didn't teach me to do that. You know you didn't. So in a way, you could say this is really all your fault."

She moaned. I laughed.

"Oh, Morgan, only you can turn this around to make it all my fault."

"I'm not making it all your fault. It *is* all your fault."

And then she sobered. "What you are doing is insanely dangerous."

"Helping Detective Jordain?"

"Meeting Cleo's clients."

"I didn't tell you I was doing that."

"You told me you were thinking about it. And since you were a kid that has been code. You always had an oh-so-clever way of telling your father or me something that you wanted us to know without actually telling us."

What she didn't say, what we both knew she was referring to, was the phone call I had finally made to my father when I was eight years old and watching my mother disappear in front of me.

"Daddy, maybe one day you could come over. Not today. But when Mommy is feeling better. But not yet. She'd be mad if I asked you to come."

He hadn't listened to me. Or rather he had listened to what I wasn't saying and he had come. But he had been too late.

39

That night at the bar was disappointing. The third man I met with seemed incapable of having anything to do with Cleo's disappearance because he had Parkinson's disease and walked with the help of two canes. I couldn't imagine he'd have the strength to hurt anyone. But what was on my mind the next day was that a certain thing particular to him was again part of Cleo's description of the fifth man: the Healer.

This last client had a scar on his right cheek—another of those details that she attributed to the Healer in the memoir. It was a small, inconsequential thing alone, but along with the money clip and the taste for Cristal, the deception was curious.

Why had she only mixed up the details when she was writing about the Healer? Was it a writerly technique she had been playing with and hadn't gotten around to fixing? Was she just trying harder to protect his identity? Or was it more complicated than that? Why describe the others, but not this client?

During my eleven o'clock session, Elias called. The machine

answered and he left a message asking me to call back. When I did, only twenty minutes later, he sounded frantic and desperate.

"Can you meet me?" he asked.

"If you want to come to the office I have an opening in a half hour."

"That's tight. I have a meeting. Do you have anything later?"

I told him I could meet him at two-forty-five at the Starbucks near my office on Lexington Avenue.

He was already there when I walked in. I had an hour before an appointment farther downtown with an antique dealer who was helping me find a special birthday present for Dulcie.

I watched him as I approached his table. The circle of people who cared about Cleo were all walking wounded. And Elias was at our center. He looked haggard and exhausted. Eyes that were huge pools of sadness, fingernails bitten down to the quick, and furrows in his forehead that seemed to be deeper and more pronounced than even a few days ago.

"If I don't do something to help find her soon, if I can't get more involved somehow, I'm going to go crazy," he said.

I knew how hard it was to be forced to sit back and feel helpless when someone you loved was in trouble.

I went to get some coffee, and when I came back he was playing with a half a dozen sugar packets that he was fashioning into patterns on the table.

As I sat down, I smelled something recognizable coming from him. It was familiar, but I didn't know why. A cologne that someone I knew had worn? A popular spice? I tried to sniff the air without attracting his attention.

It was something else. A heavy scent. Not a cologne at all. Not a woman's perfume, either. Not a usual scent, but I'd smelled it before. Frowning, I concentrated and tried to place it. But I couldn't.

"Dr. Snow?"

It was Belinda from my office standing next to my chair, and I smiled at her. She looked from me to Elias. He froze.

"Hi," I said.

"You coming back to the office?" she asked.

"No. I'll see you tomorrow."

She waved, held tight to her iced latte and walked off.

Once she was gone, Elias seemed to be able to breathe again and launched into more theories about Cleo and where she might be and what the police needed to do to find her. All the while he kept arranging and rearranging the sugar packets in random patterns.

"Will you talk to them? Will you tell them some of my ideas? Maybe if they came from you, the detectives would pay some attention."

I nodded. "How are you doing?" I asked him.

"How could I be doing? I look at her things. At her robe hanging on the back of the door. At her makeup in the medicine cabinet. At her toothpaste. At the tea bags she bought that are in my kitchen cabinet. I can't stop feeling like she's looking over my shoulder. Whispering to me: come and get me, please. Just come and find me. But what am I supposed to do?"

"Are you going to work every day?" I asked him.

"Yes. But I'm distracted."

"Are you sleeping at all?"

"A few hours. From midnight to about four."

I nodded again. "That's about the time that anxiety wakes us up. I think you should see a psychiatrist and get some medications. An antianxiety pill, or an antidepressant."

"This isn't some problem I have because my mother dragged me to church too many times every week. This is because the woman I am engaged to, the woman who I want to marry, is missing, and the only people who can really help not only won't do anything, but are sure that if anyone is involved, it's me."

My cell phone rang. I picked it up and looked at it. "It's my office," I said to Elias. "Just one second."

It was Belinda. "Hi. Your daughter just called. She only had two minutes and called here first. She said she didn't have more time to call you on your cell, but she asked to tell you that she has to cancel meeting you later at the museum. She said the rehearsal won't be done in time."

"Damn."

"At least she calls," Belinda said. "Mine never even bothers."

I laughed. Elias looked at me as though making that kind of noise was blasphemy.

"Morgan, that man you're with, you know he's one of Simon's clients?" she said on the other end of the phone.

I tried not to glance at Elias, not wanting to alert him that we were talking about him.

"As a patient?"

"Yes. A while ago. Maybe a month. Two months. I recognized him when I saw you with him. I thought it was weird, that someone would see two therapists."

"Okay. Thanks, Belinda. I'll see you tomorrow."

I hung up.

Across the table, Elias was staring off into space, a frown creasing his forehead.

I was suddenly unsure of what was going on. Why hadn't he told me? I felt a shiver of fear. Why had he not mentioned this just now when I'd suggested he see someone?

"Elias? Have you already been to see Simon Weiss? My associate?"

He nodded.

"When?"

"About five weeks ago. Maybe six weeks ago. Why?"

"When I asked you a minute ago if you wanted me to suggest someone so you could get some meds, why didn't you tell me that you'd already seen someone? You've been up to our offices?"

His expression hardened. "Not you, too? I recognize the look, the suspicion. Christ. You all look so deep beneath the surface, you miss the surface itself. Yes, I saw him and he told me that he didn't think he could help me. I didn't bring it up with you because I didn't want to say anything negative about one of your co-workers. Besides, none of it has anything to do with finding Cleo. But since you are asking, I'd be more than happy to tell you. I went to him to talk about Cleo's problems. I thought I should know about them from a professional point of view. To see if there was anything that I could do on my end to help. You don't understand what it is like to love someone with all your heart and not be able to help her. No, worse. To be part of her problem. To cause her pain because of your very existence."

"What happened with Simon?" The suspicion I'd felt was dissipating. Elias was so earnest about his pain, his guilt in not being able to help his lover out, that I was only feeling empathy. I did know what it was like to love someone who couldn't love me back the way that would have kept us together.

"He told me that it would be better if I saw a therapist with Cleo. And, as you know, I was open to that. In fact it was something Cleo and I had discussed and were planning to do...with you...but before..."

He broke off. And that pained look returned to his eyes. "She has to be out there. And someone has to find her. Please. There must be something I can do to get the police to look for her. To get them to take her disappearance seriously. What if I had a note from a kidnapper?"

"Do you?"

"Would that make them take Cleo's disappearance more seriously?"

"Of course, and if you have something like that you need to tell them about it."

A sudden excitement flashed in his eyes.

"Don't," I warned.

"Don't what?"

"Try to fake it. It will only get you in serious trouble if they find out. It's a felony. You'll be arrested."

"I don't care. Not if it helps them find her. Not if it makes them start looking for her."

40

Even though I had a month till Dulcie's birthday, I didn't like waiting till the last minute. Each year I gave her a music box. The search, at least for me, was half of the joy of giving the gift, as was the collection that graced her room.

So far there were twelve—all but two were antiques—and since she had been tiny, I'd trusted her to play with them. I hadn't been wrong; she'd never broken one of the fabulous mechanical devices.

I got in a taxi and gave the driver an address on West Broadway near Spring Street. The antique dealer was on the second floor of a building that mostly housed art galleries. I'd first met Victor Messing at the large antique show at the Armory a few years before when I noticed that he had four music boxes on display.

As the cab made its way downtown I called Simon and asked him about seeing Elias Beecher.

"I only saw him once," Simon offered.

"What did you think?"

"Let me read my notes here. I don't remember much about the

consultation..." He was quiet on the other end of the phone. I heard him rustle through some papers.

"He was having problems with the woman he was seeing. A patient of yours. Right?"

"Right. He didn't tell you her name?"

"No."

"Cleo Thane."

"Holy shit."

"Anything about that session strike you as odd, Simon?"

"No. He seemed genuinely concerned about her. I suggested they see a couples' therapist together. He was amenable to that and said that he was planning to."

I filled Simon in on my conversation with Elias, finishing up as the cab pulled in front of Messing's building. I paid the driver, headed through the lobby, then entered a waiting elevator.

It opened on the second floor inside a wonderland of antiques: an overcrowded hodge-podge of rugs piled one on top of the other, chairs sitting on chairs, smaller tables on top of larger tables. The air inside the dealer's den was musty and aged, unlike the air in the hallway just on the other side of the door.

Cinnamon, cardamom and Eastern oils perfumed the atmosphere.

Victor was a Frenchman whose store was only open seven months a year, because he traveled the rest of the time finding his treasures.

He smiled when he saw me come in and greeted me with a kiss on both cheeks, European style.

"Sit down, please, Morgan, sit. Let me go make us tea. You have time?"

I nodded. It was a relief to get away from patients and problems, from trying to solve Cleo's disappearance and Elias's morose pressure. When I had been with him, it was as though I'd felt his fingers gripping me and holding me in place, even though he'd never touched me. His eyes had pinned me to the spot, so that I was incapable of getting up, of walking away.

While Victor made the tea, my eyes wandered over the treasures and landed on an umbrella stand filled with elaborate and fanciful umbrellas. A French parasol with an ivory handle. Another with what looked like a solid-gold filigree-and-ruby handle. And then a simple, elegant black umbrella with a polished silver handle. Something about it was familiar, but I couldn't figure out why. I touched its smooth cool surface. I shut my eyes. And then I remembered. After one of Cleo's appointments, I'd watched her leave my office and had seen a man across the street with an umbrella very much like this. He'd followed her. How could I have forgotten this? It might be relevant. I'd have to call Noah and tell him. I tried to remember something else about the man. But it had been weeks ago. And I'd only seen him for ten or twenty seconds. A man in the street wearing a dark suit, with his back to me. There was nothing else to remember about him.

"I have so many things to show you," Victor said as he returned and put two steaming cups of strong green tea on the table. I sat back down. The aroma, mixed with the exotic smells of the store, made me feel as if I'd been transported to a bazaar.

"So many things? More than just the music box?"

"*Deux.* Two music boxes. And a piece of jewelry. What first?" he asked as the flecks of yellow in his brown eyes flashed. He enjoyed his business so much, and for a moment I envied him. Where was the tragedy to what he did? If he lost an antique at auction, or didn't make a sale, it was bad for business. But someone did not wind up in danger. No one's life was affected in a serious way by whether or not he did his job well. He was not responsible for someone who did not get a grasp on reality and threw themselves out of a window—still hoping their arms would turn to wings.

The first music box he showed me was made of mahogany and played "Lara's Theme" from Dr. Zhivago. The tone was lovely. But what was so exceptional was what happened when you opened the lid. Inside was an ice palace made out of crystal that rose up from a frozen pond of mirror. And inside, deep within the glass structure, were a woman and a man. In long robes. Fur against the cold of Russia's winter.

"It's a gem," I said.

He nodded. "I thought you would like it. Which makes the next one even harder to show you."

Victor put an object on the table that gleamed in the light. It was birthday-girl pink, snow-white and gold. A fancy, ornate Easter egg of cloisonné enamel. The egg was about twice the size of a real one and sat on a gold filigree pedestal. All reminiscent of Fabergé. But, I assumed, nowhere near the price. Victor knew my budget.

"Open it, the key to the music is inside."

Inside was a small white rabbit made of ivory, carved in exquisite detail and sitting atop a bronze key. I lifted it and placed it in the middle of a cabbage patch, where one bronze carrot was suspiciously shaped to suggest the key belonged there.

I wound the egg and the thin but lovely music tinkled in the air. It was from *Peter and the Wolf.* Altogether funny and beautiful.

"So, they are lovely, *mais non?*"

"They are lovely. Hard choice."

He nodded. Smiled. Said nothing and got up to leave me with the two objets d'art. I knew that Dulcie would be enchanted by either. By both. But I couldn't buy both.

"To take your mind off of those, take a look at what I found for you," Victor said, interrupting my reverie as I imagined Dulcie seeing the little ivory rabbit.

He put a suede pouch on a velvet pillow and pushed it in front of me. Opening it, I slid out a silver object and looked down at it. In my hand lay a butterfly, perfectly proportioned, expertly crafted, with vibrant fire-opal stones set in its wings. Four stones—the two larger ones in each wing on top; two smaller ones in each wing on the bottom.

The way the insect lay, it looked as if it might fly off any second, its wings trembling, that iridescent blue-purple-green color shimmering as it flew around the room.

I was afraid to ask the price. It wasn't even something that should cost money. It belonged in the Museum of Natural History alongside the specimens of butterflies preserved for as long as the museum was standing.

My cell phone rang but I didn't want to answer it, not then. I just wanted to sit and look at the butterfly while the music boxes continued playing and I breathed in the exotic smells. And after the music ended, I wanted to take the rest of the afternoon off and just walk around SoHo and then have a slow, quiet dinner in an old-fashioned Italian restaurant and maybe go to a movie.

But I couldn't shut out reality.

"Hello?"

"Morgan, it's Noah." My heart skipped one beat and I think I shut my eyes. A phone call from the detective did not always bring the best news.

"Someone else?" I asked.

"Yes. I'm sorry."

"When? Who is it? Do you know?" I held my breath.

"Sometime last night. But it's not Cleo."

"I don't know what I should say. If I tell you I'm glad it belittles whoever died."

"That's okay. I know how you feel."

"Any leads this time?"

"Maybe. But nothing big. And we need something big. We've got everyone working overtime. But I keep thinking there is some psychological aspect of this that we are missing."

Victor was looking at me quizzically. I wasn't sure he approved of me talking when there was still business to attend to.

"Is that a request?"

"Are you free?" Noah asked.

"Yes. Or I will be in half an hour. And I have something to tell you, too. Something I remembered."

"Do want to come to the station?"

I hesitated. Noah didn't let my pause last long.

"Do you want me to meet you at your office?"

"No. Actually, I have the afternoon off." I looked down at the butterfly and touched the opal with my fingertip.

"Well, I've been working for the last twenty-four hours straight and am exhausted. I could use some air. I'll meet you somewhere."

"This is a crazy idea, but can you get to the Museum of Natural History? I was supposed to meet Dulcie there to see a special exhibit but I got stood up for a rehearsal."

"Any excuse to get out of the office even if it's just for a short time." We made plans to meet in the lobby in a half hour.

I snapped the phone shut and started haggling over the price of the egg music box—"Lara's Theme" was haunting. Too haunting for a twelve-year-old.

"Maybe I'll just put the other away for you till next year." Victor's eyes twinkled. "What about the butterfly pin?"

"You'll have to put that away till my next visit, too. It's too expensive."

He took it and pinned it to my lapel and then held up a mirror for me to examine the effect.

I looked at the winged insect, poised as if it had just alighted. And while I was watching, it started to take flight. Falling straight down into my lap, the pin end stuck me through my slacks. The point was sharp and stung.

Victor must not have attached the clasp tight enough.

"I'm so sorry," he said.

I rubbed at the spot with my forefinger. Butterflies didn't sting. At least not usually.

41

I never went to the museum without thinking of tuna fish sandwiches on white bread and orangeade—the lunch the museum provided for us on our grade-school trips. The same lunch that Dulcie would describe after one of her school trips there.

Noah and I sat on a wooden bench outside the glass-enclosed butterfly house—a temperature-controlled environment where hundreds of butterflies were hatched and lived out their three-week lives gorging on plants and flitting around unaware that they were on exhibit.

"We're trying to get a jump on him and figure out where he's headed next. He gave the first woman stigmata, the second communion, the third the crown of thorns. This one was baptized. The M.E. said she'd been soaking in a tub of hot water for hours. And she was drenched in oil. There were five crystal cruets of it, smashed into shards that he used as a bedcovering. She was lying on top of them."

"A bed of glass?"

"Yes." Noah looked exhausted and his voice was hoarse. The stress of the case was obviously wearing on him.

"What is he doing?" I asked, not expecting any answer and not getting one right away.

Through the glass, I watched a monarch land on an orchid and sit there, still and folded up, just waiting.

"He is punishing them for something. For failing him somehow," he said.

"Maybe…"

"What do you think he's doing?"

"I don't know. But I think it's more complicated than that. He's trying out all these different methods. He's working on some-thing."

"What?"

I shook my head. I didn't know. I wished I did. But I couldn't even make an educated guess. "Want to go in?" I nodded toward the exhibit.

The glass-enclosed gallery was hot and humid and smelled strongly of earth. The thirty-foot-long conservatory was designed to resemble a tropical jungle with hundreds of palms, orchids, ferns and other plants and trees—the ideal environment for but-terflies.

Something flew by me and landed on a frond. Electric-green wings, orange shapes outlined in black. Powdery mosaics of col-ors.

By staring at the creature, we were also facing the glass wall and our reflections looked back at us.

Noah was much taller than me, and I was surprised to see that, instead of looking at the butterflies, he was looking at me. Turn-ing, I faced him. The shadows under his eyes made him look sad. And the haunted look in his eyes was impossible to ignore.

I was more comfortable with him now that he was in pain than I had been before. I could help him now if he wanted me to. I knew how to do that. I was at home in that role. The therapist who gave but didn't ever ask for anything back.

"This one is getting to you bad, isn't it?" I asked.

He nodded.

"Want to talk about it?"

"No. Not one bit. But I probably should."

Except he didn't. We stood there for a few more seconds, he looking down at me, me looking up at him. And then I reached out and touched his hand. I didn't know I was going to do it and it surprised me that I did. It wasn't my style to reach out to people.

Almost as soon as I touched his hand, he took mine and held it as if he had been expecting my move. It was an awkward moment—not for him, but for me—and I wasn't sure what to do. Hell, I couldn't even figure out what I wanted to do. Before I could think about it, still holding my hand, he pulled me forward, deeper into the tiny tangle of vegetation. As he walked, he told me what had happened. "It was about eight years ago. In New Orleans. We didn't get to her in time."

"Was she a prostitute, too?"

He nodded. "She had been helping us finger a drug pusher. And it was the last thing she was going to do. She had saved enough money to finally get off the street and had gotten a job. And then we screwed up. When we found her, she'd been sliced up."

I could feel the shiver in his hand and I just held on. "Did you get help?"

"You mean therapy?"

"Yes."

"For a few weeks. I'm not one of those guys who is too proud to get help. But..." He shrugged. "It wasn't a psychological problem. We'd fucked up and a sweet, funny, determined girl got killed. Therapy can't solve crimes. It can't resurrect the dead."

Inside a four-foot-square Plexiglas box there were four-dozen cocoons hanging off four rows of plastic tubing. An artificial tree of sorts where the pupae incubated. One was opening as I watched. Through the cracked caramel-colored papery outer casing a pair of orange wings were just visible and about to break free. From this mud-colored pod to a vibrant flying creature.

I extricated my hand from Noah's. "Maybe his main goal isn't to kill them," I said, turning the idea over in my mind.

"Keep going."

"You're thinking that his intent is to murder them, that that's his goal. But what if that's just the conclusion of these sessions? What if there is something else going on in that room? Some other kind of ritual?"

Noah was nodding, following me, waiting. "A ritual? Is it sexual?"

"Well, by choosing prostitutes, by definition he is dealing with these women sexually. But that doesn't mean the encounter is motivated by a sexual need."

"So dressing them up as nuns isn't just a fetishized fantasy?"

"It could be, but that's too easy."

"Okay, what's not easy?"

I shook my head. My hands opened by my sides. All that mattered was to help Noah figure this out before anything happened to another woman.

Too often the cliché has been proved. Serial killers speed up. The second killing had been a week after the first. The fourth was only two days after the third.

"How can this guy get in and out of these hotels without someone noticing?" I asked.

"Big hotels. Ordinary-looking guy."

"How does he convince the women to dress up in the nuns' habits? This case has been all over the news. I know the first woman wouldn't have understood what was happening. But these others? Once he pulls out those outfits, why don't they just run?"

"They might not have any choice by the time he gets them dressed. He might have a gun or a knife on them. He might even be dressing them himself after he knocks them unconscious."

"Knocks them unconscious? How?"

He shook his head. "I don't want to get into the details if I don't have to. We're trying to keep some of them secret in case he contacts us."

"I think he is probably smart. Educated. Obviously clever."

Noah nodded. "And fairly successful to be able to afford to leave behind all that cash."

"What kind of money are you talking about?"

"The rooms are about two hundred dollars for a night. And another five to seven hundred dollars in bills that he leaves behind. That's almost one thousand dollars a night."

A yellow-and-black butterfly, similar to one I had in a specimen box in my office, landed on a large pink flower near Noah's shoulder.

It flapped its wings, revealing reds, oranges and yellows. The colors as deep and determined as if they were applied with oil paints.

"He's educated in Catholic liturgy," he added. "He knows mass rituals. And he has access to the supplies."

"And there haven't been any robberies at churches in the last few months...don't even answer. Of course there haven't been. You'd already know that by now. What about the Internet? Can you buy all those things online?"

He nodded and patted his pocket. "I have a printout of the sales receipts for the last two months from the dozen religious-supply houses who do not require churches to have house accounts. I was going over them while I was waiting for you."

"You mean there are church-supply houses that anyone can order from? I can call them up or go online and order chalices and priests' vestments and communion wafers?"

"Well, you can't order the supplies and send them to your apartment in New York, but as long as you give the address of a church, then yes, you could. Anyone could."

"As long as it will be delivered to a parish or convent?" I asked. He nodded.

"So do you think you have a priest on your hands?"

"We are not ruling that out."

I shook my head. "I don't think so. A priest might be furious with hookers for being sinners, for tempting him, for flaunting their sexuality. But I have a hard time imagining a man who is still a priest combining his disgust for the women with disgust for his calling."

"You lost me," he said.

"I hope not."

Noah smiled. That wide easy smile. What had I said? What had he heard? I was embarrassed. I had meant it literally, hadn't I? About his following my reasoning? But there was that damn innuendo, too. And I knew too much about the unconscious mind not to realize it. Except there was no time to stop and think about myself. Not yet, anyway.

"In the process of killing the women he is defiling the sacraments," I said.

"For a nice Jewish girl from New York City, you know a lot about Catholic priests."

He knew more about me than I had told him. I was surprised that I wasn't more surprised.

"I was married to a nice Catholic man."

He nodded. "You're divorced, aren't you?"

A plain brown moth flew by us. This one was bigger than the others but shared nothing of their brilliance except when you looked closely at the designs on its wings, which were intricate. You barely noticed these creatures in the garden. Just cursed them for getting in your house and nibbling on your woolen clothes. But here, they were lovely.

"Yes. He's not much of a Catholic anymore. But he was when I married him."

"How long ago was that?"

"A little more than fourteen years ago."

"What happened?"

I shrugged. "Nothing very dramatic. Usual stuff. Are you married?"

He shook his head. "Almost. We lived together for a while. A long while. She didn't want to move to New York."

I arched my eyebrows. "That isn't much of a reason to leave someone you love."

"No. That was the excuse. The truth was she couldn't take the police work. She tried. But she got swallowed up by the darkness I'd bring home with me every night and I was too tired to figure out how to do anything about it."

I wanted to tell him how similar that was to what had happened with me and Mitch, but I didn't know how to say it in a way that wouldn't sound like I was just trying to find a common ground between us. So, in true therapist fashion, I remained silent.

He focused on my eyes for a long moment and I felt it, deep inside of me.

42

We walked out into the sunshine and stood on the wide stone steps of the museum, both of us blinking and readjusting to the noise and the light. At the bottom of the staircase, where we should have broken off and gone our separate ways, Noah took my arm in an old-fashioned gesture and we walked toward the street.

"Come with me. Coffee, a drink, something. We're up against nothing but dead ends and I need more of your fresh thinking. If we don't get a break in this case…" He didn't finish his thought. He didn't have to.

I nodded. My concentration was on my arm, where he was holding me. How was I supposed to know what kind of touch this was? Swinging between the tired embraces of my now ex and the few wildly overt connections with the men I'd met in the Diablo Cigar Bar, I just didn't know how to judge this, and that left me feeling amazingly young and stupid.

"Why are you smiling like that?" he asked.

"I didn't know I was." Now I really felt foolish.

"Well, you are."

"I'm just not walking on a street that I know. And that's an un-usual feeling for someone who has been walking these streets her whole life."

"I hope you aren't identifying a little too closely to this case."

I had to stop and think for a minute and then, realizing the un-intentional pun, laughed. "That is in terribly bad taste."

"I know. I'm overtired. I'm angry. I'm punch-drunk."

We reached the destination that Noah had picked out and went inside.

Café des Artistes is a well-known landmark in New York. A lovely restaurant graced with a mural of luscious nude women from the early 1900s.

"You know, I've never been here, either," I offered as we walked to a table in the bar area. It was just five o'clock and the crowds hadn't arrived yet.

"You've lived here your whole life and I'm showing you new sights?"

I nodded.

As soon as we sat down, Noah got up. "I'm sorry, I need to call in. If everyone is running around the same maze, and there's no reason for me to go back, I can have a real drink instead of cof-fee. Order what you'd like. I'll be right back."

I couldn't read his face when he returned five minutes later.

"So is it the hard stuff or the soft?" I asked him.

"The hard stuff. They think they have a lead on the nuns' habits, and the guys working the videotape think they have a match on a man seen at two of the hotels. Blurry, a shot from the side. But it's something. Everyone knows what to do and no one needs me looking over his shoulder. I told Perez to get out of there, too. We've both been working eighteen-hour days all week. Neither of us will be any good tomorrow if we just sit there another night, searching for a ghost on our com-puters."

The waiter arrived and I ordered a dirty martini. Noah said he'd have the same thing, then sat back in his chair and almost relaxed.

It was his fingers that stayed alert, at the ready. For what, I wondered?

"So you are a girl after my own heart," he said, his New Orleans accent making *heart* sound longer and musical. I liked listening to him, experienced an odd sensation of his words reaching out and touching my skin, as if he was stroking me with those drawn-out syllables.

Who was I here?

In session with a patient, I was probing and fearless, but flirting was virgin territory for me.

The drinks came and Noah raised his elegant martini glass to mine in a silent toast. The liquid was icy and sharp and just a little salty.

I told him about the umbrella and the man on the street, and he asked me a few questions to see if he could spark any other memory from me about what the man looked like or how he acted. But I didn't remember anything else that was helpful. "At the time it occurred to me that he might be following her…the way a moth will fly to a flame. Just because he was so attracted to her. Every man she passed on the street watched her."

Noah took another sip of his drink, just listening.

"Have you found out anything about the pink-diamond cross?" I asked him.

"Yes, we have." He pulled a notebook from his pocket and opened it to a page crammed with his loopy handwriting. He scanned one page, then another. "Perez just gave me this on the phone. We've identified two stores in the city that sell something like what you described. Graff—a place on Madison Avenue—and Cartier."

I nodded, aware of them both. Two of the most exclusive jewelry stores in the city.

"And you were right. It is extravagantly expensive. More than $30,000 if it's the same one you described. Sounds like it. Seven carats, total weight. Only five have been sold. By tomorrow morning we should have a court order to find out who purchased them."

"How long will it take once you have that?"

"If we are lucky, sometime tomorrow. By Monday at the latest. The minute we find out, I'll tell you. Do you know that much about Cleo's life that you'll recognize the name?"

"There's a good chance I will."

He looked surprised.

I took another sip of my drink and made a decision. "I need to confess something," I said.

"I'm not a priest."

"Thank God."

We both laughed, the laughs still slightly hollow and weak but deeper than how we'd laughed a half hour before.

"I've met some of Cleo's clients," I told him.

"You have?" All the relaxation in his face was gone. His eyes were focused on me and probing. He was thinking, working on a puzzle. I could see the pieces fitting together in his eyes. Did I know him that well already?

"Is that what you have been doing at the Diablo Cigar Bar?" he asked.

I nodded.

"Are you crazy? Who do you think you are that you should be doing that? You're not equipped to go undercover." A vein pulsed in his neck, his eyes narrowed with a ferocious anger.

"No one else is taking her disappearance seriously. I have to do it myself," I said accusatorily.

"There is no evidence of foul play, Morgan. For Christ's sake. We have a tap on her cell phone. We are watching her place. We can't look for someone when we have no reason to go looking for her."

"You can when she is a prostitute and prostitutes are getting murdered every other day."

"That is a very slim connection. She isn't the kind he targets."

"But she is missing, Noah. And she is my patient. And since I can't tell you who her clients are, or what their motives are, I'm doing the only thing I can do. In lieu of a formal investigation, I am conducting an informal one. I know enough as a therapist to know what I am looking for."

"Damn. You might be smart. You might be ten times smarter than me. But you are not a member of the police department. You can't just stage your own investigation. You could get hurt. Damn. Worse. You could get killed."

I waved off his words and took another sip of my drink. "I am well protected. I only meet them in public...well in a private public place but with lots of other people around. I know some self-defense. I learned when I was a teenager. It was something I needed. An extra sense of protection."

"Weren't you protected as a kid?" His eyes softened for a moment.

"My mother..." I hesitated. We were stepping into the quicksand of my past and I didn't often bring anyone to that place with me.

I stopped. It didn't make sense to be sitting in a restaurant on a Friday evening, sipping a martini, alternately worried sick about my patient and talking about my personal life with a man who was hunting down a crazy sicko whose actions may or may not have any bearing on why someone I cared about was missing. But his eyes pulled me in. Again.

Some people just have perfectly nice eyes, lovely colors, aesthetically pleasing shapes, but they don't express all that much. Not so with Noah. His eyes talked. No matter what he was saying with his words, his blue eyes spelled out other things.

I had thought his eyes were too small when I first met him. But now that I knew him better, now that I had looked at him long enough and experienced the intensity of his gaze, I was glad they were not any bigger. It would have been like looking into glaring headlights. His eyes would have blinded me.

"Tell me about your mother," he said softly.

"She was an actress. And she started working when she was young. She also got addicted to diet pills when she was young. When she broke her collarbone on a set, she got addicted to painkillers. Somewhere in there she found liquor, too. Painkillers, diet pills and alcohol. She was one of the Lost Girls."

"Too many of them out there."

I smiled. "I meant it literally. She was one of the two actresses in a TV series called *The Lost Girls*. Three seasons back in the fifties. But you were right, too. She was lost and I was lost with her for a while. When I was seven she left my dad and took me with her. A year later she overdosed and lapsed into a coma. I didn't know that's what it was, but I knew she was in danger. So I called my father and then I talked to her and told her our stories until he came. But she didn't wake up. And I never saw her again. She died. When I was eight. Did I say that?"

He nodded. Then he did more. He leaned over and put his big hands on either side of my face and pulled me in to him. I held my breath but I didn't shut my eyes. Frozen, I watched his face get closer and closer and then I felt his lips on top of mine. At first it felt like a whisper of a kiss, just gentle enough to be there, to connect me to him. I think that was all it was intended to be. Just a comforting kiss: light and fleeting, as if one of those butterflies we'd seen had brushed me with its wings.

"Poor baby," he said. There was nothing condescending about it. It was Southern and slow and like another kind of kiss. I was smelling him, discerning all the different scents at once: a green scent that was woodsy and musky with undernotes of leather and beneath all that, the salty scent of his skin.

It bypassed my head and went right to my senses, stirring me. There was not a single note that assaulted me or insulted me. I closed my eyes and saw sunlight filtering through tall pine trees and dust motes dancing on the air. He smelled the way a bolt of maroon-velvet fabric falls when you let it loose to show off the nap; he smelled the way the horizon disappears at night and you don't know where the water ends and the sky starts; and he smelled the way a fire sparks up from the first embers, slow and then violent.

He smelled like something I had been waiting for.

"You are sniffing me." He pulled back from the kiss, laughing for real for the first time all afternoon. Almost as if the case and my confession and all the awful things that were sitting on his shoulders and weighing him down had lifted. And his laugh lifted something in me that I had not even known was so heavy.

"Well, you smell good," I said.

"You smell too much."

"It's this sensitivity I have."

"I'd bet there isn't anything about you that isn't sensitive."

There was a glimmer, playful and sexy, in his eyes.

Then he came at me again, and we both dove down into another kiss.

When we pulled apart he grabbed the check. "I have a date. Every Friday night. Do you want to come?" he asked as he put some bills down on the table.

My eyebrows went up. "I've never gotten an invitation quite like that." I was trying to keep it light but I was confused.

"Don't look at me that way. You are the most transparent woman I have ever met. You'll love her."

"Me, transparent? You have got that wrong. I studied opaque. I learned from the masters. My patients complain that they can't figure out a single thing that I am thinking. And that is important to me, I work for it."

"But I am not, thank the good Lord above, your patient. You couldn't go on a date with me if I was. You certainly couldn't go home with me afterward if I was a patient. And then you'd miss out on chicory coffee and homemade beignets. Have you ever had a homemade beignet?"

I shook my head. We walked out the door onto the crowded street.

"Covered with powdered sugar. And I'll serve it to you on a silver tray—damn I don't have a silver tray—well, I'll serve it to you on a bamboo tray and the powdered sugar will get all over you here—"

He reached out and brushed his fingers over my lips. I shivered.

"And I'll just have to kiss it off...and then lick my lips."

He bent down and kissed me once more. We stood there on Central Park West with the traffic going by and the lights changing and people passing us by and I kissed him back.

* * *

The date was with a piano, in a restaurant in the Village. I sat at a table for two and listened to him play and stared at his fingers making love to the keys and imagined how they would feel if they ever played me.

His music was like his voice. Jazzy, full of riffs, slow and sexy and then dark and sad. And if there had been any question before of whether or not I was going to go home with him afterward, if he still invited me, it was answered while I watched him at the piano.

The combination of his sensitivity to the music, to me, the cool glance he gave most of the world around him and the hot one he bestowed on me, the insouciant, almost arrogant walk, the certainty that he knew how to do his job, but his curiosity about what he didn't understand, the hard-edged, piano-playing detective who carried a weapon and liked to cook Cajun food was about as complicated as they came. That scared me. And I wasn't sure I'd ever been afraid of a man before.

43

He was coming. She could hear the footsteps. She knew that there would be thirteen steps and then he would be on the other side of the window and that with him would come light.

What was worse? When he came to her or when he left her alone for hours in this darkness. She did not know how many hours passed, but she had tried to count the minutes before her mind would drift off into a horror fantasy about what was going to happen to her.

She knew something was eventually going to happen. He would not keep her here indefinitely. He couldn't. Someone had to be looking for her. There were people who cared about her. She knew that, too. She counted them. She said their names over and over in her head in the hours that he left her inside this confessional. She would have prayed to them to come and get her, to find her, but she didn't believe in prayer. There was no way that any God would let her be locked up like this inside a holy place all day for so many days. How many? More than a week. More than two weeks, she thought. But like the minutes, she had lost track of the days.

She heard the door open.

"I'm back, back for you, back to help you," he said. His voice was smooth, calm, soothing. Not to her, but in the abstract, she knew it was a soothing voice.

Was it better when he was away or when he came back?

She was confused. She had been there so long she didn't know what she was supposed to think anymore. The things she craved were different than they had been ten days ago. Or was it eleven? She wasn't sure.

Now she wanted ice water. Not the lukewarm water he left for her on the floor with the tall straw sticking out of it. He left two glasses every morning. One of water. One of some thick drink that he told her was full of nutrients. But she didn't want liquids when he was gone because they would only make her go to the bathroom, and of all the terrible things about being in this terrible box, she could not stand the thought of soiling herself. He seemed almost disappointed when he came to see her in the middle of the day—around one o'clock she had guessed—and brought her the makeshift toilet and found that she had held her water.

She was too fastidious to do anything but starve herself during the day so that she would not have to go to the bathroom. At night she drank as much as he would give her and ate every bit of the solid food he offered. There was no problem eating at night. She knew that she would be able to go to the bathroom in the morning before he left—a real bathroom. He took her to the small white-tiled room with her eyes blindfolded, hands bound, but once she was there he unbound her hands, removed her blindfold and let her have the bathroom to herself for fifteen minutes.

During those hours while he was gone and she sat on the bench or stood against the wall and stared at the wire-mesh window that she could not see beyond, she craved peaches. Or sweet strawberries. She knew it was summer; she could imagine the fruit in the store, in the little wooden baskets, jewel-toned ruby raspberries. And she wanted ice. Cubes of ice, to suck on, to keep her lips wet, because they were parched. In the small, darkened closetlike space that was not made for a human being to live in, she tried to keep herself sane by picturing the manuscript pages of her book and rewriting them in her mind. To work on the words. But it was hard to concentrate. The cravings took over and obsessed her. What did sweet summer air actually smell like? Or how did a breeze feel?

The door opened and he came inside. The light was so strong it blinded her. He took the tape off her mouth. Her lips were torn by now and dry and when she moved them, the pain was excruciating.

And then he was gone again, shutting the door behind him. She heard the sound of wood scraping wood and knew he was pulling the chair up to the door. He would now sit down on the other side of the mesh. Ready to listen to her sins. Ready to absolve her. And to torture her more.

"Have you thought about your sins?" he asked.

"I have." She knew the drill by now, and it was far easier to go along with it than to try to be logical or outwit him or even make an attempt to figure out what was going on. She didn't know. He was waiting for her to say something specific. But what? She might be able to figure it out if she wasn't so confused.

"Tell me your sins," he said.

She was Catholic and had grown up confessing. But that had been simple. She and her girlfriends used to get together right after confession and they would compare what they had offered up, what they had held back, and what the priest had demanded of them in terms of penance. Usually Cleo got off the lightest. Not because she had done the least, but because she had lied the most. And she could lie now.

"I fornicated outside the sanctity of marriage."

"And are you truly sorry for that?"

"Yes."

"Why is that, my child?"

"Because I debased the sexual act."

"And why is that?"

"Because the act of sex is reserved for marriage. And it has a purpose. The procreation of children."

"Have you committed other sins?"

"Yes, Father."

"Tell me."

"I use birth control. I take money for having sex. I sleep with other women's husbands."

"How do you feel about these things?"

"I feel guilty. I am being punished. I know this is my punishment."

She was an actress here. The way she was at work, when she did the things her johns required of her and paid her so well for. She was gone, then. The person she was had absented herself from her body. Stepped away. Stood on the sidelines. And some other woman took her place and entered her body and her mind. This other woman, this actress, who had been born thirteen years before when Cleo was fourteen, who had come into being to protect Cleo from her stepfather, had no fear. She just lied.

She lied about how good-looking men were. About how good they smelled. About how well built they were, how smart they were, how funny they were, what good, wonderful, great lovers they were, how well endowed they were, how big and thick they were and how fucking fabulous it felt when they entered her. The actress, she thought, who did not have a name because she had never stepped forward and claimed one of her own, was here with her now and was saving her.

She was pushing forward, and Cleo was slipping backward. Soon she would be gone from this wooden cell that smelled of rich church incense and cedar. And when he left again, the actress would retreat, give Cleo space, let her breathe, and she wouldn't have to remember any of what had happened tonight. The actress would shoulder that burden.

The actress was talking now. Speaking through Cleo's mouth. Words that Cleo did not even understand.

"These are your sins and this will be your penance," he said. "One day you will be so clean a halo will shine above your head. But for now, you are still dirty. You need to pray."

Cleo didn't hear anything after that.

44

Noah and I walked the four blocks from the restaurant to his apartment on Broadway and Eleventh Street. The lamplight shone off the brass doorknob set into the ornate wrought-iron door.

"How old is this building?"

"Around 1920."

I admired the art nouveau design of the door. As we passed through, I looked back. You could barely see the design from the lobby. Inside was just as ornate. Parts of the octagonal white-and-black ceramic floor were cracked, but that didn't detract from the effect. The walls were papered in a pattern that I recognized as William Morris. Faded now, the blue flowers with small mustard-colored centers and the full green leaves were from another era. The steps were carved from heavily veined white marble and the center of each was worn.

"It's like walking into another century," I said.

"You aren't kidding. Wait till you see the kitchen and the bathroom. My tub has claw feet."

Two flights up, Noah opened the door to his apartment, turned on the light and let me precede him inside. The ceilings were ten-feet high and the walls were wainscoted halfway up in lovely warm oak panels. The floors, covered with random scattered Oriental rugs, were also oak. The windows, framed in ornate molding, looked down on the back of a church garden.

The furniture was simple but classic. Arts and Crafts couches, chairs and table. All upholstered with William Morris patterns. Lithographs and posters from the same late-nineteenth-century era hung on the walls. In one corner stood a baby grand piano.

There was a small kitchen off the living room with glass-fronted cabinets and an old stove and sink that, despite their age, were in pristine condition.

Everything was subtle, subdued and masculine, but beautiful.

"I'm impressed."

"That I have taste?"

I shook my head. "No. At the quality of these reproductions. These pieces look original."

"That's because they are."

There was no way I could ask him how he could have afforded all this on a detective's salary, but he knew what I was thinking.

"I've actually written a few songs that have been published. I don't sell much. But what I've sold has done well."

"The pieces you were playing tonight? They were yours?"

"Some of them."

I shook my head. "You can do that, but you still stay on as a detective?"

"Yes, ma'am."

"Can I ask why?"

"Being a detective is a part of me. What my dad did. What I always wanted to do. I play piano real easy. I need it for balance, but first I'm a cop."

I nodded.

"The same way you need to do those stone sculptures."

There wasn't anything to say. I never talked about my sculpture and didn't think about them in words. The abstract shapes weren't anything I wanted anyone to judge, or question. They were not important once they were finished. It was just that the process kept me sane when little else could.

"Can I get you anything?" he asked.

"No. I'm fine."

I suddenly felt awkward in his apartment. Inexperienced, tired, not sure of myself. In some strange way, Noah didn't seem attractive anymore, and being in his apartment seemed like a mistake. I was suddenly afraid in a way I wasn't even at the Diablo bar with Cleo's clients.

"Why don't you sit down. I'll make some coffee."

He went into the kitchen. I looked at my watch. If I left now, I could get home and be asleep before eleven.

"You take one sugar, right?" he called from the kitchen.

"Yeah, thanks."

"Would you like some brandy in it? Or Sambuca?"

"No, I'm fine."

He brought out two mugs, put them down on the coffee table and sat down beside me. Sipping the coffee, I grimaced. It was too hot. Not sweet enough. I could taste the chicory and it was bitter.

"You know, I should go. This wasn't a good idea."

He looked at me for a long time. Then he nodded. "Let me drive you."

"No."

"I insist."

"No. That's silly. It's just uptown."

"Okay. Then let me go downstairs with you and get you a cab."

"Too much trouble. You are exhausted. There are a million cabs."

"Fine. But first, just tell me what just happened. All of a sudden you seem like you're ready to jump out of your skin."

I shrugged.

He leaned forward and kissed me, but this time there was nothing about it that connected us. Two separate sets of lips crashing together but not touching.

Noah was trying to melt down my reserves, but it felt like an assault. All the smells, the touches were an invasion. His skin was rough on my cheek, his warm touch was hot on my hand. Moving away from the kiss and his smell and his hands, I scooted forward on the couch and reached for my coffee.

"I can't explain——" I started.

"I'm not asking you to."

"But I should."

"No, Morgan, you don't have to."

The surprise must have registered on my face. "I'm not used to people telling me what to do and what not to do."

"I can believe that. But you're not out there with 'people' now. You're here. And I like seeing you sitting there. No one has ever sat there that way looking as right as you do. So indulge me. Let's not have a postmortem on an abortion. Just stay awhile. Let me play you some music. All you have to do is listen. And then I'll drive you home."

Noah was smiling at me. Not the kind of look I would expect a man to have etched on his face after being rebuffed.

Now that the pressure was gone, I should stay and let him drive me home. It would recement the working relationship. It would dissolve the tension.

He got up, went to the CD player, looked through a pile of cases, then popped out what was already in there and put in new disks.

Soft, heady music, the kind my mother had loved, flooded the apartment. Old-fashioned crooners sang their songs: Frank Sinatra, Tony Bennett, Ella Fitzgerald, Nat King Cole. I sipped more of the coffee. I was getting used to the bitterness and starting to think that I actually liked it.

Noah sat on the chair catty-corner to the couch, his eyes focused on a point to my right.

For ten minutes he didn't say anything. And I sat there just listening to the music, forgetting that I should be doing something or saying something or explaining myself or trying to explain the situation.

He took out two glass balloons and poured an inch of brandy

into each. Pushing one toward me, he lifted his own, inhaled and then took a sip.

"So, tell me. How do you separate what you do from who you are?" he asked.

"I'm not sure what you mean."

"You listen to people talk to you about their sex lives all day. About what turns them on that shouldn't. Or at least they think shouldn't. About what works for them in bed and what doesn't. I'm sure you hear all the things I see. Violence, S and M, bondage, autoeroticism, fairy tales without any happy endings, prostitutes who fuck for drug money, for abusive pimps, for Gucci shoes...crap. Nothing that is very pretty. Six years of being a sex therapist, years of being a general shrink before that. How do you get away from it?"

I looked down at the brandy. "I don't. I don't want to."

"But you need to, don't you?"

"When I'm with my daughter, with Dulcie, I don't think about my patients."

"Yeah, having kids must help."

I felt something stuck in my throat. I took a sip of the brandy. It was my first sip, and it burned, hard and hot in my throat. I almost gasped. I coughed. He looked at me. Hard. Holding my eyes.

"But when she's not there, they haunt you, don't they?"

"Trying to help them haunts me. The sadness of some of my patients' problems is hard to walk away from just because the clock says the workday is over. You don't stop thinking about a woman who wants to be tied down and have her lover wear a mask and use a cat-o'-nine-tails on her. But it's not just the extremes. There are women who crave pain and men who crave being demeaned. The couples who don't understand that seduction is as important as sex. Who have lost the art of touch. Who have an easier time spending money than spending time together. Every part of the body is connected to someone's problems, someone else's neurosis."

"So how do you separate from all that?"

"It's part of your training to know how to leave…" My voice became more bitter. Like the coffee. And that surprised me. "I can't separate from it. I see my patients' lives, like movies, playing out in my mind when I get into bed at night. I try to figure out what I can say to them. What I can suggest. Where I can lead them. How far I can push. It's what I do."

He nodded. Listening. Leaning forward. "But where are you in all that?"

"I don't think about that." My voice sounded slight to my own ears.

"What happened to your marriage?"

"I was happy in my marriage. It was Mitch who said it wasn't fair to either of us to live the way we were living anymore. Sex is great…but animals have sex. Animals don't talk. They don't share each other's pain the way humans can. There is nothing so sacred about sex that you have to break up a family over it." The words were spilling out like the stupid tears that were coursing down my cheeks. I was embarrassed, but too upset to do anything about it. "The ways that people turn their lives inside out for sex can be dangerous. They forget it's not just the act, not just the release that matters, it's the needing and the being needed, too."

"Do you ever think about someone touching you again?" he asked.

"Of course."

"But?"

"But what?"

"But why did you freeze the minute you knew I was going to touch you?"

"Every single sex act already belongs to someone else. The women and men who talk to me, they do all those things to each other. And I listen. Nod, take it in. I wade through their bedrooms, invisible and silent, taking notes, filming them and snapping their photographs. And then I go home. Dulcie and I eat dinner, I help her with her homework. We watch a movie, she goes to sleep. I go to my study. And I chip away at a stone."

"What are you looking for in the stone?"

"An untouched place."

He put his hand on my arm. It was not a sexual gesture this time. Just a connection. He was making contact.

"When you carve stone, there is this sound the chisel makes on the marble. It's loud. Have you ever heard it?" I asked.

"No. How loud is it?"

I could feel his fingers on my hand. The heat came off him in waves.

"It sounds like a jackhammer in my ears. You'd never hear this over the sound of the mallet on the marble."

His hand moved up past my wrist, up my arm, and then with his other hand he pushed the hair off my face. He leaned in. When he spoke now he was almost whispering.

"Does the sound drown out the patients' voices?"

"Yes."

He was not kissing me, but I could feel his lips near my ear as he spoke to me. Soft pressure, light rain. His right hand was unbuttoning the cuff of my shirt while his left hand stroked the space behind my ear. Not an erogenous zone. But bare skin. And it was sending an alarm, a shocking thrill, to the center of my body.

"But the voices come back, don't they, Morgan? The images start to flood your brain and you hear the patients' voices in your head again? Touching and kissing and fucking become all words again, all pictures that have other people in them but you?" His fingers were still on that patch of skin, and they felt more like the wind than someone's touch. I lost the words he was saying for a moment because for the first time in a long time, sensation was overpowering thought.

"How does all that make you feel?"

I should have laughed at how he was turning the tables on me and asking all the questions. "I get angry. I want to help my patients find their center, be able to make love, to enjoy their bodies, their partners, except I want the same thing for me, too."

He leaned over and kissed me, but before I could respond his mouth moved down my neck, down farther. He kissed the skin above my bra, moved his mouth back up my neck, trailing kisses, pressuring his lips against my collarbone, using his teeth. Shivering, I moved closer to him. He was reaching me somehow, miraculously, after all this time.

"What do you do when you get angry?" He began to work the rest of the buttons on my blouse. And then slipped it down my shoulders and pulled it off my arms. The fabric sliding off my skin was yet another embrace, as if he had imbued the shirt with erotic powers so that the very movement of the silk was some sort of lovemaking.

"What can I do?" I asked.

"You can tell me about it, Morgan."

"I just want to find my own images again." I wasn't thinking about my words but about how this man's hair was soft against my chest. How his breath was hot on my stomach and how his hands were kneading the knots out of my shoulders.

What were we doing with this odd combination of bloodletting, massage and seduction? I didn't want to stop to figure it out. My body was quivering, I couldn't get close enough to him. My hands finally, after all this time of him touching me, moved up to his arms, and I gripped his muscles.

"Tell me all about the things that have gone wrong in your life, about the things that you've rationalized because you are too smart to get mad, Morgan."

"I don't rationalize."

"Bullshit."

Almost immediately, my fists came up, curled tight, and attacked him. It was easier than I could have imagined to rain punches on him while he kissed me.

As hard as I was hitting him, his kisses were gentle. His tongue barely grazing mine, playing a hide-and-seek game, holding back as much as he was giving.

His hands were on my back, holding me tight against him. I didn't want that; I wanted to push at him and knock him down, and I wanted to hurt him, to crash against him.

I stopped long enough to unbutton and unzip my pants, pull them off, then go to work on his, struggling with the buttons and his fly. He did not help. He made me work at it on my own. I moved with the angry energy that had been building up for so long. The stillborn passion that I had not found any outlet for exploded. Feelings I had been so sure didn't exist in me anymore erupted.

As soon as we were both naked and lying on the floor, the whole length of us was touching, and his hands moved like butterflies alighting on my skin, sending hundreds of electric shocks through me and up and down my body, he made me give him more of what was buried inside me.

"This is something. It's real now," he whispered. "Isn't it?"

The anger was moving out of me, replaced by something hot and thick and sweet that pulsed through my body.

This was just want. Not love or even something as sane as lust. This was just want. Everything was gone now. There were not even memories of this in me from some long-ago college night or early courtship. My mind was not running in a logical path. I pulled back, away from him, to look at him, to take it in with my eyes, this object that was under me. This thing that I needed so badly.

I slid down his body. With both hands I held his foot, I bent down and used my teeth and lips and tongue and worked my way up, tasting his skin, smelling his body, stopping to touch myself between my legs, then moving my wet fingers up his leg. I was marking him in some primitive ceremony, and when he saw me do it once, he took my hand and made me do it again. Touching myself, taking my own slickness, I finger-painted him. His thighs. His stomach. His chest. His nipples. His erection. The scent was around me, a smell that I had never immersed myself in before. My own smell. On a man. All over a man.

He picked me up, saw my startled face and laughed.

"I am not used to this," I said.

"Good."

"I don't like it."

"Too bad."

"You have all the control," I complained as he carried me into his bedroom.

"Yes." He laughed again. Deeper in his throat. The kind of intimate laugh that I have heard other couples share at a dinner party when they think no one else is listening. "It is such torture. Poor Dr. Morgan Snow is not in control. That's what it will be like with me. You'll have it. Then I'll take it back. We will be intimate. And that is the worst thing you can think of, isn't it? You won't like it, will you?"

"No, I won't like it."

"Shh." He kissed me quiet and lay me down on his unmade bed, which was redolent with his scent. I rolled over on the cool cotton sheets and buried my head in his pillow, feeling the cold air from an air conditioner bathe my back. Luxuriating in the bouquet of smells in the pillow, I lost him for a minute. Forgot about everything, breathing in a whole other world.

And then, from behind me, he lowered himself onto me. His arms on my arms, his chest on my back, his stomach on the small of my back, the top of his thighs on the back of my thighs. I was blanketed by him and there was no more cool air but only skin, warming me...no, heating me...as he slid inside of me...and a long, slow, aching moan slipped out from between my lips. A "Yes" that was so stretched out that it was a sound, not a word.

He moved like jazz. He riffed inside of me. He made some bluesy kind of music out of movement. Never fast, just easing along, changing the rhythm, the cadence and the tone. I danced under him to music that I hadn't ever heard.

We were wet, sweating despite the cold, moving so intensely together, striving not to get to the end of the song, letting each note play out long and slow, touching some of the keys with intensity and others much more softly.

When I thought I was going to stop breathing and just break apart, he turned me around, carefully, and then he just looked down at me.

We were both panting. He took a glass of water from beside the bed, drank from it, and then put his head close to mine and fed me water from his mouth. The shock of it didn't diminish the pleasure.

"More...please..."

I didn't know what I was asking for. More of the water? More
of the jazz? More of him playing me?

He took more of the water, but this time, instead of putting it
in my mouth, he dripped it on my chest, on my breasts, on my
neck. And at the same time he started to move in me again.
Slowly, beating out a new rhythm that was more insistent and less
gentle than the one before. It was still too slow for me. I was in a
hurry and I thrust up at him, but he wouldn't let me change the
pace.

"No control, Morgan." He smiled.

I gave up then. Just let go. Stopped being. Whatever thoughts
still lingered were lost in the sensations that were flooding my in-
sides. He went so slow that it turned into some kind of pain. And
there was real pain, too. Because I was reaching up, kissing him
on his shoulders, his neck, using my teeth, gnawing his bones, and
he was biting on mine. He found a spot where my neck met my
shoulder—by accident, because he knew, because our bodies were
mirror images of each other's, because I had found this spot on
his body without knowing it. It didn't matter, he found this spot,
this two-inch-wide circle, and he kissed it and then bit into it and
I arched up and screamed. It was as if the feeling between my legs
and the sensitivity of this spot were connected by a live wire and
he was jiggling it. Shocks. Fire. Pain. Bursts of cold, spasms of hot.
Sounds. Loud, held-out notes. Music. Circles circling on one another. There was nothing anymore at all. Eyes shut. Skin. Teeth.
Full up inside. So full, too full, and too much sensation, lifting me
up, taking off, spinning, pain, no control, his hair on my cheeks,
falling on me, his lips on my lips then back at that spot while he
spun inside of me, and I was circling again and again until the circles widened and I let go, shuddering and crying out and digging
my fingers into his back to get him in me farther, and then farther, so that I might split apart and finally get to the heart of the
feeling. But it wouldn't come. I kept reaching for it. How do you
have this much feeling after so long and let it go?

He knew that, too. He waited for as long as he could. Noah
strung out every second of sensation, like the longest note you

have ever heard on a piano. And then he just stopped moving. There was no sound. Neither of us breathed.

There was nothing but that bed and our bodies and the empty fullness I felt. Brain drained, satiated with being satisfied. We were both waiting. Still connected by the tip of him hovering on the edges of me. Holding back, holding out. He was up on his elbows, looking down. I opened my eyes and he caught me in his glance.

Waiting. More silence.

Then he smiled, like a little kid, with a secret.

"Now, Morgan. With me, now," he whispered in a musical kind of singsong invitation.

And he swooped down and slid in, and the surprise and quickness and the heaviness and tightness and fullness and the quickened rhythm and the fast pace and the intense, pure pain of it after so many hours of being teased toward it was all it took. And I did let go. Finally.

45

He made us omelettes early the next morning before the sun was up. They were fluffy and filled with ripe summer tomatoes, juicy and fat, that softened into the melted Gruyére cheese. We gorged on the eggs and the promised beignets sprinkled with powdered sugar and that bitter coffee that tasted much better to me in the morning than it had the night before. I was wrapped up in his terry-cloth robe, which enfolded me in its excess fabric. He didn't let me do anything. And I didn't mind. Come what may, it didn't matter. I'd found something that I hadn't even realized was missing. And with it some of my anger had dissipated.

While we ate, we talked about silly things. Noah asked me questions about what I liked to do, places I had been, trips I wanted to take.

"You haven't traveled a lot." He sounded surprised.

"I've been working too hard. And vacations were complicated. They made me think. Without my patients to obfuscate my own reality, it was easier not to go away unless we were taking Dulcie with us."

"We'll go to Europe," he said as he poured me more coffee and then spooned in the sugar.

I nodded.

"Do you like the beach?"

"Yes."

"Once this case is solved we'll get in the car and go up to the cape. We'll go swimming in the ocean. And it will be just a little too cold."

"You are totally taking charge?"

"You'll figure out how to even that out, but for now, yes. We'll be lovers and you'll be happy and we'll figure out how to balance it all."

The phone rang. Like a shrill reminder that there was a world beyond his apartment. Almost as if we'd both forgotten, we stared at the instrument on the wall.

And with a forlorn look he took the call.

"Jordain," he said into the mouthpiece, and then he listened.

"How many of the places checked out?" he asked.

I got up, went into the bathroom and took a shower. When I came out he had taken all the plates off the table and now it was covered with paperwork. Notes, computer printouts and faxes.

"They have a lead," he explained.

I walked over and stood beside him, looking down.

"This is a list of all the religious-supply houses that have had orders for those nuns' habits in the last six months. Who ordered them, how they were paid for and where they were shipped. We've finally narrowed it down to four that fit the specs." And he slid the list to me.

My blood started pumping in a way that was different from the night before but with the same intensity. I read down the list.

Six habits were sent to the St. Mary's Convent in Minneapolis. Four to Our Lady of the Flowers retreat in Southampton, New York. Another six to the parish of St. Francis of Assisi in Bernardsville, New Jersey, and five nuns' habits were sent to Our Lady of Sorrows in St. Martin, N.A.

The hair on the back of my neck stood up. N.A. I knew those

initials. But I didn't know why. Sometime in the last three weeks I had seen them before.

I pointed to them. "What is N.A.?"

"Netherland Antilles. Does that mean something to you?"

I shook my head. "I don't know. I think so but don't know why."

"We have someone investigating all of these places. We may be lucky and actually connect this up. One of these places could have had a robbery. Or been used as a drop. We are getting the receipts. Court orders, subpoenas. It's the fucking weekend and we may not be able to get everything we need till Monday. But I have to go into the office."

"That's fine. It's okay."

"Will you stay here?"

I was surprised. And smiled.

"I'm having lunch with Mitch and Dulcie."

"Will you come back here, afterward?"

"I don't know. I'll call you."

"Okay." His eyebrows were raised. He was trying to read me and I wasn't making it easy.

His phone rang again.

"Jordain," he said, and listened.

I was about to go into the bedroom and get dressed, but something about the consternation that settled on his face and the nervous way his fingers started playing an imaginary piano on the table made me stop.

"When did it come in?" He listened while someone on the other end of the phone spoke. "When will the lab have results?" He listened again. "Okay. I'll be there in an hour."

He put the phone down.

"What is it?"

"Morgan, I need your help." His voice was weighted down with exhaustion even though he'd only woken up an hour before. I nodded.

"It's about Cleo."

Now the skin on the back of my neck pricked. I held my breath.

"If there is a connection…and since you think there is, I'm

willing to go with that. I need to know more about who she was seeing."

I shook my head.

"Morgan. You are withholding evidence."

"I am protecting my patient."

"But you are impeding an investigation."

"No. I'm doing my job and you are doing yours." I was suddenly back in my office the first time I met Noah. I had the book in my possession. And Detective Noah Jordain stared at me with his steely blue eyes. He wanted to know what I wasn't telling him.

"Is that what last night was about? All this? Did you bring me here and seduce me, hoping that I'd go all soft on you and just turn over the book and all my information to you? Are you nuts? I have an ethical obligation to protect my patient's privacy."

His eyes clouded over. His spine stiffened. He stepped back from me as if I had flung hot oil at him.

"Are you crazy? You think I was using you?"

"It's possible."

He didn't say anything, just turned and walked toward the bathroom. Each step taking him farther away, making it more and more possible that I was right. If I had been wrong he would have defended himself. He would have fought back. Gotten angry. But he was retreating. The way someone would if they were guilty.

I heard the water in the shower. And I started to imagine it hitting his skin the way I had with my fists the night before.

While he was in the bathroom I got dressed and left his apartment. I didn't leave a note.

He had only wanted what he wanted. But I wasn't going to give it to him. It wasn't his to have. Cleo might still be alive. Her disappearance might not be tied to the other killings. I had to operate from that assumption.

I stomped down the steps. Angry with myself. I'd thought he'd been interested in me when it was the information he'd wanted all along.

Me, who knew better. I'd fallen for the oldest trick in the book.

When I got to the street I wiped away the tears. What? I didn't cry. But I was crying. Over him? A man who had simply figured out where I was vulnerable? Good for him. No. Fuck him. Just fuck Detective Noah Jordain. And then I laughed, a choking sound with a mix of the leftover tears caught up in the ironic chuckle. That's what I'd just done, wasn't it?

46

I went home, showered again, got dressed, made coffee, drank it, and it was still only ten o'clock. With two hours left before I was meeting Mitch and Dulcie, and nothing to fill them with, I went to the office.

There were messages on my machine, and as I listened, I made a list of whom I'd have to call back. The last one was from Elias, who sounded even more exhausted than the last time I'd heard from him. For a minute, I imagined him standing next to Noah. In their own way they were both attractive. But so different from each other. Elias was polished, every inch the corporate lawyer. I could have just as easily wound up making a fool of myself with someone like Elias, I thought. He'd have less reason to use me.

"Morgan, give me a call. I sent the police a ransom note early this morning. I know you told me not to. But something has to jump-start them into finding out where Cleo is...." Then he sighed. A beat of silence. In the silence I could hear what sounded like a voice on his television. It was a woman—or a young girl—crying.

The way I felt. The way Elias felt.

I thought about calling him back and urging him to tell the police he'd planted the note, and then I thought about calling Noah and telling him that when the note came he should ignore it. But I didn't want to talk to Noah. Except I couldn't keep that information to myself. With all they had to do, I couldn't send the police off on a wild-goose chase when they were trying to solve real cases.

I called the precinct house and left a message. The operator told me that Noah was in, that I could talk to him myself, but I said no, I just had a message for him. And dictated it to her.

"Tell him the ransom note is fake. That Elias Beecher sent it to him to get him to take Cleo's disappearance more seriously."

She read it back to me and then I hung up.

As it turned out, it was the only smart thing I did that day.

47

Mitch and Dulcie were already waiting for me at the Boathouse restaurant in Central Park. Sitting on the deck, by the railing, both of them were twisted in their seats, looking out at the lake and the people who were rowing across its smooth surface. I stopped a few feet away, watching them, just enjoying the peaceful ease of the way they were together.

If Mitch and I had done a hundred things wrong, what we had done with Dulcie was right. The night with Noah bothered me even more now than it had earlier, and I yearned to go back in time to the moment when Mitch first said we should separate. This time I would have fought harder to keep us together.

My tears started up again. Damn. So before either of them noticed I was there, I left and went to the ladies' room.

After a few minutes of square breathing, and doing some internal talking to myself, I was okay. The therapist in me knew that the last twenty-four hours had been like a seismic shift, and even if my head didn't want to deal with it, my body did. My skin, my lips, my shoulders, my back, my thighs were all suddenly aware.

I had been seduced, explored, rubbed raw and made love to. I had opened up—to Noah. I couldn't just take all the pieces of me that he'd shaken up and fit them back into place. They'd swollen and altered. They didn't match up anymore.

By the time dessert came, my cell phone had rung twice, but I'd let both calls go unanswered. I checked the numbers, but only in case either was a patient in crisis.

Neither had been. One call had been from Elias. The other from Nina.

"Mom?"

This was a signal. Whenever Dulcie and I were together, and she started talking to me by saying my name with a question mark at the end of it, I knew something serious was coming.

"Yes, sweetheart?"

She looked from me to her father. This was obviously a rehearsed moment. Something was coming. Something they had talked about.

The sun, which had been hidden behind clouds for the last half hour, emerged again and lit up the red highlights in her hair. There were some edges on her face that hadn't been there a week ago. Or maybe they had been but I hadn't noticed them quite like this. Dulcie was moving toward being a teenager. It was something we would endure.

I loved my daughter. I loved her more than anything in the world. I would die for her. But I knew that the next few years were going to be impossibly hard, and like every parent of every teenage girl who is honest knows, these upcoming years would try our relationship.

"Mom, I have this incredible chance to get a lead in a great play."

Why had there been collusion between the two of them over this? She was doing a play every other week at drama school, this wasn't something I needed to be prepared for.

"What play?"

"A new musical version of *The Secret Garden*."

It was our favorite book when she had been younger. I'd read it to her out loud when she was only six, and when she was good enough at reading, it was the first book she'd chosen to read on her own.

"That's terrific. What's the problem?"

Another look between father and daughter.

"What is it—a nude production? Then, no, you can't do it."

We all laughed. But I could tell Dulcie was still struggling. In the silence that followed my question, she ran her finger up and down her water glass, making designs in the condensation.

"Dulcie?"

"It's not a play at drama school. It's actually on Broadway. On Broadway! The director came to the academy and watched us work. Then he asked me and two other girls to come and audition this week. So can I? Dad said we all have to agree."

Damn Mitch. Would it have been so hard to give me a heads-up? He was still a kid, just like Dulcie. And in one split second I remembered that it wasn't the boring sex and my work that had driven us apart and had kept me from fighting to stay married. It was this: his total inability to deal with difficult things in a grown-up way.

"When would this happen?" I asked.

"It's on Wednesday at two," she said.

"No, I mean the play. When would the play go to Broadway?"

Mitch took over now, explaining that it would be a fall premier and that the producers would provide tutoring for the run of the play.

I didn't even give it a minute. Not even twenty seconds.

"No."

"Mo-m-m." It was a plaintive plea, but it had no effect on me.

"Don't even try to talk me into this. How many times have we talked this through? It's one thing if you want to be in school plays and do things like the academy for the summer. But you are not turning pro at twelve. No. It's not happening."

"Morgan," Mitch said calmly, "I know that you think it's too much pressure on Dulcie, on any teenager, to do something like this but—"

I interrupted him, turning to my daughter. "I know how talented you are. I know how good you are going to be at this one day. But it's too soon. It's not an easy life. You have your whole life ahead of you to do what you want, but it's just too soon for you to become a professional actress."

Dulcie was crying. Softly. Silently. But large tears were rolling down her full, peachy cheeks. I pushed my food away, my appetite gone, my stomach churning. I turned to Mitch. "This is the worst kind of thing we can do. You know that, Mitch. We can't play good cop, bad cop with our daughter."

"Look at her," Mitch said, still trying to convince me. It would be like bending a steel cable with his hands. "She loves it. She's great at it. The producers bring in the best tutors."

I didn't know what to do, what to say, how to say it. Watching my daughter cry as if her damn life were ending was as painful as the memories I had of watching my mother come back from auditions that hadn't gone well.

"Dulcie, you have to understand. I know it sounds like fun, but it's work. It's pressure. You will have to worry about things you don't need to worry about now. Critics, fans. It's crazy. It throws your life out of whack...."

She wasn't listening to a word I was saying. She had shut down. Her face was a portrait of sorrow.

"Your father may not get it. But I do. I know what you are doing. Playing the part. You are so good at this, Dulcie. But I'm not capitulating."

My perfect daughter, long, silky russet-streaked hair, wide eyes sparkling with tears, rosebud mouth turned down at the corners. She looked so much like photographs of my own mother, it made me shiver.

For a second she didn't say a word. Held the moment. Where had she learned this stuff?

"You think you are helping me? Like you help those people who come to your office? You aren't. You aren't helping them, you aren't helping me. You just talk. Talk. Lots of talk. You used to help people before you went to the Butterfield Institute. When you were a regular shrink. You used to be fair then. You used to really do something. Not like now. Now you just worry about other people's sex lives and come home and make me miserable. You can make all the rules you want, Mom. But you can't make a rule about how I feel about you. And if you don't let me do this, I'll hate you forever."

My hand flew up, as if it were powered with a force of its own, but I did not make contact with my daughter's cheek. I had never hit her in my life. I wouldn't now. But I wanted to. She had made me that angry. Now the tears came to my eyes.

She just looked at me. She glared. It was an adult look, full of compassion turned to anger and real dislike. My daughter was staring at me the way I had seen people in prison look at the guards who admonished them.

Around our table there was an instantaneous hush. Other people had seen our little drama playing out and were watching intently, waiting for the next scene to start.

"Dulcie, I'm sorry I raised my hand. But when you say things like that—when you say you will hate someone forever—you have to understand how provocative that is. How hard it is to hear."

"I don't have to understand a single, solitary thing if I don't want to. You don't. You don't understand a single, solitary thing about how I feel and why I want to do this play. You haven't even asked me."

The waiter, who had been hovering, came over now to clear our plates.

"I'd like a cup of coffee, please," I said to him. And Mitch ordered one, too. "Dulcie, sweetie, do you want anything else?" I asked.

She looked up at the waiter, as if nothing was wrong, as if she were on stage and this were one of her moments. "No. Thank you. Not now."

He nodded, left. She turned to me, her small hands upturned on the table as if opening herself to me.

"Mom. The audition is on Wednesday. At two. If you aren't there, I will find some way to live with that. But I won't forget it. You know I won't."

It was an astonishing performance. Over the years she had heard enough of my jargon to be able to string the words together like that, but what was equally impressive was the presence she had when she said it, the way she spoke softly and then raised her voice just enough to make a point. If the room had been darkened and the spotlight had been shining on her, everyone would be clapping now.

The waiter brought the coffee.

"Morgan, are you all right?" Mitch asked.

I had been staring at Dulcie, trying to see her—not my daughter, but the person. The vulnerable, yearning child. Where did she pull the drama from? The characters? Why did she need to? That was the question that plagued me the most. Where had I failed her so that she needed this artifice?

Dulcie was now coolly eyeing me, sending me signals, and I knew, wishing me dead. I knew. I, too, had thought it would be easier if my mother had been dead and the burden of her love and her disappointments had been lifted away from my shoulders.

But when she was dead, I was just left, another lost girl, wishing I could have her back. And now, in a way, she had returned to haunt me.

Dulcie was so like all the women, younger and older, who came to me for help. Except I couldn't help them all. I hadn't helped Cleo and now she was missing. I hadn't overcome my own issues to help my daughter. And if I couldn't, she might go missing, too. Her eyes were telling me that.

"You have to understand—" I said to Dulcie.

"No, I don't. Not if I don't want to." She shook her head and her hair moved, catching the light. The tracks of tears had dried, but I could still see where they had stained her face. I wanted to dip my napkin into the glass of ice water and wash them away. But I knew she wouldn't let me. She wasn't my baby anymore. She was going to be thirteen in another few weeks. She had stepped up to the next rung, where you are half adult, half child.

"No, Mom, I don't have to understand anything. But you do."

48

As the taxi driver sped off, I turned around and watched Mitch and Dulcie walking in the opposite direction. I put my hand up to the window in a futile effort to touch her soft hair. But she was already far away.

She was the only thing I had ever been able to count on loving the right way. But I wasn't doing that job very well, either. Her closing barb could be written off as any angry preteenager not getting her way. But I wouldn't do that to her. Just because she was young didn't dilute the truth of what she had noticed, what she was feeling, reacting to.

When my ex-husband and my daughter were no more than dots of color in the Saturday crowd, I turned back around and tried to think through my reactions to her requests. I knew I was overreacting. But her taking the step into professional acting was a leap that had me worried. It wasn't only what my mother had done. It wasn't only how she had been shaped and then malformed by too much success and pressure too fast and at a critical time in her emotional development. It was also about the insidious culture that we lived in, which heaped so much praise and accolades on its young stars. It was even more intense now than it had been for my mother in the fifties.

If Dulcie had early success, would she be unable to deal with later realities if they were not so shiny? If she got a taste of the spotlight, she'd crave it. She would confuse the crowd's admiration with love. She just wasn't old enough to make those distinctions.

Upstairs in my office, I put my bag down and brewed coffee.

"Morgan?"

Nina stood in the doorway, smiling at me.

She was wearing jeans and a white shirt with the sleeves rolled up. Her usual formal makeup and coiffed hair had been replaced with just some blush and a hint of mascara, and her copper hair was pulled back in a ponytail. All traces of the head of the Butterfield Institute and renowned scholar erased, she looked about ten years younger than her years.

"Hi. Do you want some coffee?"

She nodded, came in and poured herself a cup. Like me she drank it black with just a little sugar. I probably had learned to drink my coffee like that from her.

"What's wrong?"

I wasn't surprised. She always knew. It was the fact that Noah had known which still had me confused.

"Not sure where to start," I said.

The institute was quiet. Closed for the weekend, only a few of us had access. And rarely did any of us use it. Nina, who was often writing—she had published three books on human sexuality and therapeutic process—was the only one who could be counted on to be here after hours and over the weekend. Beyond us the hallways were lit but empty, the office doors shut. The usual low-level hum was missing, and its absence was more obvious than its presence.

"Well, what might be wrong?" she asked.

"Among a million other things, my mothering skills."

She shook her head. "Absolutely not." She smiled. Nina was like a grandmother to Dulcie and spent a lot of time with us. "You and your daughter have a wonderful relationship. Dulcie is a very well-integrated and delightful child."

"She wants to act. Professionally, Nina. She wants me to give her permission to audition for a Broadway show."

Nina didn't need me to explain any more than that. She nodded. Looked at me. Searched my face.

"No matter how hard we try, we keep coming back to the same bridge, don't we? We think we've escaped and that we can move on to other issues, other problems, but the one that haunts us just never goes away. You are going to have to cross it one day, Morgan. Or else it's just going to keep presenting itself to you."

"It's my fault. I must have done something over the years. The way I talked about my mother, the way I missed her, Dulcie must have figured out that it would matter to me if—"

"Hey, that's a little too powerful a theory for me. You didn't make Dulcie love acting. That's taking too much responsibility and being too narcissistic, if you asked me. She's her father's daughter, too. How easy for you to forget that. He's a film director unless I'm mistaken."

I laughed, but it died halfway to its end. "Yes, no, it doesn't matter. The fact is she wants to do this thing and she is furious with me because I don't want her to."

"Are you afraid that if you let her audition you'll be giving your mother permission to ruin her life all over again?"

"Let's not do this now."

"What? Try to deal with an issue that you are resistant to?"

"If that is how you want to see it."

"It's what it is."

"According to you. Not to me. But I guess you are questioning my therapeutic skills, too. Damn. There is nothing that's working. Dulcie, you. The kind of therapist I am. Well, I'm not a very good one. One of my patients is missing. And I haven't done anything to help her."

If Nina had thought my segue from Dulcie to Cleo odd, she

didn't say. Instead, like the good therapist and friend she was, she pushed me just a little and pursued the thread.

"What do you mean, help her?"

"She's still missing and there's no proof that anything has happened to her, so the police aren't paying attention to her case. All their manpower is on that lunatic out there giving prostitutes last rites and hoping to turn them into saints."

"How do you know the police won't get involved in your client's disappearance and how do you know the murderer is giving the prostitutes last rites? I've been following the case pretty closely and haven't read anything to that effect."

If my lunch with Dulcie had been less disturbing, I might have been more careful and more conscious of what I said. Or maybe I'd slipped on purpose. My involvement with the police, with the men at the Diablo club, with my own investigation, had been weighing on me. From the first meeting I'd had with Noah, I'd been well aware that Nina would oppose everything I was doing with a vehemence that would be uncomfortable at best.

I sighed. And told her everything. Her only reaction was the color of her knuckles on the hand holding her coffee cup. The more I explained, the more they lost color. She was an expert at hiding her emotions, at listening, at not interrupting, at taking it in. She did it with her patients all day long. She'd earned her reputation by her ability to disappear and absorb. It had been her nature before she became a therapist and was why she was so well suited to the occupation. But it made her a complicated person to have in your life. She was hard to read. Except I knew how to read her. I'd made myself learn. She was my teacher. My mother substitute. My friend. When you study someone and emulate them, the way I had her, you figure out things.

"How many of these men have you met so far?" she asked.

"All but one. And he's Monday night."

"And the police? You've told them about this?"

I shook my head. "No names. No information. Not yet."

"But you've consulted with them?"

"Yes."

If I was going to tell her, I might as well tell her the rest of it. And I did.

When I finished, she got up and poured herself more coffee.

"I wish you'd told me what you were doing."

"So you could talk me out of it?"

"Yes. You are a therapist, not a detective."

"And as a therapist I am doing what I have to do for my patient. You taught me that. The only way I can protect Cleo's privacy is to help the police, find out what they know, and try to work on her disappearance on my own."

"You get uninvolved as of this moment. No more calls to Elias Beecher. Or any of those men at the Diablo bar. And no more involvement with the police." She reached for her coffee cup and drank down what was left. Grimacing, she swallowed.

"I can't stop now."

She just looked at me. Hurt. Betrayed. I knew my involvement with the police was bothering her more than anything else. I got up and sat beside her on the couch.

"Sam broke the law."

"He wasn't hurting anyone." Her voice was not that different from how Dulcie's had sounded at lunch. Small, powerless, hurt.

"But he was breaking the law, Nina."

I reached for her and she pushed me away. "They——"

"They only did their job."

"You saw what they did. They were underhanded and conniving. You agreed with me. You hated them as much as Sam did. As much as I did."

"No. I thought I did. But that was just solidarity."

"That's not true."

"Yes, it is. Why is it so hard for you to accept that I wanted to be there for you?"

"Because..." she started, then stopped.

I waited. I wanted her to absolve me. To tell me that we were as close as ever. That she could accept everything I'd told her. That she still loved me. That I could tell her a truth she didn't want to hear, could force her to think about Sam in a way that would demand she face his travesty. But she couldn't do it.

"I'm sorry," I said.

"About what?" Nina's voice was closer to its usual cadence and objective tone.

"That we are arguing. That you see my helping the police as a personal affront."

"And why is it that you are sorry that we are arguing? Where does that come from, Morgan? Why can't you argue and feel good about it? Excited by it. You are expressing your feelings. I am expressing mine. Why can't we do that without you apologizing?"

"You are getting angry again."

"Yes, but at myself now. I still haven't helped you see it, have I?"

"What?"

"That people don't disappear when they are mad at you. That fighting it out is healthy. That not everyone takes pills to fight feelings and that not everyone is going to disappoint you."

"When did this turn into a therapy session?"

We looked at each other. Both angry for different reasons. Both confronting what we had not ever really learned to confront, no matter how hard we had worked at it.

"That is what is so beautiful about human nature," she said. "The vulnerable, the sad, the helpless, all protected by the wings of hope and determination that we still, in the face of everything, wrap around ourselves and around each other."

I heard her words. But I was seeing Cleo. She had that determination, that hope, but I was sure she was helpless despite it now.

Things with Nina would be all right. We could get through the anger. We'd get to the other side of it. And I would do that with Dulcie, too. But Cleo had flown beyond my reach, out of sight.

49

Monday nights were not as busy as the rest of the week at the Diablo Cigar Bar. As I sat at the bar talking to Gil, and waiting, I watched a willowy woman with very blond hair and large green eyes stroke the underside of a man's wrist with such élan that I started to feel her fingerpads on my own skin. The lushness of the club was so seductive. The deep club chairs, soft lights and piano music, the exotic wood tables, lacquered to such a high gloss that they were like mirrors, and a rug so thick it would suffice as a bed. You didn't so much go to the club as you entered its world and were enveloped by it. It surrounded you, embraced you; it was the first thing that touched you when you walked in. Cleo and Gil had created an alternative universe where there was no sense of time or strife. In the middle of Manhattan, an oasis. The city was filled with spaces like this. Thousands of apartments high above street level, where you looked out of oversize windows, down at a silent world that appeared so lovely. When you lived in this city, you didn't see the trouble on the street. You didn't hear screams in the night. You didn't see the woman who sold sex for a living by getting into a man's car and giving him a twenty-dollar blow job.

"He's here," Gil offered as he put down a fresh club soda in front of me.

I turned slowly and scanned the room. The Slave was a man in his late fifties, trim but short, with a thick shock of gray hair and strong features. He was an ex–Wall Street guy who got out of the market in the late nineties with his fortune intact and became the dean of one of the most prestigious Ivy League schools in the country. He had been one of Cleo's clients for five years and, according to her manuscript, was someone she knew a little too much about.

Gil came around from the other side of the bar and I got up. A little wobbly in my stiletto heels. Not because I'd had too much to drink—I'd only been drinking sparkling water for the last forty-five minutes—but because my entire body was balanced on three-and-a-half inches of two thin spikes.

"Ed, this is Morgan," Gil said, introducing us.

"It's a pleasure to meet you," I said, trying for the voice I had practiced and now was using for the fourth time.

He smiled, appraising me.

"Thank you," he said to Gil. And then to me, "Sit down, please."

For fifteen minutes we talked about a movie he'd seen the night before that I, too, had seen a few weeks ago. It might have been a conversation between any couple, and that was the point. Cleo's girls were supposed to be able to handle conversation. But then he picked up one of my hands and held it in his. There was no surprise anymore to me that these moments of physical contact bypassed my brain and worked on my senses. It was the excitement that confused me. I would have been more comfortable with disgust or fear. But instead I was curious. Cautious, but wanting to know more. These men offered a look into a side of sex that, till then, I had only read about and then talked about as a dispassionate observer.

"You have strong hands," he said.

"Is that good?"

"Yes. I need you to have strong hands. You will need to hold me down. Stop me."

"Stop you?"

"From getting up, from touching you, from reaching out."

I nodded.

"Have you ever had a slave?" he asked.

I'd found out from my other interviews it was easier if I told mostly the truth. "No. This is a fairly new gig for me. I've only been working here for a couple of weeks."

His eyes lit up. "You mean at this club or in this business?"

"In the business. I recently got divorced. My financial circumstances have changed. A friend introduced me to Cleo. She's been working with me for a month. And last week...was my coming-out party."

He smiled. "Then I'll have to teach you."

"Is that something you like? Teaching?"

"Yes. Teaching you how to accept a slave. You have to be strong. And willing to punish me."

I nodded.

"Cleo was an excellent master."

My heart skipped a beat. He had spoken about her in the past tense.

Not sure of what to say, I just nodded. Listening, watching and waiting for the right moment to ask him the questions that I hoped would give me a glimpse into his darkness. So far he was comfortable, slightly nervous, but connected and not distracted.

"What made her so good at what she did?"

"She loved it. She reveled in it. Being a master came naturally to her. Sometimes, when I was on the floor, lying there naked, looking up at her, begging her to let me move, to let me touch her, to let me get close to her, she would touch herself and make herself come."

He shut his eyes for a moment as if he were reliving the scene, and then he continued talking. "My waiting for her, my needing her, my willingness to do as she said turned her on. Do you have any idea how fucking hard that made me?"

I shook my head. "Did you ever want to reverse it and be her master?" I asked in a low voice.

He shook his head now in a slow, rhythmic way. He was still in his daydream and my voice was barely interrupting.

"No. Never. Never wanted to. It's too easy. I can do that all day long. Have done it my whole life. Told people what to do, what to buy, what to sell, what to learn, what to take in… It's being helpless and having someone tell me what to do that makes me excited. Do you think you could do that?"

"Yes. I think it would be wonderful to have a slave."

"It is. Especially for a woman who can enjoy sex. Can you? Not all of Cleo's girls do. Most don't. But I need someone who does. I don't like someone pretending for me."

"Does that make you angry?"

He nodded.

"But Cleo never pretended?"

He opened his eyes wider and looked straight at me. They were the oddest color of blue. A lapis lazuli. A color I had only seen in stone, and they gave him a suddenly inhuman expression.

There was something wrong. With the way he was looking at me, with what we were talking about, with the very color of his eyes.

In her book, Cleo had described the fifth man, the Healer, as the man with eyes this color. Like the money clip that belonged to Judas, the champagne as drink of choice for Midas, and the scar that had been on the cheek of the actor who had Parkinson's.

Cleo had taken attributes of all these other clients and given them to the Healer. She had disguised him more than anyone else. He was an amalgam of how many others? Four so far. And why?

"You wouldn't have to act, would you?" the Slave asked me.

"No. I wouldn't. I don't know how to act." It was an odd sentence for me to say, suddenly bringing me back to my daughter and my mother. Confusing my real present with my fictitious one. Except I was acting. Sitting here pretending that I might possibly let this man hire me.

"It really bothers you, that someone might act," I said.

He nodded. "It is one thing that I can't tolerate to do this." He was suddenly serious. Talking about his predilection as if it didn't bother him at all. And perhaps it didn't. "I'm married. To a well-known woman. You'd know her name. You'd know who she was. She'd kill me if it ever came out that her husband needed to buy an evening of pleasure here and there. But what choice do I have? She won't…she can't… We've tried marriage therapy and couples therapy and she's even been to see top sex therapists but…"

The hair on my arm prickled.

"At first it was fine. For the first two years we were together. I guess now, looking back, it was the newness of the relationship that made the sex okay. But the longer we were together, the less interested she was, and the less interested I was. No biggie. I know. It happens to everyone. But I missed it more than others do. And divorce was out of the question. I love her. I love our life. And I love our kids. It's so hokey, isn't it? Most men I know leave their first wives. Trophy wives are a dime a dozen out there. Get tired of the old one, buy yourself a new one. But I really am happy with her. Every way but this. And this is harmless. As long as no one knows."

"Does the fact that no one knows make it more exciting?" I asked without thinking, and then was horrified. His admission had been so like one I might hear in my office that I had slipped into my role as therapist. But he hadn't noticed.

"Of course. That's one of the most important parts. No one knows I have this other life. Everyone thinks I am a master of the universe— Did you read the Wolfe book?"

I nodded. He continued.

"But I'm not. I'm a slave. I like to be ordered around. I like Cleo to use me as some kind of sex toy. I like to be able to come here and spend an hour with her and know that she is using me to give her pleasure. My wife doesn't get pleasure like that from sex. She is scared of sex. Of this kind of sex. She is scared of exploring the outer edges of eroticism. You have no idea what it is like to be tied up, my hands, my feet, helpless on the floor, and have Cleo touch me with just one finger and tease me. I get so excited. But she won't let me come, not until I do things for her. Sometimes she sits on my chest with her legs spread wide and makes me lick her. Makes me do it until she is done. Until she orgasms on my face."

He was lost. His eyes were shut again. I was lulled into listening, forgetting for a moment that I was there to figure out if he was someone who could have taken Cleo away.

"Do you like it to get rough? Do you like her to hurt you? Do you want her to hurt herself?"

His eyes opened fast and in them I saw complete confusion. His mouth puckered as if he'd tasted something unpleasant. "Hurt her?"

"I'm just trying to find out what you might want me to do. I don't like pain. Not inflicting it. Not taking it."

He shook his head vehemently. "No. No pain."

The Slave was quiet for a few moments. He looked down into his drink, staring at the cubes of ice, the three green olives and the colorless liquid.

"I have to tell you something," he began.

"Yes?"

"I don't want you to take this personally, but I don't think I'm going to ask you upstairs with me." Under the table I felt him fumble for something and then his hand took mine. It was hot and his fingers were strong. He pried my fingers open and put a wad of bills there.

"It's only been a week since I saw Cleo last. And I'm just not sure I can trust you. It's just a feeling I've got. I know I can trust her. We've been seeing each other for a few years now. I like how she does it with me. I think I'll hold out till she comes back. I'm sorry. It's not personal. Well…" He laughed, a very warm laugh. A kind laugh. "It is personal, I guess. I'm more attached to Cleo than I knew. Jeez, I have feelings for her. How strange is that?"

"That you have feelings or that you didn't know it till now?"

"Both."

"Not so strange. She makes you happy. She doesn't judge you."

The bar had become my office. And for a moment it didn't matter.

"Thanks. You just made me feel like there is absolutely nothing wrong with what I like."

"I guess because I don't think there are things that are wrong or right about what we like as long as no one ever gets hurt against their will."

He nodded and smiled at me. A genuine smile. Even gentle. "No. That's a terrible thing. That's what is wrong with our society, with a world that doesn't allow for differences and preferences to be okay. That's why what you do, what Cleo does, is so important. You give us a place where it is all right to have our fantasies. As long as we can act them out in a safe, private place, then there is no reason for anyone to ever be hurt."

I had been sure up until that moment that there was no way he could have been the man who had taken Cleo. But the very last thing he said made me stop. And wonder.

"And if someone tried to take away your private place, what would you do?"

He smiled again. I watched the pupils in his eyes. I watched a vein on his neck beat. His breath did not quicken. There were no signs that this conversation was exciting him or disturbing him in any way. Especially when he laughed again. "If someone threatened to expose this side of me? Or close down the club? There is one sad secret. I'm waiting for someone to prove me wrong, but so far no one has. When someone wants to do something that I don't want them to do, I just find out their price. The saddest thing. The worst thing about my life, Morgan, is that I have not yet found anyone who does not have a price."

He drank more of his drink.

Despite his wanting to keep his predilections a secret, I didn't think he was capable of doing anything hurtful to Cleo. He was only able to have her do something to him.

"You know, you shouldn't do this," he said. "I mean you are beautiful enough to do this. But it's a waste. You should be a shrink. You just made me feel better and understood more about what I need than any of those two-hundred-dollar therapists my wife has dragged me to."

I laughed. I couldn't help it. And luckily, he just laughed, too, not finding my reaction to his comment all that strange.

After he got up and left, I looked into my hand to see what he had put there. Tightly rolled up were ten one-hundred-dollar bills. I looked at my watch. I'd been with him for forty-five minutes. It was the most I'd ever gotten paid for a session.

50

I'd met all but one of the men who were identified in the book, four of the five suspects whom I had thought might have a reason to hurt or take Cleo. I might never meet the fifth. Despite my description of him, Gil had no idea who the fifth man could be. The identity of the Healer was still a mystery.

Unless it was Gil himself, I thought.

I was sitting at the bar while he finished up talking to a customer.

If Cleo published her book, then Gil would be ruined. He'd have nothing left. Sure he had the building and the bar, but without Cleo supplying the women, what was the place but another restaurant?

I shivered. Had I told Gil too much? Had I revealed anything I shouldn't have? Was he the fifth man? Had Cleo written about him and given him attributes of all the others to disguise him?

He turned to me. His face was hard. It was late. He had circles under his eyes and deep lines like parentheses around his mouth. It was as if he was seeing my thoughts. No. Ridiculous. He couldn't.

Was Gil capable of creating this elaborate ruse of introducing me to these men to throw suspicion off of himself? If I weighed what everyone had to lose, he was up there with all the other men I'd met here. The club had made him a rich man, it gave him power and prestige. He would not want a book to threaten that.

Nina was right. Noah was right. I was in over my head. Being a good therapist did not qualify me to figure out if someone was capable of being a kidnapper, or worse, a killer. I was someone who talked to people about their problems, not a mind reader, not a diviner of sick souls.

"Another Glenlivet, please, Gil," a customer said.

Was Cleo in this building? Was she locked in a room somewhere? Had he hidden her away to try to convince her not to write the book? Of course it was him.

Cleo would never have told her clients she was writing a book. And of the two men I knew she had told, Elias had nothing to lose. He didn't want her to publish it because he was worried for her. But that's not the kind of concern that would lead him to harm her to stop the publication. But Gil did have something to lose. He had everything to lose. Plus he was jealous of Elias. Of course he knew about him. And he must have been furious that he'd lost his girlfriend to him.

I had to find some kind of proof to take to Noah, to make him believe me, to make sure that he would investigate this.

Before Gil could turn to me, I got up.

"'Night, Gil," I called out.

"Wait a second, Morgan," he called out, urgency in his voice. But I didn't.

Out on the street, I walked to the corner as fast as I could in the high heels.

What could I do? How could I get someone to believe me? Who would help me figure it out?

And then I knew. The one person who cared about finding Cleo even more than I did. I'd forgotten all about Elias. He'd called earlier when I'd been in session and I hadn't called him back. I'd been avoiding him since he'd told me about the ransom note. I hadn't wanted to tell him that I'd alerted the police that it was a fake. I looked at my watch. It was only ten o'clock.

I dialed his number on my cell phone.

51

"Have you been thinking impure thoughts?" he asked.

She answered.

"I can't hear you."

"No, Father," she said, trying to talk louder. But she was confused. The days and nights were drifting into one another. She wasn't sure if she was ever herself anymore, or if the actress was taking over all of the time now. She hardly ever opened her eyes anymore. All she wanted to do was sleep.

And now she was angry that he had woken her up to go through this ritual again. Twice a day. Every morning and every night. Which was it now? Night, she thought, remembering that she could tell these things if she looked beyond him at the light. It was bluish low light, that meant day.

"Cleo?"

His voice came to her from a distance and she fought it. She hated hearing his voice. It crawled on her skin like a snake, slinking up, never losing contact, sinuous and cold. She knew if she didn't answer him he would just get angry. And when he got angry he did not let her use the toilet.

"Yes?"

"I asked you if you have been thinking impure thoughts?"

"No, Father."

"How have you been purging yourself of them?"

"I have been praying."

"I think we should pray together."

She shivered. This, too, was part of the ritual. And she hated it almost as much as when he withheld her bathroom privileges. She heard the door open and felt a whoosh of colder air come in with him. He walked behind her, unlocked the handcuffs, and holding her hands tightly, he brought them in front of her, where he put the cuffs back on. It was such a relief to have her arms in front of her. She could do more with her arms like this. Her shoulders ached. Not her shoulders, not her hands. The actress's shoulders ached. She had stepped in. She had to step in. Because of what he was going to make her do. Cleo wouldn't stay for this.

He unzipped his fly and pulled his erection out, placing it in her hands, slipping it up through her fingers, so that he was ensconced in her hands as he would have been if he was up inside her. But this was better, she thought. Less disturbing, less repugnant.

She shut her eyes and started to move her hands up and down his shaft, swaying just a little, moving to a silent rhythm. He moaned. Once. Twice. Again. She hurried her movements.

"I don't want to do this to you," he said. He always said this. Now he would tell her that he loved her.

"I love you."

Next he would talk about how this impurity was only because of her impurity.

"If you were pure I would not want to defile you like this."

She knew all the lines. They had performed this play so many times that she had lost track. He wanted...no, he needed to believe that this was something she forced him to do. And she didn't care. Her hands were in front of her now, her shoulders were relaxed.

"You know what I want?" he asked.

She nodded and opened her mouth, positioning it so that when he came, he would shoot up and into her.

"It is holy," he intoned.

She nodded, moved her hands faster. When he started to talk about the religious value of what she was doing to him, she knew that he was getting closer.

"You will be blessed. I will be blessing you. It will make you pure."

She nodded.

"Cleo? Do you believe in the Father, the Son and the Holy Ghost?"

"Yes, Father." This was confusing her. She was an actress. Her name was not Cleo. She didn't know why he kept calling her that. Her name was—

"Can you feel the spirit enter into you? Can you feel how you are being cleansed? When there is no more that is impure about you, when all the filth is gone, then I will be able to make love to you the right way. The way that you want. The way that will make you come, too. You want that, don't you?"

The woman wearing the nun's habit, with her wrists hand-cuffed together, who was being starved, the woman who used to be Cleo and wore designer clothes and expensive shoes, and had men pay her enough money so that she had to find ways to invest it, nodded to the man who had been the one she had been wrong about.

"Tell me what you want, Cleo. Tell me what it will be like. Tell me."

"I want you."

"You want to make love to me?"

"Yes," the actress answered. It was the same drill again.

"You want to make love to *me*?"

She moved her hands faster. "Yes."

"Tell me."

"Yes, I want to make love to you. On a bed, with you naked, with your arms around me, kissing me and loving you in holy matrimony—" All he needed was those two sentences. It worked every time. She shut her eyes again and tried to move away at the last minute, lest it get near her mouth or on her skin.

Despite her professionalism, she had lost her ability to do her job. And he knew it. And two seconds later he hit her face with the back of his hand so hard she fell backward.

"You slut," he hissed.

Tears stung her eyes. She blinked them back. If she allowed herself to cry she would not be able to stop.

Cleo knew that her life hung by a single thread. Somehow she had to convince this mad monk that she no longer was a sexual being. That she was cleansed. But how?

He knelt a few feet from her and prayed.

"Mary, mother of God, come to me now in the hour of my need. Teach me how to teach your child to void her mind of the filth that smears it with piss, shit and vomit. Teach me how to wipe her clean, how to make her worthy of your spirit and grace. Teach me how to teach her to shine so that she will come to me. Whole. Intact. A virgin, like you, like you…like you, so that she can be mine."

And then he got up and walked out of the confessional.

The screen on the door went black. She was shut off again. There was silence, and then she heard a phone ringing. She closed her eyes and hoped he would come back soon to clean her off. She hated to be dirty.

52

I dialed and heard the phone ring three times before he finally picked up.

"Elias, it's Morgan Snow. I think I've figured something out."

"You know who has Cleo? Where she is?" He sounded even more desperate than the last time we'd talked. I pictured him, eyes clouded with worry, hands trembling. This man was being pushed to the edge of a crevice and he stood there rocking with fear.

"No, I'm sorry, I don't know that."

I was on Fifty-ninth Street and Madison. The summer night was warm and sultry and at ten o'clock there were still more than enough people about that I wasn't concerned about walking and talking on the phone, my concentration not on those around me but on the conversation I was having.

"Where are you?" he asked.

"I just left the Cigar Bar. I don't know where Cleo is but I think I know which of the men she wrote about might be responsible. And I need to ask you if she told you anything about him. I'm getting in a taxi. If you give me your address, I can be there in ten minutes."

"No, I'll meet you."

"Elias, I don't want to talk about this in public."

"How long will it take you to get here?"

"Ten minutes."

He gave me the number of the building.

In the taxi on my way to the Upper West Side I called in and checked my messages. There was one from Mitch telling me how upset Dulcie was and asking me to reconsider and please come to the audition. Or at least call him so we could talk about it. And then one from Noah saying that they had a big break on the case. I listened to his slow drawl.

"I'm on my way to the station. A woman, a prostitute, was approached this afternoon by a man who asked her to go to a hotel with him. Just outside he gave her cash and told her to go inside and check in by herself. He gave her a story to give the desk clerk. To say her bag had been stolen, but that she kept emergency cash in her pocket. Once she got the key, she was supposed to go back outside and get him.

"But he was carrying a small suitcase and she'd read enough in the paper about the Magdalene murders to make her nervous, so she took off. We're bringing her in and we'll work with her for as long as it takes to get a good composite done of the guy's face. I should know what he looks like in a few hours. Be careful. Don't go to the club tonight. If it's Gil, if it's any one of those men, he's going to be disturbed and scared. He might be desperate."

I shut my eyes and rubbed them. The pressure was relieved for a minute. He was still talking into my machine in the same tone of voice but each word sounded amplified. My skin was tingling with fear. With relief. They were getting closer. They would have a drawing of him. Then they would know who they were looking for. Then they'd find him. And it would be an end to the murders. If only finding Cleo were connected to that case.

And then the message became personal.

"Please call me, Morgan. You can't take the easy way out about us. Well, I guess you can. But I don't want you to."

I was still holding the phone to my ear, listening to dead air when the cab pulled up in front of Elias's building.

The elevator opened on the seventh floor and I walked down the long hall to the right, as instructed. My feet were hurting. High heels with pointed toes were not what I was used to and I'd walked a long way in them. I wished I'd gone back home and changed, but I hadn't thought about what I was wearing; I was too excited by what I thought I'd figured out. Buttoning the silk shirt up to my neck, I wiped the crimson lipstick off with the back of my other hand. It didn't seem right to be going to see Elias dressed to attract the moths.

When he opened the door, he looked even worse than he had sounded on the phone. Bloodshot eyes, his hair standing up in unruly tufts, and wrinkled clothes. There was nothing that made you think of a partner in a white-glove law firm when you looked at him. If he had walked up to me on the street like this I would have worried and held tight to my bag.

And there was a smell…

"Do you want something? Some coffee? I have coffee already made. It's hot. Still hot."

I recognized the way he was talking, textbook stuff. He was dissembling again, grief and worry affecting him so greatly that he couldn't focus on the reality around him.

"Yes, that would be fine. Let me help you."

"No. The kitchen is a mess. Let me get it."

He left me in the living room and I sat down on the couch to wait for him.

You could tell the apartment had been done by a decorator. There was an air of perfection in the details. The ginger-jar lamps with the bone lampshades. The chenille throw over the couch. The extra-large highball glasses and decanters on just the right chrome-and-glass cart in the corner. I stopped my critical assessment—I was being too hard on him. What else did I expect from an unmarried, wealthy man who lived in New York? Why shouldn't he have a decorator make his apartment livable? Just because Noah's apartment— I forced myself to abort the thought.

In front of me on the ubiquitous glass coffee table was a stack of art books that had probably never been looked at and an opened bottle of wine: the label facing away from me. Something about it struck me as odd, and I reached for it just as Elias came back in the room with two steaming mugs of coffee.

"Do you—" He stopped when he saw me reaching for the wine and there was panic on his face. As if he'd made a terrible mistake by not offering wine to me.

"I'm sorry. Would you rather have wine?" he asked quickly, putting down the coffee and grabbing the bottle. I was worried about him. He was in no state to help me.

"No. The coffee is perfect."

As he walked away, I smelled that other scent again—not the coffee—but what I'd smelled when he'd opened the door. Familiar but foreign. A heavy scent. Sweet.

It would come to me.

He put the bottle down on the glass cart in the corner and walked back toward me.

Taking a seat in the matching leather chair, catty-corner to the couch, he picked up his coffee mug and held it between his hands. When he sipped it was as if he had not had anything to drink in days.

On the floor next to his chair was the briefcase I'd seen him carry before. It was larger than what most executives carried. And the leather was not as fine. He probably had too much paperwork to rely on a sleeker model. The case was open but I couldn't see inside of it.

"Did you mean what you said about helping Cleo?" he asked.

"Helping her? You mean finding her?"

"I mean helping her get over her problems with making love."

"Of course."

"I think I need to tell you some things about her. If you are going to help her you should know about her stepfather. Do you know about him?"

"I can't talk about that with you, Elias. I can't tell you what Cleo told me any more than I could tell the police."

"But you can listen. You can let me talk about it. And you can tell me theoretically about someone like the person I will describe."

"I suppose I could do that. But why?"

"Because it will help her."

I didn't say anything. He was becoming more and more agitated and I was worried that he might be having a psychotic break.

"If someone who was hurt and who was angry got over her anger, she might be able to reconnect to her feelings," he said. "Is that right?"

"Yes."

"Okay, then. This is what I know about Cleo. When she was fifteen years old, her mother went back to work, which required her to sometimes travel, and that left Cleo alone with him."

"Elias, I can't—"

"Just listen." His voice was suddenly louder. I knew that the best thing to do was humor him. Let him talk it out. So I nodded. I wouldn't break any confidences with my patient. I'd let Elias talk and then I'd call Simon Weiss and get Elias some help.

"Her stepfather had been her father substitute. He'd been married to her mother since Cleo was five. She trusted him. But she didn't understand that he was just another disgusting man who followed his cock. So when he came to her, she was confused. She didn't understand. She was a virgin. She hadn't even had a boyfriend yet."

Elias looked as if he might cry. Or scream. He was torturing himself.

"Don't do this. We don't need to talk about this now," I said.

"Yes. We do. We have to talk about it."

"All right. Go ahead."

He needed to tell me her story, to unburden himself, to let me know that he knew her horror. As much as I wanted to rely on professional ethics and stop him, I also wanted to hear how she had told it to him. To see if she had told us both the same way. Because it would be significant if she had told it to us differently.

"He was a needy bastard, and what he needed was disgusting. He made her take off her nightgown. He buried his head in her small breasts that weren't even fully formed yet. He put his head in between her legs. He pushed his thick penis in between her thighs. That first time he used her legs tightly pressed together as a makeshift vagina. He didn't penetrate her. Not the first time. Not the second. Weeks went by. He bought her presents. He was contrite. She was scared. Her mother was away. Excited about her work. They had never been close. Cleo couldn't tell her. And then he finally did it. He broke her. He pushed through her virginity. He desecrated her. He took her for himself."

Elias was lost in the telling of this nightmare that he had obviously often visualized. I looked away. The pain on his face was hard to watch.

I stared at a print of an iris, a blue-black photograph—exquisite, erotic, sensual—that hung on the wall. Not, not on the wall. It hung in the middle of a door that was to the right of the kitchen. The print might have been a Mapplethorpe, I wasn't sure. But it was that good. The petals of the flowers were pressed tightly together. Like hands in prayer. Like a young girl's legs pressed together.

"Even though he was committing a mortal sin, he did this selfish thing. He violated a fifteen-year-old girl in her own bed with her stuffed animals next to her," Elias continued.

I had heard stories like the one Elias was telling me too many times before. But, despite all my professional training, these were the ones that brought up the bile. This was what I could not reconcile. When Noah touched me, it was connected to men like Cleo's stepfather. It was the same act. Only the intent was different. All my listening had damaged me. Except that, for a few minutes in Noah's arms, I felt that I could be healed, too. That like Cleo, I could find a new and clean place for my own feelings, untouched by what I knew and what I had seen.

Now I'd never know if I'd been right.

Elias's voice was like a chorus in the background. I wasn't sure why I needed to listen anymore. A feeling of ennui flooded over me, as if I were drugged. As if my blood was thickening and flowing more slowly through my veins. He was talking about a little girl. A lost little girl. Only three years older than Dulcie. Only seven years older than me when my mother died.

"How did she feel, Dr. Snow? When he left her in her bed all those nights, sheets damp with his sweat and his semen, her thighs red with the pressure of him on top of her? Please tell me how she felt. How it made her like this."

"A child would become damaged and angry, furious." I was giving him textbook answers but he didn't seem to care. He was sitting on the edge of his seat, absorbing every word. "She would blame herself for this happening precisely because she was a child and she wouldn't know better than to think that."

It was all right. I could talk this one out, because I was not talking about Cleo per se. I would give him generalities. But I knew that it *was* Cleo we were talking about, and this was key to why she couldn't separate and make love to Elias the way he wanted her to. The way she wanted to.

"A young girl who lived through that trauma would have several paths to follow. She could break. Or she could finally tell someone and with help she would be able to deal with what had happened to her," I explained.

"But what if she didn't do either of those things? What if she didn't tell anyone and just went on? Would she, might she, become a prostitute to perpetuate that kind of action?"

"Yes, it would give her control over men. By charging for sex, by having the ability to stop it or start it she would be in total control. Everything she did in her work would ultimately be insulting toward men. Every time she took another client on she would be getting her revenge over and over."

"And what would make her better?" he asked.

"In therapy, if she was in therapy, a therapist could bring her through that period of time again, help her get in touch with her rage. Help her recognize she only had limited power as a child, but she is not a child anymore. I'd encourage her to vocalize her anger and give her mother the blame she deserves. We'd work through the trauma."

"And then?" He was nodding as if he were memorizing what I was saying.

"Then the need to humiliate men would start to go away. By being a prostitute, by getting paid for sex, she turned it into a job and kept her feelings at a distance. She'd have to learn to reconnect to the positive feelings of sex. Once she realized that she didn't need that motivation, that angry control over men anymore, she might be able to stop loving from a distance. She's afraid of being vulnerable. She's been drastically betrayed. She doesn't trust intimacy, she can't share much of her real self. She taught herself not to talk about herself or share her real self. It is love from a distance."

"And the book? Why would she be writing a book?"

I couldn't tell him. But I knew. She'd been writing a book because she was still so angry at men that she needed to expose them.

53

She was listening. To the voice of an angel. To the voice of someone who had come to save her. In the pitch-black confessional Cleo knew that it was up to her. Everything had come down to this. Her stepfather had come to her in the dark. And it was dark again. None of the men she took to her bed had ever asked her why there was always one small light on in the room. They never seemed to care. But she needed it. And she needed the light again. She needed to move. But with her hands and feet bound together it was almost impossible. Behind the duct tape on her mouth she screamed in silent agony. Screaming out the name of the woman on the other side of the door who could save her, who would save her if only she could tell her she was there.

Listening to the voices, using them as navigation out of her starless night, she inched forward on the floor. Four feet might as well have been four miles. She could not stand, not walk, not crawl. She was more helpless than an infant.

This was what he had made her feel like. With his large hands and his ugly whisper. She had told Dr. Snow about it. She had told

Elias about it. How his voice in her ear was even worse sometimes than his cock shoved up between her legs. She'd had to hear the same voice that had read her bedtime stories whisper about how tight she was between her legs. The same voice that sweetly asked her mother for more mac and cheese tell her that she was the sweetest girl he had ever fucked. He liked talking during sex, and that made it harder to take. She couldn't just shut her eyes and pretend that he was a handsome boy in her class or some actor from a movie she had seen. She had to know it was him. She had to know it over and over again.

Inches. Slow rocking, side to side. How far was she moving? At least they were still talking on the other side of the door. Maybe they would keep talking long enough for her to get there. But then what would she do? She had no voice. She could not move her hands or her feet.

It was hard to breathe through her nose while she made this effort. The sweat was sliding down her back. The fabric she was wearing was so heavy on her shoulders, so hot around her body. It made moving even more laborious. If only she could take it off. But she had no free hands, no free feet. She only had her body. It was all she'd ever had.

The fucking tears were there again. The damn tears. From the effort? Or from the words, coming at her, from the other side of the door? He knew she was listening. That was the point. His last chance to cleanse her. Nothing else had worked. Nothing would. He was using Dr. Snow. And when he had used her up, would he get rid of her, too? She had to stop him. But all she had was her body. It was all she'd ever had.

54

There was nothing left to hear. Or to say. For a moment, both of us just sat there with the words swirling above our heads. They even had their own sound. A soft rustle. No. That was a real sound. But what kind of sound?

"Thank you, Dr. Snow."

I nodded. Not wanting to talk. Wanting to listen. I got up and walked to the window. The sound was farther away. I walked back to the couch, and as I did I passed by the glass cart and saw the front of the bottle of wine.

It was not wine you could buy in just any store. It was sacramental wine. Sold only to churches for use during mass. Sacramental wine?

And then I knew what the smell was that I'd recognized when I'd come in the door. Incense. The kind they burned in church. I'd been to enough masses with Mitch to know the smell. I'd smelled it on Elias before. And I'd smelled it somewhere else.

I looked at Elias. He caught my eye. I looked away. Toward the door. There was an umbrella stand and in it a black umbrella with a familiar silver handle. It shined, and the glow mocked me. I had missed all the clues. And now they were crowding in on me. Everywhere I looked was one more.

I kept walking. Now I was passing his desk where there was a pile of envelopes addressed to him. But not here. Not here. The address was in St. Martin, N.A.

That was where I had seen those initials before. On Elias's business card. An office in New York City. Another in St Martin, N.A.

It was only a coincidence.

Noah had said there was a church in St. Martin that had ordered nuns' habits, but this was impossible. It was only a coincidence.

Suddenly, a loud crash broke the silence. It was the sound of something solid smashing against wood and it distracted me. It came from beyond the living room. From somewhere deeper in the apartment.

Was it a coincidence?

Could Elias be the Healer? Could I have been so blind? And if he was the man who had been killing all those women then he had to have taken Cleo. There had to be a connection. But what? Had he killed Cleo? No. I knew what I was doing. I had watched his face when he had talked about her. He was obsessed with her. He truly loved her. He had not killed her. But had he killed those other women in some sick ritual that was somehow connected to Cleo? I couldn't figure it out, not yet, not right away, not while I was so afraid. But of course there was a connection. I'd thought there was all along.

And then I heard the sound again. A thud. Soft, without much power. But loud enough for me to hear it. And for Elias to hear it. And for his eyes to narrow with anger.

As much as I wanted to go search the apartment, I knew that if I was right, and if there was someone—Cleo?—here, the only chance I had was to get myself out first. I needed to get to a phone. To call Noah. His name was large in my head now, shining, a solution. Just get out. Walk to the door. Do not look in the direction of the sound.

"I have to go, Elias."

"Yes, you have to go."

What had he read on my face? What was he thinking? Where was Cleo? I couldn't focus on any of that yet. I had to get out first. Just get past him. And through the door.

I was halfway there, almost to the door, when I realized I had forgotten my bag. I had to act normal, to go back for it or he would know for sure that I suspected the sound. If he had any idea that I was suspicious of him, and if he was guilty, as I was now sure he was, he would never let me leave. And if I couldn't leave, I couldn't save Cleo. I needed to get out for Cleo. For Dulcie. The adrenaline was flooding my blood.

I turned back to the couch. For my bag. But my eyes drifted toward the door next to the kitchen.

The picture of the blue-and-black iris was askew.

I heard the sound again. The banging was coming from behind that door. And this last impact sent the frame sliding off its hook, revealing a corner of wire mesh: the corner of a confessional screen.

55

It was too late. He saw my eyes staring at the door. He saw what I saw, knew that I knew. There wasn't much I could do: I had nothing to protect myself with. He was on the other side of the room. I was only steps from the door. I had nothing left to lose.

I opened the door. I didn't think, didn't worry. Too much had happened. Too much was at stake.

I stared into the dark space.

There she was. A nun, dressed in full habit lying on the floor. Cleo's lovely eyes weeping tears, her mouth taped up, her hands and feet bound. Her forehead dotted with sweat.

I was afraid to turn around and look back at Elias because now I was certain who I was in the room with. And I knew that there was no way the Healer was going to allow me to leave now that I'd found him out. Why hadn't I been able to put it all together sooner? I'd had the book and it was full of clues. True, in my office Cleo had referred to Elias as Caesar, and in the book she had referred to him as the Healer. But she'd also told me that she had several names for him. *She'd told me that. And I hadn't remembered.*

I shut my eyes. I breathed. What could I do? I was a fucking therapist. How could I get out of this?

I had to talk him down. It was what I did. It was all I did. I knew how to help people with words.

"Elias, let's sit down."

He shook his head. "What the fuck do I do with you now? Why didn't you leave? I don't want you here." He was close to crying.

"What do you want?"

"I just wanted to learn the secret to how to make her clean again."

"I can help you with that. If you will untie her, take her gag off. She can sit down and we can talk it out."

"Oh, please, Dr. Snow. I can't do that. I will not get caught."

"Yes, you will. Eventually, you will."

He shook his head. "No. I don't get caught. Not in hotels, not in your office. It was me who ransacked your office that day. I was trying to find Cleo's book. To take it away from you. I didn't want you to get any ideas."

So that's why he had gone to see Simon Weiss. To get into the institute. To be seen there so if he was seen there again it wouldn't be so obvious.

"No one figures me out," he bragged desperately.

"Let me help you."

"There is no way you can. You had to look, didn't you? You had to be a nosy bitch cunt and look, didn't you? Damn it. What have you done?"

"You're right. It's my fault I did look. I am nosy. Because I care about you. And about Cleo. I care about people who are confused and who don't understand and who think there's no way out."

"I've killed five women. What way out is there?"

My heart was pumping so hard and fast that I could hear it in my chest. He had been enticing prostitutes to hotel rooms to see if he could turn sinners into saints. Cleanse them. Create a halo effect that he could then use on Cleo. My eyes went to her gaunt face. Cleo was on the floor, helpless. Elias was across the room. Cleo was staring at me, sending me a message with her eyes. For just a second I focused on her. Her eyes darted to the floor, then over to the direction where Elias was. Back to the floor, a spot by my feet, then back up to my face. I knew she was trying to send me a message, but I couldn't read it.

I took a step toward her. He let me. I moved closer to her, and then closer, and then reached down and wiped away her tears.

"Holy water," he said behind me. "I even tried that. I bathed her in it. I practiced on those other bitches. I experimented with the sacraments, with the host, with everything I could think of to turn them pure."

"And when you couldn't, when they were still prostitutes, you killed them."

"So they could be saints. So they could go to the Virgin Mary. At least I could do that for them." He was stronger now. It was the bravado. One of the signatures of a psychopath. He had been brilliant. A lawyer. Coming to me and saying he was a suspect. Deflecting suspicion by taking it on.

He was rifling through a desk drawer. Pulling out papers. Searching for something else. Putting things in his pockets.

"I'm prepared for this. Totally prepared for this."

I didn't ask him what he meant. Cleo's eyes were signaling me again. From the floor to Elias. To the floor.

He was pulling things out of the briefcase now. Not law papers. It wasn't a briefcase, after all. It was a sacrament case. Out came holy water, a large, gold chalice and a purple silk vestment. He threw them all on the floor. They had failed him. He kicked at the chalice and it rolled across the room. If only it had come in my direction I could have used it as a weapon.

He hits them with a heavy rounded object.

I heard Noah telling me about the weapon. This must be it, what he used to knock them all unconscious.

He was almost finished emptying the case. What was he going to do with us when he did? Did he have a gun? He didn't need one. He had his hands. He had strangled five women. He would just—

And then I knew what Cleo was looking at. What she was trying to tell me.

Elias walked toward me, reaching into his pocket. For a gun? A knife? What was he doing?

"I'm not going to hurt you. I don't need to. I'm leaving. You and her. Leaving you both here." In his hand was a roll of the same kind of duct tape that bound Cleo's hands and feet. The silver slash that covered her mouth.

As he walked he peeled off a long strip and ripped at it with his teeth. He was getting closer. My heart seemed to have stopped. Everything in me was calculating how fast he was moving and how close he was getting and how much time I had and when I was going to have to move.

Three feet away.

Too far.

Another step. Another.

Two feet away.

Still too far. One more step.. I tried to focus all of my energy on what I had to do. On not thinking about it. Because if I thought about it too much I'd freeze.

His eyes were boring into mine. He was in a psychotic state. Not knowing, not feeling, acting out, his unconscious on the surface, his reason and rationality deep inside of him, useless to us both.

He took one more step, and trying not to move too quickly, not to alert him, I slipped off my insanely high heels and then as fast as I could I bent down and—

"What are you doing?" he shouted.

I didn't answer. I swung my arm, the toe part of my shoe gripped tightly in my hand. Muscles tensed, stretched, fingers holding tight, but I felt nothing. He watched the movement, surprised by it, not understanding the swinging arm. He was fast and he was strong but I had that one moment of shock on my side. He wasn't expecting it. He looked up for one brief second, and as he did, the three-and-a-half-inch thin heel came down toward his face and went right into his eye.

The scream was mine, the blood was his. I felt it hot and liquid on my own cheek. His hands went up to his face. Howling, incoherent, he circled like an animal, caught in the intensity of the pain he was feeling.

He was moving without knowing where he was going. One eye blinded, the other squeezed tight in agony. He made another circle. Closer to the door. He was losing blood. I had no idea how badly I had hurt him.

I needed time. To call the police, to get Cleo free. How long was his pain going to last? I opened the front door to the apartment and went at him. If he saw me, if he understood, I couldn't tell. The one open eye did not focus on me. He was still making guttural animal noises that I knew I'd never forget. I had caused that pain. I smelled of his blood. It didn't matter, none of it mattered, and with all of my strength I went at him again, praying that he was still in shock, that I'd be able to do this.

He reached out with one hand and grabbed my hair and pulled at me before I could get at him. Amazed at the power of the one-handed grip, I took the pain, let him bring me closer, and then swung again with the stupid shoe.

It hit his back and I heard a crack. Had I gotten his shoulder blade? A rib? A fresh scream ripped out of his mouth.

But still he held on to my hair, his other hand covering his eye, now drenched in a waterfall of blood. I let him hold my hair, and as if we were doing some macabre dance, we moved in more circles. Then we were at the door again, and I was maneuvering him closer and closer to the threshold. Finally, I used my head like a battering ram, and despite his hold, despite the fire on my scalp, I pushed at him and hit his chin. The force of my skull coming up against him like that must have caused some kind of fresh pain, and he fell backward into the hallway, his hand still holding my hair.

I had less than ten seconds to get up and slam the door, to lock us in, and lock him out.

Up. I swayed. Put my hands on the door, pushed. The only thing I saw was a thatch of brown hair intertwined in his fingers.

The sounds of the locks clicking into place gave me one second to breathe, to think through what I had to do next. Bottom lock. Middle lock. Chain bolt. Cleo had to be untied. I needed her help. And I had to call the police. Elias might have keys to get back in. No, I'd used the chain. Still.

I grabbed the phone off the receiver and dialed 911, shouted the address of the apartment building.

"You have three minutes. He's the Magdalene Murderer. He's in the hall. I'm barricaded inside but I don't know how long I have. He might have keys."

"Can you tell me the nature of—" the 911 operator asked.

"It's a fucking emergency. He can kill us. With his bare hands. Get someone here. Call Detective Noah Jordain. SVU. Tell him. Tell him Morgan Snow called. Fast. Do it."

I dropped the phone and fell to my knees in front of Cleo, ripping at the duct tape around her hands. I couldn't tear it. It was too thick. I bent over, mouth to her wrist, teeth bared, and I tried to rip it the way Elias had. Too tough.

Her eyes were wild. She was looking behind me at the desk. I got up. There was a simple letter opener sitting on a pile of papers. Not sharp enough. I needed scissors. But there were no scissors.

I heard the awful metallic sound of the locks clicking. Of tumblers opening. It was so loud I thought I was going to go deaf. There was no other sound in the world but the key unlocking the door. There were two keys. There were two locks. But there was a chain. I'd put the chain on.

Giving up on Cleo's hands for a minute I gripped a corner of the tape covering her mouth and ripped it. She grimaced, and as the tape came away, her scream erupted, growing louder and louder, so loud I couldn't hear the keys anymore.

"Get a knife," she said fast. As if she had been waiting to say it. "The kitchen is behind you."

I didn't look back, but ran into the kitchen and flung open one drawer, another, a third, and then saw a knife.

She smiled at me when she saw it gleam. It was such a hopeful smile that for a minute I actually believed we'd be all right. He wouldn't be able to push the door open. The chain would hold. The police would get here.

Of course he wouldn't be able to push the door open. It was a strong chain.

Slashing at the duct tape, trying to stay clear of Cleo's skin, took more time than I had. But I got it.

"Can you do your feet?"

She nodded.

I gave her the knife.

He was standing outside the door, his fingers trying to work through the space. But it wasn't wide enough. We were safe. For a minute more.

Cleo had worked her way through the tape and was standing up.

I ran into the kitchen again, to the intercom. I lifted it from the receiver.

"Hello," the doorman answered slowly.

"Don't come up here. Don't let anyone up here. Go outside and look for the police. Let them up. Find the police. Call 911. One woman is hurt. There is a killer loose in the hallway."

"Who is this?"

"Just do it. We need help."

I let the receiver drop and ran out to the living room. Cleo was standing now, looking at me, eyes wide with terror when I came back. My eyes swung over to the door. The fingers were gone, I knew he wasn't there.

"Where is he?"

She shook her head.

"Can you talk, Cleo?"

"Yes."

"Where is he?"

And then I heard the click again. Loud in my ears like gunfire.

"Where is he?"

"There is a back door. In the kitchen."

I looked around. Where were we going to go? How much could he hurt us? There were two of us. Couldn't we overpower him? I hoped so, but I didn't know. How could I know?

"Come," I whispered, and took her by the hand.

56

The terrace off the living room was about fifteen feet long by six feet wide and filled with heavy wrought-iron furniture: a table and four chairs and dozens of plants in terra-cotta pots.

We were both in black. It was night. Maybe he wouldn't see us. Maybe. Maybe we could hide in the darkness. As long as he didn't look for us here. As long as he didn't think of the terrace.

"Lie down," I whispered.

Cleo did.

I lay down next to her. And we waited. To hear the sirens coming up the block. To see Elias come into view.

He looked like a victim of a violent crime. His eye was swollen shut. His face, his shirt, his neck and his hands were covered with blood. It dripped from him, sprinkling the ground.

I held my breath even though there was no way he could hear me from inside the apartment.

He was circling the room, crazed, knocking over vases and books as if we had shrunk and were hiding there. He was almost unrecognizable, rage and blood and his injury having altered his face.

"What is he doing?" Cleo whispered. From where I had pushed her she couldn't see him.

"He's looking around. Searching for us."

"He won't think of the terrace."

"He won't."

"No, he won't."

Our words were prayers that I hoped would come true.

Until I heard the door handle turn.

"Stay down. Whatever happens stay down. The police will be here any minute. They have to be here. It hasn't been more than five minutes even though it feels like hours."

The door opened. Don't look up, I thought. Sending the thought out to her. Hoping she would keep down, keep hidden. He didn't love me, he wouldn't want to kill me the way he would want to kill her.

"Dr. Snow. You hurt me." His voice was childish. Young.

I didn't say anything.

His feet were inches from my face when I felt him reach down and pull me up by the hair. Even in so much pain, he was strong. He was going to break my neck, like he had broken those other women's necks.

Was there a police siren on the wind, mixed in with the other traffic noises? Even if there was, it was too far away. He'd kill me and Cleo and still get out before the police arrived.

"Elias, if you let me go, I will talk to the police. I will convince them not to put you in jail but to get you help."

My eyes were locked on to his one good eye. He had no idea what I was saying. He couldn't understand.

He stood me on my feet. Then one of his hands moved up to my neck. Then the other. The siren was closer but not close enough.

And then, fingers digging into my neck, he pulled me down with him, on top of him. He was lying on his back and I was on my stomach. His body was hard underneath mine. I could feel his muscles and his bones. His breath was on my face. I could feel everything except for his hands tightening around my neck, but I knew that was only a matter of seconds.

Because everything was turning black.

57

"Dr. Snow. Get up."

Cleo was standing beside him. The wind whipped around her legs and blew the nun's habit up into the classic Marilyn Monroe pose. How could I be thinking this?

She held out the knife, glistening in the little bit of moonlight that was shining down on that part of the terrace. Drops of blood slowly ran down the blade.

Below me, he groaned, but they were watery groans, diluted and weak.

With my fingertips I pried his hands off of my neck and stood up. Slowly, as if I had never stood up before and wasn't sure I knew how, I got to my feet.

The sirens were below us now. They would come up. Just a little too late.

I walked to Cleo and put my arm around her and she put her arm around me, the hand with the knife at my back. Her body did not move. I barely felt her heart beating. She was as still as a statue atop a tombstone in a graveyard. For one second. And then she shattered. Her crying was dry at first and deep in her throat, as if her body, her torso was weeping, but not yet her heart, not yet her head.

Suddenly more lights blazed on inside. Bright and too white. Four policemen in uniforms, with guns drawn, and out in front, Detectives Jordain and Perez.

Through the window, Cleo and I watched them as if they were on a stage, looking around for a body, for people, for the perpetrator, for a victim.

Neither Cleo nor I had any strength to move, to summon them.

Noah was the first one to see us. He put a hand out. As if he could reach me through the glass. He called out and I heard my name. Then the terrace door opened and all of them came out. One cop dropped to his knees and put his finger to Elias's throat.

"He's still breathing. He's got a pulse."

Someone else called out, "He's got a pulse." And two paramedics ran out onto the terrace. And efficiently and wordlessly got a blood-pressure cuff on him and began talking his vitals.

I was sorry about that.

58

After I was finished giving a statement at the precinct house, Nina took me back to her apartment, put me in her bed and sat next to me, waiting for me to fall asleep. But I couldn't.

In the morning I called Dulcie and told her only as much as I had to so that it wouldn't alarm her that I was asking her to stay with her father for a few more days. And then Nina and I took a long walk to Central Park and continued walking. All the way up to the reservoir, and then we worked our way down, stopping at our favorite spot: the Conservatory Garden, which was ablaze with flowers—roses and delphiniums, foxgloves and begonias. We sat and watched birds pecking in the dirt, but we didn't say much about anything that mattered. Not yet.

I just sat and took in the summer scents and let them erase the other odors from my head. The sun burned in my eyes and almost obliterated the images that had been seared there.

Afterward we took a taxi to the hospital where Cleo had been taken the night before. Gil was there, holding vigil, and he told us that she was fine and the doctors thought she might be able to leave in another forty-eight hours.

"And then I want to come back to therapy with you," she told me.

"Not with me. After what we've been through together, I can't. I have no objectivity left."

"You saved my life," she said, and took my hand.

"I wish I had. But it's really the opposite. You saved my life. You stabbed him."

I couldn't hear the words without shaking. Without shutting my eyes from the sight of Elias falling back and pulling me with him, from the feeling of his fingers around my neck. My hand instinctively went there now. When would I stop wanting to touch my own neck? When would the black-and-blue necklace of bruises go away?

"We saved each other." She smiled.

Nina and Gil went downstairs to get coffee and we were alone. Two sisters, related by blood, but not ours. A maniac's blood, which together we had spilled.

"How did you do it, Cleo? You'd been bound and gagged in that closet for days... How did you do it?"

"I wasn't there. Not me. I played a part. The part of a prostitute being held by a madman. She's the one who takes over when I'm with clients."

I nodded. I knew about that. It was acting.

"I really want to come back to therapy," she repeated.

I couldn't help her with the scars she had left and the questions she would need to ask and answer. "You can see Nina. She's the best therapist I know," I told her.

"No, you are. You saved my life. You can't get much better than that."

"What saved our lives were those shoes. Weapons. You told me that the first time you came to see me."

She took my hand and held it. I watched us from a distance. She was skinny and exhausted. Held captive by a man who was sure he could take a whore and turn her into a Madonna. Even if it killed her.

And it almost had.

59

Noah called on my cell phone Tuesday night to tell me what he'd found out.

"Elias Beecher had fooled us all. As a young man he'd gone to a Jesuit seminary and was preparing to become a priest when he raped a young woman. His father had it all hushed up. There was no arrest, no trial. He transferred to a secular college, graduated with honors and went on to law school. So you were right about that. We also traced the nuns' habits to Elias's office in the Netherlands Antilles. You were right about that, too."

"His office? I thought they had to be shipped to a church."

"Well, the order was sent to Our Lady of Sorrows Church at 1212 Fairway Drive. But there is no church at that address. It's an office building leased to Elias Beecher's law firm."

"And the diamond cross, did he buy that for her?"

"No. She bought that for herself."

So Gil had guessed that one right.

"We were five minutes behind you. On our way to his apartment when you called 911."

"You were? How?"

"The prostitute who ran away from him in the hotel had just finished with our artist. I recognized Elias from the composite right away."

I didn't know what to say.

"Are you all right?" he asked.

I nodded, forgetting again that he couldn't see me and then said yes.

"Are you?"

"No. Yes." I offered a weak laugh. "I have no idea."

"I'd like to see you," he said.

"No. Not yet."

"Will you call me?" he asked.

"I can't figure that out now. Dulcie has an audition tomorrow. She wants me to be there."

"That's great."

"No. It's all wrong. I don't know if I can go."

"Morgan, I'd like to come over and talk to you."

"No. I'm at Nina's. I'm tired. I'm confused."

He didn't pressure me. He was probably as familiar with someone in shock as I would have been.

"Well, when you are ready, I'm here," he said in his low, melodious voice.

When I got off the phone, Nina looked at me with a questioning glance but didn't ask me about the call. Instead she made me more tea and talked me into taking a nap. I listened to her, did everything she said. I needed her to make all the decisions for me. I was in no shape to make them for myself.

Later, after the nap and dinner, she asked me about my plans and I told her I thought I'd go home the next day. She didn't think I was ready. We argued about it, finally coming to an agreement that she'd approve of me going home, as long as I promised to come back at the first sign that I might not be ready.

"And I'll come with you when you go to Dulcie's audition tomorrow," she offered.

I was sitting in her living room, cross-legged on the floor, petting her standard poodle, Madeline, over and over, stroking her silky ears.

"I'm not sure I'm going."

"She's counting on you," Nina said in her most motherly tone.

"No, she's given up on me," I said.

"She's a twelve-year-old kid who has her heart set on being an actress. Right now you are the only one standing in her way."

"Better for her to hate me than to go out there and start dealing with the brutality of the business. At least I can save her from that."

Nina sighed.

"But your daughter isn't another woman you have to save. She's not Cleo. She's not your mother. Dulcie isn't lost."

60

It was hot out. I took off my sweater and tied it around my waist and continued walking downtown. It was a long walk from my apartment down to Broadway and Forty-fifth Street but I'd left early: I wanted to give myself time.

I had called Mitch and told him that it was okay with me if he took Dulcie to the audition. That he should tell her if she got the part I'd agree to her taking it.

"You should come with us to the audition, Morgan," he'd said. "She doesn't need your acquiescence. She needs your support."

The theater was in the middle of the block. I pulled open the glass door by its brass handle and stepped inside. This was harder than I'd thought it was going to be. Every instinct I had said I should run through the double doors, find Dulcie and carry her out of here, no matter what anyone said the "right thing" was. I wanted to protect my baby from this thing that was so large and absorbing and tantalizing. I wanted to protect her from growing up. And I couldn't. I knew that.

In my purse, my phone rang. I shut it off without even looking at it, took a breath and walked into the dark theater.

The informality of the rehearsal took away some of the magic. The house lights were on. Different people were scattered around the auditorium, talking, making notes, everyone doing something to occupy the time.

I didn't see any of the kids and didn't feel like asking anyone where they were.

As I slipped into a seat near the aisle toward the back, a tall, imperious man with heavy jowls, wearing jeans and a T-shirt came out on stage.

"Okay. We're ready to start. Bob, can you turn the stage lights up? And Janet?" He looked around.

"I'm here. I'm coming." A heavyset woman with short-cropped red hair bustled up onto the stage carrying a sheaf of papers that she proceeded to put on the piano. She pulled out the seat, sat down, opened the first piece of sheet music, looked at it to make sure it was what she needed, and then put her hands on the keys.

The man, whom I assumed was the director, called out a name and a young pale blond girl rushed on stage. They talked for a few minutes about who she was and where she went to school and she offered up a few credentials.

Then Janet began to play and the girl, whose name was Amy, sang. The sound was pure and perfect. I sighed. This was going to be so hard for Dulcie. The competition was too good. The standards would be too high. Dulcie didn't have this girl's training.

Three more young girls auditioned. Each one equally good, at least to me. And then it was Dulcie's turn. She walked on stage. Poised. Hardly nervous. Or so it looked from back here.

She was small, but she looked as if she had been poured from steel into a mold and would not bend. There was an antagonistic glare in her eye that gave me the shivers. But if she didn't know I was there, who was the look for?

Janet began to play. The same song she had played before. Original music for the play. Words I had never heard before and that were still a little hard to follow.

"Can you hear me?" my daughter belted out, her voice clear and strong and so sweet. "Can you hear me? Or are you still not seeing what I say?"

That this creature was my daughter made no sense to me. She was a girl-child still, not someone who should be standing up on a stage and singing like this. How did she know where to find the pain she was singing about? How did she know how to give herself up to a song the way lovers give themselves up to each other?

"Saying I am here isn't making it clear. Hear me. I'm here," she sang.

When she finished the song, the director talked to her a little about where she lived and went to school. And the people sitting the closest to the stage listened, leaning forward a little farther than they had for the other four girls.

"Miss Abbott, can you stay behind for a few minutes after everyone else leaves? Are your parents here?" he asked.

I knew what this meant. So did she. So did the other four girls who were crying now, silently, picking up their things and leaving the stage.

Mitch stood up and walked toward the stage.

"Yes, I'm here."

"You are Mr. Abbott?"

"Yes, Dulcie's father." I could hear the smile in his voice as he said it.

From the back, I watched our own drama unfolding. My daughter hadn't even looked for me. Not once had her eyes searched the theater. Up on stage a lock of her hair fell into her eyes. I reached out to brush it back from twenty yards away.

This wasn't what I wanted, it would make me scared every day, and it would keep me up at night. She was too young.

I stood up.

And then without having to search for me at all, Dulcie's eyes found me and she gave me a smile that didn't remind me of Mitch, or my mother, or me.

"I'm here, too," I said. "I'm Dulcie's mother."

* * *

An hour later the three of us walked out of the theater together. A perfect picture of a broken family but glued together in a way so that one of us would always have the two of us.

Mitch hailed a taxi and gave the driver the address of an elegant restaurant on the Upper East Side.

As we were getting out of the cab, my cell phone rang again. I looked down at the caller ID number on the LED display.

"You two go in, I'll catch up with you in a minute," I said.

"You've got to be patient for the patients." Dulcie laughed and rolled her eyes at Mitch, who rolled his back at her and then went inside.

But it wasn't a patient.

"Hold on a sec," I said into the phone as I watched their backs disappear into the revolving doors.

"I've been calling you all day," Noah said in that long, slow drawl.

"I know."

"You haven't answered the phone."

I didn't know how to explain that and so there was a long silence.

"Elias has been indicted. I wanted to let you know that."

I nodded my head. Then realized he couldn't see me. Why did I keep doing that with him? Thinking he could read my mind and see what I was doing even when he wasn't there?

"There is no question he'll be put away for the rest of his life. And a few lives after that."

I couldn't do anything else but nod again.

"You are probably going to have to testify unless he pleads."

Another pause.

"Morgan. Are you there?"

"Yes."

"Did you hear what I said?"

I didn't answer. I liked hearing his voice, hearing his breath in the silences between the words. Through the window of the restaurant I could see the table where Mitch and Dulcie had just been seated. My daughter looked older from a distance. Then she looked out and noticed me. Her excited wave made her look her age again. I wanted so much for her, but all I could do was step back and watch her try to take her place in a world that I knew was not always kind. But we'd be there, Mitch and I. And Nina and all of Dulcie's friends. It would be all right and it would be torture. But it was always torture with teenage girls.

"Morgan, where are you now?"

"Having a late lunch. With Mitch. And Dulcie."

"You went to the audition?"

I nodded.

"So she got the part," he said as if he'd seen the nod. "You are a wonderful mother. A lovely woman. And very scared and beat up right now."

There was so much I wanted to say that I couldn't say anything. So many words were filling my throat. I wanted to feel his arms around me and to hide my head on his chest and to say them all. Instead I stood outside the restaurant, watching my daughter and my ex-husband through the window and listening, like I always listened, to someone's voice. But this voice was Noah's and it sounded like spices and honey, swirling around me, getting inside my head, encouraging me, urging me on.

"I've said enough," he said. "After you all are finished with lunch I want you to come get in a cab and give the driver my address. You need to talk. I want to listen. I'm a good listener, Morgan. Aren't I?" And then he laughed. A long, slow laugh like a jazz riff on the piano, coming out over the wires and pulling me toward him.

And I nodded. Certain this time that he could see me, somehow.

With Thanks To:

The people who made the book happen—Loretta Barrett, Amy Moore-Benson, Dianne Moggy, Donna Hayes and the entire MIRA team.

The people who helped me shape the story—Douglas Clegg, Carol Fitzgerald, Chuck Clayman and Stan Pottinger.

The friends and family who kept me sane—Dr. Kenneth Temple, Gretchen Laskas, Anne Ursu, Caroline Leavitt, Michael Bergmann, Diane Davis, Katharine Weber, Karen Templer, Angela Hoy, Mark Dressier, Lisa Tucker, Suzanne Beecher, Simon Lipskar, the Readervillians, Richard Shapiro, Ellie, Gigi, Jay, Winka and of course, Doug.

If you enjoyed THE HALO EFFECT
turn the page for an exciting preview of

THE DELILAH COMPLEX
By M.J. Rose

The next thriller in the BUTTERFIELD INSTITUTE series
Featuring Dr. Morgan Snow

Available from MIRA Books
In April 2005

1

Warm, engulfing darkness surrounded him. Flesh moved over him. Naked legs held him viselike, rocking him, rocking him, lulling him back into a haze. Shoulders, torso, neck, blocking all light. Breaking logic. Hot breath on his neck. Soft hair in his face, soaking up his tears.

He was crying?

One wrenching and embarrassing sob escaped in answer.

No. Take me back to the threshold of coming.

Let me loose in you.

Please.

Please.

The pleasure was too much pain. He wasn't taking, he was being taken. Sensations were being suctioned out of him. No control over the pulsing now.

He didn't know what time it was or how long he had been sleeping. He only knew that he had never been used like this, never cried like this before. Never cried before at all. Like a weak woman reduced to weeping because—

He didn't know.

Why was he crying?

Because he had gone to the boundary of sensation. He was standing at the edge of an abyss of feeling, then slipped and fell. He was only propulsion now. The sticky flesh on his flesh, the arms and fingers and legs and toes and belly were gone. The envelope had been ripped open, now he was clammy and wet. Cold. Alone.

He drifted off to sleep again. For thirty seconds? For five minutes? For an hour? No way to tell. But when he woke up he was still crying. Still? Or again?

Why?

He was crying because…

Because…

It was like attempting to catch hold of clouds to push them away with your fingertips so you could see the sun.

He could taste someone else on his lips. Smell someone else in his nostrils. A sour smell. A sweat smell. Not sweet. Everything stunk of stale sex. He wanted more.

Please, come back.

Nothing for a few more minutes. Or another hour? Ribbons of sleep. Weaving in and out of unconsciousness. Fighting through the interwoven dream web.

Or had he awoken at all?

Must be in bed. Focusing, he forced his fingers to feel for smooth sheets but only felt skin. His own. Moist and frigid.

He tried to move his hands away from his chest, to his sides, but he couldn't.

Was he still sleeping?

Remember something, he told himself. Try to catch something from last night.

No memory.

So he had to be sleeping. All he had to do was wake himself up. Open his eyes. From there he'd sit up, stretch, feel the damn sheets, put his feet down on the carpeted floor and then get to a shower where he could wash away this fog.

A shower, yes.

That would fix everything. A steaming shower. Followed by burning coffee. He'd be fine. If he could just wake up, open his eyes and see the familiar view out of his twenty-fourth-floor bedroom window. The sun would be rising now over the East River because it had to be morning. The night before had to have been many hours ago.

But he couldn't be home.

The body he'd felt had not been his wife's.

Had not been any lover he'd known.

He fought, ignoring the tears, to open his eyes. To push one more time through the last vestiges of the milky-blue fog. Part of his brain, the small section that was functional and was informing the emotion that led to the weeping, knew that something was desperately wrong. This was not just about fucking. Hot streams of tears were sliding down his cheeks and dripping onto his chest. His rib cage hurt from the crying.

He wanted to give up then. Just float back on the waves of gray, formless fatigue. Forget about being saved. Give in and let go.

He gulped in the air, hoping that would help clear his head, and became aware that the air was cold.

Weak, helpless, spent, he lay there.

Why was he crying?

Because...

Because...

The hands stroked his hair. Cupped his skull. He felt himself stiffen again. Tears and erections. What was wrong with him? Fingers played with his curls. Where each hair follicle met his scalp, his blood singed, sending shivers of pleasure down his neck, his spine, to his solar plexus.

Please. Take me back inside of you.

He moved to reach up and brush the wetness off his face, but his hand wouldn't lift. The resistance of a metal bracelet dug its edge, hard and icy, into the flesh of his wrist.

Silver cuffs flashed in the darkened room.

When had he been chained?

He tried to lift up his head and shoulders and felt another pressure holding him in place. A band encircled his waist, preventing him from rising. Falling back, his head hit the thin pillow. Not the overstuffed down pillows on his own bed, but a thin excuse that offered only a few inches of padding between his head and the inflexible cot.

Was this more of the dream? It didn't matter, as long as the fingers kept playing so exquisitely with his hair. He tried to move his legs so that he could thrust up, but the same pressure that striped across his chest held his ankles. The same sound of metal against metal rang in his ears.

On his back, naked, shivering, he gave up wanting to understand.

The fingers were torture now. The rhythm of the stroking was making him harder. He opened his mouth, wanting to lick the skin he could smell.

His tongue wouldn't move. He tried to speak, but his mouth was filled with a dry thickness that absorbed the sound. How could his tongue be swollen so big? He tasted the cloth gag.

And then the fingers stopped.

He saw a glimmer of silver. Bright in the room's darkness. Heard the murmur that razor-sharp metal makes as it cuts, exacting and fast.

The only thing he was capable of bringing forth from his body was more tears.

Weak. Like a woman, he cried.

Because he, Philip Maur, who was fearless, was scared.

Scared to death.